Garden OF HER Heart

Hearts of the War, Book 1
A Sweet World War II Romance

By *USA TODAY* Bestselling Author
SHANNA HATFIELD

Garden of Her Heart

ISBN-10: 0-9980988-0-9
ISBN-13: 978-0-9980988-0-7

For permission requests, please contact the author, with a subject line of "permission request" at the e-mail address below or through her website.

Shanna Hatfield
shanna@shannahatfield.com
SHANNAHATFIELD.COM

*To those who face adversity,
with courage, strength, and hope...*

Books by Shanna Hatfield

FICTION

CONTEMPORARY

Love at the 20-Yard Line
Learnin' the Ropes
QR Code Killer

Grass Valley Cowboys
The Cowboy's Christmas Plan
The Cowboy's Spring Romance
The Cowboy's Summer Love
The Cowboy's Autumn Fall
The Cowboy's New Heart
The Cowboy's Last Goodbye

Holiday Brides
Valentine Bride

Rodeo Romance
The Christmas Cowboy
Wrestlin' Christmas
Capturing Christmas
Barreling Through Christmas

Silverton Sweethearts
The Coffee Girl
The Christmas Crusade
Untangling Christmas

Women of Tenacity
A Prelude
Heart of Clay
Country Boy vs. City Girl
Not His Type

HISTORICAL

Baker City Brides
Crumpets and Cowpies
Thimbles and Thistles
Corsets and Cuffs

Hearts of the War
Garden of Her Heart

Pendleton Petticoats
Dacey
Aundy
Caterina
Ilsa
Marnie
Lacy
Bertie
Millie

Hardman Holidays
The Christmas Bargain
The Christmas Token
The Christmas Calamity
The Christmas Vow
The Christmas Quandary

4

****★ *Preface* ★****

After the Japanese attacked Pearl Harbor on December 7, 1941, countless Americans developed distrust toward people of Japanese heritage living in the United States. The growing unease encompassed even those whose families had been American citizens for many years.

People who had once been neighbors and friends suddenly became the enemy as hatred and bigotry made an appalling situation worse.

President Franklin D. Roosevelt issued <u>Executive Order 9066</u> on February 19, 1942. The order authorized the evacuation of anyone deemed a threat to national security from the West Coast to relocation centers farther inland. More than 120,000 men, women, and children of Japanese descent were detained in assembly centers in the spring of 1942. The government established fifteen assembly centers: twelve in California and one each in Washington, Oregon, and Arizona.

Eventually, the government moved detainees to isolated, fenced, guarded internment camps located across the United States.

As a writer of romance books interlaced with tidbits from history, I strive to convey an authentic glimpse into the period. The sights and smells, the sounds and tastes, the triumphs and struggles of daily life shared in the book help immerse readers into the story.

Rather than commit a disservice to my readers, and those who endured the difficulties, by sugarcoating the spiteful cruelty Japanese Americans endured during the war, I did my best to portray history as it happened, albeit in a fictional setting and with fictional characters.

My heart continues to ache as I read and hear more Japanese American stories from World War II... stories of courage, strength, and hope in the face of great adversity.

**** *Chapter One* ***

May 4, 1942
Near Portland, Oregon

Hushed whispers started softly, intermittently, before rising in a steady crescendo that peaked at a deafening roar. The momentum of the sound stalled and plummeted to a silent lull as the bus ground to an abrupt and rattling stop.

The fierce thud of angry footsteps began at the front of the bus and ended at the last seat, where Kamiko Nishimura hid beneath an austere appearance and a broad-brimmed hat. Fear, unbidden and distasteful, rose in her throat and filled her nose with an unwelcome stench. She masked the trembling of her hands by clasping them primly on her lap, keeping her head down and eyes glued to the floor.

A pair of polished black shoes entered her line of vision, accompanied by a looming presence hovering over her.

"I want you off my bus," the driver demanded. Fury clipped his words and induced a quake in his voice.

Slowly, Miko tipped back her head and raised her gaze to meet his. Hatred darkened his eyes while a vein throbbed in his neck at a frenetic beat.

The man clenched his beefy fists and leaned toward her. "I won't stand for a Jap on my bus! My nephew died at Pearl Harbor along with many fine men. You Japs are all a bunch of..." The words spewing forth from his lips were unfit for anyone to hear, especially a bus filled with women, children, and a few older couples.

Appalled and mortified, Miko refused to cower or allow any hint of her tumultuous emotions to show.

The impassive expression on her face throughout his tirade further enraged the driver. He grabbed her arm in a bruising grip. As though the mere contact with her sleeve might impart a ghastly disease, he jerked his hand back and wiped it along the side of his trousers. "If you don't get off right now, so help me, I'll throttle you with my bare hands. Now move!"

Terrified by the thought of what the man might do in his agitated state, Miko picked up her handbag and rose to her feet. Remarkably tall, she stood a few inches above the man who appeared ready to shoot her on the spot. If he had a gun in his possession, she held no doubt he would have blasted a hole through her without blinking.

Regal and poised, she draped a dark blue raincoat over her arm and lifted her suitcase. The driver blocked her path, glaring at her as though his unconcealed malice might somehow bring about her swift demise.

Adamant that no one on the bus realize the depths of her unnerved state, she took a step forward. "Pardon me, please," she said, her tone calm and even.

The driver seared her ears with another round of his opinions about the Japanese in general and her in particular as he stomped down the aisle and opened the door.

Several people tossed jeering comments at her as she walked to the front of the bus. Miko focused straight ahead, her face unreadable, and made her way down the steps with all the grace of a queen.

"Don't you ever sneak on another bus, you dirty Jap!" the driver yelled and closed the door before her feet touched the ground. Barely giving her time to step away, he pulled back on the road with surprising speed, tossing gravel in his wake.

Miko remained unmoving until the bus disappeared around a bend in the road. The erect posture she maintained melted and her shoulders slumped forward in defeat.

No matter how many times she'd been called names or insulted in the days since Japan had attacked Pearl Harbor in December, each occurrence left her dejected and wounded in spirit.

Miko possessed a fierce patriotism for America, as did each member of her family. Yet, because of their Japanese ancestry, many people regarded them with suspicion and loathing, convinced they served as spies.

The utter ridiculousness of the idea might have left her amused if the situation hadn't been so dire.

In January, the city of Portland voided all business licenses held by Japanese residents. The ruling hadn't affected her father's business, however, and the Nishimura family continued living daily life in a normal manner for the next month.

Then President Roosevelt had issued an order in February authorizing the Secretary of War to protect the country from espionage and sabotage by removing individuals posing a threat. Nervous and dreading the outcome of the order, Miko and her family went on about their business. Like well-watered weeds, rumors flourished that the government planned to evacuate all Japanese people from the West Coast to military areas.

A few weeks later, the downtown attorney's office where Miko had worked the past five years fired her. The only explanation was a pointed look and shrug from her employer as he said, "You're Japanese."

A newly enforced curfew forbade Japanese people from leaving their homes between eight in the evening and six in the morning.

With nothing to occupy her time except worries about the future, Miko accompanied the pastor of the Presbyterian church she'd attended all her life to his daughter's home in Tillamook on the Oregon coast. Sally had been Miko's best friend since the two were old enough to talk. After Sally's mother had passed away when the girl was only fourteen, Sally spent as much time at the Nishimura household as she had her own.

Glad for company with her first child due any day, Sally welcomed her father and Miko with open arms. Although Sally's husband wanted to be home with her, duty placed him in Europe, with no hope of taking a leave from the Army or the escalating war.

Once the healthy baby boy arrived, Pastor Clark had departed for Portland. Miko had chosen to stay with her friend despite Sally's insistence she return to her family.

"I just have a feeling you should go with Dad, Miko," Sally said the evening before her father drove back to his home in a suburb of Oregon's largest city.

Miko laughed and cuddled baby Drew closer. "Is this like the feeling you had when we were ten that we should each eat a whole cherry pie? Do you remember how sick we were? I still can't stand the taste of cherry pie. Or maybe it's like the time you insisted I should go on a date with Ted Jones because you had a feeling he was meant for me. Sam Inouye took me home when Ted turned out to be a complete stinker."

Dismayed, Sally ignored Miko's attempts at humor. "Something bad is going to happen, Miko. I don't know what, or how, or when, but I know it will. Please, please go home with Dad tomorrow."

Miko argued that if something bad was indeed about to happen, Sally shouldn't be left alone with a newborn.

Pastor Clark kissed both girls on their cheeks, admired his tiny grandson, and then climbed in his car with a reminder for them to stay out of trouble.

Weeks passed without any incident, then rumblings about evacuating Japanese Americans along the West Coast became fact. Miko followed the news as civilian exclusion orders posted by the government required Japanese Americans living in certain regions of the coastal states to report to temporary housing set up in assembly centers. Several areas in California and one in Washington had already undergone evacuation.

Determined not to dwell on the bleakness of her future, Miko couldn't help but consider what might take place. Certain it was only a matter of time before Oregon would join the evacuation efforts, she wasn't surprised to answer the telephone one lovely Sunday afternoon and hear the alarm in her father's voice as he begged her to travel home as soon as possible.

"The order arrived to leave our homes and report to an assembly center in Portland no later than the fifth of May. You must come home, Miko. Right away," he said.

Shocked by the urgency, Miko felt her mind spin in a hundred different directions. "The fifth? But that's two days from now! Why didn't you let me know sooner?"

"We couldn't find Sally's number. With Pastor Clark out of town, we didn't know whom to call. Your brother finally found her number in your address book. I'm sorry, Miko. Please return home as quickly as you can. We're leaving everything at your grandparents' farm. Meet us there. We plan to report to the center tomorrow evening."

"I'll be there, Papa." Miko hung up the phone with a heavy heart.

After Sally offered a comforting hug, Miko hurriedly packed her suitcase and rushed to the bus station. Not a single ticket agent would sell her a ticket.

Overcome, she returned to Sally's home. Pastor Clark would have gladly driven to Tillamook to retrieve her, but the man had gone to London. His sister and niece lost their home in a bombing and needed his help. It would be weeks before he returned.

Sally didn't own a car. The few people she knew willing to give Miko a ride all the way to Portland weren't available.

Exhausted and frightened, the two women spent most of the night alternating between prayers and plans.

Early the next morning, Sally left Drew in Miko's care and hurried to the bus station, where she procured a ticket for that afternoon.

The hostile atmosphere at the bus station the previous day forced Miko to borrow Sally's broad-brimmed hat. As long as she kept her head down, it covered much of her face. The two women, as close as sisters, shared a tearful good-bye.

"Be safe, my friend, and don't forget to write. I need to know that you're okay," Sally said, giving Miko one last hug.

"I promise I'll write as soon as the opportunity arises." Miko wiped away her tears, kissed the baby's rosy cheek, and then slid into the cab waiting at the end of the walk. Sally stood on the porch with the baby, waving as the car drove away.

With her unusual height, most people assumed at first glance Miko was not Japanese. She hoped the misconception would now work in her favor. Cautiously, she made her way through the crowds at the bus station and took a seat at the back of the bus.

No one seemed to pay her any mind as the bus journeyed northeast. Thankful the trip had gone so well, Miko experienced a measure of confidence when she switched busses. Less than thirty miles from the end of the journey, she contemplated whom she would hire to drive her to her grandparents' farm when she stepped off the bus in Beaverton.

Lost in thoughts of reaching her family, Miko made the mistake of raising her head and looking over the sea of people on the bus. A ruddy-faced boy stared at her, then turned to his mother. Miko heard the word *Jap* and soon the entire bus was abuzz.

It took only moments for the driver to learn of her presence and leave her stranded on the side of the road.

Miko surveyed her surroundings and concluded there were many things worse than having to walk the last twenty miles home.

Before she began the adventure, she opened her suitcase and removed a pair of worn brown leather oxfords and white ankle socks. The sensible shoes replaced the fashionable heels she'd worn. Hastily tucking her gloves into the pockets of her coat, she stuffed it inside the suitcase, along with her handbag, and closed the lid.

The fewer things she had to carry, the better.

Hefting the suitcase, she walked along the edge of the road. She hadn't gone more than a few hundred yards when a car stopped. As soon as she turned to thank them, the man yelled, "I ain't helping no stinkin' Jap!" and sped away.

After the third similar experience, Miko moved away from the road and kept hidden in the trees. It made travel difficult, but at least she didn't have to deal with more insults and threats.

An hour later, rain began to fall in a light sprinkle. Miko stopped long enough to pull on her raincoat. The drizzle swiftly increased to a downpour while the temperature dropped.

Soaked to the skin, she wished she'd accepted the umbrella Sally had tried to talk her into taking. In fact, if she'd listened to Sally when she'd first insisted Miko accompany Pastor Clark home, she'd be with her family instead of in the middle of the forest, cold and afraid.

The suitcase proved to be a heavy burden, but Miko wouldn't leave it behind. With no idea of what she'd find when she arrived at the farm, she tightened her grip on the handle.

Caught between the incessant rain, the gnawing worry that she wouldn't reach her family, and the wall of trees closing around her on every side, she fought the urge to give in to despair.

Weary beyond anything she'd ever experienced, Miko stopped to rest beneath the sprawling arms of a towering tree. The branches provided shelter against the relentless force of the rain. Darkness loomed as evening gave way to night.

Miko sat on her suitcase and removed the wrapper from a candy bar Sally had tucked into her pocket as she was leaving. Grateful for her friend's care, Miko ate the candy and assessed how far she'd come. Although she journeyed through the trees, she'd kept sight of the road so she wouldn't lose her way.

A stroll through the woods at night seemed a foolhardy endeavor at best, so she decided to walk on the road and hope no one would notice her.

She rested until the throbbing pain in her feet eased, tipped her face up to the rain and drank, then drew on her reserve of strength to carry her home.

The farther she walked, the more her body revolted. Her feet hurt so badly, she winced with each step. The suitcase gained a pound of weight with each passing minute until her shoulders ached and arms quivered from the effort of lifting it.

Every mile or two she stopped to rest. Twice she nodded off to sleep and awoke when she toppled off the suitcase she used as a seat.

Hungry, chilled, and desperate, she forced her feet to continue moving forward.

The rain ceased in the wee hours of the morning. By that time, Miko was half out of her mind with fatigue and fear. Absently, she wondered what the newspaper would report when someone found her rain-soaked body on the edge of the road. Would they cheer that America had one less "stinkin' Jap" to torment with cruel words and unreasonable demands? Would anyone miss her? Why, oh why, hadn't she listened to Sally weeks ago?

Dazed and drained, Miko came to her senses as she reached a road she recognized in the predawn light. It led to a farm owned by one of her grandparents' neighbors. If she cut through their pasture, it would save her a few miles of walking.

She pushed down the wires of the fence and stepped over it, then reached back for her suitcase. The barbed wire caught her coat. Miko jerked it away from the snag and rolled her eyes in frustration when the fabric ripped.

Anger, at herself for her own arrogance and stupidity as well as the circumstances that left her walking through the woods in the rain at night, fueled her steps. Indignation lent her spent body strength as she hurried across the pasture. A few cows tossed uninterested glances her direction, but none moved her way.

Relieved when she reached the far end of the pasture, she hurried over the fence and along the edge of the trees that circled the vast acres her grandparents owned.

The first fingers of dawn stretched across the drab sky as she stepped from the trees and swallowed back a sob at the sight of her grandparents' produce stand. As long as Miko could remember, her family had sold produce from the red-painted structure filled with shelves and bins to hold every type of vegetable and fruit the fertile soil would grow.

A hundred yards behind the produce stand, a white picket fence surrounded the cheery yellow bungalow home her grandparents had built in the mid-1920s. With a wide porch and a plethora of flowers surrounding all four sides, the house appeared welcoming. Beyond the yard, a barn and large storage building, along with a collection of outbuildings, alluded to a prosperous farm.

With a prayer to find her family waiting inside for her, she raced up the front steps of the porch and tried the door. The knob rattled but didn't turn, locked from the inside. Miko set down her suitcase and rushed around to the back door. In her haste, she tripped over the body of a man as he sprawled across the back step.

Unconscious, the uniformed soldier shuddered against the chill in the air, his clothes every bit as wet as hers. At least his jerky tremors assured her he wasn't dead.

Panicked, she pounded on the door. "It's Miko! Open the door! Please!" Fist banging against the wood, she called out to her grandparents, willing them to be there.

All remained eerily silent in the house. Single-minded in her efforts to enter the dwelling, Miko stepped over the man and lifted a brick from the border edging the flowerbed. With a spare key in her hand, she jammed it in the lock and pushed the door open, rushing inside.

She flicked on the lights in the kitchen and walked through the house, stunned by the empty stillness. On the verge of hysteria, she even checked the basement, but no one was there.

Back in the kitchen, she noticed an envelope on the table with her name written across the front in her father's bold script.

Fingers clumsy with trepidation, she opened it, heartsick as she read the words.

Dear Kamiko,

I'm glad you made it safely to the farm. We waited as long as possible for you to arrive. I'm sorry we couldn't wait a moment longer. The transportation we arranged to take us to the assembly center has arrived and we must go.

The orders say anyone not at the center by noon tomorrow will be prosecuted to the full extent of the law. For your sake, I hope you make it before the deadline. You need to come to the Pacific International Livestock and Exposition Center on the north end of town on Swift Boulevard.

In the flurry of selling my business and our home, of packing up our belongings and moving them here, we simply put off contacting you. Now, I realize the grave error of that decision. I'm very sorry, daughter, that we didn't contact you sooner and give you ample time to travel home.

We all hope to see you soon, my beloved girl. No matter what happens, know that we love you. I admire the beautiful, strong, independent woman you have become.

Regardless of what the future brings, take care and do what you think is best, Miko.

All my love,

Papa

Miko reread the missive and laid the sheet of paper on the table. She had several hours to figure out a way to make it to the assembly center before the deadline.

Suddenly, she recalled the man outside and dragged him into the house using the last ounce of strength she possessed.

Worn beyond endurance, she sank onto a kitchen chair and glared at the handsome soldier as shivers besieged his body. "What am I supposed to do with you?"

★ *Chapter Two* ★

May 4, 1942
Portland Veteran's Hospital

If he possessed the strength to do it, Rock Laroux would have punched his doctor in the nose. Instead, he remained prone in the hospital bed, glaring at the doctor as he repeated what Rock didn't want to hear.

"I don't know what else to do for you, son," Doctor Ridley said, looking through Rock's charts a third time. "Your arm continues to gain mobility, your sight is nearly back to normal, the scars on your side are healing, but you aren't well."

"Tell me something I don't already know," Rock muttered under his breath.

Doctor Ridley lifted one bushy eyebrow and stared at him. "For a man who can barely get out of bed, you still seem to have plenty of sass."

Rock grinned. "That's about all I have left, Doc." He sobered as he lifted a weak hand and pointed to the chart the doctor held. "What's going to happen to me?"

The doctor set aside the chart and sat in the chair near the bed. He clasped his aged hands together and studied Rock for a long moment. "You want the truth or what will make you feel better?"

Rock pushed himself up against his pillows. "The truth, Doc. The whole truth and nothing but the truth."

The older man released a long breath and leaned forward. "You're dying, Rock, and I don't know how to fix it or stop it. You've been here two months and each day you get a little worse instead of better. Your blood pressure is low, you struggle to breathe, you fight against dizziness, and twice you've had seizures. You've experienced several bouts of stomach cramps and nausea the past few weeks. Nurse Brighton said if you don't start eating better, she'll come in here and force-feed you."

"I'd like to see her try." Rock glowered at the doctor, causing the physician to laugh. The petite nurse wasn't capable of forcing Rock to do anything, but it wouldn't stop her from trying. He gave the doctor an observant look. "Honest, Doc, I'm not ready to die. I didn't survive crashing my plane just to have a mystery illness steal my life. What can we do?"

Weary, the doctor rose to his feet and moved next to the bed. "Honestly, I don't know, Rock. I really don't know. I've put out a few inquiries with colleagues and have been consulting medical texts. My hope is that we'll find the answer before it's too late. In the event things get worse, you may want to prepare yourself to meet your maker, son. Despite your determination to survive, I can't make any guarantees."

"That's quite a pep talk," said a nurse from the doorway, her words laced with a hefty dose of sarcasm. The buxom little blonde swept into the room, capturing the gazes of the two men. A snappy white uniform highlighted her curves while the cap on her head accented the golden curls bouncing around her face.

From past encounters, Rock knew the woman's enticing appearance and friendly smile belied a backbone of steel. Her sharp tongue would take him to task if he didn't make at least a halfhearted effort to obey her orders. Nurse Billie Brighton was exactly the type of girl he'd ask for a date, if he lingered somewhere other than at death's door.

The last real date he'd been on was almost a year and a half ago, before he shipped out to Panama.

The incentive of regaining enough of his health to tease Billie into going out with him made him wish he could snap his fingers and be instantly well.

"I see your bedside manner hasn't improved, Doctor Ridley, but Rock isn't bright enough to realize you've practically given up on him." Billie winked at Rock, then lifted the chart and read the latest notations.

She shook her head at the information noted there, sending the curls around her face into a coy dance. How Rock wished he could reach out and feel the silky wheat-colored strands in his fingers.

"You know I won't give up on helping this stubborn soldier, but he needs to know the truth and be ready for what may come." Doc rose and patted Rock's leg before moving to the door. "Try not to tire him too much, Nurse Brighton. He's always exhausted after one of your visits."

Billie fisted her hands on her curvy hips while her eyes snapped with humor. "Darn tootin', he is. I'm the only one he can't charm out of doing his exercises."

The doctor chuckled. "I'll let you get to it, then."

After he left the room, Billie took Rock's temperature and checked his pulse, adding notes to his chart. She lifted his left hand in hers, forcing him to stretch it out. "You know the routine, handsome."

Rock plastered on a smile as she helped him move his injured arm through a series of exercises meant to strengthen the weakened limb. When his plane had crashed near Waller Army Airfield in Trinidad, several pieces of metal had embedded in his arm, causing severe damage. One jagged piece of metal had sliced into his forearm, leaving him unable to bend his fingers or control movement of his hand.

Due to the necessity of having two good hands to be a pilot, the U.S. Army Air Corps had honorably discharged him. Grateful the military had at least seen to his care, Rock hoped he didn't die in the hospital. Even with the doctor's dire predictions, he was too young to give up on life just yet.

"Are you ready to accept my offer and marry me, Nurse Brighton?" Rock teased the nurse as she helped him out of bed. She always made him go for a walk during her shift. Some days he made it all the way outside to the path in the courtyard. Other days it took all his strength just to shuffle to the end of the hall and back.

The frosty glare she shot him would have frozen lesser men, but Rock wasn't easily disturbed or dissuaded. "If I've told you once, I've told you a million times, Captain Laroux. I don't date my patients. Not ever."

"That's a shame, doll. I'd show you a real good time," he said, feigning a rakish look while fighting back a wave of nausea. Swallowing hard, he sucked in a deep breath, inhaling the scents of the hospital, which had become all too familiar. Medicine, disinfectant, and sickness created the underlying stench that permeated every inch of breathable air. An odd combination of fear and hope added another layer of unmistakable aromas. Occasional whiffs of tainted desperation mingled with desolate resolve in a strange, unsettling odor.

Rock took another breath, catching a hint of Billie's perfume, a tantalizing fragrance called Tabu that reigned in popularity the past several years. Many girls he'd dated wore it and gladly accepted the bottles he gave as gifts.

Although the nurses weren't allowed to wear perfume, Rock appreciated Billie's willingness to bend the rules. The fragrance defied detection unless she stood close during his arm exercises. Spice flirted with a citrus-laden bouquet and just enough soft femininity to stir

Rock's dreams of the day he would once again hold a girl in his arms and lavish her with kisses.

As though she sensed his thoughts, Billie pinned him with another glacial scowl. "You better not get any wise ideas, Captain, or I'll make sure Nurse Homer is assigned to you every single day from here on out."

Rock stopped in the hallway, right hand clutching the walker that kept him upright. "I can't believe you'd subject me, your favorite patient, to such cruel and unusual punishment. No one deserves ol' Horrid Homer, especially not in a daily dose." He shuffled forward a few steps, then gazed down at Billie. A boyish, engaging smile transformed his face as he moved a little closer to the nurse and lowered his voice. "Why don't you quit playing hard to get and agree to run away with me tonight? Be my bride, Billie. I'd take good care of you."

The nurse laughed and gently nudged him forward. "I've got enough problems without a hound like you for a husband. No, thank you."

"Why, Nurse Brighton!" He affected a shocked expression that morphed into a playful grin. "How could you insinuate—"

"Billie! I need your help in here," a nurse called, stepping out of a patient's room. Pain-filled groans grew louder, followed by the sound of metal clanging, like a tray hitting the floor.

Billie nodded, then looked to Rock. "Can you make it to your room?"

"Yes, ma'am. I'll head back right now." Rock turned and slowly made his way along the long corridor. Overcome with dizziness, he shifted most of his weight against the wall as he leaned his head back and caught his breath.

Unintentionally, he'd stopped outside his doctor's office. Through the open door, he heard the man engaged in conversation with a colleague. Rock listened in shocked silence when Doctor Ridley brought up his case.

"I don't know what to do about Rock Laroux," the doctor said in a voice heavy with worry.

The sound of shuffling papers drifted out the door to Rock's eager ears.

"Is this his case file?" the other doctor asked.

"Yes," Doctor Ridley replied, followed by a long sigh. "That poor boy will die soon if we don't figure out what's wrong with him."

More papers shuffled before the other doctor spoke again. "I can't think of a thing you haven't already tried, Ralph. How long do you think he's got?"

"At the rate he's deteriorating, I'd give him a few weeks, maybe a month at the most." Doctor Ridley sighed again. "I hate this, hate feeling helpless to help him. He's served our country with honor and bravery, yet the best we can do for him is to hand him a death sentence with no specified date or reason."

Rock didn't listen to the rest of the conversation. He forced his feet to carry him back to his room, where he collapsed on the bed. Although he hadn't wanted to face the truth, he'd known all along his condition progressively worsened instead of improved. He'd held out hope Doc would figure out the problem and remedy it before it was too late.

Faced with the grim outcome before him, Rock mulled over his options. He could continue lying in a hospital bed, surrounded by unpleasant odors and unable to enjoy the warmth of the sun or the blue spring sky. The possibility existed that he could figure out a way to end things in the near future rather than wasting away.

However, that thought barely entered his mind before he cast it aside. He might be able to do any number of things, but ending his own life wasn't one of them.

An idea, one that held a great deal of appeal, trickled through his overwrought mind, bringing a sense of calm and purpose. By gum, if he was about to die, he'd do it at home.

The little acreage his parents owned, located west of Portland, had passed to him on their deaths. There was no place else on earth he'd rather spend his last moments than the farm where he was born and raised.

The more he entertained the idea of going home, the more determined he became to leave the hospital.

Nevertheless, with his health completely compromised, Doctor Ridley would never agree to release him. Rock realized if he wanted to go home, he'd have to sneak out of the hospital and figure out the rest later.

Nurse Brighton stopped by his room an hour later with his dinner tray. Although Rock's stomach twisted and gurgled at the sight of it, he ate every bite, knowing he'd need strength to carry out his plans.

Once she left, he slid out of bed and shuffled over to the little closet. A neatly pressed uniform hung from a wire hanger while a duffle bag of his belongings rested on the floor.

As fast as a dying, dizzy man could dress, Rock pulled on his clothes. A fine sheen of sweat covered his face as he finished, but he brushed it away with the hospital gown. Hastily, he penned a note and left it on the nightstand before he lifted the duffle in his good hand and peeked into the hallway.

With no one in sight, Rock left his room and snuck onto the elevator. He pushed the button that would take him to the ground floor and prayed he'd make it outside undetected.

The moment the elevator opened, he kept his head down and crossed the lobby to the front doors.

Outside, he breathed in several gulps of clean air, filling his lungs. Afraid to take time to rest, he walked in an uneven gait to the street, where an older couple got into a car.

"Wait, please!" Rock called, drawing the man's attention.

"What can we do for you, sir?" the man asked.

Rock did his best to hurry over to their car. At least he rushed over as fast as his quivering legs and troubled lungs could get him there. When he reached them, out of breath, it took a moment before he could speak.

The couple looked at him with kindness, waiting.

"If it wouldn't be too much bother, would you give me a lift?" He tilted forward slightly and spread his legs wide to maintain his balance.

"We'd be happy to," the older man said, looking encouragingly at his wife.

"We most certainly would. Let's get you in the car, young man," she said, opening the back door of their black Packard. Her husband took the duffle bag from Rock and set it on the floor behind the driver's seat.

Once they were all in the car, the man turned around with a hand extended in greeting. "It might be nice to know your name. I'm Ernie Smith and this is Madge, my wife and reason to get up in the morning."

"Captain Rock Laroux," Rock said, shaking the older man's hand and tipping his head politely to the woman. "It's a pleasure to meet you both. Do you have a son at the hospital?"

"No. Ernie had to see his doctor today for a regular checkup. He served in the Great War in France." Madge placed a gentle hand on her husband's arm, squeezing it as though she needed a reminder he'd come home from the war in one piece.

Ernie smiled at her with a soft light in his pale eyes, then glanced back at Rock once he pulled into traffic. "Where can we take you, Captain?"

"Please, call me Rock. If you wouldn't mind leaving me at the bus station, it would be dandy."

"Are you a long way from home?" Madge asked.

"No. I grew up near Gales Creek. That's where I'm headed." Rock rested his head against the seat. The sensations produced from being fully dressed and riding in a vehicle seemed foreign to him after so much time spent at the hospital in bed. "Where do you folks live?"

"Troutdale," Ernie said over his shoulder. "But we'd be happy to drive you home."

"No, sir. That's a long, long way out of your way. The bus will do."

Ernie turned and merged with traffic heading west. "Where were you before you got hurt?"

Rock wondered how the man knew he'd been injured, but he supposed his weakened state probably gave away the fact he wasn't in prime condition. "In the Caribbean. My plane crashed a few months back."

"My heavens!" Madge turned around to study him. "Why, you must have been on one of those secret missions, gathering information on German boats." She looked to her husband. "What are they called, dear?"

The man grinned at his wife. "Submarines, honey. They're called submarines. Is that what you were doing, Captain?"

Rock smiled. "I'm not at liberty to say, but it was exciting work."

Ernie whistled and slapped the steering wheel. "Ain't that something, Madgey-girl! A real live pilot hero right here in our car."

Rock didn't feel like a hero, especially when the crash had left his unit short a capable man and a plane.

"Here we are." Ernie pulled the car up to the curb at the bus station. The couple both got out of the car while Rock summoned the strength to climb out and lift his bag.

"Are you sure we can't drive you, Rock? It would be our pleasure," Madge said, observing the beads of sweat on his upper lip and the pain-fogged glaze in his eyes.

"No, ma'am, but I thank you for your kindness. If you ever find yourself in Gales Creek, stop by and say hello. Our place is the fourth farm out of town on the left side of the highway. You can't miss the big blue barn."

"Blue? I thought everyone painted their barns red." Ernie rocked back on his heels and smiled.

"My mother's favorite color was blue, so Dad made me paint it one summer when I was in high school." Rock shifted the bag and held out his hand to Ernie. "Thank you, sir, for the ride. I greatly appreciate it."

"Anytime, son. If you ever need anything, you look us up. We aren't hard to find."

Rock took a step back. "I'll do that, sir. Thanks again."

The couple waved, then hurried back inside their car and left. Rock watched them go as he moved into the line to purchase a ticket. It was only when the agent asked him where he wanted to go that he questioned if he had a wallet in his possession.

His fingers reached to his back pocket. Nothing there. He opened his duffle, locating his wallet. Upon searching inside it, he turned up nothing but lint where he usually kept several dollar bills. Unable to recall how much had been in it before his plane had gone down, he couldn't imagine anyone leaving him penniless. Further rummaging unearthed thirty-seven cents.

"Where to, soldier?" the ticket agent asked again.

"I need to get to Gales Creek. How far will thirty cents take me?"

The agent offered him a disparaging frown, making it clear the question and Rock's lack of funds annoyed him. "I can get you as far as Beaverton. After that, you're on your own."

"I'll take it," Rock said, wondering how he'd possibly get the rest of the way home with only seven cents in his pocket. He handed over the change, accepted the ticket, and located the bus he needed to board.

He took a seat at the front and dropped his duffle bag at his feet. With an exhausted sigh, he settled back and closed his eyes. Although Beaverton wasn't far, it would at least get him closer to where he needed to go.

The next thing Rock knew, a hand shook him awake.

"Hey, soldier, I should have let you off about four miles back, but I didn't realize you missed your stop."

Groggy, Rock straightened and looked outside the bus window. "Where are we?"

The bus driver regained his seat and pointed to the open bus door. "Five miles west of Beaverton. You can catch a bus headed back into town in about an hour."

Rock lifted his bag and eased down the bus steps. He offered the driver a gratitude-filled smile. "Thank you for the ride."

"You're welcome, soldier. Take care." The driver shut the bus door and pulled away from the stop, leaving Rock on the sidewalk staring at the darkening sky. Rain splashed his face as a storm rolled in overhead.

Turning up the collar of his jacket, he lifted feet weighted by worry and fatigue, and plodded down the road, heading west. If his luck held, perhaps someone would stop to offer a ride. However, the late hour coupled with the growing storm left him doubtful of seeing too many people out on the road.

Before long, another dizzy spell assailed him, nearly knocking him to his knees. He sat on his duffle, holding his head in his hands as he waited for it to pass.

Once he could stand, he lifted his bag and continued on his way. Unable to gauge the time or distance, he staggered onward. It might have been minutes or hours. Regardless, if he stopped, someone would most likely find his lifeless body sprawled across the side of the road in the morning.

At last, he reached a crossroads and struggled to see through the dark and rain. By now, his bones ached with the numbing cold that seeped down beneath his skin, leaving him sluggish and disoriented. No longer holding any certainty he traveled in the correct direction, he bent forward, straining to see anything that might guide him.

Lightning flashed across the sky and Rock glimpsed a farm he'd seen many times in his youth. He and his father had often stopped to purchase produce there on the way home from the city. A friendly oriental couple owned the place. He recalled giggling girls helping them in the summer months.

His mouth watered at the thought of the tree-ripened peaches, plums, and cherries he'd enjoyed as a boy. Memories of tomatoes as big as his fist, bursting with sunshine and hearty flavor, reminded him of simple joys from his past.

Driven by the hope the couple might be home and give him shelter from the storm, he slogged across the road. His faltering steps carried him past the produce stand where his family had purchased hundreds of red, ripe strawberries and dozens of big orange pumpkins over the years.

No lights shone from inside the house, but he worked the latch on the gate, eventually getting it open. The effort needed to climb the porch steps was almost more than he could muster, but he made it.

Hand jerking from the chill that pervaded his entire being, Rock observed his fingers as though they belonged to another while he knocked on the door. All remained silent behind the thick wooden portal.

No footsteps. No hushed voices. Nothing.

Rock knocked again, his hand making hollow, feeble thumps against the wooden surface. He tried the knob, but it refused to open.

Mind muddled with pain and desperation, he stumbled down the steps and around the corner of the house, wobbling as he made his way to the back door.

Energy depleted, and with no reserves to draw from, he knocked, leaning against the side of the house. The last of his strength flowed out of him into the puddle of rainwater he dripped on the back step beneath the overhang above the door. His legs buckled as he slid down and passed into oblivion.

∗∗∗★ *Chapter Three* ★∗∗∗

Rock lingered somewhere between unconscious and semicoherent as someone touched his side, rotating him onto his back. A beleaguered grunt penetrated the fog in his brain as hands slipped under him, burrowed beneath his armpits, and circled around to grip the front of his shoulders.

Huffs of exertion accompanied every inch his rescuer tugged him backward. Too exhausted to open his eyes, too weak to provide assistance, he had no choice but to allow the continued dragging of his body.

Fortunately, whoever yanked and pulled on him moved him out of the biting rain. The warmth of a shelter enveloped him, even as he slid across a moisture-slickened linoleum floor.

Vaguely aware of the sound of labored breathing and the smell of something homey, he forced his eyes open and stared into the face of a Japanese woman.

Confused and not in his right mind, he arrived at the dreaded conclusion his plane must have gone down far off course. How had he crashed in the Pacific Ocean when he'd been flying in the Atlantic?

Most likely, the enemy would interrogate and torture him before running him through with a bayonet or lopping off his head.

Not yet ready to surrender, Rock prepared to leap to his feet and put up a fight.

Only the fight had seeped out of him in the rain, and the best he could do was wiggle his cold-numbed toes. Before he gave voice to a single word of protest, he passed out again.

He woke when someone rolled him onto a bed and again when the chattering of his teeth threatened to crack them a few moments before the weight of a heavy blanket settled over him. Burrowing into the comfort it provided, he let sleep claim him.

The next few days Rock slept and healed, unaware of his surroundings. Eventually, he opened gritty, stinging eyes, unable to focus. A hazy figure with dark hair soothed him, placing a cool hand on his feverish brow. She held a cup of hot brew to his lips that slid down his throat and into his empty belly with welcome warmth. After a few sips, he returned to sleep.

Hours later, the scent of something soft and floral brought to mind tropical flowers on an ocean breeze and lured Rock from slumber.

No one at the hospital carried that scent. A second breath revealed no stench of disinfectant, medicine, or sickness. The faint yet acrid, smoky hint of cigarettes didn't hang in the air.

In fact, no hushed conversations or footsteps clacking down the tiled floors of the hall reached his ears. No one coughed, no radio at the nurse's station played popular tunes. Everything was quiet. Too quiet.

Perhaps he'd dreamed the whole thing about being in the hospital, sentenced to die. Maybe whatever he had eaten for dinner the previous evening had caused him to have an outlandish, yet entirely realistic nightmare. Indigestion was most likely to blame for the horrific thoughts in his head.

Though he was normally up and around early, the weariness of both his mind and body kept him lingering in bed. The empty state of his stomach, though, accompanied by a few fierce growls, assured him it was past time for breakfast.

In no rush, he rested on his right side and opened one eye. A well-crafted waterfall dresser he hadn't seen before stood in front of a wall painted a pastel hue of green.

The unfamiliar sight sent him onto his back. He scrubbed a hand across his eyes, hoping he merely saw things that weren't there. Nonetheless, when he opened them, the mahogany dresser and pale walls remained.

Light spilled through two windows, filling the room with a golden glow of sunshine. Dust motes shimmered in the ribbons of sunbeams that almost reached the bed where he rested beneath a white-and-green crocheted coverlet.

Crisp white sheets that smelled of fresh outdoors and the Oxydol detergent his mother had always favored surrounded him as he struggled to raise himself on his elbows. Lacking the strength, he collapsed against the pillows, sinking into the soft bed.

He turned his head to the left and noticed a black-haired woman asleep in a chair. Head down, her chin rested on her chest while a blanket swathed her form.

A vision of a Japanese woman hovering above him darted through his mind, making him question if he was caught in a hallucination or a dreadful reality.

As he snuggled beneath soft covers in the comfortable bed, though, it seemed more like a pleasant dream than impending doom.

Before he could give more thought to the woman or his situation, his eyelids slid closed and he returned to sleep. The next time he awoke, he looked to the chair, finding it empty.

His gaze traveled around the room, taking in the polished hardwood floor covered by a green rug accented with pink and yellow flowers. Several pieces of matching waterfall furniture sat around the room, including a nightstand near his head, where an alarm clock read seven.

From the subdued light, he wasn't sure if it was morning or night.

A cheerful set of paintings hanging above a chest of drawers featured bright pink cherry blossoms with little birds preening on the branches. The Japanese artwork seemed out of place among the American furnishings.

Rock strained to see out the window to the right of the bed. Green grass, trees, and a wooden fence made him wonder where, exactly, he'd wound up, and what had happened to the woman he'd seen earlier.

As though his thoughts prompted her appearance, she stepped into the room carrying a tray.

"You're awake," she said, her face expressionless as she approached the bed.

Weak, Rock nodded and pushed against the mattress in an effort to elevate his head.

With quick, efficient movements, she set the tray on a table beside the chair where she'd slept and stacked more pillows behind him, helping him sit upright.

"Better?" she asked.

"Yes," Rock whispered in a raspy voice. Dumbfounded by the grating sound, he wondered when he'd lost the ability to speak. As he contemplated the possibilities, she set the tray across his lap and stood back, observing him.

"Eat," she said, pointing to the tray, then turned and left the room.

Wary, Rock watched her go. Not a single doubt existed in his mind she was Japanese, but she was tall, incredibly tall, for a woman. Like so many other women of the day, she wore her hair rolled away from her face and pinned. The gemlike shade of the dress floating around her willowy form made him think of the vibrant blue-green hummingbirds he'd seen flitting around flowers in Trinidad.

After she left the room, he dropped his gaze to the tray. Two boiled eggs, two pieces of toasted bread, and a mug of broth, redolent with the appealing aroma of chicken, caused his stomach to growl in hunger.

He lifted the mug and sipped the rich, flavorful brew. If he was a prisoner, it didn't seem as though they planned to starve him to death. The nourishing broth lent him strength as he ate the eggs and enjoyed the light, airy bread covered with fresh butter.

Appetite satiated, he relaxed against the pillows and waited for the woman to return. Once again, his eyes grew heavy and he struggled to remain awake.

He must have dozed, because the next time he opened his eyes, it was dark. A sliver of moonlight shone through the window, providing enough illumination that he could see the woman curled into the chair by his bed, covered by a thick blanket.

Fully awake, Rock felt better than he had for a long time. Quietly, he folded back the covers and swung his legs over the mattress, realizing the only thing he wore was his underwear. Dizziness threatened to swamp him, so he sat on the edge of the bed, inhaling deep breaths, waiting for it to pass.

When it did, he rose to his feet and, with painstaking effort, made his way out of the room. To his left, he noticed a doorway and stepped inside, feeling along the wall. His fingers connected with a toggle switch and he flipped it up, glancing around the bathroom.

He made use of the facilities, then stood in front of the sink, splashing tepid water over his face to remove the vestiges of sleep. He finger-combed his hair, looking in the mirror and wondering when it had grown so long. Typically, he kept it cut short, with the barest hint of a swoop in the front. Most women found it hard to resist.

Since he'd been in the hospital, he hadn't cared whether it was long or short, although Nurse Brighton had twice cajoled him into allowing her to trim it.

Suddenly, he recalled every detail of the last few days, of hearing the doctor's dire predictions for his future, and walking away from the hospital.

He remembered stumbling through the rain and coming upon the produce stand owned by Mr. and Mrs. Yamada. Had they taken him in? Who was the girl in the chair?

Relieved he hadn't fallen into enemy hands, he released a long breath and looked around the bathroom. Honeycomb-patterned tile covered the floor while white tiles layered the walls up to a chair rail. From there, light green walls, the same color as the bedroom, rose to the ceiling. Everything sparkled, as if someone had recently executed a thorough cleaning.

A slight floral scent wafted in the air. Relieved to smell something other than the odors of death and despair so prevalent in the hospital, he breathed deeply.

Strength waning, he flipped off the light and made his way back to bed. For several long moments, he sat on the edge of the mattress, studying the woman asleep in the chair.

A strong chin, straight but short nose, and full bottom lip complemented her oval face. Flawless skin glimmered like porcelain in the silvery moonlight. His fingers itched to reach out and touch it. Dismayed by the absurd direction of his thoughts, he shook his head and climbed beneath the covers, turning his back to her.

A Japanese woman, particularly one so tall and thin, held absolutely no interest for him. None at all.

★ *Chapter Four* ★

Bright sunlight streamed through the windows the next morning as Rock opened his eyes. Flat on his back, he stretched his toes and raised his good arm above his head, bumping it against the polished mahogany headboard.

He took stock of his aches and pains. It didn't hurt to breathe as much as usual, overwhelming dizziness didn't assail him as it normally did upon awakening, and his stomach gnawed with hunger instead of painful cramps.

Slowly, he sat up and cast a glance to his left, noting the empty chair where the woman had slept. A neatly folded blanket draped over the back of the chair.

Curious, he pondered where she'd gone and if she'd bring him breakfast. He strained to hear sounds of movement in the house. After several moments of uninterrupted silence, he wondered if she'd left.

With effort, he swung his legs over the edge of the bed. His foot collided with his duffle bag on the floor. He reached out with his right hand and lifted it beside him. Inside, he found clean underwear, a white undershirt, and a pair of trousers.

The thought of taking a bath held a great deal of appeal. A grunt of exertion escaped him as he took his things to the bathroom. Elated to find a shower nozzle mounted to the tiled wall surrounding the bathtub, he turned the water on and stepped beneath the hot stream.

He couldn't recall the last time he'd had a shower, at least a private one with all the hot water and soap he wanted. A bar of Ivory soap produced a satisfactory number of iridescent bubbles as he lathered it between his hands before getting down to the business of scrubbing himself clean.

Once he rinsed off the soap, he continued to stand beneath the steamy spray, hands braced on the tiled wall, relishing the feel of water against his skin.

Reluctantly, he turned off the water and stepped out of the tub. He lifted a snowy white towel from a nearby hook and buried his face in the soft, sun-drenched material. Leisurely dressing, he used his index finger to brush his teeth with the Calox tooth powder he found inside the mirrored medicine cabinet above the sink.

He rinsed his mouth, hung the towel up to dry, and opened the bathroom door. After hastily shoving his dirty underwear into his bag, he made his way through the empty house.

The front of the house offered a spacious living area with a room off it that appeared to be an office. Bookcases lined the walls and a large desk occupied much of the floor.

Down the hallway, he looked inside a second bedroom before making his way through the dining room to the kitchen at the back of the house.

A plate covered by a blue-and-white striped dish towel sat on the table. A note on top of it read, "Help yourself."

Hungry, Rock removed the towel covering a crumb cake. Cinnamon filled the air and his mouth watered. He lifted the knife the woman had left by the platter and cut a generous slice. After he located a plate and a glass, he retrieved a pitcher of milk from the refrigerator.

Stomach growling, he filled the glass with milk and sat at the table. He offered a brief prayer of thanks, feeling blessed by the meal and the fact he hadn't died in the storm. The severity of his condition, from what he'd overheard his doctor discuss with his colleague, left Rock surprised to be alive.

As he ate the delicious spice-laden treat and sipped the wholesome milk, he contemplated who the woman was, why she was there, and what she planned to do with him.

Strength rapidly waning, he finished his milk and the last bite of cake. He rinsed his dishes and left them in the sink, then made his way to the living room. Two brown leather wingback chairs flanked a large fireplace. A yellow velvet tufted sofa sat across from the fireplace with tables and lamps on either side of it. Overhead, a pale yellow chandelier glistened in the morning light. A Philco radio and a rocking chair with a basket of yarn within easy reach rounded out the room's furnishings.

Rock sank onto the cushioned softness of the sofa and rested his head on a floral throw pillow, stretching out on the long surface.

As he drifted to sleep, he pictured a tall, silent woman with a head full of dark, silky hair and cool, tender hands.

Miko stood at the foot of the sofa, studying the soldier as he slept. Since finding him in the wee hours of the morning last week, she'd nursed him around the clock, praying he wouldn't die.

It had depleted her lagging energy to drag him into the kitchen. She'd tossed a blanket over him and turned up the heat while she got out of her wet clothes and rested a few minutes. The effort it had taken to tug the big man to the nearest bedroom had left her reserves utterly empty, but she had somehow managed to remove his wet clothes and get him into the bed.

As soon as he'd ceased shivering in wracking spasms, Miko had taken a hot shower and made herself a simple meal of toast and tea. By then, she'd marveled that the power hadn't been shut off or the cupboards emptied of food. In their haste to pack up their lives and leave, her family must have overlooked a few details, such as emptying the refrigerator and giving notice to the electric company.

She'd returned to the bedroom where the soldier rested, spread another blanket over him, and settled into the chair by the bed to keep watch.

Throughout the day, she'd wiped his brow and spooned hot liquids into his chilled yet feverish body. As she kept a vigil over him, she'd soaked her blistered, aching feet, and rubbed them with her grandmother's special ointment.

Originally, she'd planned to ask her grandparents' closest neighbors, Lucy and John Phillips, to take him in after giving her a ride to the assembly center. The young couple had always been kind. They'd not only help her, but also make sure the soldier received care.

Miko hadn't planned to be so thoroughly exhausted from her ordeal and caring for the soldier. Much to her dismay, she'd fallen asleep and hadn't awoken until hours past the time she should have checked in at the assembly center.

Fearful of what would happen if she arrived late and truly concerned for the man in her care, Miko had remained at the house.

In the soft light of dawn the following morning, she'd decided to stay at her grandparents' farm and care for the soldier until he was well enough to travel. At that time, she'd have a better idea of what to do about joining her family at the assembly center.

On sore feet, she'd limped out to milk the cows, coaxing them back into the pasture. She'd assumed her family turned them loose with the hope they'd wander over to the Phillips's farm.

A bucket of feed had coerced the chickens into their pen from roosting spots around the yard and barn.

While her feet and body had healed from her trek home in the rain, Miko tended the garden her grandfather had already planted, contemplated her future, and cared for the soldier half out of his mind with sickness.

Several times, he'd referred to her as Nurse Brighton and spoken to someone named Billie. Miko wasn't sure if the nurse and Billie were the same person or two separate women he admired.

She was all too familiar with his type; his thick brown hair, straight nose, and square jaw guaranteed his popularity among females who went for strong, rugged men.

As he slept on the sofa, the thin straps of his undershirt bisected a set of broad shoulders. Despite his weakened condition, muscles remained visible in his biceps, especially with them crossed over his firm chest.

Tall and handsome, he probably left a trail of brokenhearted girls wherever he went.

Miko had no plans to be one of them. As soon as he was able to travel, the soldier was on his own. She'd then face the consequences of showing up late to the assembly center. Surely, given the reason for her delay, they wouldn't be too hard on her.

Lost in her thoughts, she didn't realize the man had awakened and stared at her.

"Hello," he said in a deep voice, husky with sleep.

"Hello," she spoke quietly. "How are you feeling today?"

"Better." He pushed himself up until he sat against the cushions, then swung his legs around to the floor. He rose to his feet and swayed with dizziness.

Miko rushed forward, slipping an arm around his trim waist to steady him. "Easy, sir."

"Thanks," he muttered, clearly embarrassed by his need for assistance.

"You are most welcome." She glanced up at him and caught his gaze. His eyes were an incredible shade of blue, so clear and bright they put her in mind of summer starlight. Before she fell into the tempting pools, she forced her attention back to the matter of providing care for the wounded man. Scars crossed his left side and he favored his left arm, as though he'd recently received the injuries. A nasty scar ran the length of his forearm. He seemed to have trouble moving his hand and fingers.

Curious when and how he'd been injured, she supposed if he wanted her to know, he'd share the details.

"Want to tell me who you are and why you're here?" she asked as they took unhurried steps toward the kitchen.

He remained silent until they were halfway across the dining room. That bright gaze dropped to hers and he grinned, flashing remarkably even, white teeth. "I suppose introductions are in order. Have you taken care of me since the big rainstorm? Was that yesterday?"

Miko shook her head. "I found you on the back step just before dawn on the fifth of May. Today is the thirteenth."

"The thirteenth!" Astonished, he gaped at her. "I've been sleeping for a week?"

"Yes, sir. You had a fever and chills and were quite ill. Your fever broke Friday night, but you were still very sick. I could tell you were much better yesterday. It's good to see you up and about today."

"It's good to be up and really good to be alive. Thank you for taking care of me." He smiled at her, a genuine smile full of gratitude. "I was trying to make it home, but due to unforeseen circumstances, I got off the bus a few miles past Beaverton and started walking home."

Miko questioned what kind of stonehearted person could turn a wounded soldier out on a cold, rainy night. Probably the same type to kick a young woman lugging a suitcase off a bus twenty miles from her home, but she kept her thoughts to herself. Instead, she latched onto the fact he had a home in the area. "Where do you live?"

"The farm where I grew up is in Gales Creek. That's where I was headed, but I've since remembered I leased the place to a neighbor's son when my father died three years ago."

"I'm sorry about your father," Miko said. She couldn't bear the thought of anything happening to her beloved papa. "What about your mother?"

A pained look passed over his face. "We lost her the last year I attended West Point."

Miko helped him settle into a chair at the table and handed him a glass of water. She took a seat across from him and waited while he drank half the contents of the glass. "Do you have any other family?"

He shook his head and took another drink of water. "No. It's just me."

Expectantly, she stared at him. "And you are?"

If he'd worn a hat, he would have tipped it. In place of it, he respectfully bowed his head. "Captain Rock Laroux at your service, ma'am."

A smile lifted the corners of her mouth. "It's nice to meet you, Captain Laroux. I'm Kamiko Nishimura."

Rock returned her smile. "It is a pleasure to meet you, Mrs. Nishimura."

Miko didn't feel the need to set him straight. It was best if he assumed she was married. She stood and moved to the refrigerator, prepared to make lunch.

With plenty of eggs at her disposal, she took out five and beat them in a bowl with milk, salt, and a little pepper.

"Is this the Yamada farm?" Rock asked, as she dropped a glob of butter into a hot cast-iron skillet. He listened to it sizzle and sputter as it melted, filling the air with a delicious, savory aroma.

Puzzled, she glanced over her shoulder at him. "It is the Yamada farm. Do you know Shig and Aiko Yamada?"

He nodded and continued watching her graceful movements as she worked. "My dad and I used to buy produce from Mr. and Mrs. Yamada every summer until I left home. They always had the best strawberries and tomatoes."

Another smile touched her lips as she poured the egg mixture into the pan. "They still do."

"How do you know them?"

"They are my grandparents, on my mother's side. I used to spend my summers here with them."

"I remember seeing girls working here in the summers," Rock said, recalling two Japanese girls with pigtails and big smiles filling sacks and cartons with the fresh produce.

"My sister, Ellen, and I worked the produce stand. My brother, Tommy, helped when he got big enough." Miko sliced bread and set a plate of it on the table along with butter and a dish of strawberry jam. She cut thin slices of cheese and layered it on the omelet as it cooked.

"Do you and your husband live here on the farm?"

The way his gaze rested on her ringless finger set her on edge. Every time he mentioned her husband, her shoulders tensed with worry.

Cautious, Miko finally admitted the truth. "I'm not married, Captain Laroux. It's Miss Nishimura, but everyone calls me Miko."

He tossed a wicked grin her direction. "Well, Miko, I suppose since you've seen me in my underwear, you might as well call me Rock."

Blossoms of pink colored her cheeks as she set the table. The man had been delirious and bedridden for a week. She'd done more than just see his underwear, but he didn't need to know that. "Very well, Rock. Would you like a glass of milk?"

"Yes, please. The milk I had for breakfast was the best I've had in a long time. It tasted fresh and rich, and so good."

She poured a glass and handed it to him, then lifted the omelet from the pan and cut it into two servings, sliding the largest portion onto his plate.

Much to his surprise, she bowed her head after she took a seat and offered a brief but heartfelt prayer for their meal.

"Are you Methodist?" he asked as he buttered a slice of bread and slathered it with jam. Many of the Japanese he'd known in his youth belonged to a Methodist church located on the outskirts of Portland.

"Presbyterian." She smiled and cut into her omelet. "My great-grandparents joined the church a few years after they arrived from Japan."

"When was that?"

Rock bit into the bread and closed his eyes, clearly enjoying the strawberry jam. Sweet and full of one of the best flavors of the summer, he chewed slowly, as though he wanted to savor the experience.

"In the 1880s. My grandfather was a young boy when they arrived." Miko took a bite of the omelet, pleased to see Rock enjoy the jam she helped her grandmother make last summer.

Rock asked about the farm, the produce stand, and her grandparents as they ate.

It wasn't until she stood to carry the dishes to the sink that he mentioned the absence of anyone else at the house.

"Where are your grandparents?" he asked.

She stopped midstride and cast him a cautious glance. "Gone."

"Oh, I'm sorry. I had no idea…"

Taken aback by his sincerity, she hurried to correct him. "Not deceased, Captain. I just meant they aren't home."

"I'm glad to hear that," Rock said, clearly relieved. He glanced around the kitchen before his gaze landed back on her. "May I help with anything?"

Miko set the dishes in the sink, then added soap and hot water. "It will only take a moment to wash these. It's a beautiful day out. You might enjoy sitting on the front porch for a while," she suggested, tipping her head toward the front of the house.

Rock got the idea she preferred to be alone. Under normal circumstances, he would have charmed her into accepting his company. However, he liked the idea of soaking up the sunshine and clean spring air. On unsteady feet, he stood and took a few steps. "Thank you for lunch."

"You're welcome." Her focus remained on the dishes she scrubbed.

She dried and put away the dishes, then set a chicken she'd killed and plucked earlier in a big pot to stew. Miko opened a door in the short hall off the kitchen and made her way down the dark stairs. At the bottom, she reached up and pulled on a string. Light flooded the basement.

Miko had never liked going down to the basement. Like most basements, it often smelled musty and spiders lurked in the corners. Her sister always refused to set foot in it, frightened by the dark dankness of the space.

Shelves lined the walls of the large open room. A kaleidoscope of color burst from the assortment of preserves filling jars of various sizes. Grandma always canned twice as much as she needed and frequently gave away the excess.

Bins that brimmed with potatoes, apples, and onions through the winter were nearly empty, waiting for a new crop to fill their bareness.

Along the far wall, a high bench with an assortment of tools, all precisely in place, gave testament to her grandfather's talent at carving wood and maintaining order.

Miko reached beneath the bench and found a hidden lever, pushing it back until a drawer popped open.

Her grandfather had padlocked the large building where he stored everything from baskets for the berries they sold at the produce stand to his 1939 Ford 9N tractor.

When she hadn't been caring for the cows, chickens, garden, and Captain Laroux, Miko had searched for the key. She'd never known her grandfather to lock anything, but since they planned to be gone for an indefinite period, she reasoned that was why he'd locked everything. She'd found the key to the building where he kept the lawnmower, tools, and cans of gasoline.

A search of the outbuildings that were unlocked hadn't turned up a key to the storage shed. Neither had a thorough hunt through the house.

As she'd washed the dishes, she recalled the secret drawer in her grandfather's workbench.

Intrigued by what she might find, she lifted out birth certificates, marriage licenses, titles to cars, the farm truck, and the tractor. In the bottom of the drawer, she discovered a ring with four keys. She returned all the papers, slid the key ring over one slender finger, and closed the drawer.

While she was already in the basement, she filled a basket with three jars of peaches, one of peas, and a jar of purple grape juice, taking them with her. In the kitchen, she set the basket on the counter, then checked the chicken, inhaling the steam from the pot as she lifted the lid. She turned down the heat of the burner, stuffed the key ring in her pocket, and made her way to the front of the house.

Through the screen door, she watched Rock peacefully slumber on a broad cane seat. Long legs stretched in front of him while his head tipped against the back of the chair. She would have brought a pillow for his head, but she didn't want to disturb him.

On silent feet, she returned to the kitchen and exited out the back door. At the storage shed, the third key she tried unlocked the padlock and she stepped inside the warehouse-sized building.

In addition to her grandfather's truck and tractor, she was surprised to see his car along with hers. She wished a hundred times she'd driven herself to Sally's home instead of going with Pastor Clark. Had she done so, she wouldn't have been left to walk home in the rain and could have been back in time to join her family before they left for the assembly center.

Then again, she wouldn't have been there to help Rock. The depth of his illness lingered in her mind, convincing her he had been only an hour or two away from perishing when she found him.

Even though his presence had thrown her plans to reunite with her family off-kilter, she didn't regret staying to care for him. He was a wounded soldier who needed a hand. Gladly, she would give him whatever she could.

Although in light of recent events, it might be precious little.

The country at large declared that Japanese Americans conspired with the Japanese, plotting ways to bring about the nation's fall. Regardless of what anyone thought, Miko and her family were patriots through and through. They all purchased war bonds, contributed clothing and blankets for the Bundles for Britain campaign, and wore V for Victory pins on their lapels.

Yet, because her family and friends shared the same ancestral blood as the enemy, the government had rounded them up like cattle and shipped them off to a livestock pavilion. Miko herself was *sansei*, of the generation born to nonimmigrant Japanese Americans. Compared to the young people she knew, Miko and her family were as patriotic as most, more so than many.

The injustice of it all made her stomach ache, especially when she considered her status as a fugitive.

Miko glanced around, wondering what her father had done with his car. Most likely, he sold it when he'd sold the house and business. Had he put the money in the bank or hidden it somewhere on the farm? Had he taken it with him to the assembly center?

For a moment, she fretted about what would become of the farm. Without her grandparents there, what was to keep someone from walking in and taking it over? She hadn't found the deed in the hidden box with the other important papers; she would have to search for it later.

Sheets covered neatly stacked pieces of furniture in one corner, surrounded by towers of boxes.

Miko hoped a few of the boxes contained her belongings. All she had were the clothes she'd carried in her suitcase from Sally's home and the few she kept at the farm for random visits when she helped her grandparents.

Thoughts of Sally made her wish she could call her friend, but she was afraid of who might overhear the conversation on the party line. With her luck, five minutes after she placed the call, the police would show up and haul her off to jail.

She'd written a letter to Sally, but had no idea how to mail it. A trip into town to purchase stamps was out of the question. Perhaps when Captain Laroux was well enough to leave, he'd mail it for her.

Miko squeezed around the end of the farm truck and sighed in relief when she found several boxes with her name written on the outside.

The first one she opened was full of her clothes, and the second box held shoes. Four more boxes of clothes, one of handbags, and two of hats sat around her by the time she decided she wouldn't unpack everything. It seemed silly to do so if she would soon join her family at the assembly center. From what she surmised, the number of belongings they were allowed to take with them was severely limited.

Closing the tops of the boxes, she stacked them, ran her hand with longing over the hood of her car, and shut the door. She locked the padlock and returned to the house to prepare dinner.

The sound of the Andrews Sisters singing "Boogie Woogie Bugle Boy" greeted her as she stepped inside.

Rock sat at the kitchen table, eating another slice of crumb cake with a glass of milk. "Hope you don't mind that I helped myself."

The boyish grin he shot her made her heart pick up tempo as she washed her hands and tied on an apron. "Not at all. You're welcome to anything I have."

His smile broadened and he pointed to the counter near the refrigerator. "Even that Snickers candy bar?"

Miko shot him a mock scowl and shook her head. "Captain Laroux, you should know better than to ask a woman to share her chocolate. It is sacred."

Rock stared at her a long moment, attempting to gauge if she was serious or joking. The corners of her mouth twitched and he laughed. "You had me going for a minute."

"Who said I was teasing?" She peeled potatoes and added them along with carrots and peas to the simmering pot of chicken. "The last fellow that tried to steal my chocolate met a bad end."

"What happened to him?"

Miko widened her almond-shaped eyes and used her index finger to make a slicing motion across her throat.

He shook his head. "You are serious about your candy, aren't you?"

"Just chocolate."

"Did you really send someone to his death for stealing your candy bar?"

"I certainly did. You'll be eating him for dinner." Miko clanged the lid back on the pot and offered Rock a playful smile.

Her face transformed from stoic to beautiful.

"A chicken?" Rock gave her a disbelieving glance. "Surely you can come up with a better story than that."

"It's true. Granddad kept a bothersome little rooster that constantly pecked my ankles and tried to pilfer anything I had in my pockets." Miko shrugged. "After he attempted to flog me while I was feeding the chickens this morning, I decided we'd eat chicken for dinner."

Amused, Rock studied her. "Remind me not to get on your bad side, Miss Nishimura. I'd hate to see what you'd do to a poor ol' soldier down on his luck."

"Indeed, Captain. You appear much more hale and hearty than you did yesterday." Miko sobered. "Are you truly feeling better?"

Rock leaned back in the chair. "Truth to tell, I feel pretty swell. I've been sick for months and no one seems to know the cause. Maybe it was something at the hospital in the air or medication that made me ill, because this is the best I've felt for a long time. It's nice to have an appetite again, although you might soon grow weary of feeding me."

"I doubt that, Captain Laroux."

His eyes twinkled as he smiled at her. "I thought you agreed to call me Rock."

"I suppose I did," Miko said, uncomfortable calling him by his first name. It seemed too... intimate. Thoughts of him, of those broad shoulders and blue eyes, unsettled her.

The music on the radio ended and an engaging male voice offered a news report.

Rock listened to the report. While he'd been sick, he'd had no interest in hearing the news and even less in reading about the war in the newspaper. It had galled him that his friends were fighting overseas while he was dying in a hospital bed.

Perhaps tomorrow he'd wake up as weak and ill as he had been the last few months. What if the symptoms returned a few weeks down the road and he ended up dead?

Today, though, he felt more alive and like himself than he had since his plane crashed.

The news touched on the recent declaration by the president that sugar would be rationed and the implementation of a national speed limit of thirty-five miles per hour to conserve both gasoline and tire rubber.

"Remember, folks, to check in with your local ration board if you have not yet received your ration book," the broadcaster said. "And don't forget to purchase war bonds. Each bond you buy helps our boys march on toward victory."

The sound of Bing Crosby crooning "Only Forever" filled the kitchen as Miko mixed a batch of dumplings and dropped them into the pot with the chicken and vegetables.

"I knew the government had started rationing tires and automobiles, but I didn't realize ration books had been distributed. Do you mind if I look at one?" Rock asked, observing Miko as she rolled out piecrust and lined a pan with it. He couldn't remember the last time he'd enjoyed a slice of homemade pie. His mouth watered at the thought of it.

"If I had one, I'd be more than happy to show it to you," Miko said, draining the juice from the canned peaches. She mixed cinnamon, a bit of flour, and a generous measure of honey into the fruit. Afternoon sunlight turned the jar of sticky sweetener into liquid gold. "They began issuing them last week."

"I see." Rock realized he was the reason she'd missed the opportunity to receive a ration book. "If you need to go to town, I'm perfectly capable of staying on my own for a while."

"No!" Trepidation mixed with dread in her response. Forcibly calming, she shook her head. "That won't be necessary."

"But, Miss Nishimura, if you..." He snapped his mouth shut at her warning glare.

"Would you like to read while I finish dinner preparations?" she asked, stirring the filling for the pie as it bubbled on the stove. "You're welcome to read any books from Granddad's library."

"I noticed he has a fine collection." Rock stood, delighted he did so without a dizzy spell. "If you're sure he wouldn't mind, I'll take a look."

"Go on. I'll let you know when dinner is ready."

Surreptitiously, she watched him leave the kitchen. When he disappeared from sight, she released a tight breath. She didn't want him to know about the assembly center or her failure to report there. Although she assumed she could trust him, a niggling fear that he might turn her in kept her from telling the truth.

Annoyed by the love song playing on the radio and the unwelcome feelings it generated in her for Captain Laroux, she switched off the radio.

After setting the table, pouring Rock a glass of juice, and dishing up the chicken and dumplings, she wiped her hands on the skirt of her apron and sauntered into the living room.

Rock sat in the rocking chair by the window, reading a Depression-era novel written by John Steinbeck. Miko hadn't liked the story, but both her grandparents enjoyed the tale of a family from Oklahoma making their way to California.

The rustle of her skirt drew his attention. He lifted his head and smiled at her, setting the book aside. "It must be time for dinner," he said, rising to his feet.

Miko merely nodded, finding it hard to speak when her tongue felt thick and dry. Something about Rock Laroux — about his handsome face, easy smile, and beautiful blue eyes — left her utterly addled.

She led the way back to the kitchen and took a seat, waiting for him to sit before bowing her head and offering a prayer for their meal.

When she finished, she draped a napkin across her lap and dipped a spoon into the bowl of savory chicken topped with soft, doughy dumplings.

Rock stared at his bowl for the length of several heartbeats before leaning down and inhaling the fragrant steam wafting upward. Bliss settled over his face as he closed his eyes and took a deep breath. "Mmm. That is one of the best smells in the world." He picked up his spoon and took a bite, again closing his eyes and tipping his head to one side. "I haven't had chicken and dumplings that good since I went away to school. Thank you."

"You're welcome," Miko said, keeping her eyes down to hide the delight she found in his words of praise. "There's plenty. Eat all you want."

"I plan to, Miss Nishimura," Rock said, sipping the cold grape juice. He swallowed and held out the glass, studying the dark purple color. "That grape juice is every bit as pretty as it is good. Did your grandmother make it?"

"She did. If it can be canned or dried, she had at least one batch of it put away."

Rock laughed. "She's a smart woman, your grandmother. When do you expect them home? I'd sure like to see your grandparents again."

Miko didn't want to lie, so she kept her response vague. "I'm not sure how long they'll be gone." That much was true. She had no idea how long the government would keep her family detained.

Afraid Rock would continue to question her about her family and their absence, she kept him distracted by asking about the farm where he grew up and sharing silly antics from her youth.

Eventually, Rock would either discover the truth, or be well enough to leave so she could get on with her life.

***★ *Chapter Five* ★**·

Miko leaned her head against the warm side of the cow, stripping the last of the milk from the pink teats. As she worked, her mind wandered to the soldier in the house.

Each day, Rock improved physically, sleeping less and gaining strength. The man's appetite returned. It kept her busy planning nutritious meals for him.

He'd been out of bed for more than a week. The first few days he had eaten, read, and napped. Numerous times, she'd caught him exercising his weak arm and hand. The day before yesterday, he'd assigned himself the chores of helping to water and weed the garden.

Although she appreciated his assistance, being near him left her so ill at ease, she'd accidentally pulled up two tomato plants and stepped on a poor little sprouting bean plant. At that rate, there wouldn't be anything left to harvest.

The news on the radio encouraged all Americans to grow as much of their own food as they could to support the war effort.

Her grandparents had certainly planned to do their part. In addition to what they ate fresh and preserved for the winter months, they'd planted acres of vegetables to sell at the produce stand, along with the bounty picked from the fruit and nut trees.

The two milk cows produced gallons of fresh milk that Miko's grandmother had turned into delicious butter to sell at the produce stand. Between the eggs and abundance of cream, Miko didn't know what to do with the excess. It was too bad they didn't have any pigs, because it would have made excellent feed for them.

Rock did his best to consume his share of the milk. He'd mentioned more than once how good the fresh whole milk tasted. During his service overseas, he said he'd often had to make do with canned or bottled milk.

Miko couldn't imagine going without fresh milk or eggs. Or the nutrient-rich food produced right there on her grandparents' farm.

Finished with the milking, she stood and lifted the heavy bucket in her hand. A resonant rumble from a deep voice in the early-morning shadows made her jump and nearly drop the bucket.

"Let me get that," Rock said, brushing his fingers over hers as he took the bucket in his right hand.

A jolt of electricity shot up her hand and threatened to short-circuit her brain. Unnerved by his presence and his handsome appearance in the muted light, she glared at him.

The smooth line of his jaw indicated he'd recently shaved. The smell of soap mingled with his unique masculine scent, befuddling her already-overwrought senses.

She picked up the second bucket of milk, turned the cows into their pasture, and shut the gate.

"I hoped to beat you out here today, but I guess I'll have to rise before the chickens to make that happen," Rock teased. They stepped into the barn, where Miko strained the milk and rinsed the buckets. An old refrigerator there kept the milk cool until she could skim the cream and work it into butter.

Ignoring her silence, Rock leaned against a wooden counter and pointed with his good hand toward the cows. "What are their names?"

Humor twinkled in her eyes when she lifted her gaze to his. "Amos and Andy."

Rock chuckled. "Are they named after the characters in the radio show?"

Miko nodded. "Yes. It's one of Granddad's favorite programs. He never misses listening to it or *Fibber McGee and Molly*, but Grandma said he couldn't name a cow Fibber McGee."

His grin broadened. "No, I suppose not. My favorite show is *The Lone Ranger*."

She gave him a long, observant glance as they walked to the house. "And you no doubt fancy yourself as *The Lone Ranger*."

With a feigned indignant expression, he slapped his hand against his chest. "I'm wounded you think I wouldn't choose Tonto."

Miko's laugh, a light, playful sound, did strange things to his heart. "You know I'm right Kemosabe."

His shoulder bumped hers and he looked down at her with mirth in his eyes. "If you're going to call me Kemosabe, that means you're my trusty sidekick, right?"

"Wrong. Everyone knows Tonto is secretly in charge." Miko marched ahead of him and stepped into the kitchen.

Their easy banter continued through breakfast and as they returned outside to work. Rock accompanied her to the garden, helping her water the long rows of tender shoots and sprouts.

Midmorning, they returned to the house for Rock to rest while Miko washed a load of laundry. In the midst of hanging towels on the line to dry, the crunch of gravel out front alerted her to the arrival of someone at the produce stand. Her grandparents had left the closed sign across the front of it, so she hoped whoever it was would read the sign and leave.

The engine quieted, followed by the sound of heavy footsteps in the gravel moving toward the house.

Panicked, she took the back steps in one leap and skidded into the kitchen, startling Rock as he filled a glass with water. He dropped the glass and it shattered in the sink.

"I'm sorry," he said, starting to pick up the shards.

Frightened, she grabbed his hand and squeezed it. "Someone is here and I need you to go to the door, Rock. Under no circumstance can they know I'm here. Please? Will you please go to the door?"

The terror in her eyes was enough to force his agreement. He released her hand and pointed to the back hall. "Go down to the basement," he ordered as a knock sounded on the front door.

Rock hurried to answer it, pulling back the heavy wooden portal, but not pushing open the screen door.

A nervous man with a head too big for his flaccid body stood on the other side, glowering at Rock with beady close-set eyes. From the man's sallow skin to the shifty way he tried to glimpse inside the house, Rock didn't trust the visitor. Not one bit.

"May I help you?" He moved so his body blocked the interior view of the house, leaning his left arm against the door frame. Pain shot from his wrist all the way up his shoulder, but he hid it beneath a fake grin.

The man smiled, revealing teeth discolored from a lack of brushing, and a large gap between the two in front. He set down the two cases he carried and blew out a breath that stank worse than rotten fish left in the summer sun. "Norman Ness is my name, selling is my game. What are you doing here?" the man asked, as though he had any right to question Rock's presence at the farm.

"I might ask you the same thing, stranger." Rock pulled the front door shut behind him and stepped outside.

He stood almost a foot taller than the nasty salesman who reeked of booze, sour clothes, and cheap cigarettes.

"I thought this place would be empty. Didn't these Japs get run off to the assembly center in Portland?" The man fairly spat the word *Japs* as he sneered.

Rock's expression remained blank as he shoved his hands in his trouser pockets to keep from punching Norman Ness in the nose. Japs were the enemy shooting down planes and blowing up boats in the Pacific. The Yamada family was about as American as apple pie and baseball. In fact, he had an idea the girl cowering in the basement had more patriotism in her little finger than the buffoon standing in front of him possessed in his entire body.

Rock widened his stance in a maneuver he'd employed any number of times to intimidate a foe. "The Yamada family isn't here, if that's what you're asking."

Norman slowly turned around, surveying the oasis of flowers and greenery around him. "They've only been gone a few weeks. How'd you move in so fast?"

"Maybe I purchased the farm from them." Rock crossed his arms over his chest. "Ever think of that?"

Norman's head snapped around. "Got a deed? If you didn't buy this place fair and square, you better start packing. I've had my eye on this farm for a long time. You don't have any right to take it out from under me! It's mine! If you want to farm, go squat on one of the other abandoned Jap places."

Rock dropped his façade and hardened his glare. His right hand clenched into a fist and he took a threatening step forward. "You try taking over this farm and it might just be the last thing you do. Now get out of here before I phone the sheriff and have you arrested for trespassing."

The man grabbed the two cases he'd set down and took a hurried step back, tripping on the top step and scrambling to keep from falling down the rest of them.

Fury rode the scowl he tossed at Rock. "You can't threaten me, soldier. I'll be back and when I do return, you'll be the one leaving."

"We'll just see about that, Ness. Now, get out of here." Rock stood firm and unyielding on the top step of the porch, presenting a formidable barrier to the house.

Norman hastened into his car and slung gravel across the driveway as he left, screaming curses out the open window.

Rock waited until the car disappeared down the road before returning inside the house. He made his way to the door to the basement and opened it. "You can come out now," he called down the darkened stairs.

Defeat rode the slump of Miko's shoulders as she climbed the steps. Without saying a word, she made two cups of tea and sat down at the table.

Rock joined her, taking a sip of the tea for something to do, not because he liked drinking the strange brew of herbs she insisted was good for his health.

"Did you hear any of that?" he asked.

Slowly, she nodded. "I heard it all."

"Do you want to tell me where your grandparents are and why you're afraid to be seen?" Rock leaned back in the chair, doing his best to appear relaxed.

He rested the weight of his gaze on Miko, staring into eyes that reminded him of an obsidian rock he'd once found on a hike with his dad. Glossy and such a deep shade of brown they were almost black, her almond-shaped peepers shimmered with shame and guilt.

From the moment he regained his senses, he'd known she was hiding something, but up until that moment, he hadn't realized what.

"Miss Nishimura, I can't help you if you don't fill me in on all the details."

Miko sighed and dropped her eyes to the untouched cup of tea in front of her. Telling the truth seemed like the best idea.

"It all started back in February, when my employer fired me because I'm Japanese. With nothing else to occupy my time, I went to Tillamook to stay with my friend until her baby arrived. Her father is the pastor of our church." Absently, she rubbed a finger around the rim of the teacup. "My father called on a lovely Sunday afternoon a few weeks ago to let me know I needed to rush home. Anyone of Japanese descent in the Oregon evacuation area had been ordered to report to the Portland Assembly Center by noon on May fifth. In spite of my best efforts, returning home proved difficult. The ticket agents at the bus station wouldn't sell a ticket to me, so my friend Sally procured one. Unfortunately, once I was on the bus, I ran into more trouble."

Rock stared at her. "What sort of trouble?"

Miko shrugged. "The bus driver took exception to having someone Japanese on his bus and terminated my privilege to ride."

A vertical line etched across his brow as he frowned. "You mean he kicked you off the bus?"

"Yes," she said softly.

"Where?"

She glanced out the kitchen window rather than meet his gaze. "About twenty miles from here."

Rock leaned forward and rested both arms on the table. "How'd you get home?"

"I walked." Miko took a sip of her swiftly cooling tea.

"You walked?" Incredulous, he rocked back in the chair, unable to comprehend what she'd done. "When did you get here?"

"About five minutes before I found you on the back step." She spoke quietly, barely above a whisper.

Rock made up for it as his voice rose in volume. "Are you crazy, woman? You walked home twenty miles in the rain, at night, on a dark road, all alone? I suppose you were lugging a suitcase, too."

Her spine straightened and she held his gaze. "Yes, I was, but I had no choice. What was I supposed to do? Wait for some heroic soldier to come along and sweep me off my feet?" A disgusted snort escaped her. "Believe me, I'd have been just one more dead *Jap* if I'd waited for that to happen. As it was, the few people who stopped to help took off like they'd encountered someone carrying the plague when they realized I was Japanese."

Rock reached across the table with his right hand, settling it over hers. "Did anyone hurt you?"

Touched by his concern, she shook her head. "No. Not physically." Another sigh rolled up from her chest and out her lips. "I'm a fugitive for not reporting to the assembly center. On top of that, I'm afraid to leave the farm unattended. You heard that horrid man, Rock. He'll come back and take over, and there isn't a thing I can do to stop him."

"Sell me the farm, Miko. Sell me the farm, give me the deed, and I promise I won't let him or anyone else take over the place until your grandparents return." Rock had no idea where the words he'd just spoken came from, but he rapidly warmed to the idea.

Her gaze lifted to his, shocked by his brash offer. "You'd do that? Keep the farm safe for them?"

"I would. If it wasn't for you, I'd be buried six feet under and waiting for summer daisies to grow. It's my fault you didn't report at the center, isn't it?" he asked, suddenly aware of what his presence at the farm had cost Miko.

At her nod, he lifted her hand and pressed his lips to the backs of her fingers. "I owe you my life, Miko

63

Nishimura, and there isn't a single thing I wouldn't do for you."

"Just keep the farm safe, Rock. That's all I ask. I suppose I should find a ride into town and report to the assembly center." Miko knew that was what she should do, but it wasn't what she wanted to do. Not at all. She looked across the table at Rock and studied him. "I'm sorry I didn't tell you the truth earlier. I was... I just..."

Rock smiled and released her hand, disturbed by how good it felt to hold her slender fingers with his. "You didn't want me to worry or feel guilty since I'm the reason you stayed. Is that it?"

Rather than answer, she took their teacups to the sink and poured out the tepid liquid, then opened the refrigerator, setting out leftovers for their lunch.

Rock moved behind her as she sliced a loaf of bread so they could eat sandwiches. His right hand settled on her shoulder in a comforting touch. "Don't leave, Miko. Not yet. Let me think through a plan before you do something hasty. In the meantime, if you know where your grandfather might have kept the deed, you better find it."

Tears blurred her eyes, but she remained stiff and kept her back to him as she worked, wondering what she'd do when the time came to tell the teasing, good-looking soldier good-bye.

****★ *Chapter Six* ★***

"Miko? Miko! Are you in there?" Rock called, standing in the doorway of the large storage building. He'd noticed the open doors and wandered over to look inside.

The past two days, he'd listened to every news report on the radio, hoping to hear more about the evacuation of the Japanese in America. Other than a story about the authorities taking a few Japanese Americans into custody for failing to report to the assembly center, the news focused mostly on what took place overseas.

Rock prayed for his friends in action and made plans for the farm, hoping Miko would agree to go along with them.

He decided to walk to the nearest bus stop and see if he might make his way into Portland. When he was cleaning the produce stand the previous afternoon, he'd found a jar of coins. There was more than enough in the jar to purchase a bus ticket.

Thoughts of taking the bus flew right out of his head as he gawked at two cars and an older farm truck. A four-door dark blue sedan appeared to be a few years old, but in excellent condition. Parked next to it was a car that drew Rock in for a closer inspection.

The new Packard convertible coupe sported white sidewall tires and enough shiny chrome to make him wish he had a pair of sunglasses.

"I thought I heard you calling for me," Miko said, climbing down a ladder on the far end of the building with an arm full of berry crates.

Rock rushed to help her. By the time he threaded his way through the packed contents of the building, she was already on the floor.

"That's quite a car," he said, taking half the berry crates from her and motioning to the convertible.

"Thanks. I bought it when I was still gainfully employed," she said, walking over to the car. "I fell in love with the color the first time I saw it and started saving my money to buy one. When the weather's nice, it's fun to drive with the top down."

Rock gaped at her. "It's your car?"

Miko grinned. "Is that a hint of disbelief I hear, Captain? Not only is it my car, but I know how to change the tires, check the oil, and siphon gas out of my dad's car when my brother, Tommy, borrows it and brings it back empty."

He laughed, setting down the crates and wiping his hands along his trousers before touching the car. "It is a beaut. What's this color?"

"Laguna maroon. Papa calls it the luna moon mobile, but I still think it's one of the prettiest colors out there." Miko opened the driver's side door and motioned for Rock to climb in.

He sank into the leather seat and inhaled the aroma as if it was the most expensive perfume.

"Like it?" Miko asked, bending down to better see his reaction to the car.

"You bet!" He settled his hands on the steering wheel, forcing his injured fingers to curl around the wheel.

"If you like the outside of the car, you'll probably be more impressed by the eight cylinders under the hood." Miko released the hood latch and Rock slid out to study the engine.

He whistled and smirked at Miko. "What's a girl like you doing with a car like this?"

"Anything I want," she said with a sassy grin. "At least it used to be that way."

Rock sobered and closed the hood, using the hem of his T-shirt to wipe away the smudges made by his fingerprints.

"I didn't realize you had cars here. I was trying to figure out how to catch a ride on the bus into Portland."

"By all means, drive one of the cars wherever you need to go." She pointed to her grandparents' sedan. "Papa and Mother must have sold their car or it would be here, too. Granddad wouldn't care if you took his." She cast a taunting look his way. "Or, if you think you can handle it, you're welcome to drive mine."

His raised an eyebrow at her dare as he lifted the berry baskets and followed her out the door. "Is that an invitation or a challenge?"

"Maybe both." She turned and sauntered away, casting a flirty smile at him over her shoulder.

Rock watched her walk toward the strawberry patch. In the past, the girls who had attracted his attention were generally petite, buxom, and most often blond. He enjoyed being the big hero to their diminutive helplessness.

If he envisioned the exact opposite of the type of girl he usually dated, Miko fit the description to the letter. Tall, lithe, graceful, and confident, she didn't need a hero. In his opinion, she was one.

The woman was in constant motion, working with a quiet steadiness that impressed him more than anything any other woman had ever done to win his favor.

Rock no longer worried that he'd been left like forgotten baggage at death's back door. Instead, he greeted each new day feeling more hearty and robust than the day before. He hadn't had a dizzy spell in more than a week, could draw in deep breaths without his lungs threatening to explode, and the pain in his stomach had dissipated.

Again, he wondered if something at the hospital had made him ill. The possibilities seemed endless as he considered the number of medications he took and the aromas in the air. He may never know what had nearly killed him, but he held hope that whatever it was had worked its way out of his system.

Most of the credit for his returning health belonged to Miko. She'd nursed him as well as anyone trained in the art, fed him nourishing food, and encouraged him to take in all the sunshine and fresh air he could handle.

Now, almost three weeks after he'd escaped from the hospital, he felt like a new man. One no longer sentenced to die an agonizing death. Because of the woman down on her hands and knees searching between the leafy strawberry plants for ripe fruit, he had hope for a future.

He carried the baskets over to where she carefully worked her way down the row, finding a few ripe early berries.

When she glanced back at him and popped one into her mouth, his heart tripped in his chest.

Surely, he wasn't attracted to her. To a woman nearly his height with gleaming hair the color of midnight and a slender, willowy form that put him in mind of some mythical legend from the stories his mother had told him as a child. The very scent of her brought to mind secluded tropical beaches and soothing ocean air.

Miko turned to hand him a berry and he was filled with an unbidden desire to kiss away the drop of red juice clinging to her enticing bottom lip.

Tempted as he was to give in to his yearning, footsteps pounding against the earth from behind the barn interrupted his amorous thoughts.

Before Miko had the opportunity to hide, a youngster appeared that represented Rock's ideal of an all-American boy.

The lad possessed a mop of red hair, a lock of which seemed determined to flop across his forehead and dangle in his left eye. A supply of freckles, one of the most ample Rock had ever witnessed, covered not only the boy's nose, but also his entire face. Blue eyes, the same color as summer skies, sparked with life and mischief.

"Golly, Miko! I'll tell the world, but they held me hostage against my will and it's taken three weeks to convince Pop to spring me. You'd'a thunk they captured a German for all the fuss that went on trying to keep me someplace I didn't want to be," the boy said animatedly. He brushed the shock of hair from his eyes as he approached the berry patch.

Miko stepped over the rows of plants and took a seat on the grass beyond the edge of the strawberry patch. The boy offered Rock a snappy salute, then plopped down beside her.

"Who's the soldier?" he asked, turning his inquisitive gaze from Rock to Miko.

She smiled and settled a hand on the youngster's back. "Petey Phillips, I'd like you to meet my friend, Captain Rock Laroux." Before turning her attention to the boy, Miko winked at Rock. "Petey's parents own the farm just down the road. His family has been friends with my grandparents for years and years."

"Are you a real, honest-to-goodness Captain?" Petey jumped back up and took a step closer to Rock, tipping his head back to stare at him.

Rock dropped down to one knee and stuck out his hand in greeting. The boy grasped it in his, pumping his little arm up and down. "I sure am, Petey. Or at least I was before my plane went down."

Miko glanced at him in curiosity, hoping he'd go into more detail. Instead, he took a seat beside her. Petey flopped down next to him, clearly struck with an immediate case of hero worship.

She leaned around Rock to speak to the boy. "Petey, you said you've been held hostage. Where were you?"

"Jeepers, but I've been imprisoned at my Aunt Nancy's house in the city. She's about as bossy and cranky as they come. The only one bossier and crankier than her is my cousin Ida. She's thirteen and thinks she's the smartest thing to hit the dirt since Plato." Petey rubbed a questionably clean finger beneath his nose, then leaned back in the grass. "One evening right after supper, Mom got sick and Dad rushed her to the hospital. Aunt Nancy picked me up there and I've been stuck at her house for half of forever."

"Is your mother well?" Miko asked, moving as though she planned to get to her feet and march right over to the Phillips's farmhouse to check on the woman.

"Aw, she's fine, but while she was at the hospital, someone gave her a dumb ol' baby. That's all she and Pop have done the last few weeks is wait on that squawking little monkey. Pop brought me out to see it twice, but he and Mom thought it best if I stayed with Aunt Nancy awhile."

"Don't you like your baby sister, Petey?" Miko asked, continuing to lean around Rock. "What's her name?"

"Alice. They named her Alice Marie. If they had to drag home a crying, pooping machine, I sure wish it would've been a boy." Petey twirled a blade of grass in his fingers, oblivious to the humor his straightforward assessment caused.

Rock did his best not to bark with laughter at the boy's description of his baby sister. Miko gave him a warning glare, then turned back to Petey. "But your mother and sister are fine, aren't they?"

"Well, sure. Granny's been staying at the house, waiting on Mom like she's the Queen of Sheba. There's been so many people come to visit, Pop might as well yank the front door off its hinges and put up an open-for-business sign." Petey sighed and shrugged. "At least they finally let me come home. If I'd had to listen to Aunt Nancy tell me how to sit in my chair like a proper gentleman one more time..." To illustrate, he sat up straight, pursed his lips, and pointed his chin in the air. "Or have Ida beat her gums, instructing me in how to scrub out my ears or comb my hair, I might'a waged my own war and left her scalped."

Rock coughed to hide his laugh, drawing a scowl from Miko and an interested look from the boy.

"In the hubbub of Princess Alice arriving, we all forgot we promised to keep an eye on the cows and chickens for your grandpa." Petey's little face held a measure of remorse. "Is he comin' home soon?"

Miko held his gaze. "Not for a while, Petey. In fact, he and Grandma may be gone a long time."

Petey frowned. "What about Mr. Jack and Tommy? Will they come out soon?"

Miko shook her head. "I'm afraid not, sweetheart. My father, mother, and brother went with my grandparents."

"Well, shoot!" The youngster thumped a hand on his leg. "If Tommy isn't gonna be around all summer, who'll play cowboys and Indians with me?"

"Would I make a fair substitute?" Rock asked, drawing a surprised, wide-eyed grin from the child.

"Boy, would you!" Petey leaped to his feet and grabbed Rock's hand, tugging on it. "Can we have a go or two right now, just to see if you'll fit the bill?"

"That can be arranged." Rock stood, then reached down, offering Miko his hand. She rose to her feet with an elegance that belied the faded cotton pants and dirt-smudged blouse she wore.

"Be gentle with him, Petey, he's still recovering," Miko cautioned before picking up the berry basket she'd filled and heading to the house. "When you boys are finished playing, I'll bring out a snack."

"Thanks, Miko!" Petey yelled, taking Rock's hand in his again, yanking on his fingers as he moved toward the barn.

By the time Petey showed him all the best hiding places in the barn and the other outbuildings, the boy concluded they had better not engage in a sham fight until the captain gained more strength.

In lieu of participating in a mock Battle of the Little Bighorn, Rock encouraged Petey to tell him what he knew about the farm and the Yamada family, Miko in particular.

"Miko's the limit, and I mean *The Limit*. You can capitalize that and take it to the bank, but she's as good an egg as ever was laid," Petey exclaimed. The boy swung on the low-hanging branch of a maple tree. "If anyone tells you different, it's applesauce with a side of baloney. On the level, Miko is the real McCoy and there just ain't any finer."

"Is that so?" Rock asked, amused by the boy's liberal use of slang. He wondered where a little lad from a farm had picked up such language. It most certainly wasn't from Aunt Nancy or Cousin Ida. Despite the manner in which the child conveyed his thoughts, Rock agreed with his assessment. He held a high admiration for Miko, whether or not she realized it.

"I told ya so, didn't I, and I'm as straight a shooter as Miko and Grandpa Yamada. Gee, but I wish they were gonna be home this summer. I used to come over and help them sell stuff in the produce stand. Grandma Yamada would make ice cream and we'd sit on the porch at night and listen to the crickets sing. The moonflowers made the air smell like ambrosia. Now there's a five-dollar word if you've ever heard one!"

"It certainly is." Little need existed for Rock to contribute to the conversation. Petey Phillips was more than happy to share what he knew about Miko and her family.

"Say, Pop said my scout troop is gonna have a scrap metal drive this summer. Could I come over here and gather up some stuff? There's a prize for the scout who gathers the most and I wanna win it."

Rock glanced in the direction Petey pointed. He'd noticed the pile of rusted metal objects in an open shed out behind the large storage building. The twisted mess of metal contrasted with the neat and orderly appearance of the rest of the farm.

"You'll have to ask Miko about that, but I don't think she'd object."

Petey let go of the tree and landed on the ground with an enthusiastic thump. He formed a fist and popped it against the flattened palm of his other hand. "I'm gonna help slap the Japs right off the map by collecting scrap metal."

Rock cast a glance at the house to make sure Miko hadn't heard the boy's statement, then gave him a disparaging glance. "Now, see here, Petey. That's not a nice name to use for Japanese people."

"Aw, for crying out loud! Don't go gettin' in a lather, Cap. I'm just telling it true. The Japs all need shot down and how!" Petey laced his hands together, extending his index fingers and lifting his thumbs. The child then executed rapid-fire shooting sounds as he obliterated an unseen foe.

"Hey, buddy, pipe down," Rock said, placing a hand on Petey's shoulder. "You don't want to hurt Miko's feelings, especially when you're standing on land owned by a very fine Japanese man — a man I thought you liked."

Petey stopped and gaped at him, mouth open and eyes goggled. "Your opticals need fine-tuning, Cap. Maybe you best get your ears in for a cleaning, too. Miko ain't a Jap. There ain't a single, solitary one to be found on this place. No siree! Grandpa and Grandma Yamada, Miko, and her folks are one hundred percent American friends of mine. I won't put up with anyone saying otherwise." Petey lifted two scrappy fists and jabbed them into the air.

A grin quirked the corners of Rock's mouth upward. "I'm glad to hear that, Petey. She's my friend, too."

The boy gave him a sidelong study, then scuffed his toe in the grass. "I'll give it to you on the up and up that I plan to marry Miko when I get big enough. But I might just step aside if you think you're man enough to get the job done. She's the cat's pajamas and then some, so you better make sure you're gonna treat her like Granny treats Princess Alice, or I ain't gonna let you have her."

Rock hunkered down and appeared solemn while swallowing his mirth. "I'll tell you what, Petey. Should the day arrive when I decide to marry Miko, I'll ask your permission first. If you decide I'm not up for the task, you can tell me."

Petey grinned. "I knew you were a crackerjack. Now, stand at attention and look smart about it, 'cause here she comes."

Miko smiled as she carried a laden tray to a picnic table placed beneath the shade of a large oak tree.

Sun-ripened berries and a generous helping of freshly whipped cream topped slices of white cake, still warm from the oven.

"Mmm, mm. Nobody bakes cake like Miko and Grandma Yamada," Petey said, taking a big bite. "Can you teach Mom how to make it like yours? Her white cake always tastes like she used cornmeal mixed with sawdust and forgot to add the sugar."

Rock choked on a bite and took a drink from the glass of milk Miko handed to him. If nothing else, the neighbor boy provided a welcome diversion.

Petey finished his cake, thanked Miko, and promised to return to check on them another day. Before he ran off, Miko caught him around the waist and sat him on the table so he was nearly eye level with her and Rock.

"Petey, you know I love you to pieces and you are welcome to visit anytime you like, but I need you to do something for me." Miko eyed the boy, glad to see he attentively listened to each word she spoke.

"You name it," he said, grinning at her. "If you want me to jump off the top of that barn, just say the word. You need me to chase down a bus, I'll run till my legs give out. You ask me to sing 'Yankee Doodle,' I'll tune up the pipes and belt it out without a band."

"It's nothing quite as elaborate or drastic as all that." She tweaked Petey's upturned nose. "You've seen the war posters that talk about loose lips sinking ships, haven't you?"

"Sure, I have." Petey leaned toward Rock. "Everybody's seen them and even if you ain't feasted your eyes on one, you hear 'em say it on the radio all the time."

"Yes, you do," Rock agreed.

Miko placed a gentle hand on the boy's shoulder. "What I'm trying to explain, Petey, is that it's very important no one knows I'm here. Not even your mom and dad. Will you keep it a secret, just between us?"

"Will I? Will I keep a secret?" The boy vaulted off the table and danced a little jig. "Boy, will I! The Germans could string me up by my toes, the Japs could poke me with bayonets, the Italians could roast me over a pit, but I ain't talking. If they ask, I don't know nuthin'." Petey shrugged and pulled an angelic, innocent face. "Miko? I haven't seen her for a long while. She went off with Grandma and Grandpa Yamada for the summer, don't ya

75

know. They're on a marvelous trip and who knows when they'll be back."

Petey turned and raced across the yard. He stopped at the corner of the barn and saluted Rock, then bowed to Miko. "These lips won't sink a ship or a girl as swell as you."

Miko blew him a kiss, then the boy disappeared in the direction from which he'd come.

"Whew," Rock said, propping his elbow on the table and resting his chin on his hand. "That boy is like a cyclone riding a twister."

Miko laughed and gathered the dishes from the table onto the tray. "Petey is lively, but once he gives his word, he keeps it."

"How old is the little scamp?" Rock asked, getting to his feet as she stood and lifted the tray. He wanted to take it from her, but he still wasn't able to bear much weight with his left hand. Rather than dwell on what he couldn't do, he hurried ahead and held open the back screen door for her.

"Petey turned nine in January. I knew his folks were expecting an addition to the family, but I forgot the due date with all that's happened the last few months. I wondered why they hadn't been around, but that explains it." Miko set the dishes in the sink, then wiped off the tray and stored it in a low cupboard. "He'll make a nuisance of himself coming to visit now that he knows you're here. The only thing he enjoys playing more than cowboys and Indians is soldiers at war."

"I could teach him more than he wanted to know," Rock said, drying the dishes as Miko washed them. His thoughts had carried him a million miles away when she handed him the last plate to dry.

She studied him, admiring his straight, broad shoulders and trim waist. Just in the last week, he'd put on weight, filling out his form as the sickness left his body.

Plenty of sunshine had tanned his skin, and hard work on the farm had tightened his muscles.

As though he sensed her perusal, he turned to her and smiled. "If you don't object, I'd like to borrow your grandfather's car and go to my farm tomorrow. I stored some things there, clothes and whatnot, which will come in handy."

"You mean you'll stay here?" Miko asked, not sure what to make of his plans.

"I promised you I'd take care of this place until your grandfather returns and I mean it. I rented out the farm my father left me, so I have nowhere else to go. Now, if you don't want me to stay here, that's another matter. However, you'll have to develop incredibly compelling arguments to convince me to leave." Rock watched her face as she absorbed his words. "I want to stay and help you, Miko. By the time the produce stand is ready to open for the season, I might even be able to run it."

"Really? You'd really stay and run the farm? You'll keep that awful Mr. Ness from trying to take it away?" she asked. The temptation to throw her arms around Rock and kiss him almost overpowered her good sense.

"I will. First, I want to go get my things at the farm. After that, I should go pay a visit to my doctor and let him know I didn't die the night I checked myself out of the hospital." At her surprised look, he motioned to the table.

They both took seats, then he leaned back in the chair and looked around the modern room. Miko told him her grandparents had updated the bathroom and kitchen the previous autumn. He wouldn't complain about the modern conveniences that made his life easier. Questions about how long they had before the power and phone service were shut off crossed his mind. He planned to get it all sorted out soon.

"The short story is this: I overheard my doctor tell another physician he had no hope for my recovery and I would only live a few weeks. I decided if I was going to die, I wanted to do it on the land where I was raised, not in some sterile hospital room. So I left." A self-deprecating look crossed his face. "Of course, I was half out of my mind with illness and not thinking straight. If I had been, I would have made sure I had more than a few coins in my possession."

"That's why you had to get off the bus, isn't it? You didn't have money for a ticket."

Rock nodded. "I had thirty-seven cents. I spent thirty of them to get to Beaverton. The driver didn't notice me asleep in my seat until a few stops later when I got off. I started walking and just when I was sure I couldn't go any farther, I recognized your grandparents' produce stand. You know the rest of the story."

"I guess I do." Unable to bear the thought of what would have happened to Rock if she hadn't happened along, she said a quick prayer of gratitude she'd found him. "If the doctor thought you'd die soon, I'm sure he'll be surprised to see you looking so well."

"I'm counting on it. He'll more than likely think he's seen a ghost. I do need to pay him a visit, though, and speak to someone about my discharge papers." Rock cleared his throat and glanced at Miko. "If you aren't opposed to it, I thought I'd go to the assembly center and see if they'll let me visit your family."

Her head snapped up and she gaped at him. "You'd do that? Go check on them for me?"

A soft light shone in his eyes as he nodded. "I'd happily do that for you. My plan is to purchase this place from your grandfather and have him sign the deed. I want it to be legal, so no one can question my right to be here. Upon his return, I'll sell the property back to him. Does that sound fair to you?"

"More than fair, Rock, and it will make Granddad so happy," she said. Introspective, she remained lost in her thoughts for a few moments. "Would you take them a letter if I write one?"

"Of course. Just be careful what you write. Someone probably reads through the letters and you wouldn't want to give away the fact you're here instead of there."

Miko sighed. "Perhaps I should just go with you and turn myself in."

"No!" Rock didn't know why he so vehemently opposed the idea, but everything in him argued to keep Miko far away from the assembly center. "Let me investigate things first. You may do your family much more good here than you would there."

"If you think it's best to wait, I will." She lifted her gaze and met his, wondering how his eyes could sparkle so brightly and with such emotion. "You plan to go to your farm first and then visit the doctor?"

"I'll go to the farm tomorrow and the doctor the day after that. Could you find the deed between now and then?"

Miko rose to her feet. "I've looked everywhere in the house. I guess I'll broaden my search outside. If I can't find it, perhaps Granddad can give you a clue where he hid it."

"May I help you search?" Rock asked, following her outside. He held the laundry basket while she took sheets off the line, folding them as she went.

"I'll look tomorrow while you're gone." Miko stopped and shot him a concerned glance. "Do you think Mr. Ness will come back soon?"

"Not if he knows what's good for him," Rock muttered darkly. At her perplexed look, he cleared his throat. "If he comes when I'm not here, stay hidden or sneak off to the Phillips place. After meeting Petey, I'm fairly certain he comes from good ol' American stock who'll rush to your assistance."

A soft smile touched her lips. "They would. John and Lucy are the nicest people. You should stop by to meet them sometime."

Rock nodded. "I will, but first let's make sure no one can get their hands on this place."

Miko took the basket from him and set it on the grass. Before he quite knew what transpired, she wrapped her arms around him and gave him a tight hug. "This place is more than just a farm. It ties my family to our past and provides a rich heritage for the future. Thank you for being such a good, honorable man."

The words he wanted to say remained unspoken as she lifted the laundry basket and rushed inside the house.

*★★ *Chapter Seven* ★★*

Sorely tempted to drive Miko's car just to see what it could do, Rock instead took her grandfather's truck and left with a jaunty wave the following morning.

Forty-five minutes later, he arrived at the farm his father had bequeathed him. Although he wanted to ignore the nationwide order to drive thirty-five miles an hour, he kept his foot light on the gas pedal and tootled along like a law-abiding citizen.

The young man who leased the farm offered Rock a warm welcome, then helped load his trunks in the truck. Enthusiastic, the farmer walked around the place, showing off the improvements he'd made and discussing the crops he'd planted. Rock thanked him for taking good care of the farm, then slid behind the wheel of his borrowed vehicle.

A few minutes before noon, Rock returned to the Yamada farm, expecting Miko to be in the kitchen making lunch. She wasn't in the house, the garden, or the barn. He checked the storage building and the other outbuildings. He even walked out to the orchard, but didn't find her anywhere.

Worried, he walked behind the barn, intent on following Petey's path to the Phillips place. A footpath made of flat stones through the grass diverted his attention. He followed it to a fence on the border of the woods towering behind the cleared ground of the farm.

Sweet peas and ivy climbed over the privet-lined fence, creating a thick barrier. More stones presented a walkway parallel to the fence for the length of a few hundred yards. Rock walked along it one way until it ended at a stone bench. He turned and followed it the other direction until the last stone disappeared beneath a large azalea bush. Perplexed by the reason for the footpath and its sudden end, he took a few steps back to study his surroundings. The fence sagged in an area to his immediate right. It seemed odd and out of place with the rest of the immaculately tended farm.

Curious if the wood had rotted, he reached out to feel the post. At his touch, a small gate swung open. Privets planted in concealed containers attached to the gate hid its true purpose.

Rock stepped through the opening in the fence, carefully shutting the gate behind him. He followed a narrow, almost invisible trail as it wound up the side of the mountain.

Several times in the past week, Miko had disappeared. Rock had assumed she worked in the barn or one of the outbuildings. As soon as he no longer required constant care, she'd taken to sleeping somewhere other than in the house. He couldn't help but notice the empty bedroom next to his she'd formerly occupied. He'd tried to ask her about it, but she'd avoided answering.

Perhaps she climbed up this trail to think or meditate. Maybe she slept in a tent up on the mountain.

For the most part, Miko was a quiet, private person. She had lighthearted moments, though. He smiled as he remembered her good-natured, relaxed demeanor with Petey the previous afternoon. She needed more opportunities to be carefree and full of the playfulness of youth.

Abruptly, he considered her age. He'd be twenty-nine in September, but he didn't think she was quite that old.

Yet she seemed wise and responsible, far more so than her years. By the fashionable way she dressed, the smooth creaminess of her skin, and her impeccable posture, he guessed her to be in her mid-twenties.

As he climbed the steep trail, Rock stopped twice to catch his breath. Below him, the house and buildings of the farm grew smaller and smaller.

At the top of the hill, he encountered a tall fortress-like fence. Anyone with plans to scale it would have to drag a long ladder up the trail.

Fortunately, a gate stood open, so he walked inside. Unprepared for the magnificence that greeted him, he looked out over an elaborate Japanese garden, complete with a waterfall and stream, bridge-covered ponds teeming with colorful carp, stone lanterns and benches, walkways, vibrant blooming plants, and trees. So many trees. Oaks, maples, pines and flowering plums were among those he easily recognized.

Awed, he ambled forward, taking in the splendid, tranquil beauty of the garden. It reminded him of Trinidad, where he'd enjoyed the profusion of flowers, trees, and birds.

He followed a stone walkway up a slight incline and around a screen of trees, breathing in the earthy aroma of the garden mingling with the sweet, zesty fragrance of the flowers. The air tasted green and refreshing, bursting with life.

Rock stepped into a clearing, surprised to discover a traditional Japanese home. Weeping cherry trees, limbs heavy with pink blossoms, flanked the house like sentinels bedecked for a party.

His boots crunched on the gravel pathway as he approached the house. Posts and lintels supported a gently sloped roof. The curved eaves extended far beyond the walls of the house, covering what looked like a veranda.

Heavy storm shutters stood ready to keep out inclement weather.

Wary of intruding, but fascinated by his discovery, he stood outside and raised his voice. "Miko? Are you here, Miko?"

Almost immediately, she appeared in the doorway, shocked to see him. "What are you doing here?"

He grinned. "I got back from the farm and looked everywhere for you. By accident, I found your gate." He glanced behind him and waved a hand, as though to encompass the entire garden. "What is this place?"

"The home of my ancestors and the garden of my heart." Miko motioned him forward. "Take off your boots, then you may come inside."

Quickly, Rock removed his boots and followed her up the steps.

Miko pointed behind them to the garden. "My great-grandparents arrived in the area in 1882. My great-grandfather took any work available to him and saved every penny he didn't have to spend. Within a few years, my great-grandparents saved enough to purchase a quarter section of land. Most people thought they were crazy for buying a hill so thickly covered in brush and trees; the land was best suited for a lumber business. They cleared the acres at the bottom of the hill, planted fruit trees, and tilled the ground for a big garden. The second year they were here, they added a produce stand. Eventually, Granddad and Grandma built a small house down below. After my great-grandparents passed away, they built the yellow house and a new produce stand."

"What about this house, Miko?" Rock asked as he followed her inside.

"My great-grandparents wanted to honor their ancestry, so the house and garden here keep with tradition. The two of them began the work to create this hilltop garden not long after they bought the land. My grandparents finished it. Granddad and I both enjoy working in the garden to maintain what our family strived so hard to create. That's why a stranger can't have this land, Rock. They wouldn't care about the garden my great-grandparents labored so hard to build out of nothing but thick trees and scraggly brush."

She led him down a corridor lined with screens made of wooden lattice covered with paper. The screens comprised both the interior and exterior walls. "Many people would log the trees and sell the land instead of preserving the beauty of this place."

Intrigued by the house, he absently nodded in agreement.

Miko stopped. "You are in the *engawa*, an outer corridor that wraps around a home, like a veranda. Traditionally, a Japanese home does not use glass. A *shoji* screen..." she pushed one of the panels back and revealed a light-saturated room "... is a sliding panel made of translucent paper set in a wooden frame. It provides shelter and privacy, and allows us to manipulate the natural light."

Rock looked into the room, noticing a mat on the floor and a low table with cushions around it.

Miko pointed to the mat. "*Tatami* are rice straw mats made for the floors. When they are new, they have the most wonderful smell. My great-grandmother made that one."

She led him to a room that had to be the kitchen. In the center was a sunken hearth. "The *irori*, or hearth, is used not only for cooking, but also to heat the home," she explained, then continued on with her tour.

Two sleeping rooms featured mats on the floors with bedding on top of them. He noticed Miko appeared to have moved into one of the rooms. A robe he'd seen her wear hung on a hook on the wall.

"Are you sleeping here?" Rock questioned. "I noticed you moved out of the house. If that's on my account, I'll sleep in the barn or somewhere else."

Miko shook her head. "No, Rock, you need a proper bed to sleep in to regain your health and I don't mind staying here. Now that you're better, it isn't right for us to sleep under the same roof." A slight blush pinked her cheeks as she spoke. Rock decided she'd never looked lovelier.

Unable to pinpoint the moment it had happened, he'd gone from viewing Miko as an unusually tall, foreign-appearing stranger to a woman who interested him more than any he could ever recall. From the top of her head of gleaming black hair to her fashionably clad toes, he thought she was one of the most graceful, lovely women he'd ever seen.

He shrugged. "If you change your mind, let me know. Amos and Andy would let me bunk with them."

"I'm sure they would," she said with a grin. The two cows had quickly taken to him when he'd declared it his job to handle the milking. Miko hadn't argued because the motion of squeezing milk from the cows provided excellent therapy for his injured arm and hand. Still, he tired easily, so she ended up milking at least one of them.

A short, deep wooden tub and shower filled the last room of the house. "It is our tradition to take a shower first before entering the tub. You never take soap into the tub. It isn't meant as a place to wash your body, but to relax and rejuvenate."

Rock grinned. "If I ever got folded into that tub, I'd never get myself out." The tub had to be all of three feet deep, but was barely wider than his shoulders.

Miko laughed. "It can be a challenge for one who is tall."

Involuntarily, his gaze dropped to her legs. Wide-legged navy trousers obstructed his view, although they complemented the white blouse she wore.

Rock wondered when he'd come to think of her legs as shapely and just how long he'd been paying such close attention to her attire. Miko had an extensive assortment of clothing and all he'd seen was of fine quality. According to Miko, her father owned a real estate business and did "well" in his business endeavors. From the finely crafted furnishings stored in the storage building to the expensive clothes she wore, Rock assumed her father had done a sight better than "well" in his business dealings.

Over the years, her grandparents had also made good money with their produce business. He'd done the math, calculating the expenses and income from the enterprise. Astounded by the projected numbers, he'd conferred with Miko about his accuracy. She assured him his speculations were close to what her family made selling the fruits of their labors, close to what he should make if he purchased the farm.

The nice bungalow he currently called home wasn't one that spoke of wealth or prestige. It was a homey, humble dwelling, filled with small, pleasant comforts. Other than the hand-carved screen door on the back entrance that featured a crane in a grouping of cattails, nothing from the outside of the house even hinted that a Japanese family owned it.

From the road, it looked like any other well-kept, prosperous farm. Even inside the house, few items hinted at a Japanese ancestry. The kitchen, done in cobalt blue and white, was modern and sleek, as was the bathroom. The bedrooms and living room were welcoming, familiar places to rest.

Yet, as Rock stood inside the house her great-grandparents had built, he couldn't help but think highly of the detail and expert craftsmanship that had gone into creating the home.

"I've never seen anything like this place, Miko. It's amazing."

She dipped her head, delighted he saw the exquisiteness of the old house. "I came up here to search for the deed to the place. Granddad hid it well," she said, taking a folded packet of papers from her pocket.

Rock grinned. "At least you found it. I began to think locating the deed was a lost cause." He followed as she stepped back into the corridor and slid the screen shut behind her, closing the room.

She walked back around to the entry where they had left their shoes and slipped hers on. "We don't have time to wander the full garden today, but you're welcome to come up here another time and I'll give you the grand tour."

"I'd love it," Rock said, studying a pine tree that had been twisted and trimmed into a shape that reminded him of a big umbrella. He pointed to the waterfall in the distance behind it. "Is the waterfall natural?"

Miko glanced toward the water that streamed down from higher up the mountain and landed in a clear pool. "It is, and so is the stream that feeds from it. Granddad figured out a way to run the stream water down to the orchard to keep it watered. His system is why we haven't had to do much with the trees out there yet."

Rock tossed her a teasing look. "And here I thought it was the rain we had this spring."

"The rain certainly helps, but the trees have access to the water and that keeps the fruit sweet even when we get a hot, dry spell in the summer." Miko cut across a pond by stepping on a series of fat round stones. Big orange-and-white carp swam through the water.

Like a youngster on a grand adventure, Rock trailed after her, agog at the colorful fish. "May we have a picnic up here sometime?"

Miko glanced back at him. "As Petey would say, 'You bet your life on it!'"

He laughed and grabbed her hand in his when she stumbled on a loose rock, helping her regain her balance.

Her gaze fell to his hand, then rose to his eyes, her own dark orbs full of unspoken questions.

Rather than release her fingers, Rock gently squeezed them and continued toward the high fence that kept the fortress of the secret garden safe.

"Who else knows about the garden?" he asked as they walked across a wooden bridge spanning a smaller pond.

"Other than my family? No one." Her eyes held his as she stared at him. "No one, until you."

"I promise to take the secret of your garden to my grave, Miko. With the state of things as they are, most Americans wouldn't see the beauty of it, just the foreignness."

"And that's why it's always been a secret." Miko pulled the gate closed and locked it. Together, they made their way down the hill. While she secured the gate so it blended flawlessly into the rest of the fence, Rock looked upward. The canopy of trees overhead effectively camouflaged the path they'd just traversed.

Rock gave one last glance up the hill before turning to Miko. "Does the rest of your family work in the garden?"

Miko laughed and moved along the stone path behind the barn. "No. My grandmother's knees prohibit her from making the climb. Papa is always too busy, and Tommy doesn't have the patience to do the work. The last thing my sister wants to do when she and her family come to visit is go to the garden. And Mother would rather be caught in nothing but her underwear in the middle of Meier & Frank's department store than set foot in it."

Rock chuckled. "I look forward to meeting your family. Did you know Clark Gable worked at Meier & Frank selling ties before he made it big in Hollywood?"

She nodded. "My grandmother is convinced he waited on her twice when she was purchasing ties for Granddad. It's so sad about his wife's tragic death." Miko appeared distraught as she walked toward the house. "Carole Lombard was such a fine actress."

"I heard about her plane crashing. Wasn't she on a war bond tour?" He opened the back door and held it for her as she walked inside.

"She was. The news reports said she raised around two million in war bond sales and was on her way home." Miko stared at the trunks Rock had carried inside and left in the kitchen before he'd gone in search of her. A saucy grin accompanied the teasing tilt of her head. "Moving in, Captain?"

He took a step closer to her. "I am, if you're sure you want me to go ahead with our plans."

"I haven't changed my mind. I trust you, Rock. You'll keep the farm safe until Granddad can return." She opened the refrigerator and perused the contents. "Why don't you put those in your room while I make lunch?"

"Yes, ma'am. If you have any of that leftover ham, I'd sure enjoy a sandwich. Your bread is as light and soft as any I've ever eaten."

He lifted a trunk, carrying most of the weight with his right hand as he took it to the bedroom she referred to as his.

Covertly, Miko watched as he moved the trunks, intrigued by the play of muscles visible beneath the white T-shirt he wore. His uniform shirt hung over the back of a chair, where he'd most likely left it when he returned from collecting his belongings at his farm.

It seemed so strange to her that a man who was a virtual stranger would willingly leave behind a farm he owned free and clear to make sure her family's farm wouldn't fall into the wrong hands.

Rock was a good, fine man, one she greatly admired.

One she was beginning to love.

Falling for the soldier would only end in heartbreak, especially when she would soon leave to join her family at the assembly center. No good would come from harboring romantic notions for Rock.

Even if, by some miracle, he returned her feelings, Oregon didn't allow mixed-race marriages. Despite how American Miko might feel, the fact remained that she was one hundred percent Japanese, at least in the eyes of the law and of the majority of Americans.

Dismayed by the notion of marriage, she shifted her attention to making thick ham sandwiches and potato salad for lunch.

Rock returned to the kitchen dressed in worn Levi's and a soft cotton shirt with the sleeves rolled up past his elbows. "It's sure nice to be back in my civvies."

At her questioning look, he rubbed a hand down the front of his jeans. "Civilian clothes."

"Did you find everything you needed at your farm?" She poured him a glass of milk and filled a glass of water for herself, setting both on the table by their plates.

"I did. Bert, he's the guy who leases it, has done a swell job maintaining the buildings. The farm ground looks well tended, too. It's in good hands for now."

"I'm glad, Rock. I'm sure it helps you rest easier knowing your family farm has been well cared for."

He nodded and took her hand in his, prepared to offer grace. "It does help me rest easier."

Hungry, he finished the first sandwich and started on a second, then motioned outside to the truck he had yet to return to the storage building. "Your grandpa's truck handles well. I was tempted to lean into the gas and see what it would do, but I stuck to thirty-five piddling miles an hour the whole way."

Miko giggled. "Perhaps it's best you didn't take my car, then. It's hard not to zip right on down the road."

He cocked an eyebrow at her. "Why, Miss Nishimura, if I didn't know better, I'd say you were a speedster."

"I might even confess to it, if you didn't know better. If I wanted to go slow, I wouldn't have purchased that Packard." She took a bite of her sandwich and coquettishly batted her eyelashes at him.

Rock tipped his head to the side and smirked. "Golly, I've never had lunch with a fast girl before. I might need to note this day on the calendar." He jabbed his thumb over his shoulder at the Coca-Cola calendar hanging on the wall by the telephone.

Miko bristled, wondering if he realized what he implied. "I'll have you know, Captain Laroux, that I am not nor have I ever been a fast girl."

His mischievous grin let her know he was teasing, something he did with growing frequency. "I know exactly what you are, Miko, and that's a wonderful woman with a big heart."

Embarrassed by his praise, she dropped her gaze to her plate and remained silent as she finished her sandwich.

While she washed the dishes, he returned the truck to the storage building and headed out to work in the vegetable garden.

After she put away the dishes and whipped up a batch of cookies, she sat down at the table to write a letter to her family.

When Rock returned midafternoon for a break, half a dozen sheets of crumpled paper gave testimony to her struggle to find the right words.

He poured a glass of cold grape juice and snatched three of the fresh-baked cookies before taking a seat at the table across from her.

"What's wrong?" he asked, motioning toward the two lines she'd written on the paper in front of her.

"I'm concerned about saying too much without telling them what they need to know. If the letter is read by someone before they see it, I don't want to get you, me, or them in trouble." Miko sighed. "Perhaps I shouldn't write at all."

"No, your family needs to receive word from you." Rock took a bite of cookie and washed it down with a gulp of juice. "What if you wrote the letter as a friend of the family who came to check on the farm? No one would think anything of that, would they?"

Miko considered his suggestion, warming to the idea. "That might work." She tapped the pen in her fingers against the tip of her nose. "I could write it as though I was a mutual friend of the family and Pastor Clark. His daughter, Sally, is my best friend and has been since I can remember."

She began writing the letter while Rock finished his cookies and juice, then went to sit in the living room, listening to a radio program while he rested. Although he grew stronger each day, he still needed to rest often or he became so weary he could hardly function.

Thoughts of exactly how strong and fit the soldier in her house appeared caused Miko to lose her focus on the letter. Instead, she recalled how handsome Rock looked when he walked into the kitchen wearing his old jeans and work shirt.

Something about Rock Laroux, something she couldn't explain or define, spoke to her heart in a way nothing else ever had. Prudence and wisdom dictated she join her family at the assembly center sooner rather than later. She had to leave before Rock realized how much she was coming to love him.

With great effort, she finished the letter and tucked it inside a plain envelope. Rock slept in the rocking chair while she milked the cows and made dinner.

That evening, he helped her churn what seemed like gallons of cream into butter to sell the following day, along with all the spare eggs, at a grocery store in town.

As they labored over the four-quart Dazey butter churns, he asked her about her family and friends.

"Earlier today, you mentioned Pastor Clark and his daughter," Rock said, glancing at her as he cranked the handle that turned the butter paddle with his good hand. "Tell me about them."

"Sally has been my best friend forever. Her father is the pastor of our church and that's how we met. Sally is now Mrs. Snyder. She lives in Tillamook and has the most beautiful baby boy named Drew. Her husband is stationed in Ireland." Miko's eyes held a faraway look as she churned the butter. "Sally used to get these 'feelings,' that's what she calls them, which always got us into trouble. One time she got a 'feeling' we should hide in the church basement and scare whoever opened the door. It didn't take long for someone to come downstairs to set out cookies to enjoy following the service. We didn't plan on it being old Mrs. Whipple. After we yelled 'Boo!' and jumped out from behind the door, the poor woman clutched her chest, gasping for breath. Papa and Mother took her to the hospital while Pastor Clark gave Sally and me another lecture about proper behavior."

Entertained by her story, he cast an inquisitive glance her direction. "Another lecture? Were you often in trouble?"

Miko smiled. "Always."

Rock studied Miko several moments. The sound of cream swishing in the churns filled the silence. "What about your sister? Did you two get into trouble together?"

A laugh escaped before she could stop it. "Ellen? No, she never got into trouble. Ellen is the perfect daughter every parent dreams of having."

He studied her, sensing a hint of resentment in the tension that settled along her shoulders. "I take it you aren't like your sister?"

"Our similarities are few, unless you think night and day are alike. Ellen is small and lovely. She was always the obedient child who never did anything wrong. While Sally and I climbed trees, scraped our knees, and waded in streams, Ellen embroidered pillowcases and attentively listened to Mother's advice on how to be a good wife and a true lady. According to my mother, Ellen never did anything wrong and I would have benefitted by following her fine example. Ellen graduated from high school and married the fellow Mother selected for her two months later. Paul Watanabe is a good man and he treats Ellen well, but they didn't marry for love. I refuse to follow in her footsteps."

The churn's handle stilled in his hand as he eyed her. "I don't suppose a girl as independent as you had much luck meekly obeying orders."

Miko laughed again. "I certainly didn't live up to Mother's expectations for me. Frequently, she reminds me of how I'm not getting any younger and life is going to pass me by if I don't settle down and raise a family. She chose to marry Papa out of love, not because of an arranged marriage. It's beyond my ability to comprehend why she expects me to do any less than follow my heart. Just because Ellen blindly did her will doesn't mean Tommy or I have to."

At Rock's veiled expression, Miko shrugged. "I dearly love my sister and I'm happy she has a good husband and two beautiful daughters, but Ellen and I never were nor will we ever be alike."

Mindful of the direction the conversation turned, he shifted to a happier subject. "How old are your nieces?" Rock had noticed a photograph of two adorable little girls in the living room. In the days he'd been at the house, Miko unpacked her grandparents' personal belongings, returning photographs to the walls and knickknacks around the rooms.

She relaxed and her eyes softened at the mention of the girls. "Winnie is five and full of sass. Ellen says she is just like me, so I can't help but feel a little sorry for my sister."

Rock chuckled and lifted the paddle from the rich, pale yellow butter. Miko drained the buttermilk, pouring it into a jar. She pressed the butter in cheesecloth to remove any excess liquid, then rinsed it in cool water before packing it into a press. While she worked, he added more cream to the jar and started the process over again. "What about your other niece? Is she like you?"

"Amy is two. I've only seen her twice, but she appears to take after her mother. She'll be Ellen's perfect little lady." Miko grinned with a mischievous twinkle in her eye. "That's why I'm glad she has Winnie. She'll keep Ellen on her toes." As though a thought had just struck her, Miko stared at him. "Do you suppose they had to go to an assembly center, too?"

"I'll ask your parents. If they don't know, I'll see what I can find out," Rock said, wanting to reassure her. From what he'd heard on the radio, most of the Japanese population along the entire Pacific Coast had been ordered to report at various assembly centers. "Where does your sister's family live?"

"Sacramento. Paul works for an insurance company there."

Rock tucked away the information and grinned at Miko again. "You better tell me more about the rest of your family if I'm going to see them tomorrow. I know your grandparents, but I don't recall meeting your parents or brother when my dad used to bring me to the produce stand."

The rest of the evening, she filled him in on what he needed to know about Jack and Margaret Nishimura, as well as her brother, Tommy.

★ *Chapter Eight* ★

Life failed to do right by Norman Ness.

At twenty-four, he had a hairline that marched in a steady retreat away from his sloping forehead, a flabby belly that oozed over the belt of his pants, and feet that ached from the cheaply made oxfords he favored. A mouth full of crooked, half-rotten teeth, a tendency to wallow in self-pity, and a malicious gleam in his shifty dark eyes didn't do him any favors, either.

Sallow-skinned and slight-framed, he'd always been the odd man out, even as a child. He wasn't bright enough to be among the top scholars, didn't possess a single athletic bone, and struggled to fit in with the other students.

The boy who bullied him all the way through high school had finally gotten what was coming to him, though. Norman worked after school at the soda fountain. He'd heard Alan, the bully, tell one of his friends he couldn't eat eggs because they made him sick. Norman added three raw eggs to the malt he made for Alan, then stood back and watched as the boy gulped it down. The glass fell from his hand and shattered on the tile floor as Alan clutched his throat, eyes nearly bugging from his head. Before anyone could help him, his throat swelled shut, his heart stopped, and he died.

Norman had congratulated himself on a job well done and celebrated with a strawberry milkshake.

Home wasn't an improvement over the misery Norman suffered at school. His parents had never lavished him with attention or affection, but the arrival of a baby brother made it seem as though he ceased to exist. Norman was seven when he held a pillow over his brother's face until he ceased breathing one winter night. No one ever questioned if he'd been the one to stop the toddler's crying. Everyone assumed the baby had died in his crib of natural causes.

Occasionally, the haunting sound of his mother's screams when she'd discovered the limp body of the baby the following morning drifted through his thoughts.

After his brother's funeral, his mother changed into an entirely different person, one nobody particularly liked. If she wasn't whining or complaining about something, she stayed in bed, too sick to see to the housework, insisting Norman do his share to help around the house.

The spring Norman turned ten, his father had the gall to get himself killed. The man worked on the Portland docks and died when a crate fell on him, crushing him beneath its heavy weight.

Often, Norman wondered if his father had jumped beneath the crate to escape the nonstop nagging of his mother. Thelma Ness just didn't know when to shut up. Nope, she never did.

In fact, she spent the last evening of her miserable life yammering at Norman to get a real job instead of continuing as a door-to-door salesman.

Norman reflected on how easy it had been to add enough arsenic to her bowl of pudding to put an end to her relentless demands. Over the course of several months, he'd given her a little at a time, watching as each dose made her sicker. Finally, he'd administered what he thought should be enough to kill her, then doubled the amount. Much to his glee, she died almost instantly. Since she'd been ill for so long, it had seemed as though she'd succumbed to whatever sickness had plagued her.

Smug at the recollection of his past success in removing unwanted obstacles from his path, Norman lurked behind the cover of rambling blackberry bushes down the road from the farm the Jap family had owned. He sucked on his favorite sour candy and waited.

The first time he stopped at the farm to see if he could sell any of the second-rate chocolates he peddled, the old Japanese man had purchased a box and had given him a free apple, polished to a high shine.

Norman had noticed the wealth of timber behind the tilled acres — cedar, oak, maple, and birch trees grew alongside pine, alder, and fir. Dollar signs danced before his eyes.

For two years, he'd had his eye on the farm. Under the guise of selling his wares, including everything from watered-down cough medicine to the poorly made shoes he wore, Norman visited the farm every few months, asking questions and making plans.

Once he took over, he'd get rid of the produce stand, hire someone to log the trees, clear the land, and sell the place at a handsome profit.

Thoughts of living like a king off the money he'd make from the tree sales alone had kept him going. The last thing Norman wanted was to work hard like the stupid old couple who ran the place.

When the no-good Japs along the Pacific Coast were ordered to evacuate, he knew it was time to make his move. Desperate to sell their belongings before leaving for assembly centers, many Japanese accepted mere pennies on the dollar.

The day he'd heard the news, Norman had sped out to the farm and offered the old man fifty dollars for the place, including all the furnishings and contents of the buildings. The scrappy geezer acted insulted by the offer and chased

Norman back to his car wielding a pitchfork, yelling at him never to return.

More determined than ever to get his hands on the prime piece of property, Norman waited until he was sure the cagey ol' Jap and his wife were long gone to drive out to the place. He'd been enraged to find a soldier had taken up residence in the house. Under no circumstance would he allow an unwelcome interloper to interfere with his plans.

Norman Milford Hess did not intend to let anyone stand in the way of getting what he wanted. With a little patience, he'd have all that timber and the land. He might even decide to stay in the house since it was far nicer than the dank place where he lived. After all, a salesman peddling marbles, shoes, and cookware barely made enough to keep himself fed.

Through a pair of field glasses, he watched the soldier and a tall woman walk out to the car. The man drove onto the road and headed off in the direction of Beaverton.

Norman hadn't realized the soldier boy was married. A perverted sneer crossed his face as he watched the woman walk inside the house. Maybe the soldier wasn't married and the girl was a fun diversion.

Quickly ducking down as the car drove past where he'd parked behind the blackberry bushes, Norman waited a few moments before driving down the road past the produce stand. He pulled over and glanced up at the looming trees overhead, popping another piece of candy in his mouth.

His gaze followed the fence that ran along the base of the hill all the way around the property. Inquisitive, he pondered what the old Jap had in there that required a ten-foot high wall.

One day soon, Norman would find out.

★ *Chapter Nine* ★

Rock smoothed a hand down the front of his trouser legs and tugged on the hem of his jacket.

Miko ironed his navy-blue suit that morning, carefully pressing two straight seams along his trousers. She made sure his white shirt appeared crisp.

Unable to manage his tie one-handed, he lifted his freshly shaved chin while she expertly tied it for him. He caught her gaze lingering on his face, her eyes full of something he hesitated to acknowledge or define.

Hastily stepping back when she finished, he held his arms out at his sides and grinned at her. "Are you sure I don't look out of style?" he asked, concerned the single-breasted suit he'd purchased three years ago seemed outdated.

Miko shook her head and reached out, straightening his collar and tucking a snowy white square into his breast pocket. "You look quite nifty, Captain Laroux."

The way her voice caressed his name made him long to trail his fingers along the silky smoothness of her cheek. Instead, he picked up a gray fedora and settled it on his head. He gathered her letter and the papers he wanted to take with him and lifted the keys to her grandfather's car from where he'd left them on the kitchen table.

"Will you be okay here on your own?" he asked for the third time as he walked outside.

The saucy grin she tossed at him almost made him miss the last porch step. "I'll be fine. In fact, I think I'll spend the day up on the hill."

Rock knew that meant she wanted to work in the secret garden. He hoped to explore it in the near future.

As it was, he anticipated being gone all day. "I'll be back as soon as I can, but most likely it will be early evening before I return."

"I know. I'll be fine," Miko assured him as he set the papers he carried on the front seat of the sedan. "Take care of yourself, Rock, and please give my family my love."

"I will, Miko. I promise." He squeezed her hand, then slid behind the wheel and started the car. "Be a good girl and I might bring you a treat," he teased, waving as he drove down the driveway.

When he reached town, Rock turned down a side street that took him to a grocery store he recalled visiting many times with his parents. The owner had been a jovial fellow with a bald head, rosy cheeks, and a broad smile. Before he was old enough to know better, Rock had thought the man was Saint Nicholas himself.

He parked the car in a space in front of the store and lifted a basket that held a paper-wrapped square of butter, half a dozen eggs, and a jar of buttermilk. Outside the front of the store, he studied a display of brooms to the left, a large Dr Pepper cooler to the right, and Coca-Cola signs in the windows. A small sign by the door promised farm-fresh eggs and milk.

It had been so long since Rock had tasted a soda, moisture flooded his mouth at the prospect. Miko had insisted he take five dollars with him before he left the house, but it seemed frivolous to spend money on a cold bottle of soda.

Determined to ignore the temptation, he pulled open the door of the store, listening to the bell jangle above his head as he stepped inside. Familiar scents of linseed oil, meat spices from the bologna and sausage made right there in the store, and dill from a crock of pickles swirled around his nose.

A round little man bustled through a doorway at the back of the store and hurried down the aisle to the counter where Rock waited.

"Morning, mister. What can I do for you?" he asked as he stepped behind the counter with a welcoming smile.

"Mr. Ross, I'm sure you don't remember me, but I used to come in here with my folks when I was a boy." Rock held out his hand toward the man.

Bill Ross shook it and studied Rock for a long moment. "Who are your folks, son?" he asked, propping his elbows on the counter and leaning forward. "Your face is familiar, but I can't quite place you."

"Jim and Susan Laroux from Gales Creek. I remember you always had those big cinnamon cookies for sale and would give me one when we'd come in. I'm Rock."

Bill slapped the counter with a meaty hand and grinned. "Well, sure, now that you say it, you do resemble your dad. My condolence on his and your mother's passing. Didn't you go off to fly planes or some such thing?"

"I did. I took a little shrapnel in my side and arm and they sent me home." Rock scooted the basket across the counter, unwilling to discuss his injuries or the disastrous end to his career.

"I'm sorry to hear that, son. Are you doing okay now?" Bill tugged the basket closer and peered inside.

"Yes, sir. I'm getting better every day. Right now, I'm staying at a farm that has an excess of milk and eggs. Would you be interested in purchasing any?"

The store owner removed the waxed paper from the butter, admiring the rich, creamy appearance as well as the star stamped into the top of it. "Mind if I take a taste?" he asked, reaching beneath the counter and pulling out a package of crackers.

"Help yourself," Rock said. He watched as the man took a knife and shaved the slightest curl of butter from the bottom of the neatly formed square.

Mr. Ross spread it on the cracker and took a bite. A contented smile wreathed his face. "That is some good butter. If the buttermilk came from it, I won't need to taste it." Bill lifted the jar of milk and eggs from the basket. "I'll take whatever you bring."

Rock grinned. "I've got eight dozen eggs, nine quarts of buttermilk, and thirteen pounds of butter."

The store owner's eyes widened before he scurried around the counter. "I'll take it all!"

After he helped carry in the milk, butter, and eggs, Bill wrote out a receipt and handed it to Rock. "Anytime you have more, just bring it in. I could use cream, too, if you have extra to spare."

"I'll get on a weekly schedule." Surprised by the amount of money he pocketed, Rock pointed to a cooler of soda near the cash register. "Is Coca-Cola still a nickel?"

"It sure is." Bill opened the cooler and removed a bottle, popped off the cap, and handed the beverage to Rock. "That's on me. It's sure good to see you, Rock. Thank you for your service to our country."

"That was my pleasure, sir." Rock took a drink from the frosty bottle in his hand and let the sweet, bubbly liquid slide with cooling refreshment down his throat. "Thank you for purchasing our butter and eggs, and for the Coca-Cola."

"Anytime, son. If my wife was here instead of visiting our daughter in Seattle, I'd have some of those cookies you like so well."

"Maybe next time I come." Rock opened the door and started to step out, then turned back. "How late is your store open, Mr. Ross?"

"I usually leave the door unlocked until six."

Rock tipped his head and smiled. "Thanks again, sir."

He left and drove to the office of the attorney who had helped him settle things after his father passed away. Mr. Collier was a school chum of his father and had been kind to Rock in the past.

An hour later, he left the man's office and drove to the bank. Pleased by the interest gained in the account that had remained untouched since he'd joined the Army, he made a withdrawal and left with a checkbook in his pocket.

He made one more stop, then drove to the hospital in Portland, wondering if he'd run into Nurse Brighton. Part of him hoped he would. While he was in the hospital, he'd had such a crush on the lovely, feisty nurse. With his health nearly restored and a different outlook on life, he questioned if the infatuation stemmed from the care she provided, or if he'd genuinely been fascinated by her.

Inside, he walked up the stairs to the floor where he'd felt imprisoned after he returned from Trinidad.

Several familiar faces peered at him from the nurse's station, but none recognized him until he asked if ol' Horrid Homer was on duty.

"Captain Laroux? Is that you?" A nurse with an engaging smile and kind eyes stood and stepped around the desk. "Gee, we weren't sure what to think when you disappeared. What in the world did you do? Find some magic elixir?"

"Something like that," he said, grinning as the women ogled him. He handed the nurse standing closest to him a big box of fancy chocolates. "I wanted to thank you all for taking such good care of me while I was here."

"Our pleasure, honey," one of the cheekier nurses said, nudging her coworker to open the box.

"I don't suppose I could get in to see Doctor Ridley?" Rock asked. The nurses would make sure he saw the doctor, even if he hadn't asked.

"Go on down to his office, Captain. I saw him head that way a few minutes ago," the nurse with the kind eyes offered encouragingly. "We're pleased to see you looking so fit."

"And handsome," the cheeky one added.

Rock flashed a boyish smile that made them all sigh dreamily, then sauntered down the hall to the doctor's office.

He stood outside the door and listened, making sure the doctor wasn't with someone before tapping on the door frame and stepping inside.

"May I help you?" Doctor Ridley rose from the chair behind his desk and gave Rock a curious glance.

"I don't know, Doc. Last time we spoke you promised I'd be dead by now." Rock stepped across the room and grinned as the doctor's mouth fell open and he gaped at him.

"Rock Laroux? How in the dickens did you go from having one foot in the grave to being a strapping specimen of health in such a short time?"

"Good food and fresh air," Rock replied, taking a seat in the chair the doctor indicated. "Seriously, Doc, I wanted to get your stamp of approval on my self-prescribed regimen to staying alive."

"By all means, whatever it is you're doing, keep doing it." The doctor took his pulse, looked down his throat, and listened to him take several deep breaths, then sat back with a satisfied smile. "You had me plenty worried when you up and left. I appreciated the note, but still, you shouldn't have just walked yourself out of here."

"I know, Doc, but I wasn't ready to die and it didn't seem there were any other options if I stayed here. Caught in the rain that night, I almost died from exposure to the elements in my weakened state, but I received excellent care. Once I bounced back from that, I made steady improvement."

"I can see that, son. You have color back in your face, your lungs are clear, and your eyes are bright. How's your stomach?" The doctor jotted notes on a pad to add to Rock's file.

"Great. I've been on a steady diet of milk straight from the source, sweet grape juice, sun-ripened strawberries, eggs right from the roost and fried in freshly churned butter, and —"

The doctor held up his hand to stop him. "You're making my stomach growl. Will you join me for lunch in the cafeteria? You can tell me where you've been and what you plan to do with yourself."

"I'd like that," Rock said, rising to his feet.

The doctor stopped by an examination room and checked the wounds on Rock's side, delighted to see the scars had thickened and slightly faded in color. "Any improvement in your eyesight?" he asked, shining a light in Rock's eyes.

"Yes, sir. I can see as well as I did before my injuries." Rock looked straight ahead without blinking.

"Excellent." Doctor Ridley lifted Rock's left arm, poking around the scar and testing his flexibility. "Your mobility appears to be improving."

"Yes, sir. I've been milking a cow twice a day. I think that has helped more than anything." Rock lifted a pen in his fingers and held it long enough to draw a line down a sheet of paper. The simple action was far more than he'd been able to do the last time the doctor had checked him over.

After lunch, the two men shook hands in the hospital lobby. "I have no explanation for the complete change in your health, Rock. Maybe you experienced a reaction to something here at the hospital. I have no explanation for the complete change in your health, Rock. Maybe you experienced a reaction to something here at the hospital. It could have been an allergy to medication or something along those lines. We'll probably never know for sure. Regardless, you seem to be in great health. Come back in three months for a checkup," the doctor ordered. "If you don't, I'll drive out to that produce stand to find you."

"Drive out anyway. I'd be happy to show you the place." Rock grinned and shoved his hands in his pockets. "You won't ever taste finer strawberries than are grown there."

"I might just take you up on that, Rock. Take care and have a good summer." The doctor waved as Rock pushed open the doors and stepped outside.

Rock jogged down the steps and turned to make his way to his parked car, running into Nurse Brighton.

"Pardon me," he said, tipping his hat with a smile. His thorough perusal began at the smart little hat on her golden head and ended at the open toes of her high-heeled shoes. "You look fetching today, Nurse Brighton."

Her gaze narrowed as she stared at him. Recognition arrived with an excited squeal and she threw her arms around him. "Good golly, Captain Laroux! I was sure you'd passed on to glory after you ran away."

Rock returned her hug, then released her, taking a step back. "I didn't run away, I merely left without asking Doc's permission."

"Well, I'm glad you did. I never expected to see you looking like this," she said, observing him from the top of his head to his polished shoes. "It's good to see you, Rock."

"You, too, Nurse Brighton," Rock said. When he'd been sick, he'd often called her Billie. Today, though, he hesitated to be too friendly with her. She was even prettier than he remembered, but she no longer claimed his interest. His thoughts drifted to Miko with her gleaming black hair and beautiful dark eyes.

Over his infatuation with the perky little nurse, he no longer gazed at her like a lovesick pup. Rock squeezed her hand and gave her cheek a quick kiss. "Thank you for taking such good care of me while I was here. I appreciate everything you did."

Her posture stiffened. "It was all part of the job, Captain." Uncomfortable, she backed toward the hospital. "I'm truly happy to see you well. Take care of yourself."

"You, too, Nurse Brighton."

She spun on her heel, rushing up the steps and inside the hospital. Absolved, he watched her go before making his way to the car.

⋆⋆★ Chapter Ten ★⋆⋆

With a fortifying breath, Rock drove to the Pacific International Livestock and Exposition Center. Recently renamed the Portland Assembly Center, the building housed Japanese Americans evacuated from their homes in the area.

Rock had no idea what to expect or if he'd even be allowed inside. He lifted the basket of strawberries Miko had sent for her family from the backseat, shut the car door, and surveyed the barbed-wire fence surrounding the buildings in front of him.

Purposeful strides carried him to the gate, where a guard waited.

"Afternoon," Rock said, smiling as he approached the young man.

"Afternoon." The guard glared at Rock. "What do you need?"

"I'd like to visit the Shig Yamada family. He and his wife are here with his daughter, son-in-law, and grandson." Rock forced his posture to remain relaxed, his smile entreating.

"What's the son-in-law's name?" The guard studied the cloth-covered basket Rock held in his hand.

"Jack Nishimura. His wife is Margaret and their son is Tommy."

Speculatively, the guard eyed him. "And you're a friend of the family?"

"Mr. Yamada has known me since I was just a sprout." Rock kept his voice friendly. "My father used to do business with him."

"What about you? Did you do business with him?"

Rock shook his head. "If I'd been in the area the past few years, I would have."

The guard's gaze narrowed. "Where've you been? Why do you care about visiting them now?"

"I served the United States Army Air Force in Trinidad until a few months ago, when my plane crashed and I was sent home to recover. I've only been out of the hospital a few weeks." Rock hadn't planned to mention his military service, but if it would help get him in to see Miko's family, he'd shout it from the rooftops.

The guard stood a little straighter. "What's your name, sir?"

"Captain Rock Laroux of the First Reconnaissance Squadron."

Respect filled the guard's expression. "And you're here as a friend?"

"That's right," Rock said. He removed the cloth covering the basket of strawberries and held the fruit out to the guard. The young man looked like he'd love to taste the berries. Instead, he carefully moved the berries around in the basket, making sure no contraband hid in the bottom.

"I'll have someone get them." Hastily, the guard motioned to a sentry who jogged over, then disappeared inside a large building Rock assumed housed the detainees. The guard pointed several yards away from the gate to a picnic table in the shade of the building. "You may meet with them at that table, but first, I need to check your pockets, sir."

"Certainly." Rock emptied his pockets on the table the guard indicated.

The soldier hardly gave more than a passing glance to the contents, made note in a log of Rock's name and the date and time, then had Rock sign it before he allowed him entry inside.

Rock gathered his belongings, stuffed them into his pockets, picked up the basket of berries, and stepped through the opened gateway.

The guard shut it behind him. "Have a seat, Captain. They'll be out soon."

"Thank you," Rock said. He ambled over to the table. Nervous, he sat down on the bench and waited. Sweat trickled down his back as the sunshine warmed the late spring afternoon. His right foot jiggled impatiently as he leaned back, resting both elbows on the table behind him.

Finally, the door to the building opened and Miko's family emerged, following the sentry. Uncertainty flickered in their eyes, but pride marked each footstep.

Rock stood in a rush and removed his hat, setting it on the table.

The guard strode over and pointed to Shig Yamada. "Do you know this man?"

The elderly man stared at Rock, visibly searching his memories for recognition. A smile broke out across his weathered face. "Mr. Laroux, it's been a while."

"It certainly has, sir." Rock grinned and held out his hand to Shig. Miko's grandfather took it in his and shook it with enthusiasm. Rock shook hands with Jack and Tommy, politely tipped his head to the two women, and motioned for them to join him at the picnic table.

The guard returned to his post, but the sentry hovered ten feet away, not attempting to disguise his interest in their conversation.

"I don't think all of you have met Captain Rock Laroux. His dad used to tell me about all the exotic places he was stationed," Shig said, thumping Rock on the back as he settled onto the bench next to him. "You're the spitting image of your father. I was very sorry to hear of his passing. He still stopped by every summer to purchase strawberries and peaches, even after your mother departed."

"He used to write me letters, tormenting me with descriptions of the delicious produce he purchased at your stand while I was stuck eating Army rations." Rock smiled at the old man. "There's nothing quite like the taste of the strawberries grown at your farm." He lifted the cloth-covered basket and watched as Miko's family gazed rapturously at the strawberries. The sweet, slightly tangy scent of the fruit filled the air.

Tommy Nishimura clapped his hands together. "Hot diggety! Fresh berries!"

Rock grinned. "Help yourself."

They all took a berry and ate it slowly, relishing the taste.

"These taste just like our berries," Shig said, taking another one and popping it in his mouth.

"That's because they are."

Five sets of eyes moved from the basket of berries to Rock, staring at him in question.

"To make a long story short, my doctor sentenced me to die and I decided I wasn't quite ready to give up. I walked out of the hospital and found myself staggering down a country road on a cold rainy night. Just when I thought I couldn't go any farther, I looked up and saw your farm. I made my way to the front door, but it was locked. Weak and half out of my mind, I stumbled to the back step and passed out. The next thing I knew, I was in a warm soft bed, feeling better than I had for a long time. A young woman named Kami Jane took me in and nursed me back to health. I owe her my life."

When Miko told him to be sure to refer to her as Kami Jane around her family, he wondered why she chose that name. As they all smiled in understanding, he relaxed a little.

Miko's father looked across the table with a hopeful expression. "How is Kami Jane? Is she at the farm?"

"She is at the farm. In fact, she arrived there shortly after I did that stormy night. Because of her kindness, she wasn't able to keep an appointment to meet with some people very precious to her, and she sends her regrets." Rock pulled the letter from Miko from his pocket and handed it to her father.

He read it once, read it again, and then handed it to his wife. Tommy leaned over her shoulder to read it before they passed it on to Miko's grandparents.

Rock had no idea what she'd written in the letter. By the tears her mother and grandmother wiped from their eyes, whatever she penned must have been heartfelt. He watched as Jack Nishimura took hold of his emotions and tamped them down before speaking.

"Thank you, Captain Laroux," Jack said, nodding to Rock. "Kami Jane is quite dear to our family. We are pleased beyond words to be assured she is well. She mentioned in the letter your interest in purchasing the farm. Is there a particular reason you'd like to buy it?"

"It's a wonderful place, one that should be maintained, not changed. I happened to be there when a man stopped by, planning to take it. Just walk in and take it. I informed him the only way he'd do that was over my dead body. After a few disparaging words, he left with a promise to return and see if I have the deed in my possession. If not, he has every intention of taking over the property."

"Who is this man, Rock?" Shig asked. Worry etched more lines on his face.

Rock met the older man's gaze. "He introduced himself as Norman Ness."

Air hissed between Shig's teeth as he released a frustrated breath. "He is a despicable, detestable..." The old man snapped his mouth shut and inhaled a deep breath. "Under no circumstance do I want Norman Ness to get his hands on our land. He stopped by the farm a few days before we reported here, ranting about logging the place. If he took it over, he'd strip every tree from it and then sell the land without a thought to preserving the true heritage of the place."

Rock smiled. "I've seen a little of the hilltop. It's quite impressive, but I agree with you, Mr. Yamada. Ness would destroy everything that has taken decades to build." Rock removed a second envelope from his pocket and extracted a sheaf of papers, handing them to Shig.

"I hope you don't find me too presumptuous, but I stopped by my attorney's office and had him draft this document. What I propose is to purchase your land, the buildings, and all their contents for the amount stipulated there." Rock pointed to a number printed on the page Shig held. "If the price is agreeable, I would make an annual payment for four years, splitting twenty-five percent of the purchase price into those four payments. Another twenty-five percent, I'll put into war bonds for you, purchasing those monthly and giving them to our friend Kami Jane for safekeeping. The remaining fifty percent of the purchase price I will pay in full on this date in five years. If, at any time, you'd like to resume ownership of the farm, you may pay me back half of what I've paid and we'll call it square. Does that sound like a fair deal?"

"What's in it for you?" Jack asked, taking the papers from Shig and reading each line.

"Well, if I get to keep the profits from the produce stand, that seems more than fair, doesn't it?"

"It's hardly fair for you, but I'm not in a position to argue," Shig said, patting Rock on the back. "Are you sure, Rock? It's a lot of work and you don't look like you're quite up to the job."

Rock grinned. "Oh, I'm getting there, sir. You should have seen me a week ago. In another month, I'll be like a new man."

Jack laid the legal documents on the table and nodded to his father-in-law. "The paperwork all seems to be in good order. For the sake of preserving the farm and keeping all that is there safe, *all* that is there, I think it would be a good idea to sell it to Captain Laroux. Kami Jane seems to think he is a good, honorable man, and his presence here would confirm her thoughts."

Rock was more than a little curious what Miko had written in her letter to her family. Apparently, whatever she'd shared about him was enough to convince them he had no evil intentions concerning the farm.

"Kami Jane sent the deed." Rock took it from his pocket and handed it to Shig. "If you're sure you are comfortable with this, you can sign it over to me, and sign this document agreeing to the terms of the sale. There are two copies of it, so you may keep one."

"No. Take the second copy to Kami Jane," Shig said, accepting the pen Rock handed him and signing the deed, then the other paperwork. "Now, you must tell me about the garden. Have the peas set on yet? How do the potatoes look?"

Rock talked about the garden, what he and Miko had accomplished in the orchard, and his plans for the place.

"Read the horticulture books in the library, Rock, if you have questions. You'll find many answers there," Shig said. He appeared at ease with his decision to sell the farm to the son of a man he admired. "You'll need help during harvest times. I can give you a list of boys in the area I have hired in the past. They are always eager for work."

"Have you met Petey?" Aiko asked, shyly smiling at Rock.

"I have, ma'am. He is some boy."

Everyone around the table nodded in agreement. "His parents are fine, fine folks," Shig said. "If you ever need something, don't be afraid to ask John."

"I will, sir." Rock's gaze lifted to the large building behind them. "Do you think I could have a tour of the place?"

"You'll have to ask one of the guards," Jack said, casting a glance at the nearby sentry.

Rock rose and walked over to him. "Would it be possible to have a tour?"

"You some kind of reporter or something?" the man asked.

"No. Just a friend of the family."

"We don't typically do that sort of thing. It..." The sentry snapped his mouth shut as the center administrator approached them.

"Are you paying a visit to a family?" the man asked, offering Rock a friendly handshake.

"I am, sir." Rock motioned to the table where Miko's family waited. "I wondered if I might have a tour of the facility."

"Well, generally we don't do such things, but I don't suppose it would hurt if you accompanied them back to their rooms. I'll give you fifteen minutes, before Private Johnson here escorts you back to the gate."

Rock tipped his head to the man. "Thank you, sir. Your kindness is appreciated."

"My pleasure," the administrator said. He walked with Rock to the table and helped himself to a few of the strawberries. "Those are delicious. Hope you folks enjoy them."

Jack nodded while the rest of them kept their eyes cast downward until the administrator left.

"I have fifteen minutes to walk you back to your rooms. Shall we go?" Rock asked, holding out his right arm in a gesture that encompassed the whole family.

As he watched them hurry toward the door, he wondered where in the world Miko had gotten her height. Tommy was the tallest of the bunch and he couldn't have been more than five-seven. Perhaps Miko was a throwback to a samurai ancestor from a previous century.

He followed as Shig led the way to their living quarters. With the need to provide a place for the Japanese detainees on short notice, the assembly center had been constructed by covering the floor of the livestock pavilion with wood planks. Plywood walls went up, forming cubicles with no ceiling and a canvas flap to cover the open doorway of each "apartment." The smells of manure drifted up in the heat of the day, permeating every inch of space in the eleven-acre building.

At least a different building was used to prepare and serve the food. Rock hoped it smelled better than this one.

Shig stopped in front of a canvas flap and turned to Rock with a grin. "Home, sweet home."

Miko's mother, Margaret, had barely said anything since Rock's arrival, but she turned on her father with a cool glare. "Don't be ridiculous, Father. This disgusting place will never be home." She turned to Rock with a look in her eyes he recognized well from having seen it in Miko's many times. "Promise you'll do whatever you can to keep Mi—" She caught herself before she spoke Miko's name. "To keep my father's farm and the beloved treasures there safe."

Solemnly, Rock nodded. "I promise."

Jack stepped close to Rock and dropped his voice to the barest hint of a whisper. "Under no circumstance should you allow our friend Kami Jane to come here. None. Understood?"

"Yes, sir, I understand." The moment he'd pulled up at the assembly center, Rock had decided he'd do everything in his power to keep Miko away from it. Armed guards with guns, barbed-wire fencing, and a living area that was nothing more than a walled-in feedlot assured him he'd done the right thing, insisting Miko wait before turning herself in. If he had to keep her hidden until the war ended, so be it, but he was not allowing her to set foot in such a place. Not while one breath remained in his body.

Rock peeked into the living quarters. A few crudely constructed shelves, narrow beds with thin mattresses, and their belongings neatly stacked against one wall filled the cramped space.

"I'm so sorry," Rock said. He contemplated how anyone in their right mind could condemn more than a hundred thousand people to spend the sweltering summer months living like animals, especially when many of those people were Americans by birth and by right.

He studied the little group. "Is there anything I can do to help, to make things better?"

Shig turned to Jack, exchanging some unspoken message. Jack took a step closer to Rock. "Send us food, crackers, things that are packaged. If they are in a tin to keep the flies out, that would be even better."

Rock glanced up at a strip of flypaper, black from the carcasses attached to it. Flies were everywhere. He could only imagine the infestation grew worse near the food and restrooms.

Fighting back a shudder, he smiled at the family studying him with alert gazes. "Before I'm forced to leave, I'm supposed to ask two questions: The first is how your daughter Ellen is faring and if you know where she's been detained. The second is if you've heard from Pastor Clark. If you do make contact with him, Kami Jane would be most pleased to see him."

"We'll send him to the farm if we hear from him. I expect he hasn't returned from his trip to London to help his sister and niece. We believe Ellen's family is in an assembly center in Sacramento, but we have not heard from her," Jack said, watching the sentry head in their direction. "We appreciate the berries and all you're doing for us, Captain Laroux."

"Please, call me Rock. If there is anything else I can do, send word to the farm." He extended his hand to Shig and nodded respectfully. "Thank you for entrusting your land and all that is there into my care, sir."

"You'll do well, Rock. If you are anything like your father, you'll do exceedingly well." Shig gave him a warm smile. "Be sure to read the book about fruit trees."

"I will, sir, and thank you again." Rock settled the hat he'd removed back on his head and followed the sentry to the front gate. He tipped his head to the guard. "Thank you for allowing me to visit my friends. I appreciate it."

"You're welcome, Captain," the guard said, offering him a salute.

"Do you know how long they plan to keep the detainees here?" Rock stepped outside the gate but held the guard's gaze.

"Word is most of them will ship out in a few months."

"To where?" Rock asked, wondering if the place they'd be shipped to would be better than the current accommodations. For the sake of Miko's family, he hoped it would be an improvement.

"Camps are being constructed as we speak in California, Arizona, Idaho, Wyoming, Colorado, Utah, and Arkansas. Word hasn't come down yet where they're sending them." The guard motioned behind him toward the living area. "Could be any of those places."

"Thank you for the information," Rock said. He tipped his head again, then hastened to the car.

He made several stops before he finally turned into the driveway at the Yamada farm — a farm that was now legally his.

Although he'd planned to have a long, decorated career in the military, he supposed there were worse things than building a life in such a beautiful place.

He parked the car near the gate by the backyard fence, but before he could step out, Miko bounded down the steps and rushed out to him.

Without hesitation, he opened his arms to her and she stepped into his embrace, holding him tightly.

"I was worried about you," she said, stepping away from him. Suddenly self-conscious, she twined her fingers together behind her back and waited for him to lift a cardboard box full of groceries. "What did you get?"

He grinned and motioned for her to precede him into the kitchen. "I've been craving peanut butter. Do you know Mr. Ross? He has a grocery store over off Fifth Street."

"I've gone with Grandma to his store a few times. He seems like a nice man." Miko watched as he set crackers, flour, sugar, and a box of assorted candy bars on the counter, along with the few items she'd requested.

He took four bottles of soda pop from the box and grinned as he handed her a bottle of Dr Pepper. "I wasn't sure what flavor was your favorite, so I brought home a few choices."

"I like most all of them, although root beer is my favorite." She set aside the bottle and began to put things away, but Rock placed a hand on her arm, drawing her attention.

He wrapped her in his arms again and kissed her right cheek. "That is from your grandparents." He kissed her left cheek. "That's from your folks." He leaned back and tugged on the end of the hair she'd fastened into a long ponytail. "That's from Tommy." Before he could change his mind, he brushed his lips over hers in the softest, lightest kiss. "And that's from me."

Her eyes glistened with emotion as she looked up at him. "Thank you, Rock." She pulled away from him and motioned to the table, set for two. "Go wash up. Dinner's ready. I roasted a chicken."

"You better stop killing off those birds, Miko." Rock grinned and took her hand, placing the money the grocer paid him for the butter and eggs into her palm. "That's what your butter, eggs, and buttermilk brought. Mr. Ross will take as much as we want to sell."

She gaped at the money in her hand, then back at Rock. "You better enjoy this bird. It might be the last one you eat for a while. Now we can purchase pork and beef."

Rock laughed and hurried to change his clothes before joining Miko at the table. As they ate, he told her about seeing her family, her grandfather selling him the place, and how they thought Ellen and her family were in an assembly center in Sacramento.

"They haven't heard from Pastor Clark, but suggested you write to Sally. If they see him, they said they'd have him get in touch." He spread a thick layer of strawberry jam over a steaming biscuit.

Miko played with the green beans on her plate. "But how were they, Rock? How were they really?"

The truth would do more harm than good. He couldn't bear to tell her the detainees lived in primitive conditions without a speck of privacy. That the food often spoiled from lack of proper equipment and made them sick. That the smells were enough to turn his stomach, and Rock had been in some awful places during his career in the military.

No, Miko didn't need to know how unpleasant life had become for her family. They went from being respected individuals to nameless faces in a mass of thousands treated as though they were the enemy. It would break her heart to hear the harsh reality of the situation.

Nevertheless, he wouldn't lie to her. "They're doing the best they can in their current circumstances, Miko. The men in your family seem in good spirits."

"But what of Mother and Grandma? I can't imagine my mother easily adjusting to such a change."

"It is harder on the women. Several of the men are working, doing a variety of things from maintenance to publishing a newspaper. It helps them to keep busy."

When she'd asked him to describe the facility, he told her each family had a cubicle in a large building where the ventilation was subpar.

"And every single member of your family begged me to keep you right where you are. They don't want you to leave the farm."

"But I should be with them," she said, setting down her fork and staring at Rock.

"Honestly, Miko, you're helping them most by staying here. If you were there, your folks would have to crowd one more body into an already small space. That is, if you were allowed to join them. From the information I gathered, you'd be arrested and possibly sent away. That certainly won't help your family through an already challenging time."

Her shoulders drooped and she sighed. "I suppose you're right. It's just hard not being able to see them or talk to them." She lifted her gaze back to his, drawn by the warmth in his bright eyes. "You did say I could write to them, didn't you?"

"Yes, you may. There wasn't any problem giving them the letter you wrote today." Rock offered her a thoughtful glance. "I'm half-curious what you wrote about me because they went from being wary of a stranger to practically calling me part of the family."

Miko grinned. "I only said that you've saved the farm and quite possibly my life, and that they owe you a hundred debts."

Rock choked on his drink of milk and coughed to clear his throat. "You did not!"

"Maybe not in those exact words..." A saucy smile floated his way. "Besides, if Grandma didn't like you, she'd never have said a word to you. She can be shy around people she doesn't know well."

"I remember that from visiting the produce stand. She preferred to stay in back and let someone else take the money and talk to customers."

Miko nodded in agreement. "That was usually Ellen or me, or one of the kids they hired in the summers to help. I'm sure I must have seen you at the produce stand when we were younger, but I can't place you."

"Well, I wasn't always this handsome, you know." Rock leaned back and ran a hand over his short-cropped hair. One of the stops he'd made that day was to a barber for a much-needed trim. It felt good to have his hair neatly cut in the military style he'd grown so accustomed to wearing.

She laughed and gave him an exasperated look. "I suppose you wore glasses, had bad teeth, and sported a hunch on your back."

Rock laughed. "See, you do remember me."

"Do you have a photograph from when you were younger?" she asked, fighting the urge to get lost in his smile.

"There are several in one of those trunks I brought from the farm." Immediately, he rose and disappeared. She finished eating the last few bites of her dinner before he returned to the kitchen with a framed photograph in his right hand.

"This is my dad and me. I was probably fifteen or so at the time. My dad, um... well, he..." Rock hesitated to give her the photo.

Miko held out her hand and took it, studying the photograph.

A tall, brawny man stood with an arm looped around Rock's shoulders, both of them wearing big smiles. One side of the man's face bore a jagged scar that started above his left eyebrow and traveled straight down, along his cheek, and ended at his jaw. Obviously blind in his left eye from the wound, the man so closely resembled Rock, she would have known him anywhere. In fact, she remembered seeing him with a boy who'd thoroughly enchanted her girlish heart when they visited the produce stand.

Rock was thin in the photograph, a smaller, younger version of himself. Longer hair flopped across his forehead, but the bright light in his eyes and the teasing warmth of his smile remained the same.

"It's you," she whispered, brushing a finger over the image she held.

"I already told you it's me in the photo with my dad."

Miko stared at the photograph. "Back when Ellen and I were silly girls, a very nice man used to visit the produce stand with his son. They came to get strawberries in June, peaches in August, and pumpkins in October. He always had Bit-O-Honey candy to share, and even though I never remembered his name, I always remembered his kindness. And I absolutely couldn't forget his son, but his dad always called him Chet. Ellen and I both thought he was something special."

A becoming blush pinked her cheeks as she glanced up at Rock. "I thought you were the most handsome boy I'd ever set eyes on. You always teased Ellen and me about something when you were here. I was thoroughly infatuated with you the summer I was thirteen, but you never came back after that August."

Rock was shocked that she remembered him. He had given up on her recalling the summers he'd stopped by with his dad. Although Miko and her sister had been far too young for him to flirt with, he did have fun teasing smiles out of them. He had no idea that Miko had liked him.

"That's when I left for college," he said.

Miko again glanced down at the photo. "You must have thought Ellen and I were absolute ninnies."

He reached across the table and touched her hand, gently running his thumb across her knuckles. "Not at all. I thought you both were cute little girls, but I don't remember one of you being taller than the other."

"I had a big growth spurt when I was fourteen. It was the most miserable year of my life. I was taller than all the boys in my class. Mother decided I was doomed to live my life alone because no respectable man would want a wife towering over him like some freakish monster. By the time I was sixteen, a few of the boys had caught up to me and my future didn't seem as tragic."

Rock grinned. "If I'd known then how beautiful you'd be now, I might have worked a little harder at making a good impression on you."

"You always made a good impression, Captain Laroux, even if I didn't know your real name." She gave him a questioning glance. "All this time, I've been trying to recall meeting a boy named Rock at the produce stand and the one face that stuck in my mind was yours. Why did your father call you Chet?"

He shifted uncomfortably on his chair and withdrew his hand from hers. "He was the only one who called me that. If anyone else tried, they generally went home with a black eye or a bloody nose."

Puzzled, she waited for him to continue. "There's nothing wrong with the name Chet."

Rock sighed. "No, but it's the full name that goes along with it that's a mouthful."

She held his gaze. When he hesitated to speak, she reached across the table and nudged his arm. "Now you have to tell me. What is your full name? You already know I'm Kamiko Jane Nishimura and that the kids in school called me Kami Jane."

"My middle name is after my dad, so I don't mind it, but the rest of it…" Rock sat in silence for a full minute before he finally blurted, "It's Rochester. Rochester James Laroux."

Miko stared at him a long moment. One side of her mouth quivered, followed by the other. Her lower lip trembled as she did her best not to laugh.

Slightly annoyed, he narrowed his gaze. "Go on, let it out."

Her giggles popped like bubbles around him, drawing out his smile. "I'm not laughing because I think your name is bizarre. It's just that Rochester makes me think of some stodgy little professor with pale skin, soft hands, and a tendency to sniffle."

Rock laughed and winked at her. "Well, I'm glad I don't live up to my name, then."

"Oh, but you do." She took his hand in hers, offering a reassuring squeeze. "In the weeks I've known you, since you've been well, anyway, you've been a solid rock in a suddenly chaotic world." Her throat tightened and she swallowed hard. "I don't know what I would have done without you."

The smile he gave her started at his lips, filled his eyes, and overflowed from his heart. "I'd be dead without you, Miko. For saving my worthless hide, your every wish is my command."

"In that case…" The sassy smile she cast his way sent his temperature climbing. The implication that she would call in a future favor made him contemplate what it might be.

Her eyes dropped to the photo again. "You and your father look so much alike. I see where you got your good looks and charm." She handed the photograph back to him. "I remember the wound on his face and that he was blind in one eye. How did it happen?"

"He brought that home with him when he returned from the Great War. Mom and I were so happy he survived, we didn't care. Dad and his two brothers all served our country, but he was the only one who made it back." Rock rubbed his thumb across the frame, staring at the image of his father. "Every generation of Laroux men has had at least one serving our country. However many generations back, my great-great-great-grandfather supposedly fought with George Washington and his men in our country's battle for independence. From then on, there's always been at least one Laroux from our family enlisted to serve America."

"Wow, Rock. That's incredible, yet not surprising." She stood and began clearing away their dinner dishes.

"Why do you say that?" he asked, carrying his plate to the sink.

"From what I've seen, being noble, loyal, and selfless is just part of being a Laroux."

**** *Chapter Eleven* ★★**

Life settled into a routine for Rock and Miko in the days that followed his first trip to the assembly center. They worked, planned, ate, laughed, and got to know one another.

One evening, they sat at the kitchen table eating vanilla ice cream they'd churned from the rich cream the cows produced and sugar Rock acquired with ration coupons. A news report interrupted the lively beat of "Chattanooga Choo Choo" and they both stopped, spoons in the air, listening.

"A battle has raged since this morning at Midway between our boys and the Japanese. The Japs delivered a striking blow to the US base there, but don't give up hope. Our men are on the job and determined to win the fight."

Miko set her spoon back in the bowl of rapidly melting creamy confection and placed her hand on Rock's left hand as it rested on the table. "I'm so sorry, Rock. Do you have friends there?"

"Most of my buddies are in the Atlantic, but a few are in the Pacific. It's always hard to listen to news about our troops heading into battle."

Neither of them had any interest in finishing their ice cream, so Miko rinsed the bowls and left Rock in the kitchen, staring at the radio.

Unable to pull himself away from the reports the next day, Rock found a radio in the barn and got it working. He set it on an old stump someone had carved to resemble a chair and listened to it as he worked in the garden.

The evening of the third day, he and Miko had just come in from cleaning the last of the bins in the produce stand when he flipped on the radio and listened to a jubilant report of America winning the battle.

"This is a turning point, folks, a real turning point in the war. We've got those Japs on the run," the reporter said.

Rock grabbed Miko around the waist and danced her around the kitchen table, then pecked her on the cheek.

"It's wonderful news, Rock." Enthused, she gave him a tight hug, then tried to step back. He held on for the length of several heartbeats before the ringing of the telephone interrupted them.

At least three times a day, someone called wanting to know if or when the produce stand would open for the season. Miko never answered the phone, but Rock grew weary of repeating the information.

A week before they planned to open, Miko carried a typewriter into the kitchen and set it on the table. "You should send an article to the newspaper about taking over the farm and the produce stand opening. People will want to know, Rock. Granddad has many faithful customers. They'll be happy to know the produce stand will continue to operate."

"That's a great idea." He sat down at the table and gave her a long look. "Would it be okay if we give the farm a new name, until your grandfather returns?"

"You'll have to give it a new name or we won't have any customers. No matter how much someone wants Granddad's strawberries, they won't buy them from a place with a Japanese name." Miko rolled a sheet of paper into the typewriter and poised her fingers over the keys. "What name do you have in mind?"

Rock grinned. "I was thinking of calling it Double J Farms. That's for your middle name and mine."

She beamed at him. "That's perfect."

Mesmerized, he watched her long, slender fingers fly over the keys as she wrote an article about the farm being under new ownership, the day they would open, and operating hours for the season.

When she finished, she pulled the paper from the typewriter and handed it to him.

"This is great, Miko. You have a talent for writing the details in an interesting, informative manner, not to mention how fast you type. I forgot you spent several years as a secretary."

She nodded. "My job gave me plenty of experience in typing and writing articles to submit to the newspaper."

Her voice held a wistful note, one Rock hadn't often heard. For the most part, Miko focused on looking forward instead of dwelling in the past. Her ability to face the unknown future with strength and determination was one of the many things he admired about her.

"What's wrong? You sound sad." He reached out a hand and settled it over hers as it rested on the tabletop.

"I guess I miss my job a little. Although my employer could sometimes be a little demanding, I enjoyed the work. I always felt like I was contributing something, doing something important. Now..." She shrugged.

"What about now?" Rock asked, gently lifting her fingers and enfolding her hand in the warmth of his.

"I don't feel like I'm doing anything of value, or real purpose." She rose to her feet and set the typewriter back in its case, then closed the lid.

Rock stood and lifted her chin with his index finger, forcing her to look at him. "Nothing of value or purpose? What do you call raising enough produce to feed a few hundred people through the winter? That's something of real value, Miko. Something of far greater purpose than typing letters for some cranky stuffed suit in a big Portland office."

The slightest hint of a smile hovered at the corners of her mouth. "When you put it like that..." She expelled a satisfied smile. "And I do so love working in the hilltop garden."

"Your whole family would agree your presence here is something of value to them. You're keeping something safe and treasured that your great-grandparents and grandparents worked so hard to build." Rock tapped the top of the typewriter case with his fingers. "As well as you write, why don't you type some stories? You know, of your experiences. You could start with getting kicked off the bus and walking home in the rain."

She wrinkled her nose, making Rock want to kiss her in the worst way. "No one would want to read that."

"Oh, someday people will be interested in stories exactly like that." Rock shot her a cocky smile. "You could add in about finding a dashing young soldier on your doorstep and nursing him back to health. How he was so overcome with your beauty and charm, he begged you to let him stay."

She laughed and playfully pushed against his solid chest. "Go on with you, Captain Laroux. You can work off some of that foolishness in the barn. The faucet out there started leaking this morning."

Rock backed toward the door, shaking his finger at her. "You're a slave-driving woman, without a speck of mercy, Miss Nishimura."

"Don't forget it!" she called after him, grinning.

A few days later, Rock went to town in her grandfather's farm truck and returned with three piglets in the back.

"I like bacon," he said as Miko helped him settle the pigs into a pen he'd built away from the house and produce stand.

"They're so cute," she said, leaning over to pet one. "I think we should name them Wynken, Blynken, and Nod."

The disparaging glance he tossed her went unnoticed. "You do know I plan to eat them, don't you? More appropriate names would be Ham, Bacon, and Pork Chop."

Affronted on behalf of the pigs, Miko glared at him and marched to the barn. Despite his warnings for her not to treat the pigs like pets, she mixed mash with warm milk and fed them every morning, crooning to them.

He'd even found her reciting the poem after which they were named. Amused, he listened to her enchanting voice before returning to the task of pulling weeds in the garden.

Petey paid intermittent visits, keeping them updated on Princess Alice and the happenings in his world.

The produce stand opened and their days fell into a steady pattern of work. She arose before dawn and spent a few hours working in the vegetable garden or picking berries. No matter how early Rock crawled out of bed, she somehow always beat him outside.

Together, they'd milk Amos and Andy, strain the milk and set some aside to sell, then take the rest into the house. While she cooked breakfast, he gathered the eggs and crated what they wouldn't use that day.

After the meal, Miko would straighten the house, wash laundry, bake, or spend time ironing. A few minutes before nine, she'd pack a lunch and head up the hill to the secret garden to spend the day out of sight.

The produce stand was open Wednesday through Saturday, from nine in the morning until five in the afternoon. Rock hired three high school boys to work the days it was open. They helped him water, weed, and pick the vegetables the garden began producing in abundance.

Two high school girls ran the produce stand and flirted with the boys, including Rock.

Once everyone left for the day, Miko would return to the house and cook dinner, then help Rock with any unfinished chores.

The time of day they both liked best was when dusk settled. They sat on the porch, sipping glasses of cold juice or tea and listening to the summer serenade of crickets and frogs. Eventually, Miko would rise and take their glasses to the kitchen, bid him good night, and walk up the hill to the house in the garden.

Loneliness settled over Rock as she disappeared up the trail, making him wish he could accompany her. On the days the produce stand was open, he missed her working beside him. He missed the soothing sound of her voice and seeing her move with grace and confidence in every endeavor. She made him laugh with stories of things she and Sally had done in their youth, and made him think when she'd ask him questions to which he had no answers.

Although he'd never planned to settle down and live a civilian life, Rock couldn't imagine anyplace he'd rather be than right there, with the beautiful woman who had stolen his heart.

He wished she felt the same about him. Despite the challenges a relationship with her presented, Rock would have eagerly faced them all with a smile if she'd hinted that he meant more to her than a friend. For all he knew, she viewed him as the older brother she'd never had.

Disappointed, Rock worked out his frustrations on the farm. He awoke each day feeling more vitalized than the day before. Strength flowed through him and he relished the hard work as it healed his body and his mind.

Even his hand, the hand the doctor assured him would never function properly, made slow progress. Although he had trouble bending his fingers, he gained more control over the movements with each passing week.

Miko not only saved his life, but also gave him a renewed purpose. In the process of helping secure the farm for her family's future, he discovered how much he'd missed the days he spent working side-by-side with his father on their land.

Determined to make the farm a prosperous place for Shig and Aiko Yamada to return to when they were released, he gave his best effort to each chore.

Despite the satisfaction he drew from the days he worked, he enjoyed the days of rest even more.

Sundays, Miko would take her time coming down the hill to help him milk. A leisurely breakfast preceded time spent listening to radio programs on the Philco in the living room. Miko would pack a picnic basket with leftovers and together they'd walk up the hill to the garden. Rock's favorite place to eat was beneath the shade of a weeping cherry tree near the pool at the base of the waterfall.

Since Miko couldn't attend a church service and Rock didn't want to leave her alone, they took turns reading from the Bible and discussing the verses. For Rock, those Sundays were among the most peaceful and pleasant days he'd ever known.

Sometimes, he fell asleep to the sound of Miko humming or the water from the stream lulling him to slumber.

Other times, they would walk around the expansive garden and she'd explain the design of a certain area to him. Through her patient instruction, he learned there were five distinctive areas to the garden.

Miko referred to the area around the house as the flat garden. Stones, clipped shrubbery, and shaped trees provided a sense of depth. The best view of it, he discovered, was from inside the house, looking out the front between the shoji screens. Rounded azalea shrubs, lacy-leafed maples, weeping cherries, and black pines surrounded a sea of raked rock. The sense of cool water created by the plants and rocks lifted his spirits.

The second garden area she referred to as the dry garden. According to Miko, Zen Buddhist priests had started the practice of raking gravel or sand around stones to focus on the beauty of bare space. Rock liked the simplicity of the pale sand, carefully swirled by Miko's rake around several large stones. She informed him the garden wasn't a place to meditate but to contemplate.

With much to consider, he often visited the area and thought about his future, the future he yearned to spend with Miko.

When he needed a place to relax and rest, he strolled through the section Miko called the rambling garden. To him, it seemed the most natural of all the areas the Yamada family had cultivated and created. Vine maple grew among the deciduous plants that had flourished on the hill for hundreds of years. Moss gathered on branches and trailed over rocks near the stream that flowed through the area before trickling down the hill to the orchard below. Quiet time spent wandering along the stone pathways there left him energized yet tranquil.

Although it seemed strange to him to draw energy from the garden, Miko offered him an indulgent look when he mentioned it to her.

Her favorite part of the garden was her grandmother's garden. Lanterns and stepping stones, nestled amid a variety of trees and native shrubs, led the way to a rustic bamboo gate. The inner garden held a large water basin and a stone table with two small benches where Miko and her grandmother used to have tea parties.

However, Rock's favorite part of the garden encompassed the water gardens. The stream fed three ponds, each with a bridge. Purple iris edged a border around the deep pool at the base of the waterfall. Large stones across the narrow end provided a place to cross from one side to the other.

"In Japan, only the wealthy would have a strolling pond garden. My grandparents have the wealth not of money, but of love, which is how this place came to be," she said when he asked her about the design of the garden.

He liked to stand on the bridge above the middle pond and watch the colorful carp dart back and forth among the cool shallows. He also enjoyed taking Miko's hand in his as they meandered along the pathways near the water. It made him want to spout poetry, but the only poems he knew from memory he'd learned in the Army. The rhymes weren't exactly fit for delicate ears.

Afternoon would give way to evening. Reluctantly, they would walk back down the hill, leaving behind the idyllic world of their own creation in the place he thought of as Miko's garden.

She might enjoy coaxing the fruit and vegetables to grow on the farm, but she thrived in the secret garden of her ancestors. The joy she took in it was palpable, undeniable, and it reaffirmed Rock's decision to do whatever it took to keep her and the land safe from harm.

One Sunday evening after they'd eaten a simple dinner, they retired to the living room to listen to the radio. Miko worked on crocheting a dainty pink-and-white blanket for baby Alice Phillips while Rock pretended to read one of the gardening books Shig suggested.

Absently flipping through the pages, he covertly watched Miko's fingers twine through the yarn and the silver crochet hook flash back and forth in the golden evening light.

A breeze blew in the open windows, stirring the curtains and carrying the scent of the cinnamon pinks blooming along the front porch.

Wrapped in an extraordinary spell, Rock set aside the book and walked over to the rocking chair, where a spill of amber sunlight surrounded Miko. Entranced, he removed the yarn from her fingers and smiled at the surprised expression on her face.

Without saying a word, he took her hands in his and pulled her to her feet, slipping one arm around her waist and holding her left hand in his right, in a classic dance position.

Vera Lynn sang about a nightingale in Berkeley Square, a perfect song for a slow dance. As though they'd done so a hundred times before, they swayed in harmony to the music, palms touching, hearts racing, hunger for each other hanging heavy between them.

When the song ended, Miko tipped her head back, studying him from beneath long, dark lashes. Rather than release her, he nudged her closer and continued dancing as Helen Forrest sang "You Made Me Love You."

Ever so slowly, Rock dropped his head toward hers. As Helen sang about someone having the brand of kisses that she'd die for, Rock thought he might die right there if he didn't claim Miko's kisses for his own. The thought of kissing her, of tasting the decadent sweetness that he imagined to be uniquely her, made his heart thump erratically in his chest.

Only a breath of space hovered between their lips as he waited. Waited for her to rebuff him, to pull away… or close the distance.

Consumed with his need for her but unwilling to frighten her, he brushed his thumb across her cheek and traced the line of her jaw. Reverently, he pressed a soft kiss to her mouth.

In willing response, her hands slid behind his neck and subtly obliterated any space remaining between them.

Rock abandoned all thoughts of dancing as he wrapped both arms around her and deepened the kiss. Lost to her, to the feelings she stirred in him, he had no idea how far things might have gone if a visitor hadn't chosen that moment to arrive.

The crunch of tires on the gravel outside made her jump away like a scalded cat. She braced one hand on the back of the sofa and held the other to the frenzied pulse throbbing in her throat. Thrown off balance, she drew in deep, shaky gulps of air.

Eyes wide, she glanced behind her toward the front window, prepared to scurry into the kitchen to hide. Much to Rock's surprise, she released an excited yelp and bolted outside.

He watched as she leaped down the porch steps and ran into the open arms of a man with kind eyes and a welcoming smile.

The man lifted her off her feet and swung her around in a fatherly embrace before setting her back down. Together, they walked up the sidewalk to where Rock waited on the porch steps.

"Pastor George Clark, I'd like you to meet Captain Rock Laroux," Miko said, introducing the two men.

"Pastor, it's a pleasure to meet you. Miko speaks so highly of you," Rock said, extending his hand to the older man.

Pastor Clark took his hand and shook it with enthusiasm, smiling broadly. "The pleasure is all mine, young man. I would have been here sooner, but I just returned from London a few days ago. I've been so busy settling my sister and niece in my home, I didn't realize until yesterday all the Japanese in our area have been carted off to that detestable livestock pen near the river."

Rock tossed the pastor a warning glance and slight shake of his head, wanting to shield Miko from the trials her family endured.

Pastor Clark cleared his throat and gave Rock an almost imperceptible nod. "I went to the center this afternoon and spoke at length with your family, Miko, as well as the administrator of the facility. He seems like a fair man who is only enforcing the orders he's been given."

"How are Papa and Mother? Are Granddad and Grandma well? Has Tommy grown?" Miko asked, leading the way inside and motioning for the pastor to take a seat. "Would you like anything to drink? Have you had dinner?"

The pastor laughed. "So many questions, Miko. Just like old times."

She smiled and her face softened with memories of happy moments from her past.

Pastor Clark squeezed her hand. "I wouldn't turn down a cool drink. I did have dinner, but I wouldn't mind a little something if you have it."

"I'll be right back," Miko said, rushing into the kitchen, leaving the two men alone.

Rock took a seat in one of the wingback chairs while the pastor settled into the cushions of the sofa. With his elbows braced on his knees, Rock leaned forward and spoke on a low tone. "I thought it best if Miko didn't know the, um… conditions of the assembly center. She's still not convinced she should stay here instead of joining her family. If she knew the deplorable conditions, I'm afraid she'd run right down there."

Pastor Clark nodded in agreement. "Most likely she would. You seem to have learned quite a lot about our girl since you met. Her parents filled me in on how you came to be here. Shig said you purchased the place with the intention of selling it back to him when he can return."

"That's right. The family has worked too long and too hard to make this a prosperous farm to have someone waltz in and take it from them. At least this way, their interests are protected and it gives me something to do until I figure out my next step."

"Jack mentioned you'd been injured. Are you doing better?" The pastor studied him, trying to picture the robust, healthy man in front of him as the damaged, wounded soldier he'd imagined.

Rock grinned. "About a hundred percent better." He held out his weak hand. "The doctor tells me this might never work like it used to, but other than that, I'm feeling much improved since I've been here. I think it's a combination of the fresh air, good food, and a wonderful nurse."

"I keep telling you, I'm not a nurse," Miko said, glaring at Rock as she entered the room. She carried a tray with glasses of iced tea and slices of cake covered in fresh strawberries and whipped cream.

"That certainly looks delicious, Miko," the pastor said, accepting the plate she held out to him along with the tea.

Rock took a plate and draped the napkin she handed him over his knee, leaning back in the chair as Miko took a seat next to the pastor.

She asked him about his trip and how long his sister and niece would stay with him. He planned to visit Sally soon and offered to take anything Miko cared to send to her friend.

"Sally said she was so relieved when she received a letter from you," Pastor Clark said. He finished his cake and set his empty plate on the tray Miko left on the coffee table in front of the sofa.

"I didn't have a way to mail her when I first arrived home. I was afraid if I called, someone would figure out I was here instead of with my family." Miko glanced at the pastor, a man who had been like a second father to her throughout her life. "Did I do the right thing, hiding here? It seems dishonest."

Pastor Clark sat forward and took her hand in his, giving it a reassuring pat. "As a pastor, I should probably advise you to turn yourself in and face the consequences. However, as your friend and the closest thing you have to an uncle, I will lock you in your room and toss away the key if you take a notion to go to the assembly center. You can do far more good for your family here than there. In my opinion, detaining everyone of Japanese descent along the Pacific Coast is one of the most preposterous things I've ever heard of in my life. The whole thing seems like a violation of rights to me, but no one asked my opinion."

Miko grinned. "If they did, they'd have received an earful and then some."

"That's right." The pastor tweaked her nose, as though she was six years old, and grinned at Rock. "I'm somewhat concerned about Miko's safety, though. If anyone discovers her, they'll turn her in and she'll be arrested as a fugitive and a war criminal. With the produce stand open, it's only a matter of time before someone figures out she's here."

Rock cast Miko a worried glance, then turned to the pastor. "The thought crosses my mind daily, but I don't know what to do about it. Without the produce stand, we wouldn't make a profit and the farm would suffer, but I do worry about Miko. She works during the day out of sight, but, as you said, it is only a matter of time before her whereabouts are discovered."

Pastor Clark sat back and crossed his hands over his belly. "After giving the matter considerable thought, I think it would be best if Miko and you wed."

Miko shot to her feet and glared at the pastor as if he'd sentenced her to marry the devil instead of the handsome man across the room.

Stunned by the suggestion, Rock gaped at the pastor, wondering if the man was a genius or a lunatic. Although he wanted nothing more than to make Miko his own, a few obstacles blocked the way to marital bliss.

For starters, marriages of mixed race were illegal in the state of Oregon. Even if that wasn't an issue, since Miko was a fugitive and considered a criminal, she couldn't march into a courthouse and apply for a marriage license.

Then there was the matter of Miko's heart. Rock hoped he sensed love starting to blossom, but it might just be wishful thinking on his part.

The look on her face as she glowered at Pastor Clark combined with her stiff, tense posture indicated she wasn't receptive to the suggestion of spending her life with him.

"It's a great idea," Rock said, drawing the gazes of both the pastor and Miko. While Pastor Clark smiled and nodded encouragingly, Miko's gaze narrowed and her eyes sparked with anger.

"A great idea?" she fumed, pacing back and forth in front of the fireplace. "It's a horrible idea! Did both of you forget it's illegal for Rock to marry someone like me?"

Rock leaned back in his chair and tossed her a devilish smile. "Since when did they outlaw marrying beautiful women? I will definitely have to write a letter to our congressman."

Pastor Clark laughed and slapped his leg, then waggled a finger Rock's direction. "I like this one, Miko. He's got a sense of humor on top of his other redeeming qualities."

"Would you both stop this ridiculousness and listen to reason?" she demanded, plopping down on the wingback chair across from Rock. "You can't change facts. We can't marry in Oregon. I'm a fugitive from the law. Besides, Rock has sacrificed enough for this family without being stuck with me for the rest of his life. Even if I did agree to this ludicrous plan, what's to keep the authorities from arresting me after we wed?"

The pastor started to speak, but Rock sent him a beseeching look and interrupted. "Miko, if you're willing to do this, we can make it work. It isn't illegal to marry you in Washington. We could drive across the river to Vancouver and wed in a simple ceremony. As for anyone pressing charges against you, I could claim that I refused to let my wife go and it's all my fault. It wouldn't be far off the truth, because I did refuse to let you go the first hundred times you suggested it."

"Rock has a good point. You'd be under his protection if you married. In regard to your wedding ceremony, I'd be happy to perform it. As a minister, I *can* do that sort of thing," Pastor Clark said with a mischievous smile.

Rock leaned forward again. "See how easy it was to overcome that worry. As for you being a fugitive of the law, maybe if you wore a hat with a veil, no one would notice you're Japanese. With your height, most people don't expect you to be anything but American."

Pastor Clark slapped the palms of his hands together and chortled in excitement. "That's the ticket, Rock. Miko, wear a big hat with something that hides your face. No one will know and everything will be just fine."

"What about my name? I have to put it on the marriage license and it's not exactly like Betty Smith or Susan Jones." Miko continued casting glares between Rock and the pastor, trying to decide which one of them was craziest. At the moment, it was impossible to choose.

"You could list your name as K. Jane Nishimura," Rock suggested. "For all they know, you could be a widow of a Japanese man."

Exasperated, she rose to her feet and began pacing again. "Fine, fine! I can't believe my pastor is encouraging me to be deceptive."

Pastor Clark shrugged. "Desperate times, my dear, we are in desperate times."

"But that still leaves the matter of Rock tying himself to me for the rest of his life." She waved a hand his direction. "I can't and won't allow it."

"You aren't allowing anything if I volunteer." Rock stood and grabbed her arms in his hands, bringing her frantic pacing to a stop. His gaze held hers and he stared into those dark eyes, searching for some sign that she was open to the idea of being his wife. Several intense moments later, he spied a flicker of longing, a spark of desire, and knew he hadn't been wrong about her interest in him.

Many long, happy marriages began with less than what he and Miko already shared — respect, admiration, loyalty, friendship, and devotion. He could do far worse than marry the lovely girl. In truth, his heart had flipped over in excitement the moment the pastor mentioned it.

He wanted nothing more than to have Miko by his side for the rest of his life. The only remaining challenge was to convince her of his sincerity.

"Please, Miko? Would you at least consider marrying me?"

She shook her head and tried to pull away from him, but he drew her closer, wrapping his arms around her and holding her. His breath tantalized her ear as he bent his head near hers. "Please?"

"I can't, Rock. I don't want to be the cause of you missing out on the love of a lifetime." She turned her head to the side and pressed it against his neck. Unintentionally, she heightened the yearning that already pulsed between them. Forcibly, he relaxed his hold on her.

"Miko," he whispered. "Look at me, sweetheart."

Unhurried, she tipped her head back, drawn into the bright warmth of his eyes.

"Miko, if I didn't want to marry you, I wouldn't offer. I rather like the idea of spending my future with you. We have more going for us than many couples who wed.

There is no doubt in my mind at all about your ability to be a good wife. Me, on the other hand..." His cocky grin brought an amused light to her eyes. "It might be challenging to be married to someone like me."

A smile curved her mouth upward and Rock tamped down the desire to kiss her again, even with the pastor watching their every move.

"Let me think about it before I sentence you to a future of misery," she said with a sassy smile. "After all, you wouldn't be getting an average wife and I'm not sure you're ready to settle down. I've heard the girls flirting with you in the produce stand and you don't ignore them as much as you should."

Affronted, Rock released her. "I'll have you know I've not done a thing to encourage them. Why, just yesterday I—"

Miko laughed and the pastor chuckled. She winked at Rock. "I had you going, Captain Laroux."

Pastor Clark stayed long enough for Rock to load a box full of tomatoes, peas, radishes, lettuce, and a basket of strawberries in his car before he left. He gave Rock directions to the courthouse in Vancouver where he needed to acquire a marriage license and told him to call when he and Miko were ready to proceed with a wedding.

When Rock returned inside the house, Miko was gone. He almost walked up the hill to talk to her, but decided to give her the time and space she needed.

If he trusted his instincts and heart, he could rest assured that Miko would soon be his.

Anger fueled each step as Miko trudged up the hill. She waited until Pastor Clark went outside with Rock to escape out the back door.

Humiliated by the pastor practically insisting she marry Rock, she needed time to think. Alone. Without Rock's alluring presence sending her thoughts into a jumbled mess.

The day with him had been marvelous. As had become their habit, they'd spent the afternoon in the secret garden, enjoying one another's company. Dinner had been pleasant and companionable. After the meal, as they'd sat in the living room listening to the radio, Miko had paid far more attention to Rock than she had the blanket she crocheted. If her fingers hadn't known the pattern as well as her mind, she most likely would have had to tug out every stitch she'd added to the baby blanket.

Long legs stretched out before him, Rock lounged in the chair with one of her grandfather's gardening books. Tan, tapered fingers appeared so big and strong against the parchment of the book's pages. The soft cotton shirt he wore only accented the breadth of his shoulders and width of his chest.

She'd forced her gaze away only to find him standing in front of her with an indefinable look in his eyes. They appeared darker than she'd ever seen them and were filled with a warmth that settled around her like welcome sunshine on a storm-clouded day.

When he took her hands in his, pulling her to her feet, she thought perhaps he wanted to show her something outside. Astounded when he took her in his arms and started dancing with her, Miko couldn't recall the last time she'd danced with anyone.

Rock's arm around her back with his other hand holding hers gave her an intense feeling of security and love. It was insane to harbor any thoughts that he could own amorous intentions for her, but part of her wished he did.

The moment the song ended, she'd expected him to pull away and offer a teasing comment. She hadn't imagined he'd keep dancing. And she'd certainly never dreamed he'd kiss her so tenderly it would make her heart ache before skittering into a frenzied beat as he held her closer and deepened the fervent exchange.

Miko had kissed several boys and men since her parents had allowed her to date. Not one of them had made her toes tingle and her insides feel as though they might combust from heat. It was a good thing Pastor Clark arrived when he did. Goodness only knew what might have happened if he hadn't.

She changed into her nightdress and opened the bamboo blinds over the window, allowing more of the night breeze to puff into the room. Fatigued, her mind whirled as she tried to relax against the crisp white sheets of her bed. Long into the night, she considered the options, wondering why Rock had kissed her and if he truly cared about her.

Her dreams of being in his arms, of knowing his kisses, were even more wonderful than she'd imagined. What if he really would marry her? Would he someday come to care for her as much as she already loved him?

Uncertain, afraid, and yet excited, Miko finally drifted into a restless sleep.

·★ *Chapter Twelve* ★*·*

Miko dried the last of the breakfast dishes, cocking her head to the side as she listened to the sound of the shower running in the bathroom. Curious, she wondered where Rock planned to go. Instead of dwelling on the possibilities, she turned her attention to her morning tasks. Hands buried in a mound of bread dough, she kneaded air into the yeasty lump when Rock appeared in the kitchen, dressed in his navy suit.

Surprised by his attire, her gaze traveled from the top of his still-wet, sun-streaked hair to the toes of his polished shoes. "Going somewhere?" she asked. Normally, he took the eggs, butter, and cream to town on Tuesday, purchased whatever groceries and supplies they needed, and returned home with a treat for lunch, like a hamburger or a sandwich from the diner.

Since it was Monday, she didn't have the butter churned for tomorrow's delivery. She wondered where he was headed looking so dapper.

Neither of them mentioned Pastor Clark's visit the previous evening. The tension crackling between them, though, confirmed that thoughts of his proposal hung heavy on both their minds.

"I have several errands I need to see to today. I'm not sure how long I'll be gone. It might be this afternoon before I make it back." Nervous, Rock twirled his fedora in his right hand. "Would you mind if I drive your car? It's such a nice day out, I'd like to give it a spin."

"Be my guest," she said, smiling at him over her shoulder. "But if you get in trouble for speeding, don't say I didn't warn you."

He chuckled, then sobered. "Will you be fine here by yourself?"

Miko scoffed. "Of course. It isn't like you haven't left me alone before. I'm not a child, Rock. I can take care of myself." She returned her attention to punching down the bread dough. If she did so with more force than was necessary, she hoped he wouldn't notice. The idea that he viewed her as a child in need of his babysitting greatly irked her.

He dropped his hat on the counter and stepped behind her, wrapping his right arm around her waist and pulling her against his solid form. His warm, minty breath brushed over her ear as he leaned down. "I would never, ever think of you as a child, Kamiko. Most definitely a beautiful, alluring woman, but never a child."

Involuntarily, she felt a delighted shiver trail through her and she leaned against him, leaned into his strength. Afraid if she spoke, she'd expose her true feelings for him, she took a deep breath, inhaling his masculine scent combined with a hint of woodsy spice from his shaving lotion.

For several heartbeats, they stood that way, her hands dripping flour and dough while he held her. If it wasn't for the mess on her hands creating an even bigger mess on the floor, she would have stayed there all day.

Finally, Rock dropped his hand and stepped back. "Be a good girl and I'll bring you a treat," he teased with a playful wink.

"Oh, run your errands and get out of my kitchen," she said, motioning with an elbow toward the door.

"I'm going." He lifted his hat from the counter, then paused. Gently, he cradled her chin in his hand, tipping her head up and pressing a soft kiss to her lips. "Bye, Miko."

"Bye," she whispered. Slowly opening her eyes, she watched him hurry out the door.

Rock forced himself to walk out to the storage building and get in the car before he raced back inside the house and confessed the depths of his love.

All night, he had tossed and turned as he pondered marriage to Miko. The more he thought about it, the more he realized he wanted to be her husband.

Perhaps with a little coercion, she'd come around to his way of thinking and agree.

Rock drove to the little grocery store where he traded the butter and eggs for the things they couldn't grow or didn't have at the farm. He greeted Mr. Ross, then filled a box with food to take with him to the assembly center. He set it on the backseat of the car next to a box he'd filled with the choicest produce from the farm that morning.

Anxious, he drove to Portland and out to the assembly center. Each time he visited the family, he brought them letters from Miko and left with letters they'd written to her in his pockets.

This morning, he hadn't told her where he planned to go because he wanted the visit to remain confidential between her family and him.

At the gate, the guard waved in greeting.

"Good morning," Rock greeted, carrying the two boxes of food he'd brought along.

"Morning, Captain Laroux," the guard said, giving the items a perfunctory glance. He snitched one strawberry and motioned for Rock to step inside.

"If you don't mind, I'd like to speak to Mr. Nishimura and Mr. Yamada before the women and Tommy join us. Is that possible?" Rock asked.

"Sure thing," the guard said, motioning for a sentry to approach him. While the young man went to find the two men, Rock set the boxes down on the picnic table where he usually visited with Miko's family and waited. He dropped his hat on the table and paced back and forth, practicing the speech he'd revised fifty times in his head that morning.

Jack and Shig hurried out of the building, uncertain why they'd been singled out until the sentry pointed to where Rock waited.

"Captain Laroux!" Jack said, walking over with an extended hand and a friendly smile.

Rock shook his hand and then took the one Shig offered. "Good morning, sirs. How does this day find you?"

"Well enough, I suppose," Shig said, eying the boxes of food with interest. He lifted a tomato the size of a baseball from the box and held it up, admiring the bright red, unblemished skin. His gaze lifted to Rock's. "I couldn't have done any better myself."

"Glad to hear that, sir. But you're the one who prepared the ground and planted the seeds. I'm just there to take care of it. Besides, I've got a good helper."

"How is your helper?" Jack asked with a smile.

"She's very well, sir. In fact, Pastor Clark paid a visit last evening. It was nice to meet him." Rock sat on the hard wooden bench after the other two men were seated. "He had some interesting things to say."

"I'm sure he did," Jack said, grinning at his father-in-law before turning back to Rock. "But what brings you here today with this abundance of good food?"

Rock dropped his voice to a whisper so the guard wouldn't overhear and looked Miko's father square in the face. "Sir, I don't know how else to say this other than blurt it right out, but may I please have your permission to marry your daughter?"

"I see." Jack leaned back, his face an unreadable mask. He remained silent for so long, Rock wanted to squirm on his seat. Finally, the man placed his forearms on the table in front of him and met Rock's gaze.

Rock expected him to demand an inventory of reasons he'd be a good husband or a list of things he admired about Miko.

Instead, her father stared at him and asked a single question. "Describe Miko in one word."

"One word, sir?" Rock asked, confused.

"Yes. If you summed up everything about her in one word, what would it be?" Jack's face remained impassive as he waited for Rock's answer.

Taken aback by his request, Rock's thoughts splintered in a hundred directions. Only a few seconds passed before the word that floated through the maelstrom in his head gained clarity. "Hummingbird."

Baffled, both Shig and Jack stared in confusion.

"Explain, please," Jack said.

Rock took a deep breath. "Before I was wounded, I was stationed in Trinidad, off Venezuela's coast in the southern Caribbean. The area is a big melting pot of combined cultures — Creole, East Indian, Chinese, African. A great diversity of flowers and shrubbery grow there, and it offers more than four hundred different species of birds. But do you know what they call the island?"

At the men's interested looks, Rock continued. "Land of the Hummingbird. While I was there, I saw many of them. The islanders believe hummingbirds are symbols of all that is good and they carry joy wherever they go. Hummingbirds are fearless, determined, adaptable, and flexible. They possess the courage of a mighty lion and the magic of mythical fairies. Hummingbirds have boundless energy and endurance. Those little birds can make the most difficult journey seem like a simple matter, and they are loyal, devoted to the garden they claim as their own. They are fiercely independent, but those who accept that can long enjoy the beauty and wonder of those amazing little winged fellows."

Jack's mouth quirked upward and he bit back a smile. "So you're saying Miko is like a demented bird who wants only to suck the sweetness out of life?"

"No, sir, that's not what I meant at all!" In his nervous state, Rock missed the teasing looks exchanged by the two older men. "She's a swell girl, one full of life and vibrancy, and intelligence. She'd make any man a wonderful wife."

Shig waggled his eyebrows and smirked. "We're just kidding with you, Rock."

The hunch in his shoulders slid away and he noticed the smiles on the faces of Miko's father and grandfather. "Will you please give me permission, sir?"

Jack nodded. "I will. In fact, I was planning on it, even before you asked, but I wanted to hear what you had to say."

"You answered well," Shig said, beaming at him. "Someday, you must tell Miko about this moment so she can share it with your children. It will make a good story."

Relieved her father and grandfather accepted him and pleased he had their blessing to marry Miko, Rock wanted to jump to his feet and shout. Rather than surrender to the desire, he slid the box of produce closer to the two men. "I'll get in touch with Pastor Clark and make arrangements."

"That's good," Jack said, standing and shaking Rock's hand. He released it and turned as his wife, mother-in-law, and son approached.

Rock stayed for another twenty minutes, catching them up on news of the farm before he shook hands again with Shig and Jack. "I'll take good care of her, sir," he whispered to Miko's father as they ambled toward the gate.

"I know you will. I wouldn't trust her safekeeping to anyone else."

Rock tipped his head to her family, then strode out the gate. He ventured into Vancouver to the courthouse, discovering both he and Miko had to appear in person to acquire a marriage license at least three days before the date of the ceremony.

Armed with the information he needed and the form they could fill out ahead of time, he left and headed back to Portland. He completed several errands, then drove to an area the locals referred to as Chinatown.

He entered a shop he'd been in a few times with his father, glad to find it still open for business.

A bowlegged little Chinese man, long hair braided in a queue down his back, stood behind a worn counter at the center of the store. The aroma of spices in the air blended with the smell of fresh fish.

"Hello," Rock said, stepping up to the counter and smiling at the man. Unless things had changed drastically in the last few years, the shopkeeper claimed not to know a lick of English.

The man said something in his native language and waved a hand around his shop. Rock pointed to a case full of ice where the fish selections of the day were on display. Salmon, trout, and sturgeon sat alongside other seafood he didn't recognize.

Rock pointed to a large fish and held up two fingers.

The old man wrapped his selections in paper and set the fish on the counter. Rock added a few things to his purchases he thought Miko might appreciate. In the time she'd been cooking for him, she'd only served two meals that he considered authentically Japanese, and they were both delicious. One meal included marinated chicken she cut into small pieces and fried in a pan of hot lard. The other was made from a jar of canned beef she found in the basement and thinly sliced cabbage.

When Rock was ready to pay, he pointed to the items the old man set into a box for him. "How much?"

The old man said something Rock didn't understand. The store owner liked to barter. The more animated the bartering, the more he enjoyed it. Rock rattled off a number half of what he thought his purchases were worth.

The store owner huffed, crossed his arms over his thin chest, and spoke so fast Rock wondered how the man's tongue didn't tie itself in knots.

"Is that so?" Rock said, feigning insult. "Well, I'll have you know my radio sprouts peaches and the cows give purple milk."

The shopkeeper waved his hands in the air, then thumped the counter, shouting something that sounded like pure gibberish.

Rock scowled and shook his finger at the man. "I bet you a dollar my sweet petunias are tastier than your pickled polecats any day of the week."

The bartering continued for several minutes, with Rock tossing out nonsensical statements since he had no idea what the old man said for the most part. He'd learned a few Chinese words and from what he could pick out, the man spewed silliness, too.

At last, Rock took out his wallet and handed the store owner what he felt was more than a fair price for the goods plus a little extra.

The old man grinned, showing spaces where teeth were missing. "Come again," he said in perfect English right before Rock walked out the door.

Entertained, Rock replayed the lively interchange as he headed home.

If someone had told him six months ago he'd be the owner of a farm, selling produce in a roadside stand, and about to beg a Japanese girl to marry him, he'd have cuffed them upside the head and called them loony.

Now, though, when he thought of home, a vision of Miko sitting beneath a weeping cherry tree filled his mind.

She had become his home, and he intended to do everything in his power to make sure she remained by his side.

No matter what the uncertain future might bring, he wanted to spend it with her.

The first thing he noticed when he pulled up behind the house was the open doors of the storage building. The second thing was that the three pigs rooted in the strawberry patch while Amos and Andy wreaked havoc in the tomatoes.

Miko was nowhere around.

"Miko!" he called as he hustled out of the car, tossing off his suit jacket and tie, leaving them on the hood.

He herded the cows back to their pasture. The gate nearest the garden was wide open. He and Miko never used the gate, so he wondered how it had gotten open.

It seemed odd both the pigs and cows had chosen to escape at the same time. He would have blamed it on a childish prank, but Petey knew better than to do such a thing. The kids who worked for Rock cared too much about their jobs to jeopardize their employment by doing something so foolish.

"Miko!" he bellowed, hoping wherever she was, she'd help him chase in the pigs. If the greedy rooters hadn't been making a dandy mess of the strawberries, he would have taken time to run inside and change.

"Captain?" A frightened little voice called from behind the storage building. "Captain!"

Rock abandoned the pigs and raced in the direction of the frantic calls. He rounded the corner of the building to find Petey next to Miko, prone and unmoving, her hand held in his as tears streamed down the boy's face. No blood pooled around her, but a thousand horrible reasons for her unconscious state tumbled through Rock's thoughts.

"What happened, Petey?" he asked, dropping to his knees beside them.

"Dilly-danged if I know. I came over to see if Miko might let me help her string up the beans out in the garden. The cows were already out and I heard the piggies squealing like the big bad wolf had arrived. I cut across the pasture, took the corner at sixty, and threw on the brakes, 'cause she was just like this. She won't wake up." Petey snuffled and swiped his face on his shoulder. "What's wrong with her?"

"I'm not sure, Petey." Rock felt for Miko's pulse, alleviating a measure of his worry as it pumped in a steady beat. Gently, he tapped her cheeks. "Miko? Wake up, sweetheart. Miko, open your eyes."

If Petey hadn't been watching his every move, Rock might have attempted to kiss her awake. Instead, he tapped her cheeks again and continued saying her name, encouraging her to rouse.

Finally, her eyelashes fluttered and she opened her eyes, appearing slightly dazed. "What...?" She struggled to sit up. "Where am I?"

"You're out behind the storage building." Rock smiled at her and braced an arm behind her, helping her rise to a sitting position. For a moment, she appeared as though she might be ill, but she swallowed twice and closed her eyes, inhaling a deep breath. "I just returned from town, but Petey was the one who found you."

"If you'd hurried any faster, you'd have beaten me to her," Petey proclaimed, rising to his feet. "I'll go chase in those slabs of bacon if you want to help her up."

The boy took off running before Rock agreed to his plan. Miko rubbed a hand over the back of her head and winced.

Rock tenderly ran his fingers through the black silk ribbons of her hair and found a large bump on her skull. "It's pushed out instead of in. That's a good sign," he said, hoping to reassure himself as much as her.

Eyes narrowed, as though the sunlight hurt them, she again swallowed hard. Swiftly gaining her feet, she took two steps over to a row of shrubs and lost the contents of her stomach. Rock followed and held her hair away from her face.

When she straightened and wiped her mouth on the back of her hand, she refused to face him. She appeared mortified that she'd been ill in front of him while he held her hair.

He didn't step away, but rubbed a comforting hand on her back. "Let's get you in the house, Miko."

He hooked an arm behind her knees and lifted her into his arms. Too upset and miserable to protest, Miko weakly let her head sink against the hard planes of his chest and wrapped her arms around his neck.

At the back door, he toed the screen open and maneuvered through the kitchen and dining room, easing her down to rest on the sofa in the living room. "Don't move," he said and disappeared down the hall. He returned with a cool cloth and placed it over her forehead. "Just rest awhile, Miko, while Petey and I round up the pigs."

Rock yanked off his shirt on the way to his bedroom, where he pulled on a pair of worn denims and his work boots, then raced outside to help the boy secure the pigs.

He found Petey chasing after the one he thought Miko referred to as Blynken with a broom, trying to get it to follow the other two into the pen. Rock cut it off as it tried to escape and the pig retraced its steps, running into the pen. Petey swung the gate shut and latched it.

"Unless Miko's little porkers set up a course with Houdini, I think something ain't quite right around here," Petey said, staring at Rock.

He clapped a hand on the boy's shoulder and together they walked back to where he'd left the car.

Petey whistled and rubbed his hands together. "Miko must like you heaps if she let you drive her car. Do you think I could ride in it while you park it?"

Rock opened the door, motioning for Petey to climb in.

"Zip ziggety!" the boy exclaimed, clambering inside.

Rock slid onto the seat and started the car, smiling at Petey.

The boy rubbed his hand along the dash. "Purrs even better than Mom's cat."

"That it does," Rock said, driving the car into the storage building. He noticed right away that one of the two gas cans was missing. Whoever had turned the cows and pigs loose must have happened upon Miko and clunked her on the head. Before the criminal had time to do more, something must have frightened him away. The war whoops Petey most generally used during his approach could have put a thief on the alert, or a passing car might have startled the intruder.

Whatever the reason, no one had been parked at or near the produce stand when Rock arrived home. He'd be willing to bet they hadn't been gone long, though.

A quick glance around confirmed nothing else appeared to be missing. He placed a hand on the boy's shoulder, drawing his attention. "I've got a box of groceries that needs to go up to the house and I better check on Miko while I'm at it. Can you start cleaning up the mess in the strawberries?"

"Sure I can!" Petey took off at a run while Rock hefted the box and carried it to the house, storing the fish in the refrigerator and leaving the other things on the counter. He checked on Miko and found her sleeping, which was probably for the best. He lifted the cloth from her head and dropped it near the kitchen sink on his way to the strawberry patch.

Petey was there, trying to lift a section of fence that had fallen over. Rock took over the job and soon had it repaired.

"From here on out, we'd better be hitting on all cylinders," Petey proclaimed, rolling his hands into fists. "If some interloper, some bandit, some dastardly villain thinks he can march right in here and cause trouble, he better watch out." The boy took a wild swing in the air.

Rock hunkered down until he was eye level with the boy. "Look, Petey, we have to be real careful that whoever did this doesn't come back and try to hurt Miko again. For now, let's keep quiet about what happened. Okay?"

Petey nodded so forcefully, his red hair flopped across his forehead and dangled in his eyes. With a disgusted huff, he brushed it out of his way and gave Rock a somber look. "You can count on me, Cap, to keep it top secret. Us men have to protect the womenfolk around here. I'd tell my pop and have him climb on board, but he's got more than he can handle with Mom and the princess."

"Let's put off telling your folks for just a little while, Petey. In the meantime, I'd sure appreciate your help in keeping an eye on things around here on days when the produce stand isn't open."

"I betcha it's one of Hitler's spies!" Petey bent his legs and crab-walked a few steps, looking from left to right, as though he anticipated the enemy jumping out at him any moment. Then, in a lightning-fast change belonging to those of innocent childhood, he spun around and smiled at Rock. "We'll catch him, Cap, and he'll leave here howling like the dickens with his tail between his legs."

Rock placed a hand on Petey's shoulder. "Do you suppose your folks would let you stay for supper? I could sure use help milking the cows, and the tomatoes need attention after the cows tore through there."

"I'm on the job, Cap! You can count on me," Petey said, jogging toward the house to keep up with Rock's long-legged strides. "I'll phone Mom and let her know she, Pop, and the princess will have to make do without me tonight."

Three hours later, Rock waved as Petey ran across the pasture heading home for the night. The boy was a hard worker and his interesting view of nearly everything kept Rock grinning as they milked the cows, repaired the strawberry patch, and did their best to clean up the mess in the tomatoes.

Together, they walked all around the storage building, looking for clues. Petey scampered this way and that, picking up an odd assortment of things he thought might be useful. He handed five candy wrappers to Rock.

A frown creased Rock's forehead as he studied the wrappers of cheap and tart candy imported from Mexico. Most people preferred a little higher-quality sweet.

He held the wrappers out to Petey. "Are these yours?"

"Golly! I wouldn't eat that stuff if you paid me. It's so bitter, it's like sucking a rotten lemon. I'd much rather have a peppermint drop or a jawbreaker any day. And even better is something with chocolate." The boy screwed up his face in thought, then smiled at Rock. "Maybe our bully boy will eat too many and keel over dead as a post!"

"There's a thought," Rock muttered as they returned to the house. He and Petey managed to put together a simple meal of sliced tomatoes with wedges of cheese. They spread thick layers of peanut butter and strawberry jam on slices of bread and served it along with tall glasses of cold milk. Instead of allowing Miko to move from the sofa, they carried the food to her and sat on the floor in the living room, enjoying an indoor picnic.

Petey told them all about finding a bird's nest in the tree that morning, of helping his father move their beef cows from one pasture to another, and riding his trusty horse all the way over to his friend Ryatt's house.

"That no-good oily-tongued door-to-door ape of a salesman was trying to talk Mom into buying the ugliest pair of shoes you ever clapped your opticals on when I got back from Ry's house. When she turned him down, he did his best to sell her on a bag of second-rate aggies for me, but I wasn't having any part of it. He coulda had gold bars straight from the US Mint, but I wouldn't buy one from him. No siree! He's a sham if there ever was one."

Rock glanced at the boy. "Is he a small man with pale skin and a potbelly? Goes by the name of Ness?"

Petey slapped the palms of his hands together with a loud *smack!* "Now you're talking! He's the one. Why, he'd sell the hair right off his granny's head if he could get a buyer."

Working to subdue his chuckle, Rock glanced at Miko and saw her grin. Concerned over how quiet she'd been earlier, he saw that her cheeks regained color and she'd eaten enough of her dinner to keep him from worrying too much.

"Did you see him around today, Miko?" Rock asked as she took a drink of milk, then set aside the glass.

"No. I didn't see anyone. I left the front door locked, as I always do. This morning, I worked inside the house, catching up on chores I've neglected. I spent the afternoon in the orchard, getting things ready to pick cherries. I think they'll be ready next week. Around four, I came back in the house for a glass of tea. Then I went out to the storage building to see if I could find more of the flat crates Granddad always uses for the cherries. I climbed up in the loft and dropped down several boxes, then started carrying them to the orchard. On one of the trips back to gather more, I thought I heard something outside and walked around the corner of the building. A sour smell, almost like rotten fruit, hung in the air. Before I could turn around, something hit my head. That's the last I remember until I woke up to find you two fussing over me."

Rock didn't say anything, but he had a good idea who'd been poking around the place, causing trouble.

If Norman Ness dared set foot on the farm again, Rock planned to let his fists do the talking. Just last week, he had run the buffoon off the place when he stopped by, demanding to see a copy of Rock's deed. Rock told him to go to the county courthouse, where he'd filed the appropriate paperwork, if he wanted more information.

It wouldn't surprise him in the least if Norman had injured Miko. If Norman was to blame, Rock held no doubt that the slimy little man would turn her in to the authorities. More desperate than ever to keep her safe, he hoped she'd agree to wed.

Bright child that he was, Petey arrived at the same conclusion as Rock about Norman. The boy had no hesitation about voicing his thoughts. "I betcha my life ol' nasty Norman Ness was the one who clobbered Miko and turned the tornado loose in the garden. Next time he comes to our house, I'll hose him down but good!"

"Now, Petey, we don't know that Mr. Ness did anything," Miko said, offering the boy a cautioning glance. "Regardless of what he's done or not done, it might be best if you stay away from him for the time being."

"I don't like it, but if you say so, I'll take a wide swath around him, for right now."

Rock had an idea that "right now" meant the rest of the day. After he walked the boy to the edge of the Phillips pasture, he warned him, as Miko had, to stay out of trouble.

"Oh, I don't climb right into trouble on purpose, Cap," the boy said, jogging backward. "It just seems to swallow me up!"

Rock chuckled, musing on the child's fun-loving personality as he returned to the house. Inside, he found Miko resting on the couch. She opened one eye when he tiptoed in to check on her.

"I'm fine, Rock. You can stop treating me as if I'm an invalid. It's just a bump on my head, not the end of the world."

He dropped to his knees in front of the sofa and took her hand in his. "I know, Miko, but if something had happened to you... if you'd..." He swallowed twice to clear the emotion from his throat. "I couldn't bear it if anything took you away from me."

Unsettled by the sudden sweep of emotions raging through him, he buried his forehead against the cushions of the sofa. He clasped her hand in his and held it to his chest. Her soft fragrance enveloped him, further ensnaring his already-overwhelmed senses. For a moment, he pictured himself on a beach in Trinidad, breathing in the scent of exotic flowers mingling with pure ocean air.

Her fingers riffled through his hair in a light caress, bringing him back to the present, back to her. She massaged his neck, then her hand moved around to his chin, lifting it.

His gaze melded to hers, bright and full of everything his heart wanted to say that he couldn't push past his lips.

"Rock," she whispered, appearing uncertain. Eyes dark and watchful, they shimmered with emotion as she peered into his face.

Gazes fused, he lifted her hand to his lips and kissed the back of her fingers. Abruptly, he stood and pulled her to her feet. When she swayed a little, dizzy from the bump on her head, he wrapped his arm around her waist and held her close to his side.

"Come on, Miko, let's get you to bed." Rather than lead her to the back door, he took her down the hall to the bedroom he considered hers.

"I can't sleep here," she said, trying to back away from him. "It isn't proper."

A half grin lifted the right side of his mouth upward. "It's proper enough, considering you can barely walk. You'll stay here tonight so I can keep an eye on you."

"No, Rock. You need your rest. I'll just…"

He shifted in front of her, standing so close, his toes butted against hers. "Get ready for bed and do not argue with me."

"But I—"

His index finger settled over her lips, silencing her. "How many nights did you sit up with me when I was sick?"

She stared at the floor instead of looking at him. He used the same finger to push up her chin until her eyes locked with his. "How many, Miko?"

"Every night until you were well."

His hand settled on her shoulder, giving it a gentle, encouraging squeeze. "Then I owe you at least one." He moved around her, shooting her a teasing grin over his shoulder as he stood in the doorway. "I'll give you ten minutes, then I'll be back to tuck you in."

She glared at him. "You make me sound like a disobedient child."

"If the description fits…" He stepped into the hall and ducked when she tossed a pillow at him.

Miko generally did everything but change into her nightgown at the house before she went up the hill to sleep. It took only a few minutes for her to brush her teeth, wash her face, and comb out her long hair. Deftly, she wound it into a long braid that fell down her back.

In the bedroom, she changed into a nightgown, one of many articles of her clothing she'd left stored in the closet, turned off the light, and climbed into bed. Resting on her side helped her head not ache quite so badly. Although she didn't want to alarm Rock, the first few hours after he'd

167

found her, she'd seen double and her ears had rung loudly. Now, though, her vision seemed normal and the ringing had subsided, for the most part.

Other than a dull ache in her head, she felt fine. It touched her that Rock wanted to take care of her. In the past few weeks, he'd become not only her friend, but also her champion and protector.

Miko had always been fiercely independent, liking to do things for herself. Something about Rock, about the tender way he cared, made her set aside some of that independence and lean on his strength.

As though thoughts of him had made him appear, Rock lingered in the doorway, watching her in the moonlight that streamed in through the open window.

"I'm truly fine, Rock. You don't need to sit up with me," she said as he picked up a side chair and carried it close to the bed.

He sat down and reached over, clasping her hand in his. "I may not need to, but I want to." Silently, he leaned back in the chair, holding her hand on his hard thigh. "Would you like me to bring the radio in to listen to?"

She smiled. "That won't be necessary. Why don't you tell me a story," she said, growing drowsy as she nestled into the fluffy pillows and soft bed. Although her bed in the house on the hill was adequate, it wasn't nearly as nice as the big bed and comfortable mattress on which she currently reclined.

"A story," he said, as though he needed a moment to think of one to share. "The summer I was eleven, my dad decided I needed to…"

Miko closed her eyes and listened to the deep, lulling cadence of his voice. As sleep claimed her, she imagined Rock holding her close and whispering words of love.

*★★★ *Chapter Thirteen* ★★★*

Earlier the same day

After several unsuccessful sales calls at homes in the area of the produce stand, Norman Ness decided to drive by the farm and see if anyone was home. The last time he'd been there, the man he'd learned was named Laroux had practically tossed him off the place.

Norman had no interest in the oversized brute manhandling him again. Cautious, he parked behind the blackberry bushes across the road and waited, watching through his field glasses.

An hour later, with no speck of movement except the two milk cows swishing their tails in the pasture and pigs rooting in their pen, he moved his car past the curve in the road beyond the produce stand and walked back to the farm.

Winded by the time he got there, he leaned against a big maple tree, catching his breath in the shade. He dug a few pieces of candy from his pocket and popped them in his mouth, sucking on the sour little disks until he felt energized enough to make his way to the front door.

Convinced no one was home, he still went through the effort of knocking, but received no answer.

He ventured around to the back door and let himself inside, taking in the photos of the Yamada family hanging on the walls. The homey smells of bread and something sweet wafted on the breeze blowing in through the open windows. Annoyed that Laroux encroached on the prime property Norman claimed as his, he wanted to stomp through the house breaking everything in sight.

As badly as he wanted to leave a path of destruction, he tamped down the urge and looked through desk drawers and the few piles of papers, hoping to locate the deed.

If he could get it, he could forge the soldier's signature and take over the farm with no one to question his right to be there. Of course, he'd have to get rid of Laroux, but that didn't bother Norman.

After an hour of searching and not turning up the deed, he headed outside. On his way through the kitchen, he helped himself to a handful of cookies from the jar on the counter.

Silently, he hunkered down behind some shrubs and ate his cookies, imagining how the farm would look once he removed all the trees, leaving it ugly and bare. The only thing the place would be good for after that was a dump.

He watched a tall, dark-haired woman unlock the door to a big building and walk inside. Curious, he followed, peering around the edge of the doorway as she climbed up a ladder to a long loft. The sound of her shuffling items preceded the loud *pop* and *bang* as she dropped flat boxes down below.

Norman sneered as he loitered in the doorway. The pretty-faced soldier boy had a girl there. Not just any girl, but one who stayed behind and worked while he went off to town.

The dames always went for the solid, all-American types, like Laroux. It galled Norman that men with big muscles and no brains were always the ones with a woman or two on their arms.

As he cursed Laroux and every guy like him he'd ever known, Norman made note of the car and farm truck.

He spied two cans of gasoline and an assortment of boxes, no doubt filled with supplies he would find useful.

Angry that the soldier had waltzed right in and taken what Norman wanted, he decided to give the girl and that arrogant Laroux a little extra work.

Stealthily sneaking away from the building, he made his way over to the pasture by the barn. It required minimal effort to open the gate and shoo the cows into the garden. He did the same with the pigs, releasing a snort of glee when they made a beeline for the strawberry patch.

High on the success of his endeavors, he picked up a hoe he found leaning against the side of a little building that held an assortment of garden tools. He swung it back and forth in his hand like a scythe as he returned to the building where the girl labored.

Outside the large storage building, he waited in the shadows cast by the open door, sucking on candy and biding his time. The girl went in and out a small side door, carrying the boxes away and returning for more.

Eventually, she cocked her head toward the big door, as though she heard an unusual sound.

It was all Norman could do not to laugh as she scrambled past the assorted boxes and stored furniture, heading his way.

He dashed around the corner and raised the handle of the hoe, holding it like a baseball bat, ready to swing.

When she stepped in front of him, he clonked the back of her head and watched her fall with a satisfying thud.

With the toe of his shoe, he rolled her over and sucked in a gulp of surprise. The last thing he expected to see was a Japanese woman. He thought they'd all been rounded up and contained down by the river in Portland.

Had the mighty Mr. Laroux helped this one escape? Was she his wife or just a lover?

Either way, Norman had no use for a traitor, and that's exactly what the soldier was... a filthy, stinking, Jap-loving traitor to his country.

Although Norman had no interest or inclination to join the thousands of men fighting in the war, he hated the Japs and Germans. If it wasn't for them, there wouldn't be a war. And if there wasn't a war, there wouldn't be so many men gone, leaving the women to work. The dames were too tired or too busy to listen to his sales pitches and buy his wares.

Norman thought about laying into the Jap at his feet with the hoe, but decided to bide his time. When he killed her, he wanted to make sure he got the soldier boy, too. With both of them out of the way, it would be a simple matter to take over the farm, sell the timber, and live the luxurious life he'd convinced himself he deserved.

The sound of a car approaching made him toss the hoe in the direction of the toolshed. He grabbed one of the two gas cans by the door and hurried as fast as he could to his car. The full gas can grew heavier with each step. Norman sucked in great gulps of air by the time he made it to the car and set the can in the back. He hustled behind the wheel and took off down the road before anyone saw him.

*⋆⋆★ *Chapter Fourteen* ★⋆*⋆

Miko awoke to the smell of something burning and the loud noise of clanging metal.

Hastily tossing aside her covers, she ran down the hall and into the kitchen. Rock stood in front of the stove waving his hand in the air, as though to cool it, while smoke rose from a pan of burning eggs.

She grabbed a potholder, lifting the pan from the stove and dumping the eggs into a pail beneath the sink. After setting the pan in the sink and filling it with water, she turned back to Rock, noticing the red tint of his hand.

"Burn yourself?" she asked, taking his big hand in both of hers and studying a rapidly forming blister.

"I grabbed the pan without thinking," he said, allowing her to lead him over to the sink, where she ran cool water over his hand. The water felt good against his singed skin, but not nearly as nice as the feel of her fingers brushing across his palm.

The braid she'd fashioned in her hair last night had unraveled. Her long hair streamed around her in a midnight mass of silken waves. The sleeveless white gown she wore, trimmed with ribbons and lace, made any number of thoughts, all of them completely inappropriate, float through his mind.

Heat churned in his belly and worked its way out to every extremity as she held his hand beneath the faucet. Struggling to keep a tight grasp on his self-control, he held back a sigh of relief when she turned off the water and carefully dried his hand.

"I have ointment I can put on that burn," she said, turning toward the hallway.

Rock reached out and stopped her with his other hand. "It'll be fine, Miko. How's your head today?"

"It hardly even hurts," she said, gingerly touching the bump on the back of her head. The swelling had gone down considerably. The ache in her head was barely noticeable, and she felt fine. He'd let her sleep far past the usual time she rose, though. "If you give me a moment to dress, I'll make breakfast."

Chagrined, he pointed to a plate on the counter where he'd dumped slices of blackened toast. "I'd refuse, but if you don't we might starve. I've never had to cook for myself." He shrugged and shot her a boyish look so full of charm, her knees wobbled. "You make it seem so easy. I figured I could at least manage to make toast and eggs."

She smiled, sidling toward the doorway when she realized she wore only a thin cotton gown and her hair was a mess. Most likely, she had a crease on her cheek from the pillow. It would have been her luck to have him discover she snored when she was overly tired, too. "Clearly, we need to schedule cooking lessons."

"That sounds like a great project for us to work on this winter." Rock leaned against the counter, not attempting to hide the fact he admired her appearance. Boldly, his eyes roved from her hair down to her toes and back to her face.

Miko fought back a shiver that had nothing to do with her exposed skin catching the morning breeze and everything to do with the fire burning in Rock's expressive eyes. Warmth curled through her stomach and wrapped around her heart at his mention of winter. That meant he planned to stay.

"I'll be right back," she said, breezing out of the kitchen. She hurried to dress in a pair of old jeans, rolling the hems up nearly to her knees, and a light cotton blouse. Quickly brushing her hair, she secured it in a ponytail then returned to the kitchen.

Rock had disappeared, but she heard him whistling through the open window. The sound made her smile as she washed the pan, dropped in a glob of butter and cracked five eggs onto the sizzling surface.

While the eggs cooked, she browned bread for toast and fried three of the sausages Rock seemed to like so well. She didn't know where her grandfather had acquired them, but they'd been stored in a cool corner of the basement in a thick crock, layered between coatings of lard.

Rock strode in with a basket of just-picked berries and set it on the counter. He selected the biggest, juiciest berry and held it up to her lips. "Go on," he encouraged. "Take a bite."

Even after so many summers of eating strawberries until she thought she might burst, Miko never tired of them. Obediently, she bit into the berry, enjoying the delicious flavor. The tender fruit contained just a hint of warmth, holding onto the early-morning rays of sunshine in each sweet bite.

Rock pulled off the stem and popped the remainder of it in his mouth. Aware of her gaze, he winked at her, then leaned forward, his finger lightly brushing across her bottom lip. "You missed a drop," he said, sticking his finger in his mouth and making her blush.

"If you can behave yourself, breakfast is ready." She did her best to ignore the foreign, yet fascinating feelings he stirred in her.

Since Pastor Clark's visit Sunday evening, Miko had given much thought to the possibility of marrying Rock. Even if they acquired a marriage license and managed to go through the ceremony without her being arrested, she still wasn't convinced it was the best idea. If they wed, it needed to be in name only, a business arrangement of sorts. That way, if Rock ever wanted out of it, they could have the marriage annulled.

But, oh, how Miko wished Rock would be her husband in every sense of the word. She'd never wanted anything in her life as much as she wanted him, wanted to be loved by him. However, love was a luxury she could ill afford.

The last bite of her breakfast was on her fork, headed toward her mouth, when Rock reached across the table and touched her hand. Unspoken questions lingered between them.

Intently, he studied her face. "Are you sure you feel okay today?"

Exasperated, she sighed. "I'm perfectly fine. Please stop fussing and worrying. It was just a little bump on the head. I had much worse when I was a child."

He lifted an eyebrow and grinned. "Remind me when I meet Sally to have her tell me all about the adventures you two had in your younger years."

Miko shook her head. "She's sworn to secrecy. If she tattles, then I get to tell her husband all the secrets she'd rather he not know."

Rock laughed and squeezed her hand. "I, um... I think that..." He cleared his throat and started over. "In light of what happened yesterday, it's best if we wed as soon as possible. I learned there is a three-day waiting period between the time you file for a license and when you can marry. If we file the paperwork today, Pastor Clark would marry us this coming Sunday. We could do it in the afternoon and that would give us a few days to adjust to things before the produce stand opens for business as usual next week."

Shocked, she gaped at him. "But Rock, I... we..."

"I know this isn't what you'd necessarily choose to do, Miko, but someone was here yesterday, someone who discovered you are Japanese. I don't know how long we'll have before he turns you in, but there's a good chance if we're married, the law will leave you alone. Please, Miko? Please marry me?" The pleading, beseeching look on his face would have convinced any woman with blood flowing through her veins to agree.

And Miko wanted to marry him.

Desperately.

However, part of her, a romantic part of her heart, thought marriage should be more than just an arrangement or a business deal. It should be a sacred and treasured commitment entered into only for love.

Several long moments passed as she considered her answer. Practicality won. "Okay."

Rock stared at her, hopeful and unsure. "Okay, what?"

"I'll go with you today to file the paperwork and get a license. But if something happens between now and Sunday, if you change your mind, I won't hold you to it."

Unable to contain his elation, Rock jumped up and hurried around the table, pulling Miko into his arms. Although no music played on the radio, he danced her around the kitchen, making her laugh.

He stopped only when they both were out of breath. With a quick peck to her cheek, he stepped toward the telephone. "I'll finish the chores and call one of the boys to come work today. I don't like the idea of leaving the place unattended with someone lurking around. Can you be ready to go by ten?"

"Yes," she said, picking up the breakfast dishes. She cleared the table while he spoke with one of the teen boys who worked for them Wednesday through Saturday, asking if he'd like to make a little extra money and come to work that day. From the one-sided conversation, Miko had the idea the boy readily agreed and would soon arrive.

"Don't forget you'll need a hat," Rock said as he sped out the back door to finish the chores without her assistance.

Miko washed the dishes in record time, set the kitchen to rights, then hurried to the bathroom, where she bathed and washed her hair. She sat on the bed in a ray of morning sunshine, combing the long strands until they dried. It took some effort, but she pinned the gleaming black tresses up on her head in a becoming style, leaving a fall of carefully fashioned waves to drape across one side of her face.

Hurriedly searching through the dress clothes she'd hung in the closet a few weeks ago, she selected a black dress she'd worn to a party the previous summer. Black ribbons crisscrossed the sweetheart neckline, giving it a peekaboo style, while a layer of chiffon around the hemline added a bit of flair.

Miko slid her feet into a pair of open-toed black pumps with a T-strap and wide heel. She rummaged through a drawer and came up with a pair of black gloves and a length of black polka-dotted netting.

She heard Rock come in and the sound of water running in the bathroom, mindful he'd soon be ready to leave.

From the back of the closet shelf, she lifted a hatbox and removed a broad-brimmed black straw hat. Artfully adding the netting, she secured it with a few quick stitches of thread and a length of dark blue ribbon.

After settling the hat on her head, she stared in the mirror and poked in a few pins to keep it in place. She tugged on her gloves and picked up a black handbag accented with a floral tapestry pattern on the front.

Ready as she could be for whatever might come that day, she opened the door to the bedroom and strode into the kitchen.

Rock stood at the sink, chugging down a glass of water. He gawked at her and gulped, choked on his drink, and coughed into his hand.

His voice sounded unusually husky when he regained the ability to speak. "Wow, Miko! You look incredible." He couldn't recall seeing her dressed in anything beyond the simple clothes she wore on the farm. Except for the summery skirts she wore on Sundays, normally she was attired in trousers and blouses to work on the farm. The outfit she wore exuded elegance and class.

She hid a satisfied smile by pretending to search for something in her handbag. Rather than the suit she expected Rock to wear, he had on his uniform. She'd cleaned and pressed it weeks ago, but the sight of him wearing it made her heart flutter. The trim jacket accented the breadth of his shoulders and chest while outlining the leanness of his waist. The pants were loose and neatly creased, but she envisioned those long, strong legs of his.

"Shall we go?" she asked, moving toward the door.

"I forgot we need to fill out these papers," he said, motioning to the forms he'd left on the table.

Miko scanned through them and quickly added her information, then held out the pen to Rock. He filled in the appropriate boxes. All that remained was for them to sign the papers at the license office before a witness and everything should be in order.

"Let's get on the road," Rock said, taking her elbow in his hand and walking with her outside to her grandfather's sedan. He helped her into the car then waved a hand at the young man he left working in the vegetable garden.

Miko slipped on a pair of sunglasses and pulled down the brim of the hat so it hid most of her face.

Rock chuckled. "Maybe Army intelligence should recruit you for covert operations. I'm not sure if you look like a movie star or a well-dressed spy."

She turned her head toward him, but he couldn't see her eyes to read her expression. "Perhaps they are one and the same," she suggested with the barest hint of a smile.

A laugh rolled out of him. "I'll keep that in mind." Aware of her nervous state, he squeezed her hand. "You might as well sit back and relax. It will take an hour or so to get to the courthouse in Vancouver."

In need of a distraction from their worry that the day might end with her in jail, he shared stories about leaving home for the first time as a new cadet at West Point.

"I'd barely stepped off the train when a kid named Zane bumped into me. He wore a big cowboy hat and had a western twang that sounded like he ought to perform on the *Grand Ole Opry* show. From that moment on, we became the best of friends." Memories flooded through Rock, both good and bad. "The upper-class cadets can make life miserable for the first-year cadets. They call the new cadets plebes and it is common knowledge the only things plebes outrank are the superintendent's dog and the commander's cat."

Miko smiled at his joke and he continued. "Well, Zane and I decided to stick together and make it through what they refer to as hazing. The upper-class members give plebes such a hard time, I've actually seen it reduce some of the new cadets to tears. They'd get in your face and yell about your buckle not being polished to a high shine or they'd order you to run twenty laps and you had to do it. While some might think their actions cruel, and some of the boys were mean-spirited, the purpose was to level the playing field, to make all the new cadets equal. It also helped us learn valuable lessons. A graduate from the academy survived daily inspections, rigorous training, physical exertions that pushed his body to the outer limits, exacting academic requirements, high standards of personal appearance, and a stalwart code of honor that would not be altered or bent."

Although the dark sunglasses covered her eyes, Rock felt her perusal as she studied his face. "Did you graduate at the head of your class?"

Her simple question made him want to puff out his chest with pride. He shot her a grin. "No. As a matter of fact, Zane and I both vied for that position. We got so embroiled in our competition, we didn't notice when a smart aleck named Gilbert Redding raced right past us and took top honors."

She laughed. "Serves you right."

"Yes, ma'am, it did." Rock glanced over at her, pleased to see her relax and enjoy his stories. "The academy trains cadets in a variety of lessons, as you may have gathered from what I shared. Zane grew up on a ranch and excelled at anything that had to do with horses. I'd ridden our farm horses enough that I got by better than most. When we had a rare moment of spare time, Zane shared what he knew about horses. Before long, we were among the top riders. One afternoon, orders came down for our class to practice mounted combat skills. We rode out to the practice field, half of us on one side, the rest on the other. One of the upper-class cadets took it as a personal challenge to cause Zane and me as much grief as possible. When we weren't looking, he managed to not only loosen the cinches on our saddles, but also stick burrs beneath the blankets. The moment Zane and I swung onto the saddles, the horses bucked and reared to beat the band. With the saddles loose, they slid off and there we were, two idiots, with all our classmates laughing at us."

"Oh, Rock, that's awful," she said, trying to hold back her giggles. "Were you boys injured?"

"Just our pride," Rock said, remembering how badly he wanted to pop the upperclassman in the nose. At the end of the year, he'd instead thanked him because the trials they'd endured at his hand had helped shape them into good cadets.

"What other things did you learn?" she asked, genuinely interested.

"We had a rigid academic program that included everything from mathematics, chemistry, physics, history and geography to literature, foreign languages, psychology, and constitutional law. Hours were spent in military training. Physical training helped us learn any number of skills. Zane and I had a lot of fun fencing. And our moral and ethics training will serve us well for a lifetime." He looked over at her and smiled. "My favorite classes were those that began my second year, when they started an Air Corps detachment to familiarize cadets with the construction, types, and capabilities of airplanes. Zane and I both loved to fly."

"Where is Zane now? Is he in Trinidad?"

Rock shook his head. "No. Zane was stationed at Pearl Harbor. He survived, thank goodness, but last I heard from him, he was headed to a base in the Pacific, although he couldn't say where. I'm praying he wasn't one of the casualties we've heard about recently, but I have no way of knowing."

Miko reached out and placed a hand on his leg, a gesture meant to offer comfort. "I'm so sorry, Rock. I'll keep him in my prayers and hope he is well."

"Thanks, Miko." Rock cleared his throat and glanced out the window, staring at the water of the mighty Columbia River as they crossed over it to reach Vancouver. Boats braved the choppy water, heading both up- and downstream.

One of the few things he missed about Trinidad was the beautiful turquoise water. He'd never seen anything quite like it.

Tugging his memories back to the present, he noticed Miko stared out the window, lost in her thoughts.

He turned down a wide street and drove a few blocks, then turned down another before driving around the block and parking on a side street in the shade. After a glance at his watch, he opened the car door and jogged around to the passenger side. He opened it and held out his right hand to Miko, sharing an encouraging smile. "Ready to do this?"

"No," she whispered, afraid to leave the safety of the car, but aware she had to. She took the hand he offered and stood. As he shut the car door, she pulled the hat brim down farther in the front and adjusted the veiling over her face. She removed the sunglasses and slid them in her handbag, then accepted the arm Rock extended to her.

"You can do this, Kamiko. Just keep your head tilted down and everything will be fine." He ushered her around the corner of the building and up the steps. Inside, they walked along the gleaming tile of the foyer to a hallway and followed it down four doors. Rock peeked inside the glass window of the door.

Instead of opening it, he took Miko's elbow in his hand and guided her down the hall.

Baffled, she waited for an explanation.

"When I was here yesterday, the woman at the desk wasn't overly helpful and seemed about as nosy as a person could be," he explained as they strolled around the inside of the courthouse. "I happened to hear her mention to another girl in the office she planned to take her lunch break at a quarter past eleven today because she has a hair appointment. I think the girl who'll be watching the desk then won't ask too many questions."

He glanced at his watch. "The old biddy ought to be gone by now. Let's try again."

Miko quietly walked beside him and said nothing as he again peered into the office. He pulled open the door and settled his hand at the small of her back, urging her inside.

A fresh-faced young woman smiled as they entered and rose from the desk behind the counter. "Good morning. How may I help you?"

"We'd like to get a marriage license," Rock said, returning her smile, then casting an adoring gaze Miko's direction.

"I'd be more than happy to help you." The young woman lifted a thick black book onto the counter and opened it to a page marked by a frayed brown ribbon. "We'll need you to fill out a form and enter your names here." She tapped the book with her finger.

Rock handed her the form they completed before they left the house. The secretary read it and nodded. "I just need to see something with proof of address for each of you."

From her black handbag, Miko pulled out an envelope and handed it to the woman. "Will a piece of mail do?" she asked in a soft, cultured voice. Rock stared at an envelope addressed to Jane Nishimura.

"Yes, ma'am. That will do just fine." The girl wrote down the address in the black book then handed it back to Miko. She looked to Rock. "And for you, sir?"

Rock brought a piece of mail he'd received at the farm so he'd have a record of his current address. He also had his birth certificate. The woman glanced at both, entered the farm address, then handed Rock back the birth certificate and envelope. She held out her pen to him. "I need you both to sign here..." she tapped the book again "...and on this form."

With bold strokes, Rock signed his name, then gave Miko the pen. Her feminine script was every bit as graceful and strong as the woman who wrote on the form. Nonetheless, he hated that she had to sign everything as K. Jane Nishimura.

"We've sure had a bunch of soldiers come in with their girls, wanting to get married before they ship out," the young woman said, smiling at them as she stamped the form. "If you two are in a hurry, you can see Judge Aberlee up on the second floor. You can appeal the waiting period if you show just cause for a rush. Otherwise, you have to wait three days."

Rock shook his head. "Thank you."

The secretary shrugged, filled in a date on another form, stamped it, and stuffed it inside an envelope, then handed it to Rock. "That's the marriage certificate. Today's date is noted on the certificate. You can plan for your wedding to take place after Friday. The license will expire in sixty-days. Whoever performs the ceremony must sign the certificate and return the form to this office. That'll be three dollars."

Rock fished out his wallet and paid her, pocketing the receipt she handed to him. "Thank you." He tipped his cap to the woman, settled a hand on Miko's back, and ushered her out the door.

"Happy nuptials!" the young woman called, waving as they left.

Until they sat in the car, neither said a word. Miko slid the sunglasses back on as Rock pulled into traffic.

"By jingo, Miko, we did it!" He slapped the steering wheel with the palm of his hand. "How on earth did you come up with that letter?"

"Two summers ago, I attended a party hosted by the company where I worked. They have offices in Portland, Vancouver, and Salem. People attended from all three offices as well as a number of clients and other guests. One of the clients in attendance took an interest in me. I told him my name was Jane, trying to be evasive. Anyway, he mailed a letter to me at our Vancouver office. I kept the letter because I found it amusing. Sally thought it was hilarious."

Rock waggled an eyebrow. "May I read the letter when we get home?"

"Absolutely not." Miko hugged her handbag against her chest. "The client was really nothing more than a boy, a rich one, but a boy all the same. Through flowery prose, he professed his undying love and devotion. Funny, but I didn't answer the letter and never heard from him again. I suppose he probably found a new girl within a week to lavish with his words of love."

"Most boys are fickle," Rock mused. Miko's weighted silence made him laugh. "Okay, so that also includes many men."

"Yes, it does." She leaned back against the seat and sighed in relief. "I was so afraid they'd call the police and have me arrested." The hand she held out in front of her still trembled. "It may take some time for my heart to stop racing."

Rock wanted to take her hand and hold it in his, but he couldn't use his left hand to drive. He planted a swift kiss to her veiled cheek. "I had no idea you were that nervous, Miko. You seemed perfectly calm and poised the whole time. That girl was half-convinced you were some sort of celebrity."

"No. I assumed she thought I was a widow. Dressed all in black, I certainly look like one." Miko brushed a speck of lint from her skirt. "Perhaps if a lot of soldiers are coming in for licenses, they don't ask too many questions. It was a good idea to wear your uniform."

Rock nodded. "I hoped if any of them saw me yesterday when I was there to get information, no one would recognize me in my uniform."

Miko remained silent, unwilling to shatter his delusion that a change of clothes would keep him from being noticed. With a fine-looking face like his, and a tall, muscled body to go along with it, she couldn't imagine any woman who'd seen him forgetting the experience.

In high spirits, they drove into Oregon and headed toward home. Rock veered off the highway onto a road that took them into one of the many small towns around Portland and parked in the far corner of a drive-in restaurant.

"What are you doing?" Miko asked, sinking deeper into the seat and checking to make sure the veil fully covered her face.

"Taking my best girl out for lunch," Rock said, giving her a broad smile.

Surprised he referred to her as his best girl, she appreciated his words but didn't think eating in a public place was wise. "What if someone sees me? Isn't this a little risky?" Miko tipped her head down as a carhop approached.

The girl wore wide-legged blue trousers with a red gingham blouse and a bright red belt. From the corner of her eye, Miko observed the girl had to be a Betty Grable fan, based on the pile of blond poodle curls bouncing on top of her head.

"Hi, soldier," the girl said. A wad of gum snapped in her mouth as she pulled a pad from her pocket and smiled at Rock. "What can I get for you, handsome?"

Rock placed an order for two hamburgers, French fries, and two sodas.

"Comin' right up," the girl said, leaning closer, trying to get a better glimpse of Miko before she flounced back across the parking lot.

"Everything is fine, Miko. Don't worry so much." Rock lifted her gloved hand in his and gave it a squeeze. "Have I raved about your breath-stealing beauty today?"

A blush heated her cheeks, hidden from his view by the hat and sunglasses. "You might have hinted at it in passing."

"In that case, I suppose I should tell you that you look like a queen. If Petey was here, he'd probably say you're the cat's whiskers or something along those lines."

Miko laughed. "That sounds about right." She studied her hand, held so tenderly in Rock's. She liked the way their hands fit together, felt together. "I don't believe I mentioned how splendid you appear in your uniform. It's no wonder that Betty Grable look-alike was all agog when you gave her our order."

"All agog? For me?" Rock slapped his hand to his chest. "Surely you're mistaken. I'm just an innocent little farm boy, out for a day on the town."

A giggle burst out of her at the way he placed his hands beneath his chin in an angelic pose and rolled his eyes heavenward. "I'm not falling for that nonsense, Rock Laroux." Playfully she thumped his arm. "There isn't anything about that statement that's remotely true."

"I am a farm boy. You have to give me that one."

"Okay, but only if you tell me about growing up on the farm in Gales Creek." Miko plucked at the fingers of her gloves, pulling off first one, then the other. The silver bracelet on her left wrist refracted shimmering prisms of summer sunlight, drawing Rock's interest.

Without thinking, he reached out and touched it, tracing his finger across the silver links that joined a filigreed oval with a diamond set in the center. "That's lovely."

Miko glanced down, wondering if his finger on her wrist would melt right down to her bone. "Papa's parents gave it to me for my eighteenth birthday."

Rock moved his hand away and lifted his gaze from her wrist to her face. "You've never mentioned them. Do they live around here?"

Sadly, Miko shook her head and fingered the bracelet. "No. They died in an auto accident when I was nineteen."

"I'm sorry, Miko." Rock took her hand in his again, bringing it to his lips and giving the back of it a kiss. "At least you have Mr. and Mrs. Yamada. I really like your grandfather."

"I'm pretty keen on him myself, and Grandma, too. They've always been special to me. In fact, they are the reason I'm the only one of my siblings with a Japanese name."

"How's that?" Rock asked. He shifted until he leaned with his back against the car door so he faced Miko.

"Mother insisted her firstborn have a thoroughly American name, so she named my sister Ellen Louise. When I came along, she told Papa to choose my first name, but my middle name had to be Jane. He turned right around and asked Granddad and Grandma to choose my first name. Kamiko was my great-great-grandmother's name." Miko offered him a saucy grin. "When my brother came along, Mother didn't give Papa a chance to name him, declaring him to be Thomas Jack. We used to call him Tommy Jack until he entered high school. He threatened to run away from home if we kept referring to him by that name, so we had to stop."

Rock chuckled, then turned as the carhop approached with their order. She handed them the food and accepted the money Rock gave her, thanking him for the tip.

As they ate, Rock encouraged Miko to talk more about her family. He didn't want her to notice the way the carhop or the two others working the lunch crowd kept pointing at their car and whispering behind their hands.

Unless the girls possessed some sort of magical powers, they had no way of knowing Miko was Japanese. He'd meant what he said about her appearance. She was so beautiful, she nearly took his breath away.

He didn't know how she appeared so regal and proper as she ate the hamburger and munched a few fries behind the veil of her hat, but she did. She seemed to enjoy the cold soda pop as much as he did. Before they could leave, the carhop reappeared and asked if they needed anything else.

When Rock said no, but thanked her, she thrust her order pad in the window and waggled it in Miko's direction.

"I'm sure you get asked for autographs all the time, Miss Russell, but will you please sign it for me?" the girl asked with a hopeful expression on her face. "My name's Ellie."

Miko took the pad and scribbled, "To Ellie: Best wishes," followed by a few illegible scribbles, handing the pad back to the girl.

Ellie squealed with delight. "Oh, wait until my friends find out about this. Thank you, Miss Russell. I absolutely loved you in *His Girl Friday*. It's one of my favorite movies!"

"Thank you," Miko said, in a polite, reserved tone, her head tipped down.

The girl raced off and Rock started the car before anyone else came over seeking an autograph.

"Imagine that! I'm about to marry a bona fide movie star and I didn't even know it. I thought you just looked like one. You've been holding out on me, Rosalind."

Miko giggled as he pulled onto the road. "How could that girl possibly mistake me for Rosalind Russell? We look nothing alike."

"I don't know. There might be a slight resemblance through the chin and those kissable lips of yours." Rock grinned. "But you're far prettier."

Heat burned up her neck and filled her cheeks at his words. Convinced he teased, she missed the sincerity in his voice and the admiration in his eyes as he gave her a quick glance.

Mindful of her embarrassment, Rock changed the subject. "You never said what Sally mentioned in her last letter. And didn't I see one come yesterday from your sister?"

"Sally's doing very well and so is baby Drew. She said he's already gaining weight and getting chubby little cheeks and legs." Miko smiled at Rock. "He's going to be a little chunk, but don't tell Sally I said that."

"She won't hear a word from me," he said, shooting a fun-loving smirk her way. "What about your sister? Did she say how things are there?"

"Ellen described everything in detail. I feel so bad for them, Rock. Winnie and Amy think it's a grand game, but it has to be so hard on Ellen and Paul to be crammed into a tiny little space with two rambunctious children." She turned in the seat to face him and pulled off her sunglasses. "I know you and Pastor Clark have been painting a rosy picture of the way things are at the Portland Assembly Center. Tell me the truth, Rock. What is it really like for my folks?"

He hated to ruin the day by sharing the stark reality of the situation with her, but he wouldn't lie. "It's similar to what you've said about the place where Ellen and her family are located. The rooms, if you could call them that, are small, and crowded. There is no privacy. They all have to share bathrooms and they eat in a big mess hall. It probably doesn't bother your folks as much as most since they are very Americanized, but the food they serve isn't traditional Japanese fare. The flies are awful. It's smelly and hot, and boredom seems to be the worst problem. From what I've seen, though, your family is carrying on with strength, dignity, and honor."

She sniffled and pulled a handkerchief from her handbag. He'd never seen her cry, not in all that had happened since the day they met. But the thought of her family suffering filled her eyes with tears and made her lower lip quiver.

"Miko," he said, trying to keep one eye on the road and one on her. "They'll be okay. It's hard, but they will make it through and come home again."

"I know, but it's..." She dabbed at her eyes and released a choppy breath. "I should be there with them. It's not fair that I'm the one enjoying all the good food I can eat and a comfortable place to sleep and..."

"Your family wouldn't want it any other way. Even your mother has said how glad she is you aren't there."

"Mother is probably suffering ten times more than the rest of them. She... it must be so hard for her to have no privacy, no real space of her own." She sniffled again. "There must be something I can do to help them."

"I'll keep taking them food. Although there isn't much space, if there is something you think they'd enjoy, I'll get it for them." Rock gave her a tender smile that nearly broke her fragile hold on her emotions. "The best thing you can do for your family is to pray for them."

Unable to speak past the tears choking her, Miko nodded her head and slid on her sunglasses.

**** *Chapter Fifteen* ****

"Are you ready to do this?" Rock asked. He took Miko's hand in his and helped her out of her grandfather's sedan.

A curt nod accompanied her quiet response of "yes" as she settled her hand on his good arm. Together, they walked across the park in Vancouver where they would exchange their vows in a few minutes.

"Did I forget anything?" Rock smiled at her, wishing she'd calm down. From the moment they'd left the house, tense anxiety had ridden her every move. She more closely resembled a woman sentenced to the gallows than a bride on her wedding day.

The dark blue dress she wore, sprinkled with a smattering of pink flowers and trimmed in lace, elicited his admiration. The black hat that hid her face so well on their last trip into town covered her head. In her hands, she carried the bouquet Rock had ordered from a florist and hid in the refrigerator in the barn after picking it up the previous afternoon.

"I believe you covered everything," she said, lifting the fragrant blooms of pink and yellow roses accented with ivy closer to her face. The decadent scent mingled with the enticing aroma of Rock's shaving lotion in a heady combination. "Petey said you asked his permission to marry me and it had been granted. His exact words were, 'If you ain't gonna wait for me to grow up, then I reckon

Cap will do. He's a dandy one, Miko, a real royal-stepping doozy, so you better treat him nice and be good to him.'" She glanced up at Rock and grinned. "He had several words of wisdom, but I don't believe I care to share all the details."

Rock chuckled. "I got a few of those words myself, along with a threat that if I ever made you cry, I'd have to take whatever punishment he dishes out and like it."

Miko laughed, allowing herself to relax for the first time all day. "Petey is just an all-around about-right kind of boy."

"I heartily agree," Rock said, guiding her around a muddy patch in the grass. "In fact, I wouldn't mind having a few boys just like him someday. Will you be up for the challenge?"

Miko stumbled. She would have fallen if Rock hadn't slipped his arm around her waist and kept her upright.

"Rock," she said in a low voice, "don't tease me so. I know this isn't a real marriage and I don't expect you to treat me like a true wife. We will continue with things as they are until my family comes home. I'm sure we can get an annulment then, if you don't ask for one sooner."

Before he could refute her statement, before he could confess his love and undying devotion, she waved at Pastor Clark. The man waited beneath the branches of a weeping willow tree in a secluded section of the park.

After acquiring the marriage license, Rock had called the pastor and asked him to perform the ceremony that weekend. The pastor had agreed Sunday afternoon would be a perfect time for the wedding and suggested the location of the park. Most of the people in the park picnicked with children in an area where there was a slide and swings. Back by the weeping willow tree, there wasn't another soul around, except for Pastor Clark, his sister, and her daughter. The two women had agreed to serve as witnesses.

Although Rock had purchased the bouquet for Miko and she'd baked a cake to enjoy later, the day didn't seem like a real wedding to him.

Miko should have had an elaborate satin-and-lace gown with half a dozen attendants, and a church overflowing with flowers and friends. Her father should have walked her down an aisle strewn with rose petals. Music should have filled the church from a resonant organ. Rock should have stood, clad in his dress uniform, next to Zane and his other close friends, eagerly awaiting the appearance of his bride.

Instead, he walked with her across the lush grass of the park toward a man she considered an uncle and two strangers neither of them had ever met. At least the sun shone brightly around them. He would have hated for rain to pour down on their wedding day.

In spite of the fact Miko didn't realize how much he loved her, Rock intended to make her his bride in every sense of the word. He vowed to keep the commitment he would soon make for a lifetime, not just until her family returned. Regardless of what the future might bring, Rock planned to remain faithfully by Miko's side.

However, convincing her of that might require a great deal of effort on his part. He slid his hand down from her waist, resting it at the small of her back as they neared the pastor. She turned her head his way, but he couldn't see her eyes through the veil and the dark sunglasses she wore.

He wondered if she planned to leave them on during the ceremony. The thought of not being able to see into her eyes didn't set well with him. When she removed the glasses and stowed them in her skirt pocket, he released a relieved breath.

"Miko! You are lovely," Pastor Clark said, stepping forward and enveloping her in a fatherly hug. He shook Rock's hand, then motioned to the two women standing beside him.

Both of medium height, they looked more like sisters than mother and daughter. A faint resemblance to the pastor was evident in their eyes and the mirthful lines of their lips.

"This is my sister, Bernice, and my niece, Hadley." Pastor Clark smiled at his family, then at Miko. "I'd like you to meet Miko Nishimura. She's been Sally's best friend since the girls were old enough to walk, and like a daughter to me all these years. The fellow with her is Captain Rock Laroux. He recently purchased her grandfather's farm."

Politely, Rock tipped his head to the two women. "How are you enjoying America?"

"It's wonderful," Hadley said, grinning at her mother. "Everything here is so green and lovely. It's nice to be somewhere we don't have to worry about bombs going off."

"It has been a welcome reprieve and we have settled in nicely at George's house, for the time being." Bernice motioned toward her brother. "He promised to take us to visit Sally next week. I can scarcely wait to see her and the baby."

"He is a marvelous little thing," Miko said, fondly recalling her time spent with Sally and the newborn.

"Shall we get on with things?" Pastor Clark asked, motioning for Miko and Rock to step beneath the tree. The branches drooped so low, they provided a private screen from the rest of the park.

Miko took her place on one side of the pastor while Rock stood across from her, holding her hand in his. Tension and fear radiated from her in a flagrant force.

Bernice and Hadley moved behind them, then Pastor Clark smiled. "Let us begin. Is there any reason either of you should not be joined in matrimony?"

Rock expelled a heavy sigh, drawing a worried glance from Miko as his face took on a repentant expression. "I suppose now would be as good a time as any to mention that this will be a mixed marriage."

Four pairs of eyes glared at him as though he'd stated the obvious and to do so proved unforgivably inappropriate.

"Rock, if you…" Miko started to pull her hand away from his. Not giving it release, he held her fingers tightly in his and winked.

"Miko is Presbyterian and my family raised me as a Baptist." Rock offered Miko a raffish smile. "For the sake of love, I suppose I can convert."

Hadley hid a laugh behind a cough while Bernice smiled and Pastor Clark smirked. "That's quite valiant of you, Rock. Now, shall we continue?"

"Yes, sir," Rock said. His teasing served its purpose as Miko's tension melted away and she smiled.

The pastor read a few verses from the Bible in his hand and asked them all to bow their heads in prayer. After the last amen floated away on the warm afternoon breeze, the pastor observed Miko and Rock.

Noisily, he cleared his throat, then spoke. "I realize the circumstances bringing the two of you together are far from usual. Life has a way of tossing storms and challenges at us when we least expect it. How we weather those storms makes all the difference. When you leave here today, you will have a partner who will help you face any adversity that comes your way. You'll also have a friend with whom to celebrate every triumph and joy. Learn to lean on each other, to trust each other, to cherish each other every day. Most of all, love each other. There will be times when you don't very much like your spouse. There will be times when you are ready to walk away and never look back. In those trying times, remember this moment. Remember the vows you've made to each other. Remember the love you feel in your hearts for one another."

The pastor fell silent, allowing a moment for them to absorb his words.

Rock embraced the wisdom of the older man. He pondered how he could love Miko more tomorrow than he did right at that moment, but he knew he would.

"Do you have a ring?" the pastor asked.

Rock nodded and took a ring from his pocket.

Pastor Clark tipped his head toward Miko. "Rock, please take her left hand and repeat these vows after me."

Rock said his vows in a strong, clear voice, then slid the ring onto Miko's hand. She stared at the sparkling diamond set in a silver band accented with a flourish of roses and poppies. "It was my mother's," he whispered, offering her a soft smile.

The pastor handed Miko a plain gold band.

Gently, she lifted Rock's left hand and held it as she repeated her vows in a voice that gained confidence as she spoke. She slipped the ring on his finger, giving it a nudge over his knuckle to slip into place. "With this ring, I thee wed and with it bestow upon thee my pledge of faithfulness and enduring love."

Bernice and Hadley sniffled while Pastor Clark cleared his throat again and swiped at the moisture gathering in his eyes. He smiled at the couple. "Inasmuch as you, Kamiko Jane, and you, Rochester James, have thus consented in holy matrimony, pledged your troth to one another, and have witnessed the same before God, then, by the authority vested in me, I do hereby pronounce you husband and wife. Therefore, what God hath joined together, let no man put asunder. May all your days together be blessed." The pastor turned to Rock. "You may kiss the bride."

From the moment Rock first considered marrying Miko, he'd thought about this kiss. The first kiss as her husband. Slowly, he lifted the veil, pushing it back over her hat brim before cupping her chin with his right hand

and staring into her dark eyes. A flicker of heat burned in their depths, giving him all the encouragement he needed.

"My beautiful bride," he whispered in a husky voice. His lips lowered to hers in a tender, emotion-filled kiss while his fingers trailed down her throat and settled on her shoulder.

Hadley and Bernice sighed at the romantic sight the couple made while Pastor Clark beamed with joy.

Rock raised his head, gave Miko a private smile, and kissed her cheek before pulling her against him in a tight embrace. "Thank you for marrying me, Miko."

She nodded, her cheek pressed to his as he ducked beneath the wide brim of her hat. "It's I who should thank you, Rock, and I do."

The pastor clapped Rock on the back while the women both hugged Miko. Hadley produced a camera and snapped several photos, promising to get them developed soon.

The five of them spoke for a few moments. Rock invited the pastor and the two women to come out to the farm for dinner one evening when they returned from visiting Sally.

"We'd love to visit the farm," Hadley said, giving Miko's hand a friendly squeeze. "I want to see where those delicious strawberries we've eaten are grown."

"Come anytime," Rock said, taking Miko's elbow in his hand, ready to escort her back to their car.

Sensing his plans, she slipped on the sunglasses and flipped the netting of the hat back down.

After taking one rose from the bouquet, she glanced behind her. "Heads up!" she called and tossed the bouquet.

Surprise followed by an exasperated glare settled on Hadley's face as the flowers landed in her arms.

Bernice clapped in gleeful anticipation of seeing her daughter wed.

Hadley shook her head and cast a disparaging frown at Miko. "You have no idea what you've done!"

Miko laughed. "I can guess." She waved at the two women. "Thank you for being here today."

"Our pleasure," Bernice said, brushing at more tears.

Rock waved again, then guided Miko toward the car. When they were halfway there, Pastor Clark called out, "Wait!" The couple stopped as he jogged to catch up. When he reached them, he took a key from his pocket and placed it in Miko's hand.

"I almost forgot to give you this. Yesterday, when I saw your family, your mother asked me to give you that key. She said you are to open the red leather trunk as soon as you get home."

Rock watched as Miko worked to control her emotions. She stared at the key in her palm for the length of several heartbeats before lifting her gaze to the pastor. "Thank you, Uncle George." She wrapped her arms around him and held on as he patted her back and kissed her cheek through the netting.

"You haven't called me Uncle George since you and Sally graduated from high school. I like hearing it again." He reached beneath the netting and brushed away the salty teardrops gliding down her cheeks. His eyes held moisture as he leaned close to whisper in her ear. "You go on home with this fine man, Miko. If I had to pick someone for you to wed, I couldn't have done any better. He'll take good care of you."

"I know, Uncle George, but do you think he'll ever love me?" Miko voiced the words that had relentlessly taunted her throughout the last week.

The pastor chuckled and patted her back, as though she was but a small child. "Oh, Miko, you are in for a surprise." He moved away and shook Rock's hand again. "Take good care of our girl, Captain. She's one of a kind."

"I know, sir. That's why I plan to treat her like a rare and precious jewel."

Pastor Clark took a few more steps back. "See that you do or you'll answer to me."

Rock chuckled. "And her father, and brother, and grandfather. Oh, and the neighbor boy has threatened to slather me with honey and feed me to the bears if I ever do so much as look cross-eyed at her."

The pastor laughed. "We're keeping an eye on you, young man. Now, go on, kids. Enjoy this blessed afternoon and have a wonderful life together."

"Thank you, Pastor Clark," Rock said, shaking the man's hand again before settling his hand at Miko's waist and walking to the car.

Once they settled onto the bench seat, Miko studied the ring on her finger. The diamond glittered in the sunlight and she lifted her finger to get a better look at the detailed flowers fashioned into the silver band.

"Do you like it?" Rock asked, staring at her with a hopeful expression.

"It's beautiful, Rock. You didn't need to give me a ring, especially not one that belonged to your mother." She started to pull it off, but his hand closed over hers.

While holding her gaze, he lifted her fingers to his mouth and kissed the back of them. "Leave it right there, Miko. You are my wife and I plan to keep it that way. I was going to have the ring sized, but it fits you perfectly."

Her head bobbed in agreement as the flames in his eyes held her captive. Finally, she blinked and pulled away.

Rock sighed and started the car. "Anywhere you want to go?" he asked as he left the park. He wanted to take her out for dinner or to a movie, but it seemed far too risky.

"I wish I could see my family." The wistful tone in her voice made his heart ache.

He folded the fingers of his left hand around the steering wheel and reached out to her with his right, patting her on the leg. Her gaze dropped to where his hand rested on her thigh. Bright pink color suffused her cheeks, but she didn't push his hand away. She turned to him and he leaned over, kissing her cheek through the netting hiding her face.

"Today had to be hard for you, Miko, and nothing like you probably imagined for your wedding, but I do appreciate you marrying me. I will work very hard to build a happy future with you."

"I want you to know..." Her head whipped up and she reached for the steering wheel. "Rock!"

Unable to steer well with his left hand, he'd drifted into the oncoming lane of traffic. Taking control with his right hand, he maneuvered the car back onto the proper side of the road seconds before they ran into a farm truck loaded with chickens.

Unsettled, but unwilling for her to know it, he cracked a grin. "That would have made a memorable mess."

"You think?" she asked with a teasing smile, setting aside her fright.

"What did you start to say before you were so rudely interrupted by our near demise?"

His playful grin helped her relax. She leaned against the seat, releasing her stiff posture. "I started to say that I never really gave much thought to a wedding. When we were girls, Ellen used to talk all the time about what she wanted at her wedding. She cut pictures out of magazines and saved color swatches, pasting them into a book. When Paul asked her to wed, she already had everything planned down to the color of his tie."

Rock laughed. "What about you? You didn't have any visions of how you wanted your wedding?"

Miko again sighed and studied the ring on her finger. "No. Not really. The majority of men aren't comfortable around a woman as tall as or taller than they are. Add in my tendency to be independent and think for myself, and most men don't want a thing to do with me."

"They're all idiots," Rock muttered.

Heat filled her cheeks again and she dropped her left hand back to her lap. "Be that as it may, I didn't hold out any hope of finding a man who would marry me. Mother and Papa might be very modern about most things, but they had it in mind I needed to find a nice Japanese boy. That's when the height issue came into play. The few who came close to my height didn't ask for a second date after they found out I had no intention of sitting at home, catering to their every whim."

Rock affected a shocked expression. "You mean you aren't going to greet me at the door each evening with my slippers in one hand and the newspaper in the other? You aren't going to fluff my pillows and cook whatever I want whenever I want it, and treat me like a superior intellect presiding over our domestic kingdom?"

Miko laughed. "I most certainly am not and you know it."

The look he shot her, full of mirth, longing, and affection, made her bones liquefy. "I do know it, Miko, and I wouldn't want you any other way. I'd much rather marry a girl with some spunk and sass than one who chases after me like an obedient dog."

They traveled in companionable silence for a while. Miko took the opportunity to study her husband from the fedora on top of his head to the polished toes of his shoes. The suit he wore was dark gray with a black pinstripe. A white shirt with a lighter gray-and-black tie appeared formal and gave him a striking appearance, especially with the hat tipped at a rakish angle on his short-cropped brown hair.

"I thought you'd wear your uniform today." She reached out and fingered the sleeve of the expensive suit. Since he hadn't asked her to press it, he must have taken it somewhere in town to have it done.

"I was concerned it might draw more attention than a man in a suit with a beautiful girl on his arm." He cast a quick glance her direction. "Do you not like my suit? I purchased it for Dad's funeral."

"Oh, I do. It's a fine suit, very distinguished," she said, mustering a measure of bravery. "But you cut such a dashing, rugged figure in your uniform. I'm sure you broke many hearts wearing it."

Rock waggled an eyebrow at her. "Whether I did or not is of no importance. The only heart I care about is yours and I don't plan on ever breaking it."

Stunned by his words, she remained quiet until she realized he wasn't heading back to the farm.

"Where are we going?" she asked, staring out the window as they drove south instead of turning west.

"I thought it might be nice to go for a drive this afternoon. You've been stuck at the farm for weeks, other than our hasty trip to the courthouse for the license." His head tipped her direction. "With your hat and sunglasses on, no one will give a thought to where you supposedly belong, unless of course someone mistakes you for another movie star."

Grateful for his lighthearted comment, she joined in the fun. "In that case, I hope you brought along an extra pen. I might run out of ink signing autographs, and then where would we be?"

Rock chuckled as they continued on their drive.

Although gas and rubber were rationed commodities, he decided the splurge in taking a long drive was worth it for their wedding day. He drove to Salem, then headed west on country roads before turning north toward home.

Miko enjoyed the ride, visiting areas she'd previously not explored. They talked about the small towns they passed, crops growing in the fields, and how they'd need to hire more help to pick the cherry crop.

Suddenly, she removed her sunglasses and turned to him, placing her hand on his arm. "If you don't want to talk about it, Rock, I understand, but I'd like to know how you were injured. You've never told me the whole story."

Rock hesitated. He didn't like to talk about it, but not for the reasons Miko thought. It was because he felt like such an idiot for accidentally ending his military career.

She patted his arm, then pulled away her hand when he hesitated to speak. "It's okay, Rock. Forget I asked."

A resigned sigh weighed heavy between them. "No. I'll tell you, Miko, but I'm afraid you won't like me quite as well when you hear the story."

Her hand settled on his shoulder and she rubbed it encouragingly. "There isn't a thing you could say that would alter my opinion of you, Rock Laroux."

He stared at her for a moment, then spoke in a subdued tone. "I told you the other day about graduating from West Point. The squadron I joined trained aircrews, took part in maneuvers, and participated in air shows."

Miko grinned. "I can picture you as a daredevil pilot, charming all the girls with your breathtaking performances."

Rock smirked. "Maybe I did, a little." He turned his head far enough to kiss her fingers where they rested on his shoulder. "Eventually, I shipped out to the Panama Canal. A growing need existed to tighten security there, enlarge and improve the airfield runways, and send out more long-range air patrols as the conflict with the Japanese and Germans escalated. Folks in Trinidad noticed an alarming number of Nazi boats prowling along the coastline, intent on destroying allied shipping enterprises. Waller Army Airfield was established in Trinidad last year and I ended up there, training pilots and overseeing a fine company of men."

"How long were you there?"

Rock gazed out the window, recalling the days he'd spent in the tropical locale. "I arrived last spring. The Army wanted to create a flying facility within reach of Fort Read, to protect the oilfields and refineries, and to guard the ships in the area. We flew patrol over cargo and merchant ships and kept an eye out for the Nazis. A few times, we shot at planes spying on allied ships. They'd locate a lone ship or a small convoy and send the location to one of their submarines. Then they'd show up and torpedo the ship."

"Oh! That's horrible." Like all good Americans, Miko and her family had followed the news of the war, but much of it seemed so far away. Their focus shifted from what happened in the world to the pressing issue of what would happen to Japanese Americans.

"It is horrible. Anyway, we were down to five planes, held together mostly with bubble gum and bootlaces." Rock grinned at her.

"You're teasing," she said, returning his smile.

"Mostly." He winked and continued. "One of the planes had been down for repairs and I took it up for a test flight. It seemed to be working fine, so I took it a little farther out, and a little farther. Movement off to my right caught my eye. I ended up chasing a German plane. We exchanged fire and flames burst from his plane, but by then an encroaching storm made it nearly impossible to see. I headed back to the base and realized my plane had sustained considerable damage as it continued losing altitude. The closer I got to the island, the more the storm raged, blowing me off course. The landing gear refused to function, so I crash-landed in the trees. The plane was destroyed. I woke up with shrapnel peppering my side, the inability to use my left arm, and no vision."

"My goodness!" Miko had no idea his injuries had been so extensive. The wound to his arm was obvious, and she'd seen the scars on his side when he'd been sick, but she'd had no idea about his loss of vision. "But you see okay, don't you?"

"I do, but it took a while for my vision to return to normal. My side has healed, but my hand…" He glanced down at the left hand resting on his thigh. The wide band on his ring finger glittered in the sunlight spilling into the car. The gold circle and all it represented made him wish his injury would miraculously heal overnight. He hated to burden Miko with a husband who wasn't completely whole. "I might never regain full use of it."

With her trademark optimism, she offered reassurance. "It's so much better, Rock. You've gained so much ground in the past month. When you first started helping on the farm, you could barely move your arm. Now, you're using your hand. Soon, you'll have control of your fingers." Miko reached across him and brushed her fingers over his hand in a comforting gesture. "I'm sure it will continue to improve."

"That's because I have a slave-driving wife determined to rehabilitate me." By concentrating on his movements, Rock turned over his left hand and grasped her fingers.

"See, look at that!" Miko beamed at him. "You'll be able to milk both cows blindfolded before you know it."

A smirk held a hint of accusation. "You're just saying that so you won't have to help with the milking anymore."

"Maybe," Miko said, glancing out the window as they turned down the familiar road that would take them home.

Home. The place she wanted to start a future with the man she loved… the amazing, generous, kind man beside her. Thoughts of him ever leaving made her snap her head around and stare at him in question. "Will you ever go back to the Army?"

Rock shook his head as he drove past the house and parked the car outside the storage building. "No. The Army doesn't have much use for a fighter pilot who only has one usable hand."

Relieved, she handed him the key to the door, and he jumped out of the car, unlocked the door, and pushed it back. Miko slid across the seat, drove the car inside and parked it. Rock opened the car door and gave her a hand as she climbed out.

She squeezed his fingers. "I'm sorry your career ended so abruptly, but you went out a hero."

He scoffed. "A hero? I don't even know for sure that I hit that Nazi, and in the process I destroyed one of the few functioning planes we had left. I used to holler at my men about not doing anything foolish, keeping an eye on the weather, and treating the planes like they were made of gold since we weren't getting any more in the foreseeable future. Then I did everything I warned them not to do."

Miko looped her arm around his after he locked the door and they ambled toward the house. "I don't care what you say, you are a hero. I know for a fact you're one, or we wouldn't have just come from having Pastor Clark marry us."

Gratified, Rock smiled as they reached the back step. He unlocked the door with the key she'd given him weeks ago. "Marrying you has nothing to do with being a hero, Kamiko. That is an entirely selfish move on my part."

At her baffled countenance, he swept her into his arms and carried her into the house, setting her down in the kitchen as they both laughed.

"Oh, how lovely!" Miko smiled at a tall crystal vase with a bouquet of fragrant summer roses on the table. A note beside it encouraged them to look in the refrigerator. She hurried to open the door and smiled at the sight of a picnic basket sitting on the shelf, loaded with a variety of tempting treats. Whirling around, she glared at Rock. "Who did you tell?"

Sheepish, Rock rubbed a hand along the back of his neck. "I thought it best if John and Lucy Phillips knew the truth. When I went over yesterday to get Petey's stamp of approval on our plans to wed, I told his folks about you being here, about us getting married today. Lucy said she wanted to do something for us and that she had a spare key your grandfather had given them. I told her it wasn't necessary, but the flowers and food are from her. John said he'd take care of the milking this evening. Petey volunteered to feed the future slabs of bacon, as he refers to your three little pigs, and check on the chickens."

"Oh, that's so sweet," Miko said, relieved her friends knew the truth. The family's care and gifts touched her heart. "I'll have to take over the blanket I made for Alice now that they know I'm here."

Rock nodded. "Lucy said she looks forward to seeing you. In fact, it would be nice to invite them for dinner one evening."

"I'd love to have them over." Miko removed her hat and dropped it on the table along with her sunglasses. "Perhaps we can plan something soon. I can't wait to see the baby who earned Petey's title of princess."

"She's a cute little thing," Rock said, removing his jacket and loosening his tie. "I've got a few things I need to see to, then how about we take the picnic basket up the hill to the garden?"

"I'd like that." Miko glanced at the clock. "Shall we meet back here in the kitchen in an hour? I'm dying to see what's in the trunk Mother wants me to open."

"Sure. Would you like me to carry it in here for you?" he asked.

"I'll go out there. If it's something we aren't going to use right away, there's no need to pack it in and right back out."

"That sounds reasonable." Rock backed toward the door with a rakish smile on his face. "I'll be back in an hour, wife of mine, so don't go running off anywhere. I've got a thing or two to show you this evening you might enjoy." Before she could say a word, he rushed out the door.

⋆⋆★ *Chapter Sixteen* ★★⋆⋆

Miko watched Rock jog off in the direction of the barn as she stood on the back step with the key to the trunk in her hand. Speculating about what he had planned, she both feared and anticipated finding out.

She strode to the storage building and opened the side door, then hurried over to the stack of boxes where her family had left her things. A dark red leather trunk with brass fittings rested at the bottom of one pile.

Hurriedly, Miko set aside boxes of winter clothes, secretarial supplies, and her collection of books on flower varietals to reach the trunk. Nervous, she jammed the small key into the lock with shaking fingers, and pulled down the latch when it clicked open. She lifted the lid, and the scent of sandalwood blended with herbs wafted to her nose.

Origami sachets, similar to those she and Ellen used to make to tuck into drawers and the linen closets, claimed her interest. She picked one up and sniffed it, then set it aside. Her gaze returned to the trunk, and she noticed an envelope with her name written on the front.

Impatient to read what her mother had to say, she slid a fingernail beneath the flap and lifted the sheet of parchment from inside, unfolding the monogrammed stationery. Miko lifted the paper to her nose and sniffed, inhaling the fragrance of her mother's perfume.

She closed her eyes and pictured her mother sitting at the dressing table in her room. The woman dusted powder on her nose and applied just a dab of perfume behind her ears and on her wrists, schooling her daughters in how to appear alluring yet remain wholesome.

A pang of regret and homesickness, not for a place but for her mother, hit her with unexpected force. She sank down on top of one of the boxes and held the letter for a long moment before she read the words.

My darling daughter,
(And yes, Miko, I mean you, not your sister!)

Miko blinked the moisture from her eyes and continued reading.

Your father arrived home tonight bearing the news we must report to the Portland Assembly Center next week. You'll probably think I've lost my grip on sanity if you somehow find this letter, but I had the strangest sensation I needed to write this to you.

I don't know what tomorrow or next week, or even next year, may hold for us. War is a scary, uncertain, humbling thing.

If, for some unexpected reason, we end up separated, I want you to know how precious you are to me. Although we don't see eye to eye on most subjects, I greatly admire you and the woman you've become. You are all the things I could never be: independent, strong, witty, and determined. You were always that way, even as a tiny girl.

In spite of your plans to remain single, Miko, someday you'll find a good man who will turn your head and capture your heart. When you do, the contents of this trunk will serve as your hope chest. Your sister and grandmother helped with the embroidery. And your father even added a few things.

You will always be special to me because you have such a fierce loyalty to your family, a gentle spirit, and a loving heart. Stand tall and proud, Miko, and never stop being uniquely you.

With all my love, dear girl,
Mother
P.S. This trunk belonged to Great-grandmother Yamada and came with her from Japan.

Miko sniffled and blinked away tears as she tucked the letter inside the envelope and set it to one side. She opened a box and removed the tissue paper covering a teacup from her grandmother's porcelain tea set. Pink chrysanthemums blossomed on the side of a bright white cup, surrounded by dark blue flourishes and gold trim. When she visited her father's parents as a child, she and her grandmother would often sip tea from the cups. A note in the box said, "From Papa."

Carefully wrapping the cup, she returned it to the box and lifted it from the trunk, eager to see what else it held.

Dainty crocheted lace edged several sets of fine linen pillowcases, embroidered with flowers, leaves, and birds. Miko recalled seeing her mother do the intricate stitching, but hadn't given a thought to them one day belonging to her.

Deeper inside the trunk, she found two sets of sheets, three tablecloths with matching napkins, and a stack of dish towels. A beautiful crystal pitcher shimmered in the fading afternoon light as she pulled it from a box with eight matching glasses.

A thin white box tied with a pink bow drew her interest. She removed the ribbon and lifted the lid. An exquisite peignoir set rested on a bed of white tissue. Airy lace and pearl buttons trimmed the blush-colored robe and gown. A note in the box from her mother offered a few words of instruction a naïve new bride might like to know for her wedding night.

Embarrassment sizzled in her cheeks as she considered her mother's advice. Heat churned in her midsection when she envisioned the look on Rock's face if she went to him wearing the seductive gown.

Unsettled by her thoughts, she dropped the filmy creations back in the box and retied the ribbon. No matter how much she loved Rock, no matter how desperately she truly wanted to be his bride, she wouldn't tell him. He'd already sacrificed far more for her and her family than anyone had a right to ask. She refused to tie him to her through a marriage that was nothing more than a farce.

A few blankets, assorted pieces of her great-grandmother's dishes, and a lovely box of handkerchiefs rounded out the remaining contents of the trunk.

She repacked everything, her fingers lingering on the box with the peignoir set. Rather than set it back inside, she took it with her when she returned to the house and stuffed it in the bottom dresser drawer in her bedroom. Miko took a moment to tidy her hair, then wash her face and hands before returning to the kitchen.

Rock rushed inside, wearing an excited grin and his uniform.

Her gaze traveled over his broad shoulders and chest, down the length of his long, solid legs, and back up to his face. "What are you doing?"

He wrapped his good hand around her waist and pulled her against his chest. "My wife said she wanted to see me in my uniform today, and so she shall."

Miko laughed. "You are crazy, Rock Laroux."

"Just about you, Mrs. Laroux." Rock opened the refrigerator and took out the basket of food Lucy Phillips had left for them to enjoy. "Are you ready for dinner?"

"Yes, I believe I am." Miko started to gather plates and cutlery, but Rock took them from her hands, set them on the counter, and nudged her toward the door.

"Everything is ready. All that's needed is the food and my beautiful bride." He ushered her outside, then held out his arm to her as he carried the basket.

Miko took his arm, secretly thrilled by his attentiveness, as she regarded the hard muscle beneath her hand. "You don't have to keep pretending to be the doting groom, Rock. Really, I don't expect you to put on a charade for my benefit."

His smile wilted as he gazed at her. "I'm not pretending or putting on a charade, Miko. I couldn't be more pleased or happy to marry you."

Unconvinced, she cast a wary glance at him as they made their way up the hill to the garden.

Once they entered the gate, Miko released Rock's arm and gasped in wonder. She'd never seen the garden look lovelier. Every stone lantern glowed with light, and over by the pond beneath their favorite weeping cherry tree, he'd spread out a blanket. Candles glowed from where he'd set them on rocks all around the picnic area. The sound of music drifted on the evening breeze from the radio Rock stashed nearby.

"Oh, Rock, it's like something from a dream!" She clasped her hands beneath her chin to keep from wrapping them around the remarkable man she'd married. "This is the best gift you could ever give me."

He kissed her cheek and motioned for her to precede him to the picnic blanket. Instead, she looped her arm around his left arm and walked beside him, committing to memory every detail of the amber-lit garden.

Romantic, fanciful notions fluttered through her thoughts. Miko would have said love was in the air, if Rock returned her affection. It lingered on her tongue, filled her senses, and danced before her eyes in the golden glow of candles and lanterns.

At the edge of the blanket, he set down the picnic basket, then offered Miko his hand. Gracefully, she folded her long legs beneath her to one side and placed her hands on her lap. Rock settled so close their hips touched, then he reached for the picnic basket.

The unfamiliar sensations his proximity produced left her overwhelmed. His efforts to make the day special for her, combined with the sheer enormity of what had transpired, made her waver between the need to weep and the urge to laugh.

She released a contented sigh and watched the muscles play beneath Rock's shirt. He filled a plate with thin slices of seasoned roast, pieces of cheese, crusty bread, and chunks of tomato and cucumber sprinkled with salt and pepper. After he handed her the plate, he filled one for himself and sat back, taking her hand in his as he offered thanks for their meal. When he included his gratitude for their wedding and asked the Lord's blessing on their life together, Miko bit her lip to hold back her tears.

They dug into the food Petey's mother had provided for their first meal as husband as wife. The food wasn't fancy, but it was good, filling, and easy to eat with their fingers.

Rock lifted a jar of grape juice from a pail he'd filled with ice and unscrewed the lid. He poured two glasses and held one out to Miko. "I propose a toast. To Miko, my magnificent bride. May the seeds of love planted today grow into a bountiful, rich garden."

She held her glass up to his. "To Rock, a man full of surprises with a heart even bigger than his charm. May the time we spend together give you happy moments and lovely memories."

Her toast took Rock aback. She made it sound like he'd only be there for a limited time, as if he'd leave her as soon as her family returned to the farm. He didn't know how or when, but someday he'd convince her that he'd meant every word of the vows he'd made and planned to keep them until his dying body exhaled its last breath.

Now wasn't the time, though. Not as they sat in the wondrous garden planted by her family and tended with such care by her own hands. The lanterns and candles gave it a magical appearance and Rock was glad he'd thought to light them.

He'd spent considerable time that morning hauling the candles he'd purchased the previous afternoon up the hill and placing them around. The blanket and radio he'd carried up and arranged, wanting to make the evening special for Miko.

By the look on her face as she'd stepped into the garden, he was sure she appreciated his efforts.

As he devoured the sandwich he'd made of bread, meat and cheese, he watched her eat. She held herself with such poise and dignity, he wondered, again, if her family tree included a royal branch or two somewhere along the way.

He grinned as he pictured the energetic, amiable Shig as a formidable tyrant.

Miko noticed his amusement and raised a dark eyebrow. "What's so funny?" she asked, wiping her mouth on one of the napkins Lucy had included in the basket.

"I was picturing your grandfather as a Japanese warrior or emperor. He seems far too friendly and fun-loving for that role."

She nodded in agreement. "You might be surprised at what he could do if he needed to, but he is easygoing and playful for the most part."

"I've noticed he's most always smiling. His attitude is one of the things I most admire about him. Despite what's going on in the world around him, he doesn't let it alter the happiness within him."

Miko smiled. "That's Granddad. Grandma is more of the pessimistic, cautious one of the two. Obviously, she passed that along to my mother."

He didn't want to incriminate himself by saying anything he shouldn't about his new mother-in-law, so he changed the subject. "Speaking of your mother, did you locate the trunk?"

Miko held the napkin in front of her face, trying to hide the blush that bloomed in her cheeks at the thought of what she'd found in the trunk. "I did find it. There were several things for setting up a home. I'll leave most of it in the trunk for now. If we do invite the Phillips family over for a meal, it might be fun to use a few of the things, though."

Rock ate another sandwich as they listened to the radio and talked about the additional boys he'd hired to help pick cherries in the coming week. Seven boys would show up Tuesday morning, ready to work. Miko walked him through the process of picking. They hoped to be finished by the end of the week. They'd agreed she would stay in the house and prepare lunch each day. Rock would carry the food outside for their workers to enjoy.

Once she finished her dinner, Rock set out a bowl of strawberries he picked that morning. Selecting the plumpest, reddest berry, he lifted it to her mouth, nearly insisting she take a bite. He watched her every movement. A drop of crimson juice clung to her ruby lips, and he fought back the desire to cover her with kisses.

Miko might have convinced herself that this would be a mock marriage, but Rock hadn't agreed to it. He'd never wanted a woman as much as he wanted her. Now that she was his wife, he would do everything in his power to woo her and make her his own.

Enchanted with her mouth, ensnared by her floral scent, entranced by the lights flickering in the garden that offered their own little slice of heaven, Rock leaned toward Miko, intent on stealing a kiss.

Her eyes widened and she abruptly stood, brushing crumbs from her skirt and nervously repacking the basket.

Rock moved behind her and settled his hand on her waist, causing her to jump. Part of him hoped she jounced not because he'd startled her, but because the feel of his hand sent her nerve endings into a frenzy similar to the one he experienced every time they touched.

"Would you like to go for a stroll?" he asked, holding out his arm and offering his most charming smile.

"That would be lovely." Her voice was soft as she spoke, sounding a little shy and uncertain.

In no hurry, they meandered along the footpaths, strolled over a bridge, and gazed at the lantern light reflected in the pool at the base of the waterfall. Rock kept the conversation light when they bothered to speak at all.

Eventually, they wandered back to the weeping cherry tree where Bing Crosby crooned "This is My Night to Dream" on the radio. Rock couldn't imagine a more perfect song to dance to at that moment. Slipping his left arm around Miko's waist, he took her hand in his, kissing the backs of her fingers.

"May I have the pleasure of dancing with my bride?" he asked.

Starlight seemed a dim reflection to the bright light twinkling in his eyes.

Miko tipped her head in consent, her feet moving across the grass, keeping time to Rock's steps.

He hummed the tune as they swayed in the glow of the candles with a sliver of moon shining down on them from a clear night sky.

Possessively, his hand splayed against her back and he turned into her, pulling her closer. Relief and torment, ecstasy and misery washed over his body in a confused jumble as they danced. Rock discovered his home was right there with her in his arms, her body swaying against his to the music.

Confident with enough time and patience that he'd win her affections, he smiled. Suddenly, he understood what his father had meant when he said love from the right woman gave a man a reason to hope for tomorrow.

Miko gave him hope that went far beyond the boundaries of war and death and fear. The love he felt for her buoyed his dreams and made the impossible seem completely tangible.

"*This is my night to dream,*" he sang in a husky tone then hummed a few lines. He thought the words about being in love with no idea what he might do exceedingly appropriate for the moment the two of them shared.

Slightly pulling back, Miko studied his face. Rock held her gaze, his dark and full of yearning.

With a sigh, she moved closer again and nestled her head against his shoulder. Rock's feet continued the dance while his heart hammered so loudly, he was sure she would hear the staccato beats. Time stood still and the rest of the world fell away in that moment as he held her in his arms, breathed in her luscious scent, and reveled in the wonder that she was his wife.

His wife!

The glorious, mysterious, thoroughly fantastic creature in his arms was his bride. His to have and to hold, for as long as they both should live.

Rock had in mind there would be a lot of holding and having in the years to come.

First, he had to convince her he truly loved her. The realization that he'd never said the words to her flashed across his mind. No wonder she doubted his sincerity when he'd not forced the most important words a man could say to a woman past his lips.

The moment the song ended, he dropped a soft kiss to her temple. She lifted her head and he saw the truth in her eyes, the wanting and hunger there as strong as his own.

"Miko," he whispered in a raspy, deep tone as his thumb grazed the long column of her throat. Unable to stop himself, to hold back any longer, his lips ignited a fiery trail along her jaw before settling on her mouth.

Surprised and pleased when she parted her lips, Rock kissed her deeply, thoroughly, lovingly as he continued to hold her in his arms. "Kamiko, I love you."

Rather than reply, she pressed against him, wrapping her arms around the back of his neck to remove any space lingering between them. Her heart pounded against his. Rock marveled that he'd survived so many years without the pleasure of her kisses, without the warmth of her embrace. Languidly, his hands slid along her back, past her waist, caressing, massaging, stirring her to respond.

As suddenly as she melted against him, she jerked back, chest heaving as she glared at him. "I'm not some floozy you can woo into your bed, Captain Laroux."

Stunned, Rock reached out to touch her, but she took a stumbling step away from him. "Miko, I meant what I said. I do love you. I've loved you since the first time I opened my eyes and saw you sleeping in the chair next to the bed. Nothing will change how I feel about you."

Shaking her head, she closed her eyes as she backed farther from his reach. "No, Rock. You've been stuck here with me for weeks on end, and this isn't love. I've read about men who think they're in love with the women who nurse them. I wouldn't be wrong in saying you had feelings for a nurse at the hospital, would I?"

His guilty look told her all she needed to know. "I appreciate all you've done for me, for my family. The sacrifice you made today by marrying me is more than I can comprehend, but if you... if we... consummate this marriage, it will only bring you problems."

He stepped forward and grabbed her hand, holding it against his heart. "Do you feel my heart racing, Miko? You do that to me. You are the only girl who has ever made it feel like it might explode right out of my chest. You're the only girl I've ever told I love, and I won't love another. It's you, Miko. Only you."

"Rock, no. Stop it." She yanked her hand from his and turned away. "I won't have you burdened by a future with me. I just won't. You know how people will treat you, what they'll say about you."

"They'll say I'm a lucky man to have talked such a beautiful, incredible, intelligent woman into marrying me." Rock moved behind her again, pressing a moist kiss to her neck.

She wavered at his touch. A shiver of desire coursed through her, and he saw goose bumps rise on her skin. Without a doubt, he knew he could seduce her, but she'd hate him for it and so would he.

Resigned, he stepped back and lifted the picnic basket in his hand. "I won't touch you again, Miko, until you ask me to. When you decide you'd like to truly be my wife, come to me anytime, day or night, I don't care. Come to me and tell me you love me, and I'll be yours forevermore. Just come to me."

Silently, he turned and left the garden. Once he disappeared out the gate, Miko sank onto the blanket and cried. Pretending she didn't love Rock, pretending she didn't want him more than she craved air to breathe, was the hardest thing she'd ever done. No matter how much it hurt her, she would spare him the misery of being shunned because he'd taken a wife most of his friends would consider an enemy.

✶✶★ *Chapter Seventeen* ★✶✶

The peignoir set taunted Miko. Four days had passed since the beautiful picnic beneath the weeping cherry tree. Four days since she'd spurned Rock's affections. Four days that his words had echoed in her head and tormented her heart.

As though the filmy bit of fabric trimmed in lace had a voice, the peignoir set persistently called to Miko. Multiple times, she'd gone into the bedroom and opened the dresser drawer, fingers lingering on the box.

No matter how much she wanted to slip it on and go to Rock, she just couldn't do it. Convinced what he felt for her was lingering sentiment from her nursing him back to health, she knew in time he'd get over his infatuation and set his affection on someone else. Someone better suited as a sweet, obedient, dutiful wife. Someone who wasn't a fugitive.

In an effort to rid herself of the nagging voice in her head telling her to surrender, she took the peignoir set up to the house where she slept. At least there, it wouldn't tempt her during the day. Although she could have easily stored it back in the trunk where she'd found it, Miko didn't give that a moment of consideration.

In spite of how hard she worked to block thoughts of being his wife from her mind, she couldn't help but wonder if being loved by Rock would be as amazing as she imagined.

She was determined never to know. After all, it was in Rock's best interest that she refused to consummate their marriage. However, acute pain stabbed her heart as she thought of Rock loving another, but it was for the best. Rock Laroux was the finest man she'd ever met. He deserved so much more than being burdened with a wife who would only bring shame and scorn to his door.

Having resolved to ignore her feelings and tamp down her emotions, Miko focused on cooking for the crew Rock had hired to pick the cherries. She wanted to be out in the orchard helping pick the dark, ripe fruit, but they couldn't risk one of the boys reporting her.

So she stayed in the house and cooked doughnuts for a morning snack, fried chicken for lunch, baked cookies for an afternoon break, and set out drinks she made by blending crushed strawberries and their juice with cold buttermilk.

Rock behaved as though nothing had happened, teasing and joking as he always did when they were together. If she'd hurt him by refusing his amorous advances and tossing his love back in his face, he didn't show it.

There was nothing she wouldn't do for him, except allow him to permanently tie his life to hers. She'd asked Pastor Clark in a moment of private conversation about annulling the marriage if it remained in name only. The pastor chuckled and assured her that it was a possibility, but the option most certainly would not apply to her.

Lost in her reflections about what he had meant, she didn't notice Rock come in for dinner until he placed a quick kiss to her cheek.

"Hiya, sweetheart. What delicious thing have you made for dinner?" he asked, leaning around her to peer at the pan of savory gravy she stirred.

Miko grinned at him over her shoulder, pleased by his playful mood. Although he had kept his hands to himself since Sunday evening, he still kissed her cheek often and frequently brushed against her in passing.

In spite of herself, she enjoyed every bit of his attention, whether it was intentional or not.

"I traded Lucy a flat of strawberries and two gallons of cherries for a beef roast and four packages of ground beef. I made the roast for dinner tonight. With all the cherries you and the boys picked today, I figured you'd be starving."

"I am starving." Rock backed toward the doorway leading to the rest of the house. "I think we got the better end of the bargain with Lucy, though. Did you notice the strawberries are all but gone?"

Miko nodded. "I picked the last of what was ripe this morning. Granddad planted three different varieties and they all are everbearing, though. We'll have more in a few weeks. I noticed the berry plants on the south end of the patch are already getting new blossoms."

"That's good to know. I wasn't sure if we'd have more." Rock tipped his head in the direction of the oven, where mouthwatering scents emanated from the roasting beef. "If you give me a minute to wash up, I'll carve the roast."

"Thank you. I'd appreciate that." She gave him a parting glance as he disappeared down the hallway. From observing his habits, she knew he'd strip off his shirt on the way to the bathroom. He'd wash his hands and face, hastily run a comb over his short hair, and then grab a clean shirt on his way back to the table. Since the weather had been so warm, he wore sleeveless undershirts to work in, although he did usually put on a cotton dress shirt for dinner.

He returned to the kitchen, fastening the last buttons of a shirt the same color as his bright blue eyes. "Give me the weaponry, wife, and turn me loose on that hunk of cow."

Miko laughed. She handed him the carving knife and fork after he pulled the roast from the oven and removed the lid from the roaster. He leaned forward and inhaled the aromatic steam as it rose from the meat. "Mmm. That sure does smell good. Even if it makes the kitchen thirty degrees hotter than normal, the suffering is worth it."

He carved the roast while she spooned mashed potatoes into a bowl, poured the gravy into a boat and set them on the table. Rock carried over the platter of sliced roast and gazed at the feast. Miko had gone to considerable effort to make a nice meal.

"Everything looks wonderful," he said. "You didn't need to go to so much trouble."

"I was stuck in the house, anyway." She shrugged. "I've had time to clean and get caught up on the laundry. This morning I baked enough bread to last for a week."

"And here I thought you might sit by the radio with your feet up, listening to one of your favorite programs." He winked at her as he took her hand in his, then offered a brief prayer of thanks for their meal.

Rock opened his eyes and glanced down at the salad plate before him. "I haven't had stuffed tomatoes for a long time. The ones I've eaten were never this pretty." He dipped his fork into the creamy filling and took a bite. "That's very good, Miko." He motioned to the lettuce beneath the tomato, providing a frilly green base. "Is the lettuce from our garden?"

"Yes. I picked a bunch of it this morning and left the rest of it in bundles in the produce stand. The girls you hired seem to do a good job of arranging the produce when they aren't ogling you or the boys."

Rock chuckled and tossed a pointed look across the table. "Are you going to tell me you never ogled boys at that age? I recall you telling me there was one handsome boy who caught your eye. What was his name again?" he questioned in jest.

Her gaze narrowed as she smiled indulgently. "His name must have been Arrogant Conceited Blowhard, because that's what he appears to have grown up to become."

"Touché."

Throughout the meal, Rock paid Miko compliments on how good the meal tasted. She watched as he spread a thick layer of cherry jelly she'd made the previous day over his dinner roll. He took a bite and closed his eyes, leaning back in his chair as he chewed. "That is so good, Miko. I've never had cherry jelly before."

"Oh? We always make cherry jelly, and grape, peach, and plum. And there's strawberry and blackberry jam. Oh, and Grandma always makes apricot, but it's not my favorite. If you don't protest, I might skip it this year."

Rock wiped his mouth on a napkin. "I'll eat whatever kind you make, but apricot isn't my favorite either. Strawberry and grape are what my mom most often made. When will you start canning the produce?"

"I've done a little already, but the bulk of it is in August and September. It's far too hot to do it now, and we always like to sell all the fresh fruit we can at the beginning of the season."

He nodded and added jelly to another roll. "That makes sense. If things go as well tomorrow as they have the past few days, we should finish with the cherries around noon."

"That's great, Rock. The peaches and plums look like they'll be ripe in a few weeks. In the meantime, the vegetables are really starting to produce. If you wanted to have the boys plant more peas where I pulled out the old plants, we could have some later in the season."

"I'll have them do that tomorrow afternoon."

They discussed more garden plans, then Rock returned outside to see to the evening chores while Miko washed the dishes and cleaned the kitchen. When she finished, she went out to milk the cows. It took her half the time it took Rock to complete the chore, with the fingers of his left hand still not functioning properly, and he had enough things to do that evening.

After she strained the milk and rinsed the bucket, she worked in the vegetable garden until it grew too dark to see. She returned to the house and took a shower. Hastily scribbling a note, she let Rock know there were still a few pieces of cake left from the previous evening if he wanted something sweet. Then she made her way up the hill to her empty room in the quiet house.

Although she opened the blinds to encourage more air to blow through her room, unrelenting heat kept her tossing and turning. Sleep eluded her for hours.

Finally, she rose and ambled outside, walking around the garden, seeking relief. The relief she needed wouldn't come from a cooling breeze, though.

Images of Rock's broad shoulders, tanned from the time he'd spent outside in nothing but that thin scrap of white cotton he called an undershirt, raced through her mind. The dark, rich taste of his kisses filled her mouth with excess moisture while an excited fluttering in her belly made her long to have his arms wrapped around her again.

Miko rushed back inside the house and tossed her nightgown aside, pulling on the gown and robe from the peignoir set. Her fingers trembled as she hastily unwound her braid and shook out the long waves of her hair.

Determination and desire fueled her steps as she hurried down the hill in the midnight darkness.

Thousands of stars sparkled overhead, and she paused to admire how much they resembled the twinkling light in Rock's eyes.

The moon, full and clear, washed the world in silvery hues and lit the way as she crossed the stepping stones behind the barn and strode toward the house. Rather than go straight to the back door, she walked around to the side yard and stood on the other side of the fence that surrounded the house.

No light glowed from inside the house, although she heard the faint notes of a song as the radio played. Rock sometimes listened to it to lull him to sleep. The radio quite often greeted her when she entered the house in the early hours of the morning before he awakened.

Struck by the awareness of what would happen if she walked into the house, she hesitated, staring at his bedroom window with her hand on the latch of the yard's side gate.

Uncertain and undeniably afraid, not of Rock but of their future, she lingered for several silent moments. Torn between doing what she felt was right and following the pleading of her heart, she wavered at the gate. What if he rejected her? What if he didn't love her? What if he regretted his offer for her to come to him anytime?

A long, weary sigh rolled past her lips as she spun around and scurried up the hill to her lonely bed.

Rock walked through the darkened kitchen and flipped on the radio. He filled a glass with water and guzzled it, then paced through the house, perturbed by the stifling air.

Heat permeated every corner of the house as if the entire thing rested inside an oven. Even the breeze blowing in the window brought no relief, just sweltering warmth that left him irritable and exhausted, yet unable to sleep.

He marched back toward the kitchen, catching his toe on a chair in the dining room. Hopping the rest of the way on one foot, he muttered words that would have earned him a thorough tongue-lashing from his mother if she were alive.

The linoleum on the kitchen floor, often comfortably cool and pleasing at this time of night, still held the day's warmth. Annoyed, he jerked open the refrigerator door, fanning it back and forth in an effort to cool his overheated body.

Dressed in nothing but his cotton underwear, he knew part of his problem stemmed from his longing for Miko. When he came in for dinner, he stood at the door and watched her for the length of several heartbeats before he stepped behind her and made his presence known.

A great deal of self-control was required to do nothing more than kiss her cheek and tease her through the delicious meal she prepared. He wanted to pull her into his arms, carry her to his bed and...

He shook his head to chase away the thoughts that would only increase his current condition of misery. Briefly, he considered stuffing his underwear into the freezer section of the refrigerator for a few minutes.

A grin lifted the corners of his mouth as he envisioned Miko opening it in the morning and finding them lodged between a package of ground beef and a tray of ice cubes.

Mindful that nothing in the kitchen would help his agitated state, he made his way back to the bedroom. He stood in front of the window, absorbing every bit of the evening breeze and staring at the full moon shining above the trees.

Movement drew his eye to the far edge of the yard outside his window. Spellbound, he watched as Miko slowly approached the fence. Whatever opalescent lace-trimmed thing she wore skimmed her curves and stoked the fire already searing through his veins. Everything in him shouted for him to run outside and claim her as his.

He wondered if this was what a primitive cavedweller felt as he watched his woman in the moonlight, or perhaps a knight gazing upon his fair lady. The possessive, protective, utterly unreasonable emotions swarming through him had to be the direct result of the depth of his love for Miko. Nothing else could explain the need he felt for her, the painful longing for her to belong only and forever to him.

Hesitant, she stood with one hand on the gate to the side yard, as though she couldn't make up her mind if she would bravely follow her heart or retreat.

"Come on, Miko. Open the gate, sweetheart." Rock's whispers held a hint of desperation.

As though to mock his suffering, Glenn Miller's "Moonlight Serenade" played on the radio. How appropriate for someone else to sing about two lovers on a June night while Rock silently pleaded for his lover to come to him.

Nerves jangling and muscles taut, he remained at the window, hopeful, waiting. Completely attuned to her every move, he willed her to come to him, to love him.

"Open the gate, Kamiko," his husky voice encouraged. "Please, open it and come to me."

Disappointment unlike anything he'd ever experienced sucked the breath right out of him when she turned and ran. His forehead pressed against the glass of the upper window as he watched her pale figure race across the pasture behind the barn and up the path to the house on the hill.

Despondent and weary, Rock sank onto the edge of the bed and held his head in his hands. He knew all along he needed to be patient with her, not push her, but oh, how he wanted her.

Rising to his feet, he considered running after her, following her to the soft bed on the floor of the house her great-grandparents built, but sense prevailed.

To go to her now would only drive her further away. Although he hated it, hated the very thought of it, he had to dredge up enough patience to wait until she was ready to love him as much as he loved her.

··✶★ *Chapter Eighteen* ★✶··

Norman popped a sour candy into his mouth and watched the last of the hired help leave the farm for the day. From past observations, he knew the soldier boy would milk the cows, feed the pigs and chickens, and complete an hour's worth of chores before going to the house.

He'd seen Laroux's woman go out to the barn a few minutes ago. She spent a lot of time out there and rarely returned quickly once she went that direction.

Determined to get his hands on the deed, Norman left his car parked across the road and quietly made his way to the house. He crept along the shadows created by the trees in the yard to the back door and let himself inside. The smell of roasting meat mingled with the aroma of chocolate.

His mouth watered at the sight of a frosted cake sitting on the counter. While Norman ate a steady diet of canned goods and candy, that pretty-boy soldier was living the good life.

It wouldn't be long before Norman put a stop to it for good.

Intent on locating the deed, he made his way to the office at the front of the house. The big desk seemed a likely place to keep important papers. He sat down in the leather chair and opened a drawer, inspecting the contents before feeling beneath it to make sure nothing important was hidden on the backside of the drawer.

After searching through each and every drawer, Norman wondered if the deed was in the house. It could be anywhere on the farm.

Rather than get caught and have to face the soldier, Norman decided he'd leave and come back on a day when Laroux wasn't home. There were ways to make the woman talk. Ways that Norman would purely enjoy enforcing.

He stepped out of the room and made his way back to the kitchen. Unable to help himself, he lifted a knife and cut a large slice of cake, picking it up on his hand. He took a big bite, relishing the delicious, moist flavor before he ambled down the hall to the back door.

The moment his hand reached for the knob, the door swung open. The Jap woman stared at him in surprise.

Norman rushed forward, giving her such a hard shove, she tumbled backward off the steps and fell to the grass. He tore around the corner of the house and raced to his car as the woman yelled for Laroux.

Gravel spewed from beneath Norman's back tires as he gunned the engine and roared down the road.

In the rearview mirror, he saw Laroux run out to the road and shake a fist his direction.

Relieved he escaped without having to deal with the man, Norman finished eating his cake as he drove toward town.

Unconcerned about the soldier following him, Norman slowed his speed and ambled along, plotting how he'd torture the information about the deed out of Laroux's woman. From the look of terror on her face earlier, he'd enjoy every single moment of making her suffer.

Lost in his thoughts, Norman failed to notice the car speeding behind him until it pulled alongside his car. Laroux glared at him, motioning for him to pull over.

Norman's foot hit the gas, but the soldier kept up with him. When an oncoming truck would have forced Laroux to drop back, he zoomed ahead and pulled in front of Norman, then slammed on his brakes.

To avoid a crash, Norman whipped his wheel to the right. His car bounced over the ditch running along the side of the road, and spluttered to a stop in a thicket of berry bushes.

Before he could attempt to start the stalled car or climb out to assess the damage, his door swung open and Norman was pulled from the vehicle.

The enraged soldier shoved him against the back of the car, holding the front of his suit and shirt in his clenched fists. Norman's feet pedaled air as the soldier held him above the ground.

"If you ever set foot on the farm again, even think about setting foot on it, I'll bury you so deep in the ground not even worms will be able to find you," Laroux threatened.

Norman gaped at the soldier, noting the raw anger in the man's eyes and the vein bulging in his neck. Wishing he had a knife in his hand, Norman would have dearly loved to sink it into that pulsing vein.

Instead, he struggled against the hold of the solider, once again feeling like a bullied child. "You have no right to touch me, Laroux. Get your hands off me."

"No right!" the man yelled into Norman's face. "You assaulted my wife. That gives me every right."

"I did no such thing," Norman said with a calm detachment. At least now he knew the Jap woman was married to Laroux. That made things even more interesting. Norman bet she was related to the old Jap who used to own the farm. The soldier probably took advantage of the girl and forced her into marriage just so he could get the farm.

Incensed someone had beat him to a devious plan, Norman had no intention of losing out on owning those timber-rich acres.

Laroux gave him a vicious shake, nearly rattling the teeth in Norman's head. "Stay away from me, my wife, and our farm, Ness, or it will be the last thing you do."

"You don't scare me. Now let me go. You have no proof, other than the word of that stinkin' Jap. Who do you think the police will believe? Me or her?" Norman sneered. "Oh, but then you can't go to the police because your wife isn't supposed to be there, is she? Wouldn't the authorities love to know you're hiding a Jap on the farm."

Norman didn't anticipate the soldier hitting him with such force, blood spurted from his nose. Pain seared through his head.

Stunned, he whimpered and held his hands to the geyser flowing from his nose.

With another shake, Laroux turned him loose and let him drop to the ground. "Stay away from us, Ness!"

The soldier stomped back to his car and drove away while Norman reached into his pocket and pulled out a handkerchief, holding it to his nose.

It would give him immense pleasure to kill Laroux and his wife, just as soon as he had the deed in his hands.

✶✶★ *Chapter Nineteen* ★✶✶✶

Infuriated, Rock drove into town and parked outside the sheriff's office. After wiping Norman's blood off his hands with a rag he kept in the car, Rock jogged up the steps and inside.

An older woman eyed him over the glasses perched on her nose as he moved in front of her desk. "May I help you?" she asked in a nasally tone.

"Yes, ma'am. I'd like to speak with the sheriff, if he's available."

She gave him a studying glance. "May I say to which matter this regards?"

Rock sighed. "A man just broke into our home, assaulted my wife, and ran off. It's the second time he's done it and I want him arrested."

The woman's mouth formed an "O" while her eyes widened. "Just a moment please, sir." Quickly rising to her feet, she disappeared down a hallway and soon returned. "Right this way, please."

Rock followed her into a large office. Maps covered the walls and papers piled over the surface of a large desk. A friendly-faced man sat behind it, speaking on the phone. He held up a finger to Rock, indicating he'd be right with him.

Impatient to get back to Miko, Rock was tempted to pace back and forth with nervous energy, although he managed to remain still.

The sheriff hung up the phone and stood, holding a hand out to Rock. "Evening, I'm Sheriff Bentley."

"Rock Laroux, sir." Rock shook the man's hand then took the seat the sheriff indicated. "A man has trespassed twice on my property and assaulted my wife. The first time, I didn't have any proof it was him, but this time, I saw him shove my wife off the back step and run through the yard."

"Do you know his name?" the sheriff asked, frowning as he opened a notepad and wrote down notes.

"Norman Ness."

The sheriff lifted his gaze and rolled his eyes. "Somehow that doesn't surprise me. Ness is a sneaky one. You'd be surprised how many complaints I get about him, but no one ever catches him in the act. Do you want to file charges against him?"

"You bet I do." Rock sighed and forked a hand through his hair. "And to be entirely truthful, I ran him off the road about three miles out of town and bloodied his nose pretty good. I also threatened to do worse if I caught him on our place again."

The sheriff grinned. "I wish I'd seen that. Thank you for your honesty, but it doesn't change the fact he's been on your place, and bothering your wife. Is she okay?"

"Yes. Just shaken up, but no worse for wear this time. The last time, he clunked her over the head and left her unconscious."

The sheriff's eyebrows inched upward as he jotted notes. "Where do you live, son?"

Rock gave him the address. "It used to be the Yamada farm. My wife and I purchased it not long ago."

"And what's your wife's name?"

"Miko. Shig Yamada is her grandfather." Rock couldn't see any point in telling the sheriff anything but the truth. He just hoped it wouldn't put Miko in any danger.

"I see." The sheriff gave Rock a narrow glance that lasted the length of several heartbeats. "Is your wife's family at the assembly center in Portland?"

"Yes, sir." Rock wanted to squirm in his chair. Maybe he should have handled Ness on his own without going to the sheriff. He'd been so intent on getting Ness locked up to keep him away from the farm and his wife, he hadn't given a thought to what the authorities might do if they found out about Miko.

"Is there a reason your wife isn't with them?" Sheriff Bentley folded his hands on top of his desk, as though he waited for Rock's explanation.

"Yes, sir. She's been taking care of me. I was in the hospital, ringing the bell at the pearly gates at the first part of May. I decided if I was going to meet my Maker, I'd rather it be at home, beneath a blue sky, so I released myself from the hospital. I almost died after I arrived at the farm, but Miko took great care of me, nursing me back to health. She stayed behind because I needed her."

The sheriff didn't say anything as he took more notes. Rock wished he could see what the man wrote, but the sheriff's hand blocked his view of the notepad. Finally, Sheriff Bentley lifted his gaze. "Is your wife a threat to our national security?"

Rock shook his head. "No, sir. Not at all. In fact, she reminded me just yesterday to purchase more war bonds on my next trip to town. She's filled boxes with clothes and blankets for the Bundles for Britain campaign. She even saves all the waste fat and grease from cooking for me to take to the butcher for munitions."

Sheriff Bentley studied Rock again. "Were you in the military?"

"Yes, sir. I was a captain in the U.S. Army Air Corp. I planned to make a career of it, but my plane crashed earlier this year and that was the end of that." Unconsciously, his gaze dropped to his hand.

"Thank you for your service, Captain Laroux." The sheriff took a few papers from a desk drawer and filled out information, then slid them across the desk for Rock to sign. "These documents state you are filing charges against Norman and the reason for it. If he shows up out at the farm again, call us immediately. In the meantime, I'll see if I can track him down. He has a place his mother owned where he'll most likely be. I'll let you know when we arrest him."

Rock signed his name on the documents, then stood. "Thank you, sir, for your assistance. It's greatly appreciated."

"Anytime, son. Now, about your wife..." The sheriff appeared thoughtful as he walked Rock to his office door. "Before I decide what should be done about her failing to report to the assembly center, I'd like to come out and meet her. If you don't object, I'll plan to be there in the morning."

"Yes, sir," Rock said, devastated by the sheriff's request. Vainly, he'd hoped the sheriff would let Miko's situation slide.

Contemplative on the drive home, he rushed inside the house after he parked the car in the storage building. Miko met him at the door with a hug.

"I was worried about you. You shouldn't have chased off after Mr. Ness like that," she admonished as they stepped into the kitchen. Miko poured Rock a glass of iced tea as he washed his hands then took a seat at the table. The food had grown cold, waiting for his return, but he wouldn't utter a word of complaint.

After asking a blessing on the meal, he told Miko about catching up to Ness and threatening the man. Conveniently, he left out the part about punching him in the nose. He told her he'd gone to the sheriff's office to file charges, and what the sheriff had said about wanting to meet her.

"I shouldn't have mentioned you to the sheriff, Miko. I'm so sorry," Rock said, pained by the trouble he'd brought right to their door.

Miko's fork returned to her plate and she held Rock's gaze. "You did the right thing, Rock. Don't give it another thought. You and I both know I should have been at the assembly center all along."

"No," he barked, then softened his tone. "You belong here, with me. If you aren't here, how will any of us know what to do in the garden? It's your guidance that's keeping the farm going, not me."

She reached across the table and patted his hand, offering reassurance. "Everything will be fine, Rock."

The next morning, they both nervously awaited the sheriff's arrival. At five minutes past eight, Sheriff Bentley parked his car at the end of the walk and made his way to the door.

Rock opened it and welcomed him inside. "Good morning, sir."

The sheriff smiled and removed his hat. "Good morning, Captain." He looked over at Miko and politely tipped his head. "Hello, Mrs. Laroux."

"Good morning, Sheriff."

"Sir, I'd like you to meet my wife, Miko Laroux." Rock moved to settle a hand on Miko's back, offering her what comfort he could give.

"It's a pleasure to meet you, ma'am," the sheriff said, taking the seat Rock indicated after Miko settled onto the couch.

"May we offer you some refreshment, Sheriff?" Miko asked, smiling warmly at the man.

"Thank you, Mrs. Laroux. That would be appreciated."

He accepted the cup of coffee and slice of coffee cake Miko handed to him. Rather than get down to business, he took a few bites of the cake and a deep swallow of the coffee. He glanced at Rock and grinned. "You're a lucky man, Laroux, to have a lovely wife who can cook, too."

"I am lucky, sir," Rock said, placing a kiss on Miko's cheek as he draped an arm around her shoulders. The dark blue dress she wore appeared both professional and polished, especially with her hair rolled back in the popular victory style. A small U.S. flag pin on her lapel made it clear what side she supported in the war.

Much to Rock's surprise the sheriff didn't discuss what would happen once he arrested Miko. Rather, Sheriff Bentley inquired about the crops on the farm. "My folks used to bring me out here when I was a boy. Your grandfather always grew the best watermelons. I hope you've planted some this year."

Rock grinned. "We do have melons planted. They're off to a good start. Right now, we've got strawberries coming out our ears."

"Strawberries?" the sheriff asked with a hungry look. "I sure do enjoy a slice of strawberry pie, although this berry cake is very good, Mrs. Laroux."

"Thank you, sir," Miko said, demurely.

Rock thought she looked like a queen holding court as she sat straight and proper on the couch.

The sheriff finished his slice of cake and cup of coffee, then asked to see the house.

Rock and Miko showed him the office, the bedrooms and bathroom, the dining room and kitchen. He even went down to the basement and took a look around before they escorted him on a tour of the outbuildings and the produce stand. While they were there, Rock picked up a flat of berries. "We'd like you to take these with you, sir."

"Thank you, Captain Laroux. I appreciate that. I can almost taste that strawberry pie right now," the sheriff set the berries in the back of his car. Miko and Rock stood together, waiting for the sheriff to put her in handcuffs and direct her to get in the car.

Instead, the man leaned back against the passenger door and smiled. "I don't know if the two of you have heard, but the assembly center recently began to release a few of the women who are married to Caucasian men. The main stipulation is that their homes be predominately of American influence." The sheriff waved a hand toward the cheery yellow bungalow behind them. "I don't think you can get much more American than that. I don't see any reason for Mrs. Laroux to leave here."

Rock reached out and pumped the sheriff's hand in gratitude. "Thank you, sir! Thank you!"

Sheriff Bentley laughed. "You're welcome, son. All I ask is that you save me one or two juicy melons when they're ripe."

Rock looked to Miko and smiled. "We'll save you a dozen if you like."

The sheriff laughed and opened his car door, sliding inside. "You both should know we couldn't find Norman Ness last night. His place looked like it had been cleared out in a hurry. I've got men keeping an eye out for him, but for all appearances, he's left the area."

Relieved, Miko leaned against Rock. He patted her back and nodded to the sheriff. "That's good news, sir. I hope he stays gone."

"Me, too." He shut his door and started the car. "Stay out of trouble and make sure you keep those melons watered. I want mine extra juicy." With a wave, he left.

"Whew!" Rock said, giving Miko a hug and swinging her off her feet. "That was close."

"I can't believe the sheriff allowed me to stay here," she said, walking with Rock back into the house.

"I can't either, Miko, but I'm so grateful that he did."

**** *Chapter Twenty* ***

June melted into July without more trouble from Norman Ness. Convinced Rock had scared him enough he left the area, they didn't give another thought to his disturbing presence.

The heat wave continued and the garden exploded with ripe vegetables. In addition to lettuce, radishes, tomatoes, cucumbers, and early carrots, Miko and Rock harvested beets, beans, onions, and the first golden ears of sweet corn.

They celebrated Independence Day with the Phillips family, inviting them over for a picnic in the backyard, complete with sweet cherry and chocolate ice cream.

Pastor Clark arrived early one morning with the news that the Portland Assembly Center released another group of women to rejoin their non-Japanese husbands.

"Do you know what that means, Miko?" he asked, smiling at her as he closed the door to the chicken pen behind her.

"No, Uncle George, but I'm sure you'll tell me." She carried the eggs to the barn, where she set them in cartons and noted the date on the side.

His grin broadened. "It means there is no reason for you to continue to hide. No one will think anything of you being here with Rock, now that other women are returning to their homes. The only stipulation the administrator mentioned is the homes have to be traditionally American, with no Japanese influence."

Miko waved a hand toward her grandparents' charming bungalow. "That's what the sheriff said when he visited. This house has never been anything but traditionally American, just like the occupants."

"I know, Miko, I know." Pastor Clark patted her on the back with sympathy in his gaze. "In light of this development, you may come and go as you please. There is no need for you to hide."

She shook her head as the pastor followed her to the garden, where she filled a large basket with fresh produce for him to take home. "I still think it's best, for Rock's sake and the success of the business, if I stay out of sight."

"Oh, bosh. If you want to stand behind the counter at the produce stand and greet every customer, go right ahead. Most people will be happy to see you, Miko. And those who aren't, well... don't worry about them. I'm sure Rock doesn't." The pastor accepted the basket she held out to him and followed her back to the house.

"Would you like to come in for a cup of tea or some breakfast? I made muffins this morning. Rock must not be feeling well today because he left three of them behind instead of eating every last one of them."

The pastor laughed. "No, Miko, I need to get back to town, but I wanted to make sure you heard the news as soon as possible."

"Thank you for delivering it, Uncle George." She walked with him out to where he'd parked his car. "Have you visited the folks recently?" she asked, shoving her hands into the pockets of her pants and swirling the toe of her worn blue canvas shoe in the gravel by his front tire.

"I saw them yesterday. The fire department had been there. Since it is so hot, they thought it might help to hose down the outside of the building. It did cool the interior for a while, but the water soaked into the manure beneath the floor." The pastor wrinkled his nose as he set the basket in the backseat of the car, then turned back to her. "Goodness, but that did smell. Other than that, though, your family is doing well, Miko. Your grandfather and a few of the other farmers have planted a large garden and that keeps them busy. Your father and brother are also doing work around the center, and your grandmother has been teaching some of the younger girls how to embroider and crochet."

"I'll have to purchase some thread and yarn for Grandma," Miko said, brightening at the thought of her family keeping themselves occupied.

"I know how badly you want to see them, Miko, but that is the one place I would advise you not go. Let Rock take whatever you want to send."

Miko nodded, then gave the pastor a hug. "If you talk to Sally, tell her I mailed another letter with a little something for Drew."

"I'll do that." The pastor pulled a package from his car and handed it to her.

"What's this?" Miko gave him a questioning glance.

"Hadley asked me to give these photos to you. She took them at your wedding." He slid into his car and gave her a wave before pulling away.

Miko walked back to the house, and Rock caught up with her on the front porch.

"What do you have there?" he asked, motioning to the paper-wrapped parcel she held.

"Photographs from our wedding."

Rock pointed to a porch chair and waited as Miko took a seat, then folded back the paper. She lifted an ornate gold picture frame in her hands and stared at the photo. Hadley had captured them beneath the feathery branches of the weeping willow tree.

The setting appeared tranquil and beautiful, but the look on Rock's face held her interest. Adoration shone from his eyes as he gazed at her in the image. Did he truly care for her? Love her? From the emotion on his face Hadley had caught, she wondered if it could be true.

Rock leaned over her shoulder and smiled. "That's a nice photograph. Hadley has quite a way with a camera."

"She does," Miko agreed, taking a packet of photos from the paper. Together she and Rock studied them.

"I like this one best," Rock said, holding out a picture of the two of them laughing. He couldn't recall what had been said at the moment, but something had struck them both as funny.

With a critical eye, Miko shook her head. "The one Hadley framed is my favorite."

"Let's hang it in the living room." Rock took her hand in his, helping her to her feet. "Where should we put it?"

Miko followed him inside. Together, they decided to hang the picture on the wall where the wedding photos of Miko's grandparents, parents, and sister were on display.

As he pounded a hook into the wall to hold the frame, she shared the news Pastor Clark had delivered about women leaving the assembly center to return to their husbands.

"I agree with Pastor Clark. You should stop hiding. If you want to work in the produce stand or the garden or just laze the day away in a chair in the front yard, do it."

She laughed and swatted his arm. "How many times have you seen me laze a day away?"

He grinned. "Never, which is why it might not be a bad idea for you to take a day off to do nothing but relax."

"There's too much work to be done around here for such foolishness," Miko said, waving her hand outside as their helpers arrived for the day.

Rock hung the photo and stepped back to look at it. "If you change your mind, come out to the corn patch. The boys and I plan to pick all we can out there today."

"Perfect," she said, kissing his cheek in thanks for his work. He wrapped a hand around her waist and gently squeezed it before rushing outside to give the boys their work assignments for the day.

Even if she didn't intend to pursue her feelings for him, she did enjoy his attention.

That afternoon, she made a big batch of brownies, although she hated to heat the house by using the oven. While the decadent smell of chocolate filled every corner of the kitchen, she squeezed the juice out of several ripe peaches Rock had carried in that morning, mixing the sweet liquid with a bottle of ginger ale.

She took a tablecloth outside to the picnic table where their helpers often ate their lunch in the shade of the storage building and spread it over the surface. A vase of cheerful blossoms adorned the center of the table.

Miko carried out glasses and a stack of paper napkins her grandmother always kept on hand for days such as this.

Finally, she filled the juice pitcher with ice and carried it with the brownies out to the table.

She donned a broad-brimmed straw hat and her sunglasses, then went in search of Rock. She found him and the young men they employed gathering up gunnysacks full of corn to carry back to the produce stand.

Rock glanced up and beamed at her as she approached them. "Hey, sweetheart. What are you doing out here?" He leaned over and kissed her cheek.

"I set out a little something for you all to enjoy," she said, slightly nervous as she balanced on the balls of her feet with her hands behind her back. Afraid her normal farm attire of rolled-up jeans and an old blouse might embarrass Rock in front of the boys who worked for him, she'd changed into a cotton summer dress and slipped on a pair of wedge sandals. The ensemble wasn't the best choice to wear out to a corn patch, but the clothes made her feel confident and fashionable.

"That's wonderful," Rock said, grinning as four boys stared at his bride. "Guys, this is my wife, Mrs. Laroux."

The boys all smiled politely, albeit a little shocked to meet their employer's wife. They had assumed he had one since someone obviously made food while they harvested the cherries, but they hadn't seen her.

Impressed by the tall, elegant woman with a beautiful smile, the boys appeared caught up in the spell of her charm.

Miko smiled at them, then turned to her husband. "And who are the boys, Rock?"

He made the introductions, then motioned for the young men to heft sacks of corn and head back to the produce stand.

Miko preceded them and introduced herself to the two girls working there. Since it was nearly closing time, she invited them to join in the refreshments and helped them close down the stand for the evening.

"Gosh, Mrs. Laroux, I love your dress. It's perfectly peachy!" The more outgoing of the two girls chatted about clothes and current fashions as Miko walked with them to the picnic table.

The boys and Rock soon met them there with hastily washed faces and hands. While Miko poured drinks and passed out the glasses, the girls cast flirty glances at the boys. In turn, the boys covertly watched Miko.

When all the teens left for the day, Rock settled an arm around Miko's shoulders and tugged her against his side. "I'm so proud of you for coming out to meet the crew today, Miko. As you can see, the kids are quite taken with you."

"That's only because they have no idea I'm different from them," she said as she set glasses on the empty brownie platter and carried it inside.

Rock held the pitcher in one hand with the tablecloth draped over his arm and followed her. "Those boys are so smitten, they wouldn't notice if you came from a different planet. And in case you missed it, both the girls emulated your every move."

Miko set the platter on the counter, then removed her sunglasses and hat. With a disbelieving glare, she took the empty pitcher from him and placed it in the sink. "I doubt that. I'm sure you were mistaken." She washed the pitcher, then soaped the glasses. "It was nice to meet the kids you talk about all the time. I've seen them from a distance, out the windows, but they are a nice bunch."

"They are, although the girls become distracted if I let the boys linger around the produce stand too long."

She laughed and began drying the dishes. "Imagine that... a good-looking boy distracting a silly girl."

"Well, this boy is very distracted by his lovely wife." Rock tugged the dish towel from her hand, then walked in a circle around her, intently studying her from head to toe. "Have I seen this dress before?"

"No," she said, and snatched the dish towel, desperate to tamp down the syrupy warm feelings he inspired in her midsection with his perusal. "I haven't had much occasion to dress up since you've been here."

"I suppose not," he said. It was a shame she didn't wear dresses more often, especially with those long, long legs of hers. The floral-print dress hugged her waist and swished around her knees. It wasn't anything fancy, but it certainly sent his thoughts zooming off in a husbandly direction.

Before they got too far out of line, he reeled them back in and once again removed the towel from her hand. "Since you're all dressed up, why don't I take you out for dinner tonight?"

The idea held a great deal of appeal, but she hesitated. "I think we better—"

"Hurry and get ready to go," he said, interrupting whatever she planned to say. "Give me a minute to clean up and I'll take you to that burger place on the way into town. If you wear your hat and sunglasses, no one will bother you. We can stay in the car if you like."

Resigned to indulging him, she smiled. "Fine, but you better hurry or I'll leave without you."

"Yes, ma'am."

★ *Chapter Twenty-One* ★

Miko stretched and grasped a juicy, ripe peach in her hand. The ladder wobbled beneath her and she gasped, reaching for the pail on top of the ladder's platform to keep the fruit she'd picked from spilling.

Three pairs of hands hurried to steady the ladder.

"Thank you, boys," she said in a smooth, velvety voice, beaming at the young men who had rushed to her rescue and gazed up at her with unbridled adoration.

"Sure thing, Mrs. Laroux."

"Our pleasure, Mrs. Laroux."

"Anything for you, Mrs. Laroux."

Rock rolled his eyes and swallowed the urge to holler at his crew to get back to work.

Since the day she'd offered them brownies and sweet peach fizz, all the kids they'd hired, even the girls, had been fascinated with Miko.

Fashionable, funny, witty, and smart, it was no wonder their hired help thought she was the best thing to come along since soda pop. The boys fell all over themselves trying to impress her, and the girls asked her advice about clothes, hairstyles, makeup, and boys.

Rock was happy they all doted on his wife. He wasn't sure any of them had even noticed she was Japanese since she kept her sunglasses on most of the time when she was outside. Beyond the shape of her eyes, it was hard to deduce her ethnicity, especially with her long legs.

Those legs, the ones that danced through many of Rock's dreams, were on full display as Miko carefully turned around on the ladder and smiled at the boys lingering below her.

After lunch, she ventured out to the orchard to help them pick peaches. A pair of high-waisted navy-blue shorts with white buttons marching down both sides along the front replaced the rolled-up denims she'd had on that morning. A white blouse trimmed with red piping and a pair of dark blue canvas shoes gave her an all-American appeal. To embellish the image, she'd taken time to curl her long hair into a bouncing, shimmering midnight mass. A red polka-dotted scarf knotted into a headband with a jaunty bow held her silky tresses out of her face while she worked.

Perched on the ladder with an alluring smile on her ruby lips, she could have posed for a pinup poster. Experienced with the ideas and comments those posters generated among men starved for the attention of women, Rock scowled. The notion of Miko being the object of anyone's lustful thoughts besides his caused raw anger to boil in his belly.

Jealous of the attention she gave the boys and annoyed by their rapt interest in his bride, Rock wished she'd head back to the house before his patience completely unraveled.

Astutely sensing his unease, Miko lifted an inquisitive eyebrow above her sunglasses. He felt the weight of her gaze even though her eyes remained hidden as he balanced on top of a ladder in the tree next to hers.

"Rock, darling, would you mind terribly if I head back to the house?" she asked, providing a reason for her to leave. "Dinner will be cold sandwiches if I don't get something started." The flirtatious smile she threw in his direction would have caused lesser men to topple off the ladder.

Rock set the bucket in his hand into a fork in the tree and scrambled down so fast he skipped the last half dozen rungs of the ladder. Before one of the teens could offer to help Miko, he moved in front of them.

One tempting step at a time, she descended the ladder facing forward, clutching the pail of peaches beneath her bosom in such a way it enhanced her curves. Any number of thoughts raced through Rock's head, none of which would help him accomplish any work.

As soon as she was within reach, he took the pail from her and handed it to one of the boys, then placed both hands on her waist, swinging her to the ground.

"I think it's a great idea for you to head in, sweetheart." Rock pecked her cheek with a quick kiss. "We'll wrap things up here just before five."

"I'll see you boys later." She waggled her fingers at Rock's helpers, then turned to him. "Especially you, Captain."

"Go on with you, you tease." He leaned close and whispered so only she could hear. "If you don't stop your movie star performance and skedaddle, the boys will be worthless the rest of the day."

Her grin widened and she moved away from him. Rock swatted her backside with the flat of his hand, causing her to spin around and raise both eyebrows at him before she left.

Shaded by the trees, four males watched her leave while the sweet scent of peaches mingled with Miko's unique floral scent.

Rock inhaled a deep breath, filling his lungs with the aroma before thumping his hand on the shoulder of the young man closest to him. "Let's get back to it, men. The peaches won't jump into the buckets without a little help."

A satisfied smile buoyed Miko's spirits all the way back to the house. She waved at four boys who worked in the vegetable garden, watering and weeding. After checking on the girls in the produce stand and bringing them a cool drink, she decided to work in the flower bed around the house.

With every weed she pulled, she thought of the jealous spark in Rock's eyes as the boys waited to help her off the ladder. Miko no more needed their help than she needed a second nose, but she'd enjoyed seeing Rock's reaction to their attention. Since the day he'd introduced her to the teens he'd hired, she'd done her best to charm them all.

She genuinely liked the kids and enjoyed spending time around them, but for Rock's sake, she needed them to accept her. And they had.

Admittedly, she might have been trying to get Rock's attention back in the orchard as she'd stepped down the ladder. Between the women peering at him at the produce stand and the innocent flirting of girls they employed, Miko felt defensive and unreasonably upset.

Even if she was his wife in name only, she still held the possessive feelings of a married woman. Perhaps Rock had gotten a dose of his own medicine today.

Her lips tipped up in a grin as she recalled him referring to her as a tease and playfully swatting her backside as she left the orchard.

Pleased with life in general and her husband in particular, Miko planned the dinner menu in her head as she worked. She compiled a mental list of chores she planned to accomplish the following day as she tended to the flowers.

She stood to carry a pile of weeds to the compost pile behind the pigpen when she heard the sound of running footsteps. Quickly turning, she watched Petey race across the pasture.

Tears streamed down his freckled cheeks and the breeze fanned his hair without his cap to hold it in place.

The weeds fell from her hands and she opened her arms to the boy. Petey vaulted into them, crying against her neck with distraught wails.

"Petey! My gracious! What in the world is the matter?" she asked, carrying him over to a stone bench beneath a maple tree and taking a seat, holding him tightly in her arms.

He continued to cry, unable to speak as he sucked in ragged breaths between sobs.

"It's okay, honey. It's okay," Miko said, rocking back and forth. Soothingly, she rubbed her hand up and down his back.

From out of nowhere, Rock appeared, dropping onto a knee in front of them. A callused hand settled on the back of Petey's head as he looked at Miko with unspoken questions. She shrugged and continued to rock the boy.

"Petey? Can you tell us what's wrong? Are you hurt? Did something happen to your sister? To your folks?" Rock asked, brushing the boy's hair away from his face. "What happened, Petey? Did someone harm you?" The big man leaned back to get a gander at the child, to surmise if there were any visible wounds.

The trembling little body in Miko's arms stilled and he swallowed a big gulp. Petey sat up and swiped his nose across one sleeve, his eyes across the other, and pulled himself together.

"Harm me? Harm me!" The boy shook his head, sending his bright red locks into greater disarray. "Heck no! No one harmed me, unless you call ripping out my heart and stomping it to pieces harmed. If that's the case, if that's the way of it, then you bet your life I've been harmed!"

Miko kissed his cheek and continued rubbing his back. "What happened, Petey? Who broke your heart?"

"My friend Ryatt, that's who. I've never had so much everlastingly awful trouble as I've had today," Petey said. He sniffled and wiped his nose on his sleeve again.

Just when Rock thought the boy might hop off Miko's lap and scamper home, he leaned into her and sighed again, as though he'd found a place of rest.

"What kind of trouble?" Rock asked, continuing to hunker in front of Miko and the boy.

"The kind no one should have. Ryatt's folks... well, they..." Petey's eyes sparkled with tears and his lower lip quivered, but he took another deep breath. "Those nasty, rotten blighters in the Pacific, well, they shot up Ryatt's dad pretty good last month. An officer knocked on the door this morning to let them know his dad had... his dad was... dead."

"Oh, honey," Miko wrapped her arms around Petey again and kissed the top of his head. "I'm so sorry."

"You can't be that sorry yet. You ain't heard the worst of it." Petey jerked upright and looked from Miko to Rock. "It's about the most horrible, awful story that'll ever pass through your ears. Ryatt's mama was plenty shook up this morning, but she needed to see to arrangements, that's what she and my folks kept calling them, arrangements, for Ryatt's dad. So she brung him over to our house to stay while she went to town. Poor ol' Ry was trying hard to be brave and act like life was just as swell as ever, but he stayed close to Mom and sat real quiet with her and the princess. Well, Pop decided to head into town and see about making some arrangements of his own. He wasn't gone any time before he tore up our lane, sending grass and gravel flying and yelling at Mom to get on the phone and call the sheriff. There'd been an accident."

"Oh, no," Miko whispered, anticipating the rest of the story.

"Oh, yes," Petey said, unable to contain his tears. They rolled in great sorrowful drops down his cheeks as he finished the tale. "Pop thinks Ryatt's mama was so upset by the news of his daddy dying that she missed the curve in the road down by Mr. Donald's place and ran the car right into a tree. I wasn't supposed to listen, but I snuck into the kitchen and hid under the table while my folks were talking. Pop said Ryatt's mama was in bad shape, but she squeezed his hand and said it was an accident and she didn't want to leave her baby. Before Pop could do anything to help her, she up and died."

Miko's tears mingled with Petey's as she held him close again and rained kisses on his head. "Oh, you poor thing."

Petey pushed upright once again and slid over onto the bench. He held onto Miko's hand and leaned his head against her side. "If you keep a- lovin' on me, Miko, I'll never get through this. This whole danged day is mixing up things inside here..." Petey pointed to his chest "... that ought not to be stirred. But I'll tell it to the world I'm not the one who needs a hug and your tears, that'd be Ry. When my folks told him about his mama, he took off running down the road. Pop had to hit the floor with all cylinders pumping to catch him before he got to the wreck. He carried him back to our house. Mom called Granny to come watch the princess because her hands are about full to overflowing with handling Ry. He cried so much, he almost suffocated, but he finally went to sleep. I just couldn't swallow any more of watching him, seeing him hurt so bad, so I hotfooted it over here."

"Does your mother know you're here?" Rock asked, rising from his crouched position.

Petey gave him a disgusted look. "Mom and Pop have plenty enough worries without me piling on more today. A' course she knows I'm here. I always play the game square and today ain't no eggception."

Rock hunkered back down and placed a gentle hand on the boy's shoulder. "I'm really sorry about your friend and his family, Petey. It's a terrible loss for you all."

"Thanks, Cap." The boy jumped off the bench, barely able to contain his nervous energy.

"May I walk you home, Petey?" Rock asked, rising to his feet, then giving a hand to Miko as she stood.

"I'm not ready for home just yet. Mom is hovering over Ry and he's sniffling and crying in his sleep. Granny is walking around with a hankie in one hand and the princess in the other, muttering about the bomb nations of war, whatever that means."

"Abominations," Rock supplied.

"Yep, that's what she said. Anyway, Pop went back to the wreck and was going to go with the sheriff into town and make arrangements. There's that word again. Ry's aunt is on her way from her ranch, but won't be here till tomorrow. I can't go back to all the tears at our house. Not just yet. Can you put me to work pulling weeds or picking peas or even cleaning up after the three little pigs? Please? I'll do anything." Petey turned pleading blue eyes up to Miko, then Rock.

"Sure, pardner." Rock ruffled the boy's hair. "How about you stay with Miko while I run over to see if there's anything I can do to help your folks?"

"That'd be swell, Cap." Petey wrapped wiry, tanned little arms around Rock's legs and squeezed, then looked up at him with a watery smile. "I knew you were a straight arrow."

Rock grinned, bending down to hug the child. "I'm glad you think so." As he straightened, he glimpsed Miko's face. She brushed at her tears with the palms of her hands so he handed her his handkerchief. "Will you be okay for a little while?"

"Yes, of course." Her low voice made something inside him thrum, but he ignored it. She fussed with the handkerchief, wiping her eyes and dabbing at her nose. "Please give them my condolences and find out if there's anything we can do. I'd be happy to send over food or help with whatever they need."

"I'll be back as soon as I can." Rock delivered a hasty kiss to her cheek, gave Petey an encouraging nod, and strode off through the pasture in the direction of the Phillips farm.

Petey watched him go with an open look of admiration. "I sure like him, Miko. Since you wouldn't wait for me to grow up, I'm glad you married him."

She smiled and settled a hand on the boy's thin shoulder. "Me, too." With a quick glance around, her gaze fell on the boys working in the garden. She recalled three more worked in the orchard. "Do you really want something to do, Petey?"

"You betcha. Point the way and I'm on the job." The boy clicked his heels together and gave her a snappy salute.

Miko laughed softly. "In that case, would you run up to the orchard and tell the boys they may go home for the day as soon as they carry the boxes they've filled down to the produce stand. And when you finish with that, would you pop over to the garden and tell those boys the same? The girls in the produce stand will know to close things up on time."

Barely had the last word left her lips before Petey took off at a dead run for the orchard. Miko hurried into the house to begin preparing a mountain of food to send over to the Phillips family.

Rock returned an hour later with his mouth set in a grim line. At Miko's concerned glance, he shook his head and looked pointedly in Petey's direction.

Miko nodded and suggested Petey might like to help Rock milk the cows. When the chores were finished, she called and spoke with Lucy Phillips. Ryatt continued to alternate between tears and sleep, so Lucy agreed it was fine for Petey to eat supper there.

After the three of them partook of the frankfurters on split buns, baked macaroni with cheese, and slices of tomatoes Miko served for dinner, Rock and Petey helped her box the food she'd prepared for the Phillips family.

"Gosh, Miko, do you think we'll have an army camped at our house?" Petey asked as he carried a box with two pies out to the sedan Rock had parked near the back gate.

"No, but I expect you'll have plenty of extra mouths to feed. Does Ryatt just have one aunt?"

Petey nodded his head and followed her back to the kitchen, where she handed him a tin full of chocolate cookies. Together, they returned outside. "Yep, but his Aunt Dee makes up for only having one. Talk about a real, royal, bee's knees kind of girl, Ry's Aunt Dee is it." With care, he placed the tin on the green grass, then his small palms slid together with a smack to illustrate that "it" was indeed something special. The boy turned to Rock. "She's almost as spiffy as Miko." An endearing grin came from the freckled imp as he picked up the cookies and ran to the car.

Rock drove while Petey sat next to Miko on the front seat, leaning against her. They'd barely crossed the gravel of the driveway before the boy fell asleep.

"He's completely exhausted," Miko said quietly, feathering her fingers through the disheveled red hair.

A sudden, unbidden vision of her doing the same to a child with black hair and his own blue eyes hit Rock in the chest with the force of a hammer. The realization that he wanted a family, a family created by his love for Miko, left him contemplative as they made the drive up John and Lucy Phillips's lane.

Miko carried Petey inside and handed him to his father while Lucy and her mother helped Rock pack in the food.

Lucy and Miko shared a reassuring embrace, then Rock and Miko returned to their farm.

By unspoken agreement, they sat on the front porch swing in the gathering darkness and watched the stars come out.

"That poor little boy," Miko said, leaning her head back and realizing Rock had draped his arm along the top of the swing. Without giving a thought to her actions, she scooted closer to him, resting her head against the curve of his shoulder. After such an unsettling day, she needed the comfort of another human's touch.

Rock drew her closer and kissed the top of her head. "I can't even imagine what the Danvers boy is going through. To lose both parents in one day, it's more than anyone should have to bear, especially one so young."

Miko nodded against his chest. "What will Petey do? Lucy said Ryatt's aunt plans to take him back to her ranch in eastern Oregon. Those two boys are inseparable. You've seen how they spend nearly every waking moment together."

"Maybe we can find a few chores to help keep Petey occupied. School will start in another month or so, won't it?"

"Yes, but I imagine that won't be any easier. Those two boys were in the same class. Petey has other friends, but Ryatt is his best friend." Miko wrapped her arms around Rock's waist and gave it a tight squeeze. "Thank you for being so wonderful with him today. You're very good with children."

"I haven't been around them much, but I like them just fine." Rock glanced down at her in the darkness. "I think it would be more than fine to have a few with you."

Abruptly stiffening, she would have pulled away, but Rock held on, keeping her close. "Don't run off just yet," he whispered against the fragrant shadows of her hair. "Days like this make me wish wars didn't exist. Good men shouldn't have to die to stop those bent on destruction and terror."

Filled with a sense that Rock's need to be held was as strong as her own, Miko lingered. In silence, they listened to the symphony of crickets and frogs, of the breeze blowing through the trees, and breathed in the heady aroma of the moonflowers blooming in the flowerbeds.

At length, she kissed Rock's cheek, then stood.

"What was that for?" he asked, rolling his head back to look at her with a lazy grin on his face.

She almost sat back down. Almost took his hand and pulled him inside the house with her. But she didn't.

Instead, she took a step away from the temptation her husband presented. "For being such a good man, Rock Laroux." The night closed behind her as she rushed around the house and disappeared on her way up to the secluded hilltop home.

★ *Chapter Twenty-Two* ★

Steady streams of rain drizzled from a concrete-hued sky on the attendees of Carol Danvers's funeral.

Next to Petey, Ryatt leaned against his aunt, Delaney, withdrawn as his mother's body was laid to rest.

At the end of the service, Delaney Danvers thanked everyone for coming, then ushered Ryatt to the car that would take them to catch the afternoon train to Pendleton.

Petey followed, flinging his arms around his friend. "I'll never, ever, ever forget you, Ry. You'll always be my best friend. I'll write all the time and I'll think of you every day."

Delaney bent over and hugged Petey. "Thank you for being such a good friend to Ryatt, Petey. You are always welcome to visit him at the ranch. Don't forget that."

"I won't." Petey's lower lip quivered as Delaney nudged Ryatt, numb and silent, into the car. Before the car pulled away, the traumatized boy lifted a hand and pressed it against the glass of the backseat window.

Petey buried his face against his mother's skirts and cried, great wracking sobs, for the loss of his friend and for all his friend had lost.

Miko fought back her own tears, grateful when Rock took her elbow and escorted her to their car. It was the first time she'd been at a public gathering since May. At least her broad-brimmed black hat with the thick netting hid most of her face. Beneath the dark umbrella Rock held over their heads, no one had paid her any mind.

In the days that followed the funeral and Ryatt's departure to his aunt's eastern Oregon ranch, Petey spent a considerable amount of time at the Double J Farm, helping Miko and Rock. With their permission, he showed up one sunshiny morning with troops of Cub Scouts and Boy Scouts. The boys and their fathers loaded every piece of scrap metal from the open shed near the barn.

Miko brought out refreshments and watched as the boys loaded everything from wagon wheels to broken scythes.

Rock took the glass of lemonade she held out to him and drank deeply. "With the care your grandfather put into keeping everything neat and tidy on the farm, I don't understand why the shed was full of rusted junk."

Miko poured lemonade for the boys and passed out cookies. "None of that belonged to my family."

At his baffled expression, she explained, "When my great-grandparents bought this property, the neighbors around here didn't like having foreigners in their area. People treated them terribly. They'd bring all their garbage and dump it in my great-grandfather's garden. Chickens were stolen. Cows were turned loose. Once, someone even took an ax to their wagon and hacked it into pieces only usable for firewood."

"Why did your great-grandparents stay?" Rock asked, shocked by the horrid treatment they'd endured.

"Because this was their home. In time, the neighbors stopped seeing them as a foreign enemy and began to trust them as friends. Among the few people who were kind to them was John Phillips's grandfather. He bought the ground and started his farm not long after my great-grandparents moved here. They worked together and helped one another."

Rock smiled. "It's nice to see the good traditions continue." He inclined his head toward Petey as the boy gave his fellow scout members a tour of the vegetable garden and berry patch, then introduced them to the three pigs.

"I'm glad to see Petey showing a spark of life again." Miko sipped her lemonade. She'd used a portion of her sugar ration to make it, but it was worth it. "I worried about him."

Rock settled his arm around her shoulders and gave her a tender hug. "From what I've observed, children are resilient. John said Petey received a letter from Ryatt and that made all the difference in the world."

"Oh, I'm glad to hear Ryatt wrote to him. I feared that poor boy might never find his way back to the land of the living. He seemed so..." Miko struggled to find the right word.

"Lethargic?"

Miko nodded. "That's a good description, but more than that. Almost like his spirit had wilted. I'm sure his aunt will have her hands full once Ryatt returns to normal."

"She certainly will if Petey ever takes her up on the offer to visit." Rock chuckled. "Can you see those two little ruffians running wild over a cattle and wheat ranch?"

"John and Lucy might never get Petey to return home if they let him go," Miko mused, watching as the boys finished their snacks. The youngsters thanked her and Rock for helping the war effort and for the refreshments. The troop left in a flurry of waving hands and shouted goodbyes.

Once the trucks disappeared down the road, Rock helped Miko carry the dishes back inside the house, then she helped him load the car for his weekly trip to town.

Hurriedly, he changed into a pair of creased trousers and a shirt with a tie, carrying his suit coat over his arm as he returned to the kitchen. As he did each Tuesday, he planned to take the excess butter, cream, buttermilk, and eggs into town. After he left Mr. Ross's store, he would visit Miko's family, attend to other errands, then pick up groceries they needed on his way home.

"Did you get the yarn and embroidery thread for grandmother?" Miko asked, following him to the car he parked outside the back gate.

Rock grinned as he tossed his suit coat on the seat, then turned back to her. "I sure did. I have the letters you wrote them, the gloves for the men, and the magazines for your mother."

She nodded, pleased he'd remembered everything she wanted to send to her family along with the produce, crackers, cheese, and cookies he always gave them. "It looks like you have everything," she said, rocking back and forth on the balls of her feet.

"Do you want to come along? You could wear your hat and wait in the car while I see your folks." Rock reached out and grabbed her hand, pulling her closer to him. "I'd enjoy your company."

"That's sweet, Rock, but I better stay here. There's plenty of work to keep me busy, and I don't like to leave the place unattended too long. You know something strange always happens when we do."

"I know, but I worry more about something happening to you." He brushed his knuckles over the smooth skin of her cheek. The day of Mrs. Danvers funeral, they'd arrived home to find all the chickens loose. Another evening after that, they returned from a picnic supper in the hilltop garden to discover the cows grazing on the flowers around the house and several pumpkin plants pulled up by their roots.

He would have blamed Norman Ness for the trouble, but no one had seen him since the day Rock had bloodied his nose. Sheriff Bentley let them know Norman seemed to have left the area for good.

Concerned about leaving Miko alone, but knowing he needed to go, he wrapped his arms around her and held her close. "Please be careful while I'm gone. I'm sure Lucy wouldn't mind if you wanted to go over there for a visit. Most likely, Petey will show up once he finishes with his scrap drive. From what John said, those boys have picked up every piece of metal that isn't nailed down over at his place."

"They probably grabbed a few that were, too." Miko grinned and returned Rock's embrace. It was getting harder and harder for her to fight her feelings for him, to subdue her desire for her beguiling husband.

The more time she spent with him, the deeper in love she fell until she couldn't imagine a future without him in it. Rock was so much more than physically attractive. He embodied all the characteristics Miko admired most: kindness, loyalty, dedication, gentleness, and tenacity. He laughed easily, worked hard, and treated the teens that worked for them fairly and with patience.

Miko could spend a lifetime searching for someone she admired, respected and loved as much as Rock, but she had an idea she'd never find anyone who measured up to the standard he set.

With one final, tight hug, she stepped back and smiled at him. "Give everyone my love and tell them the plums should be ready next week."

"I will, Kamiko," Rock said in a husky tone, cupping her chin with his right hand. "Why don't you spend the day reading or soaking up some sunshine? Do something fun for a change. You work far too hard."

She tipped her head to the side with a masked expression. "I'll consider the idea."

Rock chuckled. "That means you'll think about it long enough to say you considered it and then go on with whatever you already have planned." His hand released her chin, but he surprised her when he slid it beneath the heavy weight of her ponytail and rested it on the back of her neck.

His lips brushed across hers in a light, tentative touch before he kissed her with a rising longing that made it hard for him to pull away. Much to his delight, her hands slid up his shoulders and she returned his kiss.

"I better go," he whispered, resting his forehead against hers.

"Yes, you should." Her eyes remained on his lips as he dropped his hand and stepped back.

One smoldering glance later, he got into the car and closed the door. "Stay out of trouble," he called with a wave as he drove past the house and down the drive to the road.

★ *Chapter Twenty-Three* ★

A scowl plowed two deep horizontal furrows across Norman Ness's pallid brow. He dabbed at his clammy forehead with a grayed handkerchief and stuffed it back into his shirt pocket, sinking lower into the lumpy seat of his car.

He'd waited as the noisy, obnoxious kids and their do-gooder fathers had loaded the scrap metal in a truck and hauled it away from the old Jap's farm.

Normally, the pretty-faced soldier boy would already be on his way to town to peddle fresh eggs and butter. Norman knew that because he'd spent plenty of time observing the comings and goings at the farm. He also knew how good the butter tasted and how fresh the eggs were. In the last month, as he lurked around corners and learned the habits of the occupants of the place, he'd helped himself a few times.

Thanks to Laroux reporting him to the sheriff, Norman had to leave his childhood home and rent a cheap apartment in a run-down part of town. He figured helping himself to some of the produce was a fair trade for the money the soldier cost him by making it impossible for Norman to return to his home.

During his weeks of surveillance, he'd observed that a bunch of giggling, gangly teens descended on the farm every Wednesday through Saturday, working from early morning until the stand closed each evening.

Sundays, Norman liked to sleep in late. After lunch, he visited a woman named Verlene who only charged two dollars for an afternoon of her services. By the time evening rolled around, he wasn't in a mood to go anywhere. He had no idea what happened at the farm on Sundays, but he couldn't imagine it was any different from Mondays. The man and his woman worked outside, pulling weeds and watering crops.

Every Tuesday, pretty boy would leave midmorning and return late afternoon.

Twice, Norman had followed him, just to see where he went for the day. He'd envisioned some tawdry dalliance, but both times Mr. Upright Citizen had dropped eggs and butter at a little grocery store owned by a man Norman greatly disliked. The nosy old coot asked too many questions and seemed incapable of minding his own business. Why should he care if Norman wanted booze and cigarettes for lunch instead of one of the smelly bologna sandwiches he offered?

From the grocery store, soldier boy generally ran a few errands, stopping places like the telephone office, the electric company, or the bank.

Then he made a long drive to the far side of Portland. Norman had choked on the piece of candy he accidentally swallowed when he realized the man went to the place where the government had rounded up all the Japs in the area.

Mr. Goody Two-Shoes turned out to be a true traitor, carrying boxes of food to those stinkin' Japs.

Norman didn't care a whole lot about his country and even less about patriotism, but he despised the Japs. Most of his hatred stemmed from the fact they seemed better off and happier in life than Norman had ever been.

The reasons they were successful and cheerful never entered his narrow mind, just the notion they had something he wanted.

And what Norman wanted, more than anything, was the Yamada farm. Oh, he'd heard the interloper had given it a new name, calling it the Double something or other. Norman didn't care.

He'd teach the soldier a lesson, and his Jap woman, too.

Norman mused over his plans and sucked on a piece of his favorite sour candy, waiting across the road from the farm to see if this Tuesday would pass like the others.

After what seemed like hours, the pretty boy and his woman walked outside. Norman sneered as they embraced and slid farther down in his seat when the soldier drove by on the road. He hoped the man was too distracted to notice his car partially hidden behind the blackberry bushes.

Norman waited a few minutes, then followed the car into town. He parked a block away, watching as the soldier-turned-farmer carried butter, eggs, and cream into the store. More than thirty minutes passed before he left the building, waving to the crazy old goat inside.

While he sat in the sweltering car, Norman sucked on sour candy, mopped at his forehead, and fought down a woozy feeling. Tired beyond endurance, he wanted to curl up on a soft bed and sleep for a week.

Later, there would be plenty of time to rest. First, he had to gain control of the farm and earn money from logging the trees.

In an effort to find out exactly the kind of money he would make off the place, he'd escorted a tree expert out there one day. He had parked well away from the house and produce stand on the far side of the property, where thick trees rose from the road up to the skyline behind the fence that surrounded the property. The expert had walked around, studying bark, staring at trees. The man nearly danced a jig when they found half a dozen trees of some rare variety. According to the fancy-suited schmuck, those trees alone would bring in enough money to make Norman very comfortable, and he'd still have the rest of the trees and property to dispose of as he chose.

Norman wished he'd written down what type of tree the man had said they were, or even what they looked like. The past few weeks, he'd struggled to remember things. Blame for his memory loss landed squarely on the burly soldier who'd caused him so much grief by his untimely arrival at the farm Norman had eyed for his own.

Attribution for the ache in Norman's joints, the constant prodding pain in his stomach, and his lack of appetite went to Laroux, too. Norman hadn't felt like himself for weeks. The root of all his problems started with the soldier who'd marched right in and purchased the farm Norman had planned to claim.

None of it would matter after today.

By the time evening rolled around, Laroux and his woman would no longer be an issue.

Norman thought long and hard about the easiest way to kill them both. It wouldn't take much effort on his part, just a little more patience.

He wiped the beads of perspiration from his brow and spied on the soldier. The man ran a few errands, then headed north.

Rather than follow him to the stockyard for Japs, as Norman referred to the assembly center, he turned his car in the direction of his place. He had time for a nap before implementing his plans.

Norman awoke four hours later, drenched in sweat and fuzzy-headed. His stomach roiled, a sharp pain throbbed behind his left eye, and, for several seconds, he couldn't remember anything except his own name.

Eventually, he recalled returning home for a nap and drinking two beers before falling asleep. A glance at the clock on the scarred bedside stand jolted him off the rickety bed. If he didn't hurry, he'd miss his window of opportunity and have to wait another week before taking possession of the farm.

With shaky movements, he pulled on the shirt he'd discarded earlier and fumbled with the buttons. Tremors combined with the numbness in his hands left them barely functioning. Norman released a string of curses as he forced his fingers to cooperate and finished buttoning his shirt. He stuffed it into the waist of his trousers, shoved his swollen feet into shoes, and hurriedly picked up his ill-fitting suit jacket. After sliding it on, he settled his father's straw panama hat on his head, picked up a box of supplies he would need, and rushed out to his car.

Out of breath and so tired he could hardly hold himself upright, he shook his head a few times and sucked on a piece of candy. The moment the wooziness subsided, he drove out to the farm and parked his car in front of the produce stand. He popped two more pieces of candy in his mouth, took a rag from the box on the seat beside him, moistened it with liquid from a bottle, and stepped out of the car.

Dizzy and chilled despite the heat of the day, Norman leaned against the car, sure the Jap woman would appear when he didn't leave. A few minutes passed and he began to think she wasn't home. His patience paid off when she strode out of the house and down the front porch steps disguised behind a broad straw hat and a pair of dark sunglasses.

If he didn't know better, didn't know she was a worthless Jap, he'd never have guessed it from her current appearance. She just looked like a tall dame with a lovely face and legs that went on forever.

Norman tipped his head down and continued leaning against the car as she made her way out the front gate and over to him.

"I'm sorry, sir," she said, offering a friendly smile. "Our produce stand isn't open today. If you'd like to come back another time, we're open Wednesday through Saturday."

Pretending he didn't hear her, Norman remained perfectly still, waiting for her to move within his reach.

"Sir?" Her footsteps ground against the gravel as she approached him. With his head down, he watched her feet enter his line of vision. "Are you well, sir?"

A few more steps and she stood beside him. "Pardon me, sir? Do you..."

Norman lifted his head and jeered at her, slapping the rag over her face before she could protest. Although she stood inches above him, Norman had the element of surprise and the strength of desperation fueling his efforts. She clawed at his fingers, trying to pull them away from her face, but Norman held fast. A satisfied smile transformed his features from those of a sullen, sallow specter to a demented lunatic when she limply fell to the ground, unconscious.

He tossed her hat aside and looped his hands beneath her arms, dragging her across the gravel and into the yard behind the house. Uncertain how long she'd remain unconscious, he hurried back to the car for the box of supplies.

Winded by the time he returned to her, he took a minute to allow air into his lungs, then tied her feet, bound her hands behind her back, and lashed her inert body to a tree. To make sure she remained silent, he shoved a rag in her mouth.

All he needed now was the deed to the farm. Once it was in his hands, he'd have a little fun with Laroux's girl, then shoot the soldier in the head when he returned home.

He lumbered up the steps into the house and began digging through cupboards and dumping out drawers.

Agitated and growing more anxious with each passing moment, Norman glanced up from the office desk he riffled through at the sound of an approaching vehicle.

Slinking into the living room, he peered out the window and watched Laroux park his car out front. He stooped and picked up the woman's hat, then eyed Norman's car before opening the gate and jogging down the front walk.

Norman didn't waste any time in taking a pistol from his pocket and holding it with trembling fingers.

Under his breath, he cussed a blue streak, willing his hands to be steady, at least long enough to put a bullet between the man's eyes.

The front door opened and the pretty boy stopped short, shocked to see Norman across the room, pointing a gun at him.

"Ness! So help me, I'll wring your scrawny neck if you —" Rock crumpled to the floor as a bullet found its mark.

Norman pocketed the gun and hurried to the back door. He'd just have to force the girl to tell him where to locate the deed.

In his haste to claim the farm as his, Norman didn't take into account the arrival of Petey Phillips.

✱✱★ *Chapter Twenty-Four* ★✱✱✱

Petey whistled as he dashed across the pasture and cut through a stand of trees to come out by the storage building on the Yamada place. He knew Rock and Miko had changed the name, but he'd always think of it as Grandpa Yamada's farm.

Excited to tell Miko all about turning in the scrap metal and holding the record for the most collected in his troop, he raced past the outbuildings and garden, looking for her.

He altered his course, scampering toward the house, wondering if she was inside baking chocolate cookies or a cake. He opened the back gate and stopped at the sight of Miko tied to a tree.

Scared, Petey listened, waiting for the sound of footsteps, but heard only banging noises from inside the house. Silently, the boy crept around until he could peek in a front window. He watched Norman Ness toss papers and upend furniture in a crazed frenzy.

Petey hurried back to Miko and took a pocketknife from the assortment of treasures in his pocket. Carefully, he cut through the ropes binding her and released the knot holding the rag over her mouth. Elated when her breath blew on his hand, even if she remained incoherent, he left her propped against the tree and formulated a plan of attack.

With the bravery borne of one too young to know better and the fearlessness possessed by a child, Petey set out to show Norman Ness he had a thing or two to learn about resourceful little boys.

On nimble feet, he ran out to Norman's car and opened the back door, locating the man's door-to-door sales cases. He carried one to the back step of the house, then raced over to the compost pile behind the pigpen. Several rotten peaches and tomatoes went into a bucket he'd grabbed on his way past the garden shed. He stopped to gather a handful of rocks from near the pump by the barn and continued on his way.

The rumble of a car as it crunched across the gravel in front of the house gave him hope that help had arrived. He zoomed back to the house with his bucket. Making as little noise as possible, he opened the sales case of marbles and spread out the contents of every marble bag across the back steps.

The boom of a gunshot burst around him, causing him to flinch and cover his ears. "Well, that's that," Petey whispered, hastening off the back step.

Miko had yet to awaken. Her champion positioned himself several feet away from the back door, set the bucket of malodorous produce at his feet, and yanked a well-used slingshot from his back pocket.

The boy dropped down on one knee to balance his arm, loaded a peach, and waited.

The second Norman stepped outside, Petey let the peach fly, hitting the man smack dab in the middle of the face.

Norman took a threatening step forward, only to have both feet fly out from beneath him on the marbles.

"Why, you sneaky, grubby little brat! When I get my hands on you…" Norman sat up and shook a fist at Petey, shock and anger pulsing off him.

Splat! A tomato found its mark, hitting Norman in the mouth.

Petey reloaded and rose to his feet. "Don't you beat your gums at me, you skunk. You're nothing but a four-flushing, gimpy-noggin thief. If you think I'll let you jitterbug out to your ugly ol' jalopy, you're even screwier than Pop says."

Norman's eyes darkened in fury and he again tried to stand, his feet sliding back and forth on the sea of marbles. "You are dead, kid. Stone cold —"

Plop! Chunks of fermenting peach joined the tomato dripping down Norman's face, stinging his eyes. He wiped his face on his saggy suit coat sleeve and spat out a chunk of decomposing fruit. "I'll hang you by your toes and —"

Pop! A rock found its mark on the back of Norman's hand as he tried to reach into his pocket. He howled in pain and shook his fingers.

"So help me, I'll skin you alive, kid!" Norman again attempted to gain purchase for his feet, but each time he did, the marbles rolled and he would slam down on the step.

Encouraged by Norman's inability to move, Petey let another tomato missile slap the man in the face. "Keep your hands where I can see 'em, you dirty, low-down cheat. If you want off that step, then crawl like the slithering snake that you are. Crawl through that juice on your slimy ol' belly."

Norman reached his hand toward his pocket again. Petey darted closer and sent a plum-sized rock sailing through the air.

Crack! The unmistakable sound of bone breaking reached the boy's ears only a second before Norman screamed and slumped back. The wounded hand, clutched to his chest, began to swell while blasphemy poured from his lips.

"You best button your lip or the next rock that flies will land square on that foul thing you use as a yap trap and knock out all your smelly teeth," the boy warned.

Norman violated the air with more curses. Petey launched a rotten peach, followed by another tomato that hit the downed man in the mouth. Juice and rotten tomato flesh squirted up his nose and into his eyes, causing him to howl in pain.

Miko awakened to the sound of Norman hollering. She saw him sprawled across the back step while Petey waited a few yards away with a slingshot in his hand. Slightly disoriented, she struggled to rise to her feet, weaving slightly when she finally stood.

"Can you hold him there, Petey?" she asked. To clear the lingering fog in her mind, she shook her head.

"You betcha I can hold him here! I can hold him from now till tomorrow if that's what you want, Miko." Petey cast a quick glance at her over his shoulder before he bombarded Norman with more decaying fruit, keeping the man effectively pinned in place.

If Norman moved over a few inches, he might reach the doorknob and sneak inside the house, but Petey determined that wouldn't happen. Not while a breath remained in his tightly wound, tension-strung little body.

Miko took a few staggering steps, attempting to regain her balance.

Intent on keeping the would-be murderer occupied, Petey continued to shoot rocks and rotten produce at Norman until the man curled into a cowering ball on the back step, whimpering.

Rock staggered around the corner of the house into the backyard, head dripping blood and eyes filled with unease as he held a pistol at the ready in his hand.

"Are you both okay?" he asked, forcing wobbly knees to carry him across the yard.

"We're swell, Cap! Golly, it's a jim-dandy doozy thing to see you." Petey fired his last tomato at Norman, hitting his exposed ear. The man yelped and curled into a tighter ball. "I thought for sure when the shot went off we'd have to bid you a final farewell. I'll tell it to the world, Cap, I surely will, but I'm pretty keen on you and Miko. This has played out to be a real humdinger of a day."

Rock lost his battle to remain upright and sank onto the lawn beside the boy, who grinned as if he'd just won a year's worth of free chocolate bars. Miko hovered above them, keeping one eye on the pathetic thief crying on the back step a few feet away and the other on the man she loved as his lifeblood dripped onto the lush green grass of the yard.

Miko wrapped her arms around Rock, helping him lie back in the cool grass. Gentle fingers probed the wound on the side of his head. A prayer of thanksgiving rolled up from her soul and joined her heartfelt sigh of relief that Rock would be fine. The bullet had barely grazed his head just above his ear. Although it bled like the dickens, he would recover.

She looked to the boy who had defended them and her home. "Petey, would you run inside and phone the sheriff? If you ask the operator, she can connect you. Please tell him his assistance is needed and give him our address."

"I'm on the job, Miko!" The youngster shoved his slingshot into his pocket and raced around to the front porch. The sound of his footsteps pounding through the house vibrated out the open windows. The excited tone of his voice drifted to the adults on the breeze although his words were not distinguishable.

When Petey returned, he held a wet towel in one hand and a glass of water in the other. He rushed over to where Rock had raised himself to a sitting position and pushed the towel against the wound oozing blood all over Rock's fine clothes.

"The sheriff is on his way. I told him to be quick about it since we got a wounded soldier and a crazy man with a gun in his pocket." Petey handed him the glass of water, then hunkered down, resting on his haunches. "Gee, Cap, but ol' Norman sure made a mess out of your nice suit."

Rock drained the glass and glanced down. "I guess he did, but this doesn't seem like much compared to the mess he made in the house."

"I've never seen such a cyclone!" Petey whistled and waved a juice-streaked hand toward the back step where Norman continued to cower and whine. "Gosh, do you think we ought to tie him up until the sheriff comes?"

Rock forced his gaze to focus on his wife. Although she stood, she looked unsteady on her feet.

"Why don't we —" Rock gasped and rose to his feet as Norman screeched an unearthly sound and lunged toward Miko, struggling to draw the gun from his pocket with his wounded hand.

Marbles scattered beneath him and he fell down the steps. Rock used the butt of the pistol in his hand to knock Norman senseless. The criminal tumbled into the grass at Miko's feet.

"Let's do him up right!" Petey retrieved the rope he'd removed from Miko and rushed back, handing her a length of it. She took the gun from Norman's pocket, then knotted a piece of rope around his hands while Petey wrapped the man's ankles. The boy promised to keep watch if she wanted to help Rock back inside.

Brushing aside the marbles with her foot, she opened the back door, then wrapped an arm around Rock's waist, guiding him into the kitchen. Carefully cleaning the wound, she'd just finished wrapping a piece of gauze around it to keep it clean when wailing sirens announced the sheriff's arrival. Two speeding vehicles approached the farm, red lights swirling on top of the cars.

"I don't know what Petey told them, but they certainly hustled to get here," Miko said, helping Rock to his feet. Together, they walked to the front door and down the steps to greet the sheriff and two deputies.

"Afternoon, sir," Rock said, holding out his hand to the sheriff, pleased to see the man he considered a friend.

"Afternoon." The sheriff looked around, expecting to find a yard littered with bodies from the frantic message relayed to him. "How many bodies are there?"

"Bodies?" Rock asked, gaping at the sheriff. "There's one would-be murderer trussed up in the backyard, but that's it."

The sheriff's face remained impassive. "Shall we take a look?"

Miko and Rock led the way to the back of the house, where Norman remained curled on the grass, shooting venomous daggers from his glazed eyes. Petey stood nearby, brandishing a pitchfork he'd grabbed from the garden shed.

The sheriff's eyes widened and he bit back a grin at the sight of the boy and Norman Ness. Over the past few weeks, he'd embraced the hope he'd never set eyes on the salesman again.

"Norman, fancy meeting you here." The sheriff bent down and removed the rag Petey had stuffed into Norman's mouth. "You got anything to say for yourself?"

Norman appeared drunk as his eyes rolled back in his head and he muttered gibberish no one could understand. His breath came in short little puffs that reeked of sour candy while sweat rolled off him in waves. Although adrenaline had fueled his strength earlier, he now seemed as harmless as a wrung-out dishrag.

"Interesting." The sheriff turned to Petey and hunkered down. "Do you live around here, young man?"

"Yes, sir. That way." Petey pointed to the path he took to cut through the pasture to his house

"Is that right?" the sheriff asked. "Are you the one that phoned our office?"

The boy nodded with such vigor, his mop of red hair flopped into his eyes. "That was me, sir. Miko was busy keeping Mr. Nasty-Pants Norman from getting away and Cap was down for the count, so calling in the cavalry was up to me."

The sheriff chuckled and motioned to the stone bench beneath the maple tree. "How about we sit down and you tell me all about your afternoon adventure while my deputies take Mr. Ness to jail?"

"Are you gonna stake him out in front of a firing squad and everything?" Petey asked as the deputies half carried, half dragged Norman around to their waiting car.

"Not just yet. I'll have plenty of questions to ask him first." The sheriff took a seat on the bench and Petey plopped down next to him. "Let's start at the beginning. What did you see when you arrived?"

Petey answered the sheriff's questions, his little body strung so taut with lingering excitement, it appeared he might combust at the slightest provocation. He'd just reached the point in his story about hearing the gunshot from the house, when John Phillips arrived, racing into the backyard, concern evident in every line of his face.

"Petey! Are you okay?" he asked, scooping his son into his arms and hugging him close.

"By jingo, Dad, I done good! Boy, you should'a seen me in action. I was a regular terror, but I tell ya, I'm about played out." Suddenly sapped of energy, the boy sagged and rested his head on his father's strong shoulder.

John looked to the adults for an explanation. Miko spoke of finding Norman at the produce stand, then waking up to Petey cornering the salesman like a rabid animal on the back step. Rock shared what little he knew of the story. The brave little boy filled in the gaps the two adults hadn't been conscious to witness.

The sheriff sent Petey home with his father after praising him for his fine work. Miko handed over the pistol she'd taken from Norman. The sheriff pocketed it and accompanied the couple inside the house, inspecting the damage Norman had caused. After taking detailed notes, he glanced around in disgust at the mess.

"What was he after?" the sheriff asked as Rock and Miko walked him out to his car.

"We think he wanted the deed to the farm. He had it in his head if he found it, he could take over the farm," Rock said.

"You won't have to worry about him bugging you again, Mrs. Laroux. He'll be gone for a very long time," the sheriff said, then pointed to the produce stand. "Are the melons ready yet?"

Miko hurried over to the stand and returned carrying one of the few early watermelons she harvested that day. She handed it to the sheriff with a shy smile. "Thank you for your help, Sheriff. We appreciate it."

He took the melon with a grin and set it on the floor in his car. "I'm not sure I'll be able to wait to taste that until I get home. My wife and kids might never know about it. Maybe I'll bring them out here one of these days."

"You're welcome anytime, sir," Rock said, settling his arm around Miko's waist again.

The sheriff nodded. "If we have any questions, we'll be in touch." The man pointed toward Rock's head. "You might want to have that graze checked by a doctor. Most likely it just stunned you, but head wounds can be tricky things."

"Thank you, sir, and thank you for coming out so quickly," Rock said, shaking the sheriff's hand, then watching as the man slid into his car.

"If you ever get in another fix, I sure hope the Phillips boy is around. Now that's a young one with some spunk." With a wink, the sheriff backed up and left.

Rock and Miko watched him drive away before turning toward the house. Neither wanted to clean up the monumental mess Norman had created.

With heavy steps, they crossed the front walk and mounted the porch, but the sound of another vehicle approaching drew their gaze to the car pulling up at the front gate.

One of their work crew bounded up the walk and stared at them. "Are you both okay?" he asked, fear clearly expressed on his face and in his voice.

"We're okay, Jared," Rock assured him. "What are you doing here?"

"I was working just down the road, over on the Donald place, when I heard the sirens and saw the flashing lights speed by. I had to finish my work, or I would've run over right then. Anyway, I wondered what brought the sheriff out this way again. It hasn't been that long since Mrs. Danvers's wreck. I was almost to your lane when the sheriff pulled onto the road." The young man took in Rock's bandaged head and the blood all over his clothes. "Jeepers! What happened?"

Rock looked down at his filthy clothes. "You know that salesman, Norman Ness?"

Jared's nose wrinkled. "The smelly one who eats that stinky candy, and then breathes all over you when he talks?"

Miko couldn't contain her smile. "That's the one."

"He's a sick man, Jared," Rock said. "He got it into his head that if he killed me and Mrs. Laroux, he could take over this place."

"What!" Jared's eyes widened. "That's crazy!"

"Yep, it is. Anyway, he tied Mrs. Laroux to a tree, tore the house apart looking for the deed to the farm, and shot me when I arrived home from town." Rock gingerly touched his head. "I'm lucky he isn't a better shot."

Eager to hear the rest of the story, Jared leaned forward. "How'd you stop him?"

"Petey Phillips," Rock said with a broad grin. "I wish I'd been awake to see the whole thing, but Petey kept ol' Norman cornered on the back step with his slingshot and a bucket of rotten produce he nabbed from the compost pile."

Jared laughed. "That kid is a regular firecracker. Boy, I wish I'd seen it, too." The young man sobered. "But you both are okay? Did the sheriff take Norman to jail?"

Miko smiled at the teen. "We're fine. Norman will be in jail for a long time to come," she said. "I don't have a thing put together for supper, but I could probably find some cookies and iced tea if you're interested."

"Thanks, Mrs. Laroux," Jared said, following them through the open front door. He stopped inside the threshold and whistled, looking around the disastrous mess. Norman had dumped drawers, pawed through cushions, turned over lamps and tables, broken picture frames and tossed papers and books in his search for the deed. "Well, if this ain't a dirty gyp of a thing, I don't know what is."

The young man stepped over a broken vase and glanced from Rock to Miko and back again. "You both have been so good to us this summer, it's our turn to help you. Do you mind if I call the gang to give you a hand?"

"Oh, Jared, that's so sweet, but I'm sure you must be tired from a long day of work at Mr. Donald's place."

"I've got plenty of juice left to squeeze," the teen said with a jaunty grin. "Point me to the phone and I'll send out a call for help."

Miko shrugged and looked to Rock. He led the boy to the kitchen and showed him the telephone, then went to change his clothes. Miko retrieved a tablet of paper and began a list of everything that had been broken or damaged.

Rock returned to the living room pale-faced. Once they righted the sofa, she insisted he rest.

Within seconds of his head hitting the cushions, he fell asleep. Jared helped Miko until two carloads of young people arrived. The two girls who worked for them carried brown paper sacks full of hamburgers.

Miko poured glasses of juice and she and the teens ate an improvised picnic outside, then set to work cleaning the house. Rock roused when they returned inside. Miko gave him a hamburger and a glass of milk, ordering him to stay on the sofa. Unable to sit still while others worked, he moved into the office where he and one of the boys shelved the books Norman had scattered across the floor. John Phillips phoned, letting them know Petey had fallen asleep on the way home and awakened just long enough to eat a sandwich before drifting back to sleep.

When they finished, it was well past ten that evening. Not one of the teens left until the house was sparkling clean and everything that hadn't been broken was put away.

Miko hugged Jared when he lingered behind as the other kids left. "I don't know how to thank you, Jared. What you did was wonderful and so appreciated."

Red crept up the embarrassed teenager's neck, and he glanced down at his feet. "Aw, it wasn't anything, Mrs. Laroux. We're glad we could help."

"You're a fine young man, Jared." Rock clapped him on the shoulder, then held out a hand for him to shake. "Thank you for what you did for us today, and for all you've done working for us this summer."

"Well, shoot, everyone knows this is the place to work. It's good pay, good hours, and Mrs. Laroux makes the best brownies."

Miko smiled. "Perhaps we should have brownies tomorrow, then."

"That's a swell idea." Jared grinned and jogged down the steps. "See you in the morning."

Miko and Rock returned inside the house, relieved the mess was gone, and grateful for the amazing young people who had swept in and completed the bulk of the work.

Rock slumped onto the sofa and Miko sank down beside him, resting her head on his shoulder. Not one usually given to great shows of emotion, she sniffled as tears burned her eyes and clogged her throat.

"What's wrong?" Rock kissed the top of her head as his hand rubbed comfortingly up and down her arm. "Did Norman hurt you? Did something happen you didn't mention earlier? If he laid a hand on —"

Miko melded her lips to Rock's, silencing him. Caught off guard, he didn't want to frighten her away. He meekly accepted the kiss like a treasured gift and didn't press further when she pulled back.

"I'm fine, Rock. Norman didn't hurt me, other than my pride. I'm rather overwhelmed by the fine young people we know. First Petey, and then Jared and the gang. On top of that, I'm grateful you'll be fine. If Norman had shot even a centimeter closer, you wouldn't be here with me right now. I can't bear to think of how close I came to losing you today."

Tears rolled down her cheeks and she buried her face against Rock's throat. He wrapped her in his arms and held her close, murmuring words of comfort.

"If I wasn't bone-tired and incapacitated, I'd show you just how happy I am to be alive and here with you," Rock teased when Miko lifted her head.

She offered him a lopsided smile and released a choppy breath. "I better take a look at your head before you go to bed. Do you have a headache?"

Rock hated to admit it, but his head felt like it might split in two. It had been that way since he'd come to his senses after Norman grazed him. His ears rang as if someone incessantly clanged a bell inside his noggin. Any quick movements of his head made him nauseous. He suspected he had a slight concussion, but he didn't want to worry his wife.

On the other hand, if it would keep her close, he could let his tough, rugged persona slip to the wayside for one night.

With an anguished expression, he held a hand to his head. "My head feels like it might explode and my ears have been ringing like church bells for hours."

Miko stood and fisted her hands on slim hips. "Why didn't you say something earlier? I would have driven you to the hospital. Get up and I'll take you right now." She took two steps before Rock caught her fingers and tugged her around to face him.

His eyes fluttered open and closed, then he expelled a weary breath. "A good night's rest is all I need. It's probably just a little concussion."

"A concussion! Good grief, Rock Laroux!" She plopped down next to him, making him wince, and then bounced back to her feet. "That's it. I'll take you straight to the hospital."

"Honest, Miko, I just need to rest. I'll be fine tomorrow." He made a great show of lumbering to his feet and weaving his way down the hall to the bathroom. In the mirror, he examined the wound on his head, glad it wasn't any lower or it would have taken part of his ear. Any higher, and it might have been impossible to hide the scar it would leave behind. Incredibly blessed to be alive, Rock decided the inconvenience of a headache was a small price to pay.

He took a fast shower and brushed his teeth, then entered his bedroom to find Miko there. The covers on his bed were turned back, his pillows fluffed. The curtains blew in the soft night breeze from the open window. The fragrance of moonflowers and cinnamon pinks drifted in, filling the room with a succulent scent that reminded Rock of his days in Trinidad.

Although his wife lingered in his bedroom, she didn't appear ready to join him in bed. Fully dressed, she stood with hands at her sides, ready to offer assistance.

When he walked into the room dressed only in his underwear, he'd hoped to stir a reaction from her, but she hadn't so much as blinked. A man less confident in himself might have felt slighted at her lack of interest or expression.

Had he not known how much she loved him, he might have given up hope. But no matter what she did or didn't say, love lingered in her touches. He could see it in the light that shone from her dark eyes, and hear it in her voice when she said his name.

One day soon, she'd admit how much she loved him, needed him, and wanted him.

However, tonight was not the time to pursue his wife. Not when his head really did feel like it might explode.

"I better bandage your wound," she said and disappeared into the bathroom, reappearing with salve and more gauze. After she finished, she brought him aspirin and a glass of water, then watched as he settled into the bed and pulled the sheet up as far as his waist.

She brought a cool cloth and wiped it over his warm brow, bringing welcome relief. He smiled and caught her hand, kissing her palm.

"Talk to me, Miko. Tell me something about you I don't know."

She left the cloth on his brow and took a seat beside him. "Do you remember seeing a big sword up in the garden house?"

"Yes," he said, relaxed by the soothing tone of her voice. "It's on the wall in the main room."

"It belonged to my great-grandfather's great-grandfather. The *katana* sword is one owned by a samurai, a fighter. The swords were quick to draw and served well in close combat."

"I knew you came from a warrior ancestry." Rock grinned sleepily, finding it hard to keep his eyes open.

Miko smiled, brushing her fingers lightly through his hair. "Granddad taught both Tommy and me in the art of using it."

"What about Ellen?" Rock asked.

She laughed. "Ellen would never, ever pick up a sword. She might stab you with a knitting needle, but not a sword."

His chuckle made her heart flip in her chest. "I'd like to see you demonstrate what you know sometime."

"Maybe I will," she said, thinking how much she would enjoy showing Rock all the traditional things her grandfather had taught her.

"You're so beautiful, Miko, so brave and wonderful," Rock murmured as sleep claimed him.

"So are you," Miko whispered. "I love you so much, Rock Laroux. My heart wouldn't survive losing you." Leaning over, she pressed a tender kiss to his lips before leaving him to his dreams.

★★★ *Chapter Twenty-Five* ★★★

Rock and Miko barely had a minute to themselves the rest of the week. All the young people who worked for them stayed close, excited to listen to Petey retell the story of defeating Nasty Norman, as the boy referred to the salesman.

Like a celebrity, Petey held court in the produce stand. Animatedly, the youngster shared the story of saving the day until it was time for him to run home to do his chores.

Lucy and John Phillips were so proud of their boy, they nearly floated as they walked, especially when Miko and Rock repeatedly told them they owed Petey a debt of gratitude along with their lives. If the little rascal hadn't arrived when he had, goodness only knew what Norman might have done.

Pastor Clark heard the news and drove out to make sure Miko and Rock were well. Reassured everything was fine, he promised to keep the incident from her parents, unless they asked about it.

The sheriff arrived the afternoon after the incident with the news that they'd found Norman dead in his jail cell shortly after his arrest.

"The doctor looked him over and decided Ness had some kind of poisoning, although he hadn't any idea from what. Most likely, from something he ate. That man was sick in both mind and body before he ever set foot here.

Although, the Phillips boy's skill with a slingshot didn't do Ness any favors." The sheriff shook his head as he looked from Rock to Miko.

"No, it probably didn't," Rock agreed, walking with the sheriff from the front gate of the house in the direction of his car. "We do appreciate you coming all the way out here to tell us, sir."

"Well, shoot, I could have telephoned with that news, but I wanted to thank you both for that watermelon. By gosh, it had a wonderful ripe flavor, just like I remember from when I was a boy." The man grinned at Miko. "I'm almost embarrassed to admit it, but I took the melon into the office with me. My deputies and I ate the whole thing and didn't share with anyone else."

"Then we best find another for you take home to your family," Miko said, smiling as she led the way to the produce stand.

The sheriff left fifteen minutes later with two watermelons, a basket of candy-sweet plums, and an assortment of vegetables.

Another heat wave descended on them, lasting through the next few days as people flocked to the farm, hungry for the fresh produce and gossip about Norman.

The temperature spiked Saturday afternoon. Rock and the boys finished picking the plums and partook of the refreshments Miko had left on the picnic table in the shade, but she remained absent.

Ready for peace and quiet, Rock closed the produce stand early and sent the young people home, promising to pay them for the extra hour and a half they didn't work.

They left amid cheers with plans to go swimming.

Rock had plans of his own. A scab covered the wound on his head, the headache was gone, and he was tired of waiting for his wife to admit they were meant to be together.

If he had to spend hours pleading with her to listen to reason, he'd do it. If he had to get on his knees and beg her to love him, he'd drop to the ground and grovel.

He didn't care what it took, but he wouldn't stop until he held her in his arms as his true wife.

Since the incident with Ness on Tuesday, she'd kept a close eye on him, worried about his health. Frequently, she'd touched him, placing a hand on his back or feeling his forehead for a fever.

While he appreciated her care, what he wanted was her love.

Rock stepped into the kitchen, expecting to find her there, but the house was silent. She wasn't in the barn, the storage building, the garden, or anywhere in his line of sight.

The only place he hadn't looked was in the secret garden on the hill. Inspired to do something special, he decided to take a picnic to her for their supper. They could linger in the cool shade of the trees and forget about the rest of the work until tomorrow.

Swiftly formulating a plan to woo his wife, Rock rushed to feed the pigs, milked the cows, filled the water pan in the chicken pen, and locked all the buildings for the night.

Hot and sweaty, he returned to the house and jumped into the shower. He shaved and dressed, then hastened to the kitchen. A large basket soon held ripe plums, wedges of cheese, slices of smoked ham, half a loaf of bread Miko had baked the previous morning, and a handful of chocolate cookies. The remains of the pitcher of tea he found chilling in the refrigerator went into two canning jars that he added to the basket. He tossed in napkins, a few candles, and a book of matches before snatching the quilt they used for picnics off a shelf by the back door and striding out the back gate.

Behind the barn, he followed the stepping stones to the gate and slipped inside. Up the hidden trail he walked, aware of the temperature cooling as he climbed higher.

At the top of the path, he stared at the high fence for a moment before walking inside the open gate. He wandered along the winding path that took him to the weeping cherry tree where they most often picnicked on Sunday afternoons. Quietly, he spread out the blanket and set the basket on one corner of it, then covered the food with a napkin before searching out Miko.

The path he followed led him to the house. He removed his shoes and stepped inside, but Miko didn't linger in the cool recesses of any of the rooms.

Rock stood in the doorway and glanced around the garden, wondering where she was. The gleam of light glistening off a dark head drew his gaze to the pool below the waterfall.

With a broad grin, he tugged off his socks and jogged to the pool at the base of the waterfall.

Silently, he lingered at the edge, entranced as his wife rose out of the water like a magical, mythical water nymph.

Crystal beads clung to the smooth surface of her bare skin and shimmered in the beams of bright summer light. Eyes closed, she arched her slender spine and tossed back her glorious hair with a carefree grin on her face.

Heat churned in Rock's belly and zinged through his veins with a force he couldn't deny and didn't want to control. Determined to claim his wife for his own, he moved to the shallow end of the pool.

Oblivious to the presence of her husband, Miko dove beneath the surface.

Tired of all the noise and busyness of the produce stand and in need of a few moments of quiet, she'd gone up the hill, seeking solitude. The past week, she'd hardly spent any time in the Japanese garden, and today planned to work there for an hour or two, until it was time to make dinner for Rock.

She'd worked for an hour, watering plants and pulling weeds. Overheated and sticky with sweat, she'd decided to take a refreshing swim in the pool beneath the waterfall before returning to the bungalow. She, Ellen, and Tommy used to swim in the pool all the time when they were younger, but Miko hadn't played in the cooling waters for years.

Safe from prying eyes, she gave no thought to leaving every stitch of her clothes piled on the bank by a seat made of smooth stones. No one but Rock knew about the garden, and he was busy with the boys in the orchard.

She waded into the water, gasping at first as the cooling liquid swirled around her calves. Wading deeper, she immersed her body in the pool, enjoying an unhurried swim.

As she dove and then shot to the surface, she grinned at the warmth of the sunshine on her face and the earthy smells around her. She caught a hint of Rock's scent — a spicy, woodsy aroma combined with his unique masculine fragrance — but that was impossible. He had another hour of work in the orchard before he would finish for the day.

The scent of him, the rough texture of his skin, and the shining brilliance of his eyes were so firmly embedded in her mind, so intimately familiar to her, she could conjure them on a whim.

Convinced her longing for him filled her senses with his scent and created the tingling wonder of his presence, she again dove into the pool and swam several strokes before heading to the shallow end.

Her feet touched the rocks on the bottom of the pool and Miko continued forward, focused on wringing the water from her hair as she moved to the bank.

Goose bumps broke over her skin, the type that came from being watched. Frightened, she snapped her head up.

Rock stood less than ten feet away from her at the edge of the pool. He wore a pair of khaki trousers with a sleeveless undershirt that accentuated his muscles and tanned skin. That was it. No shoes, no shirt, not even a belt. Miko swallowed hard, unable to drag her eyes away from the breadth of his shoulders and chest.

"How's the water?" he asked, boldly staring at her sun-drenched body, covered in tiny droplets of sparkling water.

"Refreshing." Her cheeks burned with embarrassment, but she remained unmoving, fighting the urge to turn and dive back into the water. As much as she'd tried to convince herself otherwise, she wouldn't continue pretending she didn't want or need Rock's love. She craved it, yearned for it, dreamed of it.

While her face grew hot and blushed under his intense perusal, so did the rest of her.

His gaze settled on hers and a puckish smile crossed his face. "It's time, Miko."

"Time?" she asked, confused. Thrilled by the fiery light burning in his eyes, she worked to make sense of his words. "Time for what?"

"Time for you to admit you love me." He yanked the undershirt over his head and tossed it on top of her pile of clothes. "You let me into your secret garden, Mrs. Laroux. It's far past time to let me into your heart." He dropped his trousers and stepped out of them, encouraged by the wild look of wanting on Miko's face. "It's time..." Rock slipped off the last bit of cotton fabric covering his skin and stepped into the water "... for this ridiculous farce that you don't really want to be my wife to come to an end. You have sixty seconds to tell me no, Miko. Otherwise, I'm going to make this marriage one you can never annul."

He moved toward her until they stood a foot apart knee-deep in the pond, his skin so hot he thought it might catch fire, hers cool from the water. Admiration mingled with love, desire with hope, as they stared unabashedly at each other.

"Rock, I..." Miko couldn't think. Not with him so close, not with her dreams within reach. She needed to tell him no, to remind him they'd agreed to a marriage in name only.

They had both agreed to it, hadn't they?

With the heat of his body enveloping her every bit as much as his tantalizing scent, all ability to think fled. His clean-shaven jaw practically begged for her lips to taunt it, taste it.

"Thirty seconds, wife of mine." Rock took one step closer, his smile enthralling as he reached out and traced the shape of her lower lip with his index finger.

"But, Rock, we... I..." Miko didn't know why she even pretended to protest. She wanted to close her eyes and yield to whatever Rock suggested.

"Fifteen seconds, Kamiko." The husky rumble of his voice sent the butterflies in her stomach into a whirlwind of flight.

His thumb trailed along the delicate column of her neck and slid across her collarbone. He closed the distance between them, wrapping both arms around her and pulling her flush against the hard strength of his body. "Time is up, sweetheart. Any protest?"

"No," she whispered and closed her eyes, surrendering to Rock, to her consuming love for him.

His first kiss was gentle, a kiss of beginnings. The next was more demanding. The third kiss, full of passion and hunger, made her knees so weak she couldn't stand.

Rock swept her into his arms and carried her to the blanket beneath the weeping cherry tree. The place where they'd spent hours becoming friends seemed fitting as the place where they would spend hours becoming lovers.

Later, with the moon casting silvery light among the shadows, and stars twinkling like illuminated fragments of glass, Miko rested in Rock's arms, staring up at the sky, happier and more content than she'd ever been in her life.

"I love you so much, Rock Laroux," she whispered, pressing a kiss to his chest where she rested her head.

He smiled at her, that roguish smile she'd finally come to understand was meant only for her. "And I love you, Kamiko Jane Nishimura Laroux."

She laughed. "That's a mouthful, don't you think?"

"Then I guess I'll stick with Miko, or sweetheart, or my beloved wife." Rock kissed her with such tenderness, tears gathered in her eyes. "You know, anytime we want to take a honeymoon, all we have to do is walk up the hill to claim our own little corner of sweet paradise."

She hugged him tightly, as though she'd never let him go. "I'm so glad you didn't give up on loving me, Rock. I'm sorry I've been so stubborn. If this is what we would have enjoyed all summer, why didn't you give me an ultimatum sooner?"

"You would have told me no," he said with stark honesty. "Something just felt right about today. In truth, Miko, it has tested my patience almost beyond endurance to be around you, to be so close to you, to be so in love with you, and not do more than hold your hand or kiss your cheek. There were nights I thought I might go mad wanting you." He kissed her temple. "After the incident with Norman the other day, I knew then I couldn't live without you. If he'd hurt you, if he'd done anything to you, I don't know how I would have continued to live."

"Oh, Rock, how do you think I felt, seeing you walk around the corner of the house with blood streaming down your face? My heart fell to my feet and I thought the world would come to an end until I realized you'd be fine." She kissed his cheek and made her way down to his jaw. "I wanted you to love me all along. You told me to come to you, anytime, and I almost did one night. I wanted to go to you so badly, Rock, to love you."

"I know. I watched you."

Miko raised herself on one elbow and stared at him. "You did?"

He pulled her back down and nuzzled her neck. "I did. Sleep eluded me, as it so often does because of how desperately I want you. I turned on the radio and paced the house, then watched you come to the gate and hesitate. I begged you to keep coming, even if you didn't hear the words. But you ran off in a cloud of filmy fabric that made it even harder for me to get any rest. Whatever you wore that night, I'd sure like to see it up close sometime."

She grinned against his mouth. "I think that can be arranged."

Their kiss, full of acceptance and anticipation, filled both their hearts to overflowing.

Rock pulled back and cupped her chin. "Whatever the future brings, Kamiko, whatever happens, we'll face it together."

"Together," she repeated. "As long as you're beside me, I don't need another thing in this world, Rock. Only and forever you."

Mafa Chicken

As I included mentions of food in this story, I searched online for recipes from the late 1930s and early 1940s. In particular, I wanted to find "ration recipes" that people used once they had limited supplies of certain items, like sugar.

Eventually, I recalled a box of cookbooks Captain Cavedweller's grandmother gave me a few years ago. Vaguely, I recalled seeing some older cookbooks in it and crossed my fingers that one of them would be from the World War II years.

I found three "Victory" cookbooks, along with four others from the 1930s. The cookbooks published during the war years have little notes in the margins beside some of the recipes like, "A favorite with the boys at camp," and, "These cookies travel well and keep well."

There are also many recipes for selections that can be made "in a jiffy." For the first time in history, many women worked outside the home and no longer had time to plan or prepare elaborate meals.

One cookbook included tips and ideas like "how to bake a cake with chicken fat" or "extend the flavor of meat with handy minute tapioca."

In the box of cookbooks was also one titled *A Taste of the Orient*, a Japanese cookbook published by the Nisei Women's Society of Christian Service from Grandma's local Methodist church.

After browsing through that cookbook, I decided to share this recipe with you.

I grew up in an area where there were several Japanese families. In my youthful ignorance, I never gave a thought to the trials the relatives of my school friends had faced during World War II.

At family gatherings, one of my aunts often brought a platter of golden-fried chicken that had such a unique, yet utterly addictive flavor. As a child, all I knew was that one of her Japanese neighbors had shared the recipe. As an adult, I finally got my hands on the recipe and learned that this particular dish supposedly originated from some of the Japanese families in the area.

Mafa chicken is delicious fresh and hot, but I think it tastes even better the next day. Enjoy!

Mafa Chicken

2 pounds of boneless chicken, cut into bite-sized pieces
1 ½ cups granulated sugar
½ cup soy sauce
1 cup funyu (fermented bean curds)
4 eggs
flour
1 tsp. salt

Mix sugar, soy sauce, funyu and eggs. Pour into a resealable plastic bag (or you can leave in the bowl and cover with plastic wrap) add chicken pieces, and marinate overnight.

Mix flour and salt together and set aside.

Heat about 1 to 1 ½ inches of oil in a heavy skillet over medium heat. Roll each piece of chicken in flour and fry until golden brown. Drain on paper towel and serve.

Author's Note

Picture a beautiful summer day when the sky is clear, the temperature is warm, but not uncomfortably so, and the humidity is low.

On one of those ideal summer days in Portland, Oregon, Captain Cavedweller and I climbed a hilly path to visit the Japanese Garden. We heard it was "nice" and "pretty," but we had no idea what to expect.

After we topped the hill and paid our admission at the little gate booth, we walked inside the garden, spellbound by the beauty around us. For a few minutes, we didn't move, absorbed in the wonder of being transported to a completely different world in a matter of a few steps. The garden — oh, such a lovely garden. I highly recommend visiting it if you are ever in the area. There are ponds with bright orange fish, walking paths, raked sand, and a waterfall. In truth, in my mind's eye, it is Miko's secret garden, only bigger.

It was while we wandered along the moss-covered stones and stepped across the wooden bridges that the idea for this story began to percolate. What if there was a girl who lived in a secret garden? Why would she be there? What scenario would drive her into hiding in a Japanese garden up on a hilltop that no one knew was there?

As Captain Cavedweller and I ambled among weeping cherry trees and vibrant flowering bushes, I blurted out my thoughts. Then somehow, in a wonderful blending of ideas, we both arrived at the conclusion of World War II. A Japanese girl would have every reason to hide, had she the opportunity to do so, in 1942 when the government ordered all Japanese along the West Coast "military areas" to report to assembly centers.

Captain Cavedweller and I visited a wonderful museum in Portland called the Oregon Nikkei Legacy Center. Located in an area where the Japanese used to have many businesses near downtown, the museum provides a glimpse into the internment experience. The photos and stories shared broke my heart at what the Japanese Americans endured.

In this story, Miko's family is summoned to the Portland Assembly Center. In reality, the Portland Assembly Center really was the Portland Livestock Exposition Pavilion. The government housed more than 3,500 detainees under one roof there, using plywood to divide the space into apartments. The manure beneath the hastily constructed floor and the flies buzzing everywhere added to the trying conditions, especially during the summer months the Oregon evacuees were held.

Meals were served in a mess hall in shifts. Privacy was nonexistent. The "apartments" had enough floor space for about five Army cots. Rough eight-foot high plywood walls divided one family from another. With no ceiling, noises from adjoining families echoed day and night.

Notice through Civilian Exclusion Order No. 25 and No. 26 posted April 28, 1942, provided instructions about reporting to the assembly center. All Japanese in the evacuation area, regardless of citizenship or birthright, had until noon, Tuesday, May 5, to report to the center. Those who failed to report would be "liable to the criminal penalties provided by Public Law No. 503."

When that particular public law was in the works, the first draft suggested violators be charged as felons and face penalties of up to a $5,000 fine and five years of imprisonment. Agreement was reached that the penalties were too harsh, so the law passed with violations as a misdemeanor and limited the maximum prison term to one year.

As I created Miko's character, I tried to envision how desperate she would be to reach the center on time. I imagined how terrified she would feel after missing that deadline.

The evacuees were instructed to bring bedding and linens, toilet articles, extra clothing and "essential personal effects for each member of the family." All items had to be securely packaged, tied, and tagged with the name of the owner and numbered (with detail provided from the Civil Control Station, where each head of household had to report prior to the evacuation). The size and number of packages was limited to what each individual could carry.

In a matter of days, the evacuees had to either sell or find somewhere to store nearly all their possessions. Many sold their homes, their business, and their vehicles, taking mere pennies on the dollar because they had no idea if or when they would return.

"Only what we could carry was the rule; so we carried Strength, Dignity and Soul."

This quote from Lawson Inada makes me teary-eyed each time I read it, but it sums up so much of what I have read and learned about the Japanese internment.

The Portland Assembly Center functioned like a small town with various divisions. They even had a newspaper called *The Evacuazette* that came out twice weekly. Thanks to the efforts of the director of the recreation department in Portland, the assembly center had a recreation program to help combat the boredom.

By September, evacuees boarded trains and arrived at internment camps. Many were sent to Minidoka, Idaho, while others went to Heart Mountain in Wyoming, or Tule Lake in California. Guards patrolled the train cars, shades were kept drawn over the windows, and many of the evacuees had no idea where they were headed.

For more information about their experiences, a wealth of detail is available in the <u>Densho Encyclopedia</u>.

Although many don't know of it, the government did detain several thousand German and Italian residents during the war. In fact, Ellis Island served as an internment camp for German, Italian, and Japanese in the years of World War II.

A few other tidbits from the story I'd like to share with you...

As a girl, I remember seeing a big box of Oxydol at my grandma's house every time we went there. The washing machine and dryer were located in a little laundry area next to the bathroom. I can't tell you how many times I inhaled the aroma of the soap in my childhood. I will forever equate sparkling white laundry to that smell and my grandma.

The first "vehicle" I learned to drive was a Ford 9N tractor. My dad sold it a few years ago, but boy, did I love driving that thing as a kid. My grandpa also had a Ford 9N tractor. According to Dad, in 1942, Grandpa had gone on a trip to Amarillo, Texas, to get parts (they lived in Oklahoma at the time). He spotted a brand-new 9N at a dealership and stopped to see if it was for sale. After the war started, it was nearly impossible to purchase a new vehicle. Apparently, the dealership missed that memo or excluded tractors because Grandpa purchased it on the spot. As a little tribute to my dad and grandpa, I had to include a mention of the tractor.

Back in the day, I used to play the piano (or play at playing the piano). One year for my birthday, my brother gave me a subscription to a sheet music magazine. Six times a year, new piano pieces arrived in my mailbox, neatly bound inside a colorful magazine cover. The songs varied from pop selections to golden oldies. I believe it was the June issue, with a lovely moon scene on the cover, which included the song "Moonlight Serenade." I'd never heard the song before, but as I sat down and picked out the notes, I fell in love with the words and the tune.

It's dreamy. It's romantic. It's beautiful.

It embodied everything my sentimental little teenage heart longed to experience.

Composed by Glenn Miller with lyrics by Mitchell Parish, "Moonlight Serenade" became one of Miller's signature tunes. It spent many weeks at the top of the Billboard charts in 1939, and was released in November 1943 by the US Army on a <u>V-Disc</u>. V-Discs (V for Victory) were records sent overseas to troops as part of a morale-boosting program during World War II. Many popular singers, big bands, and orchestras recorded special V-Disc records.

"Moonlight Serenade" just happened to be my introduction to songs from the World War II era. I adored the soft romantic tunes, the peppy swing songs, and the big band beat. It seemed only fitting to include a few of them in this story, especially with Rock and Miko trying so hard not to fall in love.

The scene where "Moonlight Serenade" played in the background I envisioned long before I put the words on the page. Part of it came from listening to <u>Ella Fitzgerald's sing</u>. Part of it came from a piece of art I have on the wall above my desk. When Captain Cavedweller and I were last in Las Vegas, we stopped to watch a street vendor who created the most amazing paintings with spray paint (yes, spray paint!). Anyway, the idea for this book was already dancing around in my head, and the moment I saw him painting a big silvery moon above a rippling pool of water surrounded by shadowy trees, I knew I had to have it. And CC, being the awesome guy that he is, lugged the painting around for me the rest of the evening. The combination of listening to Ella's sultry voice, the fabulous painting hanging right in my line of view, and my own personal opinion that June nights are full of magic just waiting to be discovered led to the scene.

One more musical mention… I'm a big Bing Crosby fan. I've always loved the sound of his voice, especially on those love songs he croons. It seemed so right to include "This is My Night to Dream." If you've never heard the song, you can find a YouTube clip.

My search for the perfect car for Miko ended when I "clapped my opticals" on a 1941 Packard Convertible. Goodness gracious! I think I fell in love on the spot. The color, Laguna Maroon, just sounds so glamorous, doesn't it? I'm adding it to my list of dream cars I hope to see in person someday.

Originally, I planned for Rock to be a Flying Tiger, those famed heroes who flew for the Chinese and battled against Japan before the United States officially entered the war. However, because there were so few of them and because their service is so well documented, I started to worry about doing justice to the Flying Tigers.

A few chapters into the story, I switched Rock to serving in the Battle of the Atlantic instead and stationed him at Waller Field Air Force Base until his accident. The air base, named after United States Army Air Force Major Alfred J. Waller, a distinguished World War I combat pilot, was officially activated in September 1941.

You might wonder why Rock's debilitating illness suddenly disappeared, other than Miko's care. I wanted there to be a reason everyone thought he was dying, but for the source to be something simple to fix. The answer came as I researched penicillin use in the war. It was a fairly new drug in those days, but its effectiveness at curing infection had already been explored. Although I pushed the timeline a bit on having Rock's doctor administer it to him, it worked well with the story. Rock's symptoms are all caused by an allergic reaction to the penicillin that his doctor didn't recognize. Once he arrived at the farm and the medication worked out of his system, he healed. I like to think Miko's tender care helped him, too.

As for nasty Norman Ness, he died of lead poisoning by eating too many contaminated pieces of candy. The idea for the villain to give himself lead poisoning through imported candy came from articles I read about lead poisoning deaths in the 1940s... from candy manufactured in a facility that exposed their products to high quantities of lead. It seemed fitting for Norman to poison himself gradually with each piece he consumed. The candy binge the day he attacked the farm overloaded his system. Once the adrenaline from the showdown with Petey wore off, his body succumbed to the poison.

To see the visuals that helped inspire Miko and Rock's story, check out the board on Pinterest.

Thank you for reading their story. I hope you'll join me as I continue with book two in the Hearts of the War series, *Home of Her Heart*.

If you have a moment, please review _Garden of Her Heart_ online. Help other readers find great new books by telling them why you enjoyed the story. You can post your review of _Garden of Her Heart_ here.

Thank you, dear reader, for reading Rock and Miko's story. May we meet again between the pages of another book.

Best wishes,

Shanna

Join Shanna Hatfield's mailing list and receive
a free short story!

Shanna's Newsletter

The newsletter comes out once a month with the
details about
new releases, sales, recipes, and more!
Sign up today!

Acknowledgements

So many people made it possible to take this book from an idea to reality, and I owe them all a huge debt of gratitude.

Special thanks to Eliza Dee from Clio Editing for helping me tell a better version of Rock and Miko's story. Also, thank you to Anne Victory of Victory Editing for adding that last bit of polish to the book.

Thank you to Leo, Shauna, Marcia, Charity, Ann, Becky, Susan, Melanie, and all my beta readers for your help, your feedback, and for cheering me on.

To my Hopeless Romantic street team members, thank you for your encouragement, for offering ideas, and for being so awesome!

I also owe a big thanks to my dad for strolling down memory lane with me and giving me so many wonderful tidbits of information from his childhood during the war.

And to Captain Cavedweller — you are amazing and I couldn't do what I love without your love and support. Thank you for always having my back, being my number one cheerleader, and making me laugh every single day.

Pendleton Petticoats Series

Set in the western town of Pendleton, Oregon, at the turn of the 20th century, each book in this series bears the name of the heroine, all brave yet very different.

Dacey (Prelude) — A conniving mother, a reluctant groom and a desperate bride make for a lively adventure full of sweet romance in this prelude to the beginning of the series.

Aundy (Book 1) — Aundy Thorsen, a stubborn mail-order bride, finds the courage to carry on when she's widowed before ever truly becoming a wife, but opening her heart to love again may be more than she can bear.

Caterina (Book 2) — Running from a man intent on marrying her, Caterina Campanelli starts a new life in Pendleton, completely unprepared for the passionate feelings stirred in her by the town's incredibly handsome deputy sheriff.

Ilsa (Book 3) — Desperate to escape her wicked aunt and an unthinkable future, Ilsa Thorsen finds herself on her sister's ranch in Pendleton. Not only are the dust and smells more than she can bear, but Tony Campanelli seems bent on making her his special project.

Marnie (Book 4) — Beyond all hope for a happy future, Marnie Jones struggles to deal with her roiling emotions when U.S. Marshal Lars Thorsen rides into town, tearing down the walls she's erected around her heart.

**Lacy** *(Book 5)* — Bound by tradition and responsibilities, Lacy has to choose between the ties that bind her to the past and the unexpected love that will carry her into the future.

**Bertie** *(Book 6)* — Haunted by the trauma of her past, Bertie Hawkins must open her heart to love if she has any hope for the future.

**Millie** *(Book 7)* — Determined to bring prohibition to town, the last thing Millie Matlock expects is to fall for the charming owner of the Second Chance Saloon.

And don't miss Nik's story coming in 2017!

<u>Baker City Brides Series</u>
Determined women, strong men and a town known as the Denver of the Blue Mountains during its days of gold in the 1890s.

<u>*Crumpets and Cowpies*</u> *(Baker City Brides, Book 1)* — Rancher Thane Jordan reluctantly travels to England to settle his brother's estate only to find he's inherited much more than he could possibly have imagined.

<u>*Thimbles and Thistles*</u> *(Baker City Brides, Book 2)* — Maggie Dalton doesn't need a man, especially not one as handsome as charming as Ian MacGregor.

<u>*Corsets and Cuffs*</u> *(Baker City Brides, Book 3)* — Sheriff Tully Barrett meets his match when a pampered woman comes to town, catching his eye and capturing his heart.

Bobbins and Boots (Baker City Brides, Book 4) — *Coming in 2017!*

ABOUT THE AUTHOR

SHANNA HATFIELD spent ten years as a newspaper journalist before moving into the field of marketing and public relations. Self-publishing the romantic stories she dreams up in her head is a perfect outlet for her lifelong love of writing, reading, and creativity. She and her husband, lovingly referred to as Captain Cavedweller, reside in the Pacific Northwest.

Shanna loves to hear from readers.
Connect with her online:
Blog: shannahatfield.com
Facebook: Shanna Hatfield
Pinterest: https://www.pinterest.com/shannahatfield/
Email: shanna@shannahatfield.com

If you'd like to know more about the characters in any of her books, visit the Book Characters page on her website or check out her Book Boards on Pinterest.